THE MYSTERY STONE

VICTORIA MARSWELL

The Mystery Stone is entirely a work of fiction. The names, characters and incidents portrayed in it are the work of the author's imagination. Any resemblance to actual persons, living or dead, events or localities is entirely coincidental.

Scripture excerpts permissible by the World English Bible (WEB): Public Domain.

ISBN-978-1-7350135-2-7 (Hardcover)

ISBN-978-1-7350135-3-4 (Paperback)

ISBN-978-1-7350135-5-8 (eBook)

Editing Services: K.L. Adams

Cover Design: 100Covers

Logo Design: Dillon Adams

Published by: Penhallow Books | Portsmouth, New Hampshire, USA

https://penhallowbooks.com/

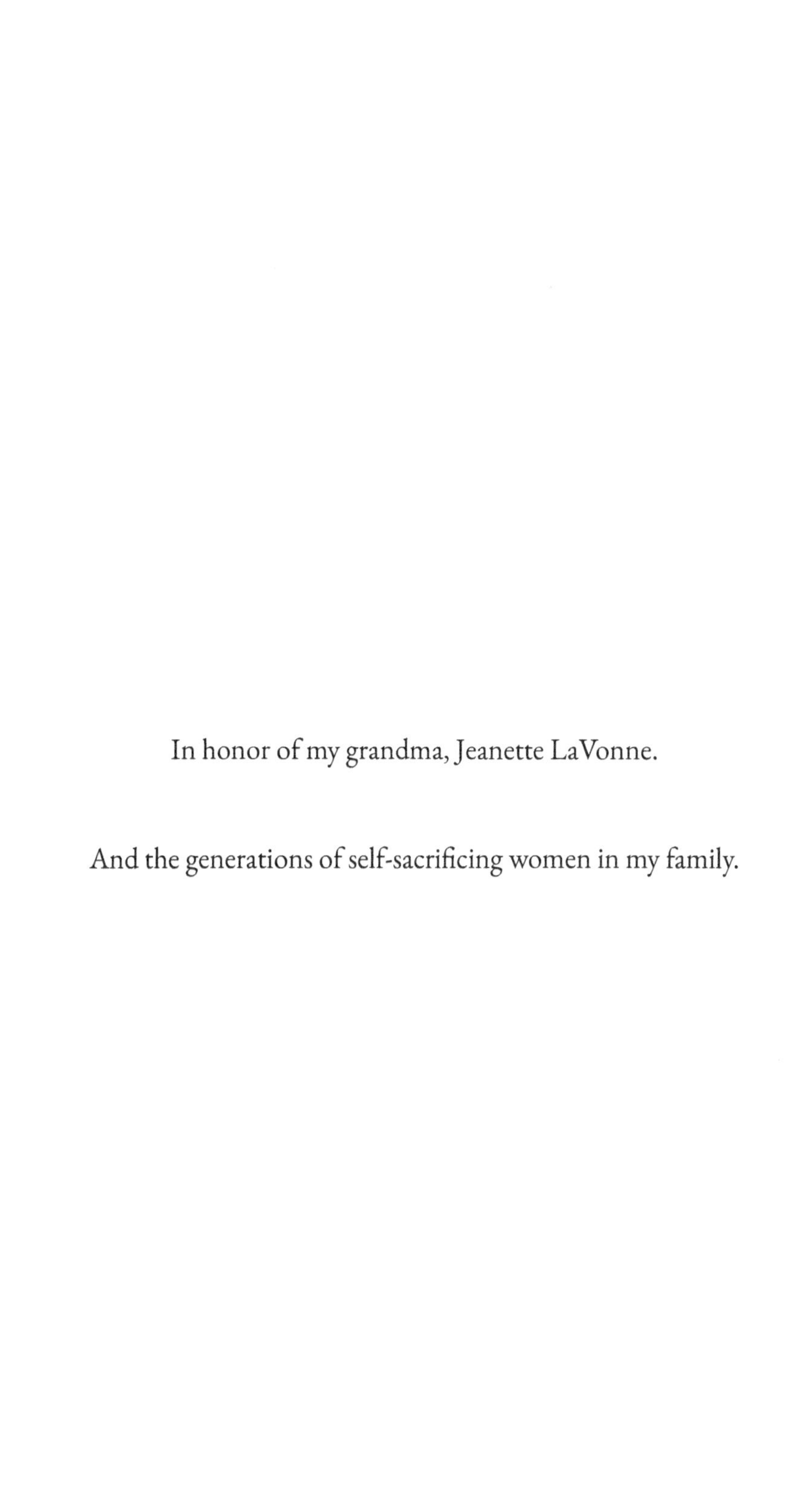

In honor of my grandma, Jeanette LaVonne.

And the generations of self-sacrificing women in my family.

ONE

Whitefield, New Hampshire–1998

The attic door creaked open with a slight push. Jeanette flipped the light switch upward and squinted at the dim, uncovered bulb hanging from the ceiling. Tom stood close, pressing against her hip.

"Stop nudging forward," she whispered through gritted teeth.

"I wanna see inside." He knocked his elbow on her rib cage.

Jeanette shifted her backside, leaning in front of the entry, and blocked his path. "Jack told us to stay downstairs. We're not even allowed up here."

"Then why did you follow me upstairs?"

"Because you're the world's most annoying little brother and always get into trouble."

"Well, you're the universe's bossiest sister and never leave me alone." Tom stiffened his torso and huffed, folding his arms across his chest.

Jeanette dropped her shoulders and exhaled long. "Let's just hurry before Jack comes home. If we're caught, Mom and Dad will never let us spend another summer in the White Mountains." She stepped aside, and Tom bolted into the center of the room.

He searched in every direction. "Whoa, cool."

Jeanette rested against a dusty wall; the smell of old books and a dampness lingered in the air. "What do you expect to find in a boring attic?" She glimpsed at the sheet-covered furniture and writing desk in a corner with stacks of boxes bordering the space.

Tom looked around at all the objects until he spied a framed pencil sketch propped on top of a chest of drawers. "Something exciting, like this picture." He scurried toward the drawing and tripped over his shoelaces. With a thud, he crashed onto the wood planks and bumped his chin.

Jeanette jolted and rushed over, dropping to her knees. She laid a palm on his body, and he shuddered. "Are you okay?" Her voice made a high-pitched squeak.

Tom's shoulders shook as he sat upright, giggling with a bloody mouth and an extra gap in his grin.

"You're missing a tooth!"

Tom spit into his hand and showed her the slimy incisor resting in a pool of pink saliva.

Jeanette scrunched her face and turned away. "Ew, so gross."

"I know you are, but—"

"Now we'll get busted for exploring Jack's house, and he'll call Mom and Dad. They'll pick us up, take you to the hospital where a doctor will perform a ten-hour surgery putting your tooth in place and we'll never, ever come back here again for the rest of our lives." Jeanette stood and brushed the thick film of dust from her favorite pair of Bongo jeans.

"You think you're so smart 'cuz you're a teen, but it's my last baby tooth and I've been wiggling it for the past week."

Jeanette stared at him and rolled her eyes. "Shouldn't you already have all your permanent teeth?"

"No." He climbed to his feet. "I'm younger and—"

"Whatever! Go rinse your mouth before Jack returns."

Tom stumbled down the hall toward the bathroom. Jeanette tucked loose strands of hair that slipped from her headband behind her ear and focused on the framed artwork. Taking slow, steady steps, she approached the dresser, fixing her eyes on the image, and her pulse increased.

Her fingers gripped the cool metal frame, and she moved under the single, dangling lightbulb for a better look at the picture. She stared at the rectangular-shaped drawing, her vision absorbing the shading around the peculiar markings on the surface surrounding what appeared to be a face, but not of human origins, and a coolness quivered throughout her nerves.

"It's an ancient relic."

Jeanette gasped and the frame slid from her fingers, smashing onto the floor. Fractured glass scattered round the paper and on the splintered wood beside her three-hole Doc Martens Oxford shoes. She twisted her torso and faced Jack standing in the doorway. Now she was totally buggin' because Tom always caused trouble and dragged her into it to take the fall.

"Um, I didn't mean to…"

"It's all right. You have a curious mind." He strolled into the middle of the room and picked up the broken picture frame. "Remember, curiosity creates innovations and leads to discoveries that drive the human spirit, pushing us beyond our perceived limitations to explore the unknown and delivers us into true freedom." Jack angled his head to one side. He shook the loose glass from the frame into a trash bin and tugged a corner, pulling the paper out.

"My grandfather told tales of mysterious stones buried all over the world." Jack leaned closer and passed her the portrait. "This drawing is a depiction of one near Bergen, Norway."

"Why are they called mysterious?"

"Archaeologists are inconclusive about their findings on the objects, and some believe ancient civilizations used the items in sacrificial rituals to the gods."

Jeanette gulped the gummy feeling lodged in her throat. "Like human sacrifices?"

"Wicked." Tom snuck behind her and snatched the drawing from her hands.

"Hey!"

"Where is it now?" Tom wedged himself between them as his eyes brightened, roving over the detailed image.

"Never discovered. Historians gave up the search and we're left with little documentation and only this sketch." Jack tapped the edge of the page. "Turn it over."

Jeanette leaned closer and opened her eyes wider, examining the simple map scrawled on the back, including the signature of their great-granddad, Sjur Hillestad.

"What happened?"

"In 1870, your great-grandfather sailed to Quebec with my grandfather. They pursued a new quest here in America, settling as farmers and this"—he poked the paper—"became a forgotten dream."

Jeanette kept her eyesight fixed on the smooth, contoured charcoal lines of the drawing. She stared so hard that her vision watered, blurring the image. Jack had a way of spinning a yarn and shared the gift of telling tales as his father did for the guests at The Glen House Hotel.

"I'm going to find the stones." Tom waved the drawing in the air.

"As if..."

"I'll be a world-famous archaeologist and discover more than one stone without you watching over my shoulder."

"Ha! You can't even walk two feet without tripping and knocking out your teeth." Jeanette crossed her arms and tilted her chin upward. "If you go to Norway, you'll probably mess the whole thing up, and get lost or injured or something worse."

"Now, now, kids. Don't say anything you'll regret." Jack raised a flat palm in the air.

"Nettie started it," Tom said.

"I did not."

"I've heard plenty from both of you. Let's go downstairs and have a nice cuppa cocoa." Jack slipped the picture from his hands and laid it on the desk.

Tom hung his head downward and slouched with a deliberate pout. Jeanette had a feeling he'd be willful enough to hunt for the stones. They played pretend archaeologist, geologist, or any kind of researcher, since the ages of four and six. She noticed the gleam in his eyes at first sight of the stone relic. As soon as he was old enough, Tom would search for it or die trying.

Jack stood between them and wrapped his arms around their shoulders, guiding them outside the attic. "Cheer up. You've got your whole lives ahead of you."

"Jack, do you think when I grow up, I'll find the stone?"

"Who knows, anything is possible." He paused and faced them. "The most important lesson I can share is whatever you choose to pursue in life, do your best, work hard and never give up, especially on your dreams."

Jeanette loved Jack like a grandpa, but she doubted Mom and Dad would approve of him putting ideas in Tom's head about searching for lost stones around the globe. Yeah, dream big, do what you love, and all that stuff. She hoped for an exciting future too—a world-renowned geologist like Florence Bascom, contributing to the scientific community, traveling internationally and exploring the oceans. Of course, she'd balance work, a family, and have at least two kids.

One thing was for sure, she wouldn't waste her time on old stones that Jack's granddad probably invented in one of his tall tales. So many discoveries laid right before them. Jeanette pivoted on her heel and followed Jack. She clasped the doorknob and glanced at the drawing of the mysterious stone one last time. An eerie sensation rippled through her body, as if the image of the etched face in the stone would haunt her forever. Jeanette wriggled her arms to shake off the feeling, flipped the light switch, and closed the door.

TWO

Kinsale, Ireland—Present Day

Jeanette trudged up an incline on Barrack Street in Kinsale, Ireland and blew out a heavy breath. Tom did it again, another international crisis for her to handle and bail him out of a serious situation.

In the past seven years, she traveled halfway around the world for Tom because of his lifelong obsession with relics. She stopped walking at the top of the hill, turned left and followed the directions toward Friary Lane. If it wasn't for Tom's boss, Simon Bonhoeffer, emailing her about his concerns and her previous work with his excavation team in Vermont, she wouldn't have left home in a spur-of-the-moment decision.

Who was she kidding? She always jumped on a plane, boat, train, or car whenever and wherever Tom needed her help to get him out of trouble. Grandma always taught that family sticks together, no matter the cost.

The street curved toward the right, leading her to a cul-de-sac. Jeanette took a deep cleansing breath and salty sea air filled her sense of smell. Her eyes fixed on the port below and she glanced at the address written on the envelope she held in her hands. She spun on her heel and squinted at the matching number posted at the end of the road, 5 Friary Lane. Her shoulders drooped and she sighed. Tom had better get his act together or else…

Jeanette stood at the edge of a gray-painted gate, skimming the front entry lined with bells-of-Ireland. The tall, slender plant with unusual cone-shaped flowers bordered the perimeter of a garden and walkway. She flipped the latch on the inside of the entrance and strolled toward the door, passing a silver bicycle propped against a wrought-iron bench. A quintessential home in Ireland, ready for a photographer to snap a picture and include the photo in next year's calendar of Irish cottages.

"Hello, what would ya be wanting?"

Jeanette whirled around and dropped her brother's letter on the wet cement. She faced the Irishman walking along a stone pathway beside the cob house. The white color was a stark contrast to the vivid pink, green, and blue buildings in the town, five minutes away.

Sunrays streaming through the clouds in the light rainfall obstructed her view of him and she flitted her lashes. "Hi, I'm looking for Conlin Murphy."

"You've found him."

She extended her arm for a greeting and propelled ahead as the rubber sole of her boot snagged a rock.

He laughed under his breath. "Ya must be Nettie." Conlin clasped her hands with a hearty shake and a wide smile.

"Jeanette Hillestad." Her head bobbed to the side, shaking her hair loose from the clip, holding a mess of tangled tresses. She must've arrived at the correct place since no one but Tom used her childhood nickname.

"Come in, come in. We needn't stand in the rain at all." Conlin brushed her hip as he crouched and picked up the dropped note. He passed it to her, then dug into the pocket of his navy wool coat, standing at the burgundy shade door, and pulled out a set of keys dangling from a tiny die-cast sailboat.

"Fáilte." Conlin moved aside, outstretching his arm. "Welcome."

Jeanette ambled under the archway. "Thanks, and I appreciate you allowing me to stop by on short notice."

"No bother." Conlin followed behind and shut the door. "May I take your jacket?"

He removed his coat, hung it on a rack, and yanked off a black beanie. Brown curls with auburn undertones sprouted below the hairline on his forehead, drawing attention to his azure-blue eyes. Jeanette averted her stare and took off her outerwear, handing him the garment.

"Make yerself comfortable." He gestured toward the couch. "Will ya have a cup of tea?"

"No, thank you."

Conlin peered over his shoulder on his way to the kitchen. "Ah, of course you will."

Jeanette rolled the cuff of her sleeve and glanced at her watch. Already a quarter till four in the afternoon, after traveling on a red-eye flight and driving for a couple hours from the airport. She staggered backward, and her shoes squeaked on the hardwood floor, forcing her into a lounge chair. Jeanette set her crossbody handbag on the seat and dug out her phone to take notes.

She didn't waste a second and got straight to the order of business. "When did you last see Tom?"

"Haven't seen the lad in three, maybe four weeks." He handed her a ceramic teacup and sat across from her on a forest-green sofa.

A lump formed in her throat, and she swallowed to make way for words. "I don't get it. Tom wrote in his letter that he was staying here for the past few months but neglected to mention why he visited Kinsale."

Conlin sipped his tea. "Sure, ye're confused and have questions." He leaned back against a cushion. "I'll tell you what I know."

Jeanette inhaled hard and held her breath, preparing herself for Conlin's news. All the worst-case scenarios filled her mind. Did Tom have an accident and sustain injuries or get into circumstances beyond his control again? Her nerves remained knotted the moment she departed from Logan International Airport and boarded the flight to Ireland. Jeanette joggled her head side to side. No point in jumping to conclusions. She raised her gaze and focused on Conlin.

He finished his drink and placed his teacup on the table. "Thomas came into my office at Inland Fisheries Ireland, in Macroom. He was looking for a group of men we questioned about illegal netting in protected waters."

"Why would Tom be interested in fishing laws?"

"They weren't catching salmon." Conlin scratched the short stubble on his chin and glanced at the ceiling. "They're part of a crew searching for artifacts."

A coldness ripped through her body. The minute Tom told her he stopped in Ireland after he visited Norway, she figured he had a lead on another relic. Discovering a piece of unwritten history motivated most of Tom's actions.

Jeanette shifted in her seat as her limbs tightened. She didn't like where the facts pointed. Her mouth opened, but she paused, listening to the rest of Conlin's information.

"Two days later, I ran into Thomas at a pub in town and he was looking for a summer rental. I offered him a lease term for our detached guesthouse." Conlin poured more tea into his cup. "Details about his involvement with the others digging for the artifacts are unclear. Y'know what I mean?"

Jeanette understood and often experienced the difficulty of keeping up with Tom's hunt for relics. "Did he tell you where he was going next?"

"The last time I saw Thomas, he took his belongings and planned on being gone for five days. When he didn't return after a week, I rang him but never got a response." Conlin's lips pressed into a straight line and his eyebrows cut low. "That's all I know."

A tightness constricted her chest and she stared at the light creamy tea. The cup warmed the chill in her fingers and steam rose from the hot liquid, infiltrating her nose with a malty scent. She took a large gulp and lifted her gaze toward Conlin. "Whenever I text or call his cell, there's no answer. Then I received a written letter and an email from his boss and thought he might be in trouble." She petted the length of her loose tresses. "Did the men that you questioned seem suspicious?"

"Em, Thomas didn't think they posed a threat." A crease between his eyes deepened as he leaned forward, resting his arms on his thighs. "I'm concerned about—"

The front door opened. A teenage girl walked in and dropped a messenger bag onto the floor of the entry. "Howya, Da?" The girl gawked and shifted her glance between the two of them as she kicked off her boots.

"How're t'ings, dear one? C'mere, meet Thomas's sister, Jeanette." Conlin extended his hand and motioned at her. "This is my daughter, Saoirse."

"Nice to—"

"Did Thomas come back?" Her tone escalated, and her body swayed, moving from one foot to the other.

"Not yet," he said.

Her shoulders wilted, dragging her feet a few inches, and she smiled thinly. "Howrya?"

"Okay, thanks." Jeanette shook her hand.

Saoirse folded her arms across her waist and bent her neck to one side, scrutinizing Jeanette's appearance. "I see a family resemblance in the color of your hair and eyes."

Jeanette fussed with her messy hairstyle, shoving several strands into a plastic hairpin. "It's the look of our Nordic mother."

Both ends of Saoirse's lips curled upward. "Are we searching for Thomas together?"

Floundering with a response, she sent an inquisitive stare to Conlin, then passed it to his daughter. "I... um..."

Saoirse bounced on her tiptoes and questioned her dad. "Did ya tell her about the gurriers lookin' for the stone Thomas found?"

Conlin wrinkled his brow with a dissuading headshake. "Pour yerself a cuppa and Jaffa's are in the press."

Saoirse exhaled aloud and swooshed her long brown hair over her shoulder as she traipsed into the kitchen.

Jeanette placed her cup on the table and lowered her hips to sit, then straightened her posture upright, unable to settle into her seat. What stone and why all the secrecy? If Conlin had additional information, he needed to divulge it and without delay.

"Yer brother made quite an impression."

"He has that effect on people." She fidgeted with her hands and grabbed her handbag. "I won't take up any more of your time, but I'd be grateful if there's anything else you can share about Tom's visit."

"You're staying in town, yeah?"

"At the Trident Hotel. I'll give you my cell number."

"Sure." He stood and pulled his phone from the back pocket of his denim jeans, handing her the device to type in the digits.

"Please call me if you hear from him or recall more details," she said.

"I will, so."

"She can stay in the guestroom, yeah?" Saoirse chewed a bite-sized round cake and washed it down with tea.

Jeanette caught Conlin peering at his daughter. "Well, I better get going." She strolled across the living area, halted at the door, and twirled around, bumping into Conlin's biceps as he followed close. "Thank you for your hospitality and accommodating my brother."

"Not a bother." Conlin stared into her eyes for a moment. He reached over her shoulder and snatched his coat from the rack. "I'll drive you."

Her posture shrank with the nearness of his body. "There's no need. I rented a car but left it at the hotel to enjoy the twenty-minute walk after sitting for hours."

"How about we meet at the pub?" Saoirse's face brightened and she nudged her dad's arm.

"Em..." He rubbed the back of his neck with an uneasy appearance.

"I've had a long day and I'm tired." Jeanette smiled and her sight trekked between them. "Nice meeting both of you."

"Do ya want me to show you the way into town?" Conlin bent closer and opened the door.

Jeanette stared at him longer than she intended and stepped outside. "I'm fine, thanks."

"All right, take care, Jeanette, and let us know when ya hear from Thomas."

"Okay." She raised a flat palm and gave a single wave.

Conlin leaned against the doorframe and returned the silent gesture, holding up five fingers. Jeanette turned and flinched at the sound of Conlin closing the door. A gusty sigh escaped her lips, realizing she traveled thousands of miles to receive minimal information and he could have answered her questions in an email. A nagging feeling that he knew more than he shared persisted, and she remained determined to get answers from Conlin Murphy.

THREE

A cool October breeze stirred and slipped underneath her plaid scarf. Jeanette tightened the knot and inhaled the briny sea air. The drizzle taunted her untamed mane, enlivening strands that embraced her nape. She swiped and pushed them back, attempting to control the wild locks. It didn't help that she grabbed the wrong jacket without a hood. She was certain her look mirrored her frazzled mood.

The confirmation that Tom disappeared rocked her senses, and the conversation with Conlin provided limited details about Tom's stay in Kinsale. Saoirse mentioned stones, but Conlin seemed apprehensive about giving her all the facts. Once again, Tom took off on one of his escapades, got into trouble, and waited for her to bail him out. Perhaps turning in early for the night would give her clarity in the morning.

A stale taste filled her mouth. The last meal she ate was the bland food during the flight from Boston to Shannon. Did she want to bother and eat now? A growl quaked her belly, and she wrapped her arms around her waist, needing strength to sort out Tom's disappearance.

Smoke billowed from the roof of a pub a couple of feet away on O'Connell Street. Jeanette pulled the brass handle on the crimson door and scanned the room. A group of men gathered at the bar and empty tables lined the perimeter.

Jeanette strolled through the center of the lounge and settled into the corner near a fireplace. She removed her damp puffer jacket, draped it on the chair, and inhaled the burning turf in the hearth. The earthy, moss-like aroma wafted from homes, pubs, and throughout the countryside on her drive from Shannon Airport to the town of Kinsale.

A server approached. "What can I get for you?"

Jeanette ran her fingers over the surface of the glossy wood table and glanced at the menu. "I'll start with a vegetarian Irish stew and still water."

"Be right back."

Jeanette admired paintings of the old town, lining the exposed brick, and a harp hanging on the wall. The fire warmed her body and she unwrapped her scarf. Unfolding Tom's letter, she read it for at least the tenth time. His choice to delete his social media accounts, setting an out-of-office automatic reply for his emails, and Mr. Bonhoeffer's call prompted her journey to Ireland. Tom's cryptic message left little to no information or leads. Perhaps Mom and Dad were right, and her search was a wild-goose chase.

Jeanette massaged her temples. Each blink weighed heavier and the dim lighting in the pub urged her to sleep. The toasty temperature had her ready to call it a night.

"Here you are." She placed the bowl on the table. "On holiday?"

"Not exactly. I was hoping to see my brother after he spent the summer in town. Maybe you've met him?" Jeanette pulled out her phone and tapped the camera roll icon. She scrolled through her digital library to a family picture from last Christmas and angled the image toward the fresh-faced brunette.

She stared at the photo for a minute. "Haven't seen him and I'd remember that face. He's a handsome fella."

Jeanette presented a courtesy smile. She grew up hearing about how good-looking, smart, accomplished, and successful her younger brother proved to be in any situation.

"What's his name? I'll ask the staff and some locals."

"Thanks. His name is Thomas Hillestad."

The server returned to the counter and chatted with a few men at the bar. Jeanette inhaled the steam circulating from her dish. Garlic clove and thyme awakened her senses. She blew on a large spoonful, and the rich, hearty red-wine tomato paste slid down her throat.

Finishing the entire portion in less than thirty minutes, she reclined on the wooden bench with a satisfied stomach. She sipped her water, washing the tangy flavor from her taste buds.

A man with shimmering silver-red hair limped toward her table. "Ye looking for the brother?"

Jeanette traded a glance with the stranger. "Yes, do you know him?"

"He joined in for a round, slagging over a few jars."

"Would you mind telling me about your time with him, Mr....?"

"Around here they call me Michael."

"Nice to meet you, I'm Jeanette." She extended an arm across the table. "Please have a seat and let me buy you a drink."

He pulled out a chair and sat. "There's a kind one, like Thomas."

Of course, like Tom... How could this man know she's the older sibling and taught him everything he knows?

"Howrya getting along?" the server asked.

"I'll have the usual," Michael said.

"Nothing for me, thanks."

"Ah, have a jar of the black stuff."

Jeanette straightened her shoulders and managed a polite grin. "Okay, just a half-pint."

"There you go now." Michael lolled in the chair, similar to Jack's posture, when he began one of his stories. "After his arrival, a group of shifty characters had taken an interest in Thomas' business and a sleeveen with a French accent caused a ruction while three others were starting.”

Jeanette wound a curl on her finger and tapped her toes to a jittery beat. Why was Tom keeping his involvement with these people a secret?

The woman brought their order and set the glasses in front of them. “Sláinte.” He raised the pint glass and gulped the thick foam layer atop the dark liquid.

Jeanette sipped the stout and squinted at the strong wheat taste, turning bitter in her mouth. She coughed and took a swig of her water. “Do you remember the last time you saw Tom?”

“It would be about a month since I’ve seen the lad. The others come in once a week.”

“Did Tom tell you what they wanted?”

“Ah, ye know Thomas is dog wide and the lad’s gas craic altogether during a session. I’d wager he left Kinsale to avoid trouble.”

Jeanette scratched her head. She struggled to understand all his slang, but Michael made it clear he had a great time with Tom in the pub, and whatever he found gained attention and initiated conflict.

Michael polished off his Guinness. He held his hand in the air and called out, “Same again.”

Jeanette took two sips and hiccuped. She wasn’t a regular drinker, and she felt the effects.

Michael said, “Ye can’t expect to keep up wit’ the brother.”

Heat roared up her neck and she eyed the glass, ready to conquer the challenge, and downed the entire drink. Straightaway the alcohol bubbled in her brain and added to her fatigue. She might need a taxi instead of staggering back to her hotel. She shut her eyelids to stop the whirling in her head.

“You discovered the best pub in town,” an Irishman said.

The voice broke through her foggy mind as her eyes popped open and she turned toward the man. Conlin and Saoirse stood at the edge of the table.

Jeanette stared at him for too long, recognizing he wore eyeglasses now, drawing her deeper into his blue irises, and she blinked hard to refocus her thoughts. "Yeah, I'm passing gas craic with Michael."

A smile peeked from behind Conlin's fist held to his lips, restraining his laughter. Jeanette's cheeks burned and she darted her gaze toward the empty pint glass.

Saoirse giggled and scooted across the bench beside Jeanette. "Gas craic means great fun."

Jeanette grazed her front teeth along her lower lip and caught Conlin's amused expression as fine lines creased the corners of his mouth.

He kept his eyesight fixed on her and removed his coat. "I'm surprised to find ya here."

Brushing loose hair strands from her forehead, she angled her chin upward. "Why? I was hungry."

"Told ya to invite her to the pub," Saoirse said.

"Right, I didn't extend true Irish hospitality." He glanced at Michael and patted his shoulder. "How's the form?"

"On me last legs. How's the Murphy clan?" Michael moved over to another chair, inviting Conlin to join them.

"Not too bad."

"We're chatting about the brother, Thomas." Michael finished his second pint.

Conlin shifted the casual conversation and spoke in an inquisitive tone. "Find out any news?"

"The guys taking notice of Tom's work sound insistent... I'm concerned," Jeanette said.

Michael said, "I explained they were giving it out to Thomas."

Saoirse rested her elbows on the counter and bent forward, perking up in her seat. "And did ya tell her about—"

"Moira." Conlin raised his hand and waved at the waitress.

She swung beside the table, leaning close to Conlin, and pulled him into a side hug. "How're things?"

"Grand. And yerself?"

"Mighty!" Her face beamed and she straightened her posture. "Will ye be having the usual?"

Conlin gave her a single nod and winked. Moira's face flushed, and she glanced at Saoirse. "A cola for ya?"

"Sure, t'anks."

Jeanette studied the interaction between Moira and Conlin. Muscles tightened in her stomach, churning a mixture of stew and Guinness. "I should go and get some rest." She shoved her arms into her jacket and tied her scarf around her neck.

Saoirse slid off the bench and moved aside. "Stay for the craic."

Jeanette's eyesight flitted round the room until landing on Conlin. Part of her wanted to hang out, yet she needed to sleep after a flight, drinks, and unsettling news about Tom. "Maybe another time."

She shook Michael's hand. "It was nice to meet you and thank you for talking to me." Jeanette turned toward Moira. "I'll take the bill now and please add everyone's order to mine."

"You're a kind soul." Michael lifted his glass in a toast and dipped his chin.

"It's the least I can do for the consideration you all showed Tom."

"Here ya are." Moira handed Jeanette the card machine and she completed the transaction.

Saoirse flipped her hair to one side. "See ya, Jeanette."

"All the best," Michael said.

Conlin reached and placed his hand upon hers. "Please, stay." A warmth surfaced under his touch, feeling a kinship, and he jerked his elbow rearward, releasing his grip as if the mutual awareness muddled his senses. "Em... we interrupted your meal."

"Not at all. I'm exhausted after a long day."

He seemed more agreeable now than he did earlier. Perhaps it was an ideal opportunity to gain more information about the stone Tom found and the men after it, but their food arrived. "Enjoy your night."

One corner of her mouth curved upward, and Jeanette stepped backward, almost knocking the plates off the serving tray. She slinked away until she reached the exit and peered over her shoulder. Conlin's gaze followed her movements and a hotness spread throughout her body. Jeanette pushed the door open and left in a hurry.

The time difference, traveling, and an overload of information about Tom mixed up in his usual circumstances intensified the headache surging through her brain. The alcohol didn't help settle her nerves, either. She strolled along the waterfront, staring at tethered boats rocking on the quay and lights twinkling on the water. Or was that in her head? Jeanette massaged her forehead with the tips of her fingers.

Why did she decide to take off on another rescue mission? Did she play the heroine everyone in the family accused her of being? Whenever Tom led explorations, he got in over his head, and she showed up looking like an overbearing sister. Then he waltzed away, appearing as the clever archaeologist, living the life of an adventurer with no worries. Yeah, because he always had a way out, his big sister, but no more of his wild escapades or putting herself on the line for her *little brother*. He needed to grow up and this time would be the last that she would come to his rescue.

FOUR

Late Thursday morning, after a pot of black tea and a modified vegan Irish breakfast, including dairy-free soda bread, Jeanette left Trident Hotel for the day. She created a list of questions for Conlin and strolled Main Street in the direction of his house; now that her physical and spiritual strength returned. Shops in a striking contrast of turquoise, fuchsia, and pistachio lined the stone pedestrian walkway. Distant wails of seagulls echoed through the marine layered sky with a breeze carrying the aroma of saltwater and freshly cut fish.

A few minutes later, when she reached Desmond Castle at the top of a hill, she paused and glanced at her watch: 11:25 a.m. Even though Conlin withheld details and information regarding Tom's plight, it didn't earn her the right to push him for answers. Although she believed he'd understand the need for him to divulge everything he knew about her brother's situation.

Jeanette inhaled, straightening her shoulders, and continued to the Murphy's cottage at a clipped pace. Conlin must recognize the importance of protecting family members and she bet he would do whatever it took to help those he loved, especially if it involved Saoirse.

Walking Barrack Street, she followed the curve along the road until she arrived at Conlin's home on Friary Lane. Cupping her hands together, she gave her tingling fingers a gentle squeeze and swallowed to make room for words. If she gathered a few additional clues about the men pursuing Tom, then she'd be on her way and out of Conlin's life.

Jeanette knocked on the entrance for their house and gazed skyward at the straight trimmed lines of the thatch roof.

Saoirse answered and stood in the entry. "Hiya, Jeanette. Come in."

"Thanks. Is your dad home?"

She closed the door. "He went into work for a couple of hours. Although he's supposed to be on holiday." Saoirse bobbed a shoulder, and she shuffled her feet toward the kitchen.

"I can return later."

"Ah, please stay. I'm wicked bored." Saoirse yanked the top off a ceramic canister. "Did ya have brekkie?"

"Yes, I ate breakfast at the hotel."

"I'm going straight to elevenses." She stuck half a biscuit in her mouth, holding it between her front teeth and placed a stainless-steel kettle on the stove.

Saoirse reminded her of herself when she was a teenager. Mom scolded her whenever she ate cookies for breakfast and Dad let it slide if she brought him one too. "You're not in school now?"

"It's midterm break and I have two extra weeks off while me mas on her honeymoon."

An unexpected release of tension streamed through Jeanette's limbs. It had nothing to do with the marital status of Saoirse's parents. She pulled an unruly ringlet straight and held her breath for a minute. Too much stress and the time change made her feel out of sorts.

Saoirse motioned for Jeanette to have a seat at the center island. "The auld man didn't take Ma's wedding well." She set a teacup and saucer in front of Jeanette. "I t'ink that's why he went to work today; he likes the distraction."

Saoirse's observations of her father impressed Jeanette, and she nodded in agreement about Conlin's position.

"You're kinda quiet." She filled her porcelain cup, placing cream and sugar on the table. "Thomas was always sharing stories about whatcha call it, the Notch?"

"Tom's quite the storyteller." Jeanette stared at the steaming liquid and blew, cooling the beverage. "I talk a lot when I'm discussing history, artifacts, and ancient cultures. So, it depends on the setting and subject."

"Like the fella Thomas told us about." She snapped her fingers and her gaze flitted around the room. "What's his name?"

"Arctic Jack."

"Yeah, that's it."

An ache pinched Jeanette's throat. Discussing Tom and reminiscing about Jack weighed heavily on her heart. No use in getting caught up in emotions, at least not in the presence of Saoirse. "I'm glad you enjoy Tom's company. It seems you both care about him and share my concerns about his disappearance."

"I was worried when he left and thought he might be in trouble." Saoirse nibbled at her lower lip and lowered her gaze.

Did Conlin notice that his teenage daughter had a crush on a thirty-three-year-old man? Jeanette envisioned his shock at the notion of his baby girl taking an interest in an older guy, or any boys for that matter. "I understand."

"Do ya think somet'ing awful happened to him?"

Jeanette glanced to one side, searching for the right answer, and correct verbiage for explaining her predicament. Although Saoirse appeared mature for her age, she didn't need early exposure to the harsh realities of the world yet. "Tom always pulls through any situation with my help." Jeanette bit into a crispy biscuit. The buttery crunch crumbled onto her tongue, and she washed it down with black tea. "As an older sister, I'm less than thrilled about the expeditions he embarks on and sometimes he gets an idea…" She shook her head. "Let's just say he's overzealous."

Saoirse's eyes gleamed and widened. "His adventures sound exciting."

"Your dad doesn't seem too impressed."

Saoirse bent her elbows and propped them onto the counter, resting her chin on a fist. "Da didn't want ya to know about the gurriers following Thomas."

"Are they the archaeologists that were picked up for illegal fishing?"

"Yeah, Da ripped into the one with a French accent outside of our house. The eejit approached me on the way inside, asking me about Thomas and if I knew about an ancient stone. I didn't even tell the auld man about that part." Saoirse smirked and crossed her arms. "Da had a row with Thomas after the incident and told him to leave. That was weeks ago." Saoirse's eyelids lowered with a downcast look on her face. "He's still fond of the lad. It was like bad timing wit' me ma's wedding." Saoirse settled back onto the stool and gulped her tea.

Was it the same man Michael saw Tom with at the pub? The person they described seemed adamant about finding Tom and the relics he discovered. It started sounding more serious than she thought, maybe worse than his usual debacles.

"I'm sorry Tom caused an unnecessary disruption in your lives." Jeanette stared at her teacup. "I know the feeling all too well."

"Are you kidding? Things were dull until Thomas showed up. He's the bizz."

Saoirse had fallen victim to the young idealist trap and under the spell of her brother's jaunts. It was best if she went on her way and didn't involve the Murphys with any of her family's issues.

"Thanks for the tea and the delightful conversation." Jeanette stood and smiled.

"Ya need to go already?"

"Now that I have a little more information about Tom and the guys involved, I should probably try to sort out what happened and go looking for him."

Saoirse drooped her shoulders. "Don't worry about me Da, he likes you."

Heat radiated from Jeanette's chest, spreading up her neck, and flooded her face.

"Um, I'm not sure about that. He seems to regret the moment I arrived."

"Ah, he's stiff around women. The folks never married and split seven years ago. Ma left for Dublin and I'm with her in the city most of the year. Da's out here by himself, but I stay some weekends, school breaks, and the summer." She flipped her hair over her shoulder. "Like he never goes out, and doesn't date, so he thinks I shouldn't at sixteen. Know what I mean?"

"I guess it's hard for parents to watch their kids grow up in the blink of an eye." A smile twitched her mouth. "Let your dad know I stopped by for a visit." She moved toward the front entrance. As she slipped her hand around the brushed-nickel knob, the handle turned, and she hopped backward. Conlin swung the door open, missing Jeanette within half an inch. She flinched, stumbling over her feet, and he halted mid-stride.

A gleam touched his expression at first sight, and in an instant, it dimmed as his lids lowered to half-mast. "What are you at?"

"Oh, I wanted to ask you a couple more questions, but you weren't home, and Saoirse invited me in for tea."

"Ah, here. I told you everything about your brother's stay in Kinsale. There's no need to question me daughter when I'm not home." His eyebrows crinkled as the crease deepened at the bridge of his nose. He shot a glance at Saoirse. "Give us a few minutes to talk alone."

"Da—" A grunt vibrated from her throat as she whirled around and headed down a hallway.

"It wasn't like that at all, and I'm not trying to cause any problems. We hung out and had a chat," Jeanette said.

"I'm concerned about Thomas' well-being and you're a kind one. Still an' all, I t'ink it's best if we leave it now." He pushed a palm through his loose curls. "I feel for your dilemma, yet I need to protect Saoirse."

Jeanette jogged her head in agreement, and a weight pressed on her chest. "Well, Mr. Murphy, I have no intentions of intruding on you or your daughter any more than I already have."

She straightened the mass of hair clumped at her nape with an elastic band and extended her arm.

"I'm grateful for the information you provided. The best to you and Saoirse." She slipped her hand into his, relishing the touch of his palm against hers as he prolonged their handclasp.

Conlin licked his lips and cleared his throat. "Slán, and good luck with everything."

She exited the cottage and walked along the pathway, fighting the urge to look back. Jeanette gained a little more insight into Conlin. The fact he solely focused on part-time parenting and his career clarified he maintained an imbalance in life with strict priorities. Now her presence added to a disruption of his daily routines, with the additional chaos of strangers approaching his daughter in search of a relic hunter.

However, his contradicting reactions to her visit troubled and piqued her interest. One minute he welcomed her inside their home, offering to help, and the next he kicked her out the door. Did she overstep boundaries? Was she unaware of some traditional Irish etiquette?

Either way, she'd have to find Tom without Conlin's assistance. A heaviness slowed her footsteps walking into town. Should she return to New Hampshire? After all, she only had a two-week leave of absence from work and used three of the days gaining minimal info about Tom's disappearance.

Jeanette's torso vibrated from her iPhone inside the pocket of her nylon jacket. She retrieved the device and skimmed the name displayed. Brian again. She sighed, clicking the side button, and declined the call. Jeanette ignored all his messages since the night she departed for Ireland.

Brian made his position clear about her decision to leave town and search for Tom. He wasn't willing to help and expected her to stay for a work gathering with his friends. As if his social networking took priority over her brother. When she called him out on his behavior, he passed it off as if she had misunderstood.

The next time he phoned, she would answer. After three years in a relationship, she at least owed him an acknowledgment and an explanation for the breakup note she left him about the different directions their lives had taken.

Pressing matters took precedence in her mind. Was Tom still searching for stones or hiding out somewhere?

The best option she had for locating Tom was considering places he would go if he needed sanctuary. Where had he gone in the past? She tapped a finger against her lips, strolling along Main Street. So much puzzled her about the circumstances leading up to his abrupt departure from Kinsale.

Perhaps it had something to do with Saoirse being approached by one of Tom's pursuers. He might not even be in danger, and she blew his cryptic note out of proportion. No, most of Tom's expeditions ended with problems, and this upsetting scenario fit his profile. Mr. Bonhoeffer's concerns also backed up her motives to look for her brother in Ireland. Great, she doubted her original reasons for traveling to a foreign country since Mom, Dad, and Brian thought she always overreacted to Tom's need for help. If the entire trip turned into a misunderstanding because of his lack of communication, she would never hear the end of it.

Of course, she prayed for his safety, yet if the situation resulted in a fool's errand, she would appear as the one needing saving.

FIVE

Conlin's gaze followed Jeanette until she was no longer in his visual field. He closed the door, and a heaviness lingered in his chest. Nothing to be done now. He had set the matter straight and freed himself of any more entanglements with the Hillestad family, except for a few belongings Thomas left in the flat. When he received a forwarding address from him, he'd mail the items. Better yet, he would text Jeanette and request she take the last of his things. Although he made it clear, he preferred she stayed away.

Conlin sighed and poured himself a cup of tea from the pot. His words seemed rather harsh as he pictured the hurt reflected in her soft hazel eyes. She hid it well and only with the deepest, intentional gaze did he see the sadness emerge.

"Why did ya accuse Jeanette of interrogating me and throw her out?" Saoirse stood across the room, setting a hand on her hip, like when her mother was cross with him.

"Don't be dramatic. I didn't boot her out the door."

"Practically, you told her to get lost and never come round here again."

Did he? If so, he didn't mean it. He never intended to cause Jeanette discomfort. No wonder she looked forlorn. 'Tis true and he tried convincing himself he didn't want to see her heart-shaped face, with hair the color of honey wheat framing her delicate features. What an eejit for saying that for no good reason. Conlin took a long drink of his favorite Barry's Gold Blend Tea, enjoying the rich and refreshing taste settling on his tongue.

"Ah, listen, I sounded callous because..."

Saoirse linked her arms around his and rested her head against his biceps. "I know. You've been testy since Ma's wedding."

"Have I now?"

She glanced upward and fluttered her eyelids. When did she grow into an observant bean óg? He kissed her noggin, and she perked up, cracking a smile.

"Will ya invite Jeanette for tea?"

"Wait a minute, I—"

"Please?" She folded her hands together and begged with a slight frown.

Conlin laughed through his nose. "Maybe, but she might leave town soon." A coldness rushed through his chest.

"Then ask her tonight, so."

Did he have the nerve after the way he treated her a few minutes ago? "I will t'ink about it."

Saoirse bounced up and down on her tiptoes. "What should we cook?" She hurried into the kitchen and sifted through the press. "Potato cakes?"

Conlin suppressed a grin and shook his head. Saoirse had him wrapped around her finger, and she knew it. "Make a list, and I'll go to the shops in a bit."

Taking sluggish steps, he walked down the hallway and out the side door. Gathering any of Thomas' belongings that he might've left behind gave him an excuse to contact Jeanette. At the detached guesthouse, he inserted the key and entered the room. He hadn't gone inside since he cleaned it before Thomas' arrival.

Conlin glanced around the flat—the single bed made, waste bin emptied, and the en suite wiped clean. He appreciated Thomas' cleanliness, yet it was obvious he didn't intend to return and his departure from Kinsale was final. A pen and blank paper rested on the nightstand. Probably the same notepad he used to write Jeanette a letter. He pulled open a drawer, discovering a black t-shirt and a pair of socks.

Conlin shuffled across the scuffed hardwood floors that he planned on refinishing, yet never had the time, and stood at the writing desk with the 19-inch telly positioned atop the fixture. He tugged the brass handle on the bottom drawer, and found nothing, then checked the one above, revealing a single pencil rolling around. As he pushed it shut, the crunching of paper hindered the drawer from sliding on the track. Reaching inside, he felt the obstacle, moved the sliders forward, and yanked the munched parchment from the rollers. Conlin unfolded the crumpled sheet, laid it on the oak desk, and smoothed out the wrinkles. He skimmed the sketch of a map with locations listed and arrows directing from Norway to Ireland and Iceland onto Greenland, continuing in the direction toward North America.

Conlin swiped a palm over his mouth and sighed. The reason Thomas withheld his plans was to prevent him from having to lie to Jeanette. Why did he snoop around? Now he had information and needed to decide whether to honor Thomas' wishes of keeping his sister out of the situation or be forthcoming with Jeanette.

Conlin shoved the sheet into his jeans. For now, he'd keep it to himself and not tell Saoirse. She seemed to take a liking, as he did, to the Hillestad siblings, yet she had no trouble divulging any and all details.

He locked the room and headed into the house, cruising past the kitchen. "On me way out for the messages."

"Here are a few t'ings to pick up." Saoirse handed him a handwritten list of ingredients on a piece of paper.

Conlin threw on his peacoat and tucked the note into the pocket of his cacks. "See ya."

He left and followed the pathway toward the village. Single parenting challenged him more than anything in his life. Although

Saoirse was his greatest blessing, most of the time he didn't know what he was doing and despite multiple mistakes, she developed into a fine iníon. The years passed too fast. Now, she reached the age of taking serious notice of boys and wanted to date. Conlin pressed his thick hair back from his forehead, relieving the pressure building in his cranium.

A sea breeze stirred the scents of salt and burning turf in the air. With a deep breath, he closed his eyes for a moment and pictured himself on his Bavaria 30 Cruiser sailboat in the harbor. He gazed at the waterfront on his walk toward Main Street. The few days he spent out on his boat gave him moments of respite and reflection.

If Thomas hadn't disappeared, he would be sailing right now instead of navigating the situation he created, with the newfound information, and all the while attempting to keep Saoirse in the dark about everything. It wasn't a simple task since she had an eye that could see around corners.

His vision settled on the choppy waves as he headed down Pier Road. Managing the hull of a sailboat in undesirable conditions seemed easier than dealing with the current undertaking of asking Jeanette to join them for tea. Conlin entered the shop and removed his hands from the front pockets of his coat.

Grabbing a basket, he perused the aisles and gathered ingredients. As he rounded a corner, he spotted Jeanette examining prepackaged sambos. A smile built at the sight of her, and a warmth filled his chest. Conlin moseyed toward her and stopped short of a few steps away. She didn't flinch, and he leaned forward to catch her attention.

"Howrya?"

"Huh?" She spun and knocked the handbasket into his gut.

The hint of a grunt blew out from a gusty breath. "Right, you'd be expecting an apology for the way I spoke to ya earlier."

"Oh no, I didn't mean to bump into you." Her cheeks reddened and she straightened her posture. "I'm picking up a couple of essentials."

He glanced at the items she collected—a bottle of water, a bag of nuts, Ready Salted Walker Crisps, shaving cream, and a disposable razor. "Busy night ahead?"

"Not really." Jeanette followed his line of vision, stiffened her torso, and flung the basket behind her back. "There's no need to apologize, but I appreciate the courtesy."

"Em, it has been a rough week."

"I understand, between me arriving on short notice, Tom causing chaos and Saoirse mentioned her mother's recent marriage."

"Ah, sure, you know yourself." A muscle twanged in his neck. They had engaged in girl talk. What else did they chat about? "Saoirse would like you to come for tea this evening."

Wisps stuck in her lashes, and her gaze flitted around the store. "That's kind of her to think of me."

"If ye're willing to put off any previous plans." He gestured, tilting his head toward her shopping basket. Conlin cringed at his comments and rubbed his nape. Saoirse knew her auld man well when she assessed he lacked the finesse to talk to women, and this wasn't even an invitation for a date.

"I don't want to impose," she said.

The reservations in her tone and meek manner conveyed he had indeed been a complete eejit. Conlin figured she would need some convincing. "I'd like you to join us as well." He grinned to put her doubts at ease.

Jeanette dipped her chin downward, and her face flushed. "Sounds nice."

How did he miss how reserved and shy she became around him? Conlin tuned into the rising heat under his collar. "Grand, how's seven o'clock?"

"Perfect. Plenty of time to finish my prior commitments." She motioned to the grocery items and a sweet laugh bloomed on her lips. "Should I bring anything?"

Ah, now she was codding him, and her personality shined. "Em..." Conlin pulled the paper from his pocket. "Saoirse made a list of a few things to pick up." Glancing down at Thomas' map, he folded it and hid the note in his coat.

"Don't trouble yerself." Conlin evaded telling her what he found for now.

For the first time since they met, she seemed comfortable with him, and he didn't want to ruin the moment.

A smile sprang across her countenance. "See you at seven." She twirled in the opposite direction.

Conlin watched her walk down the aisle and she angled her head, sweeping her tendrils over her shoulder. He pulled his sweater forward, stretching the material away from his body and allowed air flow to circulate. Most definitely, he would tell her about his findings tonight. Promise or no promise, he had to be honest.

He prided himself on being forthcoming and taught Saoirse the importance of honesty, and Conlin needed to demonstrate that example by sharing his discovery with Jeanette. Besides, the sooner he passed on the map, she would move on and continue her search for Thomas. His upper body gravitated earthward, forcing a stifled breath from his mouth. Even before meeting her, Thomas' stories about them as kids delighted him and when he first saw Jeanette's picture...

Conlin scanned the surrounding area, as if she was aware of him thinking of her within the proximity. Dinner, a conversation about the map, and nothing more. That'd be the end of his brief acquaintance with Jeanette Hillestad.

SIX

Back at the Trident Hotel, Jeanette tossed her reusable grocery bag onto a chair in the guestroom and hurled herself onto the queen-sized bed. A light scent of lavender hung in the air, and she lifted her head just high enough to see the clock on the nightstand, then flung her head back onto the pillows, letting out a gusty breath. Five more hours until seven. She flip-flopped on the mattress, then hopped up and paced the royal-blue carpet. Jeanette threw open the drapes and stared out at the boats in the harbor.

Was it too early to get ready for dinner? Did she bring anything nicer than a few thermal shirts, a couple of flannels, and a polar-fleece pullover? She shook her head. It wasn't a date. Besides, Conlin barely tolerated her presence and her intentions remained to gather information about Tom, nothing else. Still, he possessed a sweetness in his demeanor, especially with Saoirse and the way he extended his invitation for supper. Yes, Conlin's relationship with his daughter seemed special. Now her feelings for the Murphys became clear—a fondness and longing for the parent-child bond.

At thirty-five, any ideas she clung to about having children in the future ticked farther away. She didn't discuss marriage or kids with Brian, since his work always took precedence, and Jeanette never pictured him as a dad. Heck, he wasn't even much of a partner. If she got real with herself, there was no point in pressing the matter because they did not build their relationship on the same beliefs and they failed to secure a lasting connection. Sure, he fit the profile, they shared a few similar interests, and had mutual associations, yet she wasn't in love with him. Brian became comfortable and familiar.

Jeanette removed her jacket and hung it on the desk chair. She dug out Tom's letter to read it again. Best if she kept her mind on the task at hand. She laid back on the comforter and studied the note, paying careful attention to the remark at the end. It sounded like a quote, but it wasn't. He seemed to echo a thought or mimicked a phrase:

Like a voyager, discovering the new land, I set out on that same journey. An expedition from Fort Ó Cúis. I follow in their footsteps.

Jeanette skimmed it over a few more times and tapped her finger against her lips. Where was Fort Ó Cúis? Her phone buzzed and she grabbed the device to browse the internet. She stared at the screen for a second and took a gulp of air before she answered.

"Hi, Brian."

"I started thinking something happened to you... or maybe you're ignoring my calls."

"Sorry, I'm preoccupied," she said.

"Did you locate Thomas?"

"No." Her voice cracked.

"Oh, I see..."

Silence lingered on the line. Better deal with the awkward conversation. "Did you see the letter I left for you?"

"I haven't opened it yet. You know I'm busy." Brian's tone deepened and turned serious. "So, when are you coming home?"

Jeanette held her breath for half a minute. Seriously? He didn't bother to read her note. Not a surprise, just typical Brian.

"Are you still there?"

"Yeah, I'll need a few more days. Mr. Murphy and his daughter are helping me sort out the details of Tom's stay here, and where he might've headed after he left Kinsale."

"Well, don't take too long. We have a special event at work coming up soon, and Thanksgiving is right around the corner. My folks are expecting us."

"This is important, and Tom could be in major trouble."

"I'm just thinking about you, babe."

She shook the device in her hand, unleashing her bottled retorts on it instead of initiating an argument with Brian. "I need to go."

"I should get going too," he said.

"Okay, bye." She hung up and expelled a heavy sigh. It wasn't nice, but the nerve of him pressing her to come home for family festivities when Tom was who knows where and to top it off; he ignored her letter. A quiet rest, meditation, and prayer would provide the peace and clarity she needed. Too much happened, and she required God's guidance.

Jeanette stirred from a deep sleep, struggling to lift her heavy eyelids and fluttered her lashes until her vision focused. She rolled onto her side and shook the pins and needles sensation from her hand, waiting for the feeling to subside. Her phone pressed into her shoulder, and she snatched it from behind her back.

Widening her eyes, she checked the screen displaying 6:15 p.m. and leaped off the bed. Now she only had five minutes to freshen up. Hurrying toward the bathroom, she scrambled to comb out her tangled mane. As usual, brushing out her curls created frizz and the volume of her tendrils grew two times bigger. She pushed her hair backward with a fleece headband and pulled her locks into a low ponytail.

Jeanette changed into a green-and-blue checkered flannel to replace her obviously slept-in cotton shirt. Tossing on her jacket, she swung her bag over her chest and slipped on her boots. She froze and snapped her fingers, thinking she forgot something. Yes, her phone. She snagged it off the bed and glanced at the home screen. In thirty minutes, she'd be late, yet she kept having the pressing thought of Fort O... Dang it. What was the name?

Jeanette grabbed Tom's letter and verified the spelling. She typed the phrase into her internet browser and the search returned plenty of information, giving her tons of reading to do later. She bookmarked the pages, then shoved her iPhone and the note into her purse.

She made her way downstairs, through the lobby from the third floor, and strode out the double-glass doors, facing the water. Jeanette halted and considered driving the Opel Corsa in the parking lot and turned in the opposite direction. Her body yearned for the usual two-mile hikes she took at least three times a week. If she hurried, she might arrive at seven on foot. Jeanette walked along the waterfront and crammed her hands in her pockets as the seaside breeze stirred.

Trekking at a fast pace, her breath was visible in the air as the temperature dropped. She cut through residential streets right outside of town and huffed up an incline. The roads looked desolate, with lights placed at the end of each block and an eerie stillness circulated in the air. She kept her eyes fixed on the ground and maintained a steady speed. As she rounded a corner at the top of a hill, she halted inches from slamming into a broad man.

"Excuse me." She stepped aside and moved forward.

The stranger bumped her arm hard as she passed. He grabbed the strap of her crossbody bag, and an immediate force yanked her backward. Her heart skipped a beat, and she whirled around. He tugged her close and she smacked against his belly bulge.

"Hey!"

The attacker pressed his thick hand over her lips, and she snapped her jaw shut, grazing her incisors along his palm. He repositioned his fingers and she sank her front teeth into his hot, sweaty skin. The man grunted and raised his arm, crossing it over his chest, and with a heavy backhanded swoop, his knuckles smashed against the corner of her lips. Bones quaked as if solid rock slammed into her face, and she wobbled off balance.

Jeanette squeezed her eyes tight feeling the instant burning and throbbing. She licked the taste of salt and iron on her gums as her saliva pooled with blood. He shoved her torso onto the brick wall behind, forcing fluid from her mouth.

His muscular body towered above, and he drew nearer. Beads of sweat poured down his temples. "Give me the map." He bared his crooked teeth.

Jeanette stared at him and jutted her chin. "Let go of me."

He jerked the cut-proof strap on her bag and her limbs flailed. Jeanette's pulse raced and perspiration broke along her hairline.

"I'll take it by force if I have to." He slammed her harder against the stone, expelling her breath from her chest.

Rolls of fat brushed her stomach and she held in a rippling sickness. She pursed her lips, hiked her knee upward, jamming it into his groin, pressing deeper at an angle, and ramming his tender flesh until he buckled. The man howled, stumbled rearward, and doubled over.

Using the wall as a springboard, she raised her boot, shoving the rubber sole into his gut and he fell to the ground. Jeanette kicked him again in the midsection with the same strength and force she used playing soccer throughout school. The sheer power sent a numbing sensation throughout her tendons and ankle. She spun on her heel and ran in the opposite direction toward the Murphy's cottage.

Jeanette sprinted through the streets, and icy air burned her lungs. Even with her level of physical fitness, the incident rocked her senses. The bitter coldness and an ache in her jaw slowed her stamina. She arrived at Conlin's residence out of breath and her trembling hand knocked on the door.

Saoirse opened the entry, and her smile collapsed. "Janey Mackers!"

Conlin hovered behind, widening the entrance, and Saoirse stepped aside. He wrapped his arm around Jeanette's back, gently guiding her inside the house and escorted her toward the kitchen.

"What happened?" he asked.

The rush of adrenaline shuddered her limbs, and she blew out a heavy gust. "A man attacked me."

His eyes flashed wider and settled on her split lip. "God between us and all harm."

She opened her mouth to speak, but he raised a finger and paused her explanation. He directed her to the sink and dampened a cotton dish towel. Conlin poured a glass of water and placed it in her hands.

"What can I do?" Saoirse held her palm upward.

"Keep an eye on the tea, dear one."

Saoirse gave a single nod and tended to a pot on the stove. Jeanette shrank, observing the look of concern on Saoirse's face. She didn't want to alarm them. Maybe Conlin disapproved of her coming to their home since Tom had already caused plenty of trouble. She sipped her drink and rinsed her mouth.

Conlin laid a tender touch on her shoulder. "C'mere, have a seat, and tell me the details."

He helped remove her jacket, then steered her toward the sofa and sat close. Leaning forward, he placed the cloth against her bruise. His eyelids raised until he met her gaze, revealing the blue of the horizon bursting with a new day in the morning sky. The warmth of his palm clasped over her hand, lifting her arm and he passed her the towel.

Jeanette said, "Thanks."

"Did the gouger steal yer money?"

"No." She balled the cloth, laid it on her lap, and pulled out the crumpled note from her handbag. "I think he wanted to get a hold of Tom's letter."

"Why?"

"I guess he assumed it gave information on Tom's whereabouts or the relics."

Conlin tipped his head forward. "May I?" He slipped the paper through her fingers, studied the page, and shrugged a shoulder. "There isn't any mention of locations."

"The man demanded I give him the map."

Conlin opened, then closed his mouth as a deep *hmm* vibrated in his throat.

"I figured he meant this phrase." She leaned close and pointed a finger at the particular words.

"A quote? I don't get it."

"That's the idea. Tom intended for me to decode the message." The curve of her lips upward triggered a sharp pain, and she clenched her jaw. Jeanette pressed her arm against his and inched closer. "See how he wrote about Fort Ó Cúis? Well, I searched on the internet and it's a location. I haven't been able to read about it yet—"

"Let's take a breather, eat and have a proper rest now. We'll have a look at it together later." Conlin held her at the bend of the elbow, helping her onto her feet.

Jeanette dropped her shoulders, folded the piece of paper, shoving it into her bag on the couch and followed him into the kitchen.

Saoirse loitered at the stove, jerking her head upward. "Feeling better?" She continued at lightning speed without taking a breath. "Was it the man looking for Thomas?"

"Don't get overexcited. We're going to have supper, then discuss it."

"Da, I'm asking how she's doing." She pulled three plates from a shelf with a headshake.

Jeanette held back an aching smile. She enjoyed listening and observing the interaction between the two of them. "I'm fine. Thanks for your concern." She wasn't feeling well yet gathering together with them comforted her and unwound her knotted nerves.

"Do you mind if I clean myself up before we eat?" Jeanette asked.

Conlin showed the way across the living room. "Second door on the right."

Jeanette ambled down the hallway, entered the bathroom, and flipped on the light. She glanced at the mirror and flinched.

A break in the skin on her lower lip enhanced a blue-and-purple tint. She dampened a couple of facial tissues and dabbed her mouth until the blood spots disappeared. Straightening her hair and retying her elastic band holding her ponytail, she felt a little more presentable.

She exited the restroom and returned to the dining area. Conlin pulled out a chair and she sat, wringing her hands in her lap as his stare lingered. She resisted the temptation to meet his gaze. "Smells delicious."

Conlin bent over her shoulder. "Ever had shepherd's pie?"

A fluttering swooshed through her body with the brush of his breath against her cheek and the *r*-heaviness sound in his rhotic dialect pronunciation of Irish English near her ear. Jeanette smoothed her palms over her shirt and kept her reaction under control. "No, I haven't."

He clapped and rubbed his hands together. "You're in for a treat." He aimed his steps back into the kitchen and returned with two dishes, serving her a portion.

Saoirse strolled in with her plate and a glass dish. "It's me granny's recipe."

Jeanette examined the square-cut piece with a mashed potato topping and tilted her head to one side, viewing the filling. They observed her inspection of the food.

"We make it with beef," Saoirse said.

"It looks like you both put in a lot of work." Jeanette shifted her gaze between them. "I'm sure it's delightful, but I eat a vegan diet."

The cutlery clanged on the porcelain serving tray. Saoirse and Conlin stood across the table from each other with their mouths agape.

Saoirse said, "We have extra mash and veggies leftover from the pie filling."

"Sorry, I should've mentioned it."

"No trouble at all."

Conlin picked up her plate and Saoirse trailed behind him. She hurried into the room, serving her a new plate of potatoes and mixed vegetables.

"Thank you. I'm disappointed I didn't get to try your grandma's special recipe."

"We figured since it's Thomas' favorite Irish tucker, you'd like it too," Saoirse said.

Being a people pleaser was Tom's forte and it ensured he remained the life of the party. His easygoing personality made him an overall likable guy and a pleasure for everyone to be around. Always gas craic, as Michael said at the pub.

Conlin cleared his throat and placed full pint glasses in front of their plates. "I'll say the blessing." He propped his elbows on the table, folded his hands, and closed his eyes. "Bless us, O Lord, and these gifts which we are about to receive." He peeked out of one eye to ensure Saoirse followed along. "From thy bounty through Christ our Lord. Amen."

"Amen," Saoirse said and raised her glass.

Conlin looked at Jeanette and gestured toward her drink. "Beamish Red Ale, sláinte." He grinned, flashing his teeth.

Jeanette gave a single nod and raised her glass to the toast. "Sláinte."

An expansive feeling spread across her chest, and a peacefulness strummed through her limbs. Although she met them under less-than-ideal circumstances, she enjoyed the time in their company and despite Tom's constant poor choices on his expeditions; he knew how to develop meaningful friendships with trustworthy people. She would never forget the Murphy family.

SEVEN

Jeanette helped Conlin clear the place settings from the table. A slight buzz swirled in her brain now that the events of the evening settled in and mingled with alcohol in her head. Jeanette almost bumped into Saoirse as she froze and stared at her phone.

"Excuse me, it's Eamon," she said.

Jeanette smiled. Better for Saoirse to get her hopes up about a boy her age rather than have a crush on Tom.

"What's the suss?" Saoirse's tone changed from the adult nature and demeanor when hanging out with her dad to a typical school-aged girl.

Jeanette missed the innocence of youth, and her heart burned with nostalgia for her childhood. Saoirse rushed from the kitchen before Conlin reacted.

"Call me for afters." Saoirse cruised down the hallway.

Conlin whirled around and tossed a hand upward, then smacked it against his hip. "Teenage girls."

"She's lovely. Good job, Dad." Jeanette winked.

"Em..." He unbuttoned his cuffs and rolled his sleeves to his elbows. "T'anks, although she spends most of her time at Kera's, her mother."

"Yeah, but I've seen the way the two of you interact. She adores you and you've achieved a delicate balance of parental authority, along with a respectful recognition of her being a young woman."

"Is that what you see?" He playfully smirked and nudged her with his elbow. "Right now, I want to grab her phone and tell that boy to feck off."

Laughter charged out. "That's what I mean. You're a great dad when you show that level of restraint."

The ghost of a smile flickered, and his neck flushed, focusing on washing a glass. "Do you have children? Ya seem to have a keen awareness of the parent-child relations."

"Oh, no, I don't have kids." A hardness tightened in her chest, and she picked up a dirty dish to keep busy. The awkwardness hung heavy in the atmosphere, and she had a sudden urge to grab her coat and bolt.

"Sorry, I didn't mean to pry."

"It's okay. I assumed Tom already shared our entire family tree."

Conlin flipped on the faucet and took the plate from her hands. "Not quite. Most of the time, he talked about his adventures."

"That's Tom all right." Jeanette lowered her chin and spoke into her chest.

"Still, ye must be close. You're here, in another country, searching for him, and putting yourself in harm's way."

"Enough to drive each other crazy. And when he's not trying to compete with his big sister, we get along fine."

"Ah, don't I know it. I'm the middle child of two brothers and three sisters." Conlin passed her a wet, clean plate.

"That explains your understanding of relationships and your strong parenting skills." She towel-dried the dish. "It appears your parents built a firm foundation and set a great example for you. I'm sure they don't pressure you about your career and life decisions."

"Once, years ago. Mother wanted me to marry Kera after the news of her pregnancy."

"Why didn't you?" Jeanette sucked in a hard breath. "Oh, that's too personal."

"Not at all. We were kids, having a kid. Then…" Conlin stared off for a second. "Everything overwhelmed me, finishing third-level education at the university and starting a career. The panic settled in about the responsibilities of raising a child at nineteen."

Jeanette nodded with understanding, although she could only imagine. Nothing in the immediate future held any prospects for her getting married and having children. "You've made your daughter a priority and it shows."

His body tensed, and he hunched forward over the sink. "'Tis kind of you to say. The truth is, work receives most of my time and attention, now that Saoirse spends a majority of the year in Dublin."

"Sounds like you have a civil relationship with her mother."

"We manage…" Conlin shook his head and glanced at the dishwater. "Yer folks around?"

Jeanette dried the last glass and blew a thick strand of hair from her face. "Yes, and they're convinced I'm on a fool's journey going after Tom."

Conlin angled his head to one side and scrunched a shoulder, continuing to wipe a plate. "They believe he's in no trouble at all?"

"My parents don't know how Tom gets into difficult situations on his expeditions. I've worked with him in the field before, and his precarious nature results in some kind of mess."

"So, you work together?"

"The same profession, but we have different job titles. I'm a collections manager at a historical society in New Hampshire and Tom's the assistant-chief curator of antiquities at a location in Boston. We both earned our master's degrees in archaeology." Jeanette swept back her messy curls and glanced away feeling like she appeared unprofessional.

"Interesting," Conlin said.

He wiped his hands with a towel and hung it on the tea trolley. "Thomas explained he's on sabbatical. A personal mission?"

An itch prickled her skin. Ever since they entered Jack's attic as kids, the drawing of the mysterious stone tempted Tom like a possession by a supernatural entity. "I'd call it a lifetime obsession."

"Ya disapprove of his actions, yeah?"

If she confessed and responded with a firm yes, she'd sound opinionated. Although, chances are Tom already complained about how she exaggerated his need for her help, and she enjoyed acting like a bossy sister. "Most of his decisions lead to risky behaviors, and I've had to bail him out on numerous occasions."

"C'mere, listen." He slipped his fingers around her hand, guided her into the living room, and directed her onto the couch. "You've been through a lot today."

He made a turnabout, placed peat in the fireplace, and lit the briquettes until a flame flickered. Jeanette pulled out her phone and verified the name Tom wrote in his letter. A text alert popped up from Brian.

Let's talk. Call me.

Not now. She swiped the message aside and opened the internet browser for her prior search history.

Conlin crashed onto the sofa cushion beside her and expelled a heavy breath. "Want a drink or anyt'ing?"

"No, thanks." A rolling sensation filled her stomach. "Can I ask you a question?"

"Em, sure."

Jeanette angled the phone screen toward him. "Have you heard of Fort Ó—"

"Yer lip looks swollen. Let me grab the ice."

He moved, and she grabbed his arm, tugging at his sleeve. "Please, tell me if you know anything about Fort Ó Cúis?"

A wrinkle deepened between his eyebrows, and he cocked his head sideways. "Daingean Uí Chúis in Irish."

Jeanette inched forward and sat at the edge of the sofa. "Where is it?"

"Dingle Peninsula on the Wild Atlantic Way."

She gasped, flinging her arms around Conlin, and his torso stiffened. Acting on impulse, she didn't consider his reaction.

She wriggled her shoulders, and he lowered his limbs, resting them on the curve of her spine, spreading a tingle throughout her body.

"Don't worry. You'll find Thomas and everything will be grand."

Jeanette pressed her cheek against his arm. She waited weeks for someone, anyone, to say those words. Heat rose between their bodies and her pulse increased. She tilted her chin skyward and he opened his arms. A sudden yank on her locks nipped her scalp and kept her tethered to Conlin.

"Ow." She bent in the opposite direction, intensifying the discomfort.

"Hold tight, you're stuck in my watchband."

Jeanette stretched her neck and scrunched her face, squeezing her eyes shut. Conlin's fingers twisted and twirled her hair, unwinding a few strands. She sat upright and rubbed her head.

"You're having a rough night."

"Depends on how you look at it. Tom might be in Dingle, but…" Jeanette glanced around the room and settled on nothing.

"What is it?"

"Why would Tom go there and keep it a secret?"

"Let me see the note again." Conlin reviewed the paper and massaged the stubble along his jawline. "Saint Brendan."

He showed her Tom's handwriting and paraphrased. "A voyager to the new lands from Fort Ó Cúis. He's referring to Saint Brendan the Navigator. A tale of Irish monks that set off from Dingle and journeyed on a currach, a small canoe-shaped boat made of light wood with watertight skins covering the bottom," he said with longing in his eyes and a distant smile.

How did she forget the story of Voyage of Saint Brendan? "Why would Tom pursue a folklore?"

"Plenty of legends have proven to be factual."

"You don't need to convince me. I've been the hopeful believer, or as my parents always say, a fantasist, but Tom's the logical one."

"Maybe something led him to consider otherwise." Conlin bowed forward and dug into his back pocket, retrieving a folded paper. "Which might explain this map. I found it stuck inside the desk drawer in the guest room earlier in the day."

Jeanette drew in a heavy breath and snatched it from his hands. "The man that attacked me must've been after the sketch, and not Tom's letter." She skimmed the drawing and hurled her most cutting glare. "When did you plan on telling me?"

"I just did."

"Even if I had said nothing about it?" She had no right to accuse Conlin of anything or project Brian's behavior onto every guy she encountered.

"In fairness, I only came across it a few hours ago and the state ya showed up in this evening took precedence."

"I know you're trying to help."

Conlin slid his arm around her shoulder and angled his head until he caught her line of vision. The closeness of his body roused her nerve endings, and she elongated her backbone against the couch cushion.

"At least I have a clue and know where to search next."

Conlin curled his fingers, tightening his grip in a protective manner. "Don't go..."

"What—"

"If Thomas placed himself in a dangerous situation and you follow, God knows what will happen." Slackening his clasp, he reclined against a decorative pillow and massaged his nape.

Conlin's response revealed that he cared about her and Tom. The warmth of a blush suffused, and she tapped the ball of her foot, rapidly bouncing her knee. "I came here to find my brother."

"And I promised Thomas to keep you out of danger."

"That's rich coming from him, since he's at the root of all my problems."

"Ya already had to fight off an attacker."

"I managed."

"Even so, what if he..." Conlin searched her eyes, sighed, and shook his head. "Ah, forget it. Ye're as thick as the brother."

Now, he echoed the same counsel as everyone else in her life.

"What should I do? Leave Tom to deal with it on his own? These people have made it clear they mean business."

"I suggest you go to the gardaí."

"To tell them my brother ran off to chase a childhood fascination, took on more work than he could handle, and involved dangerous men?"

Conlin slouched and released a drawn-out exhale. "At least report your assault."

"Trust me, I left him with severe consequences." An unexpected smile developed. The agony the man suffered gave her satisfaction beyond her wildest expectations.

"Sure, you're a fierce banféinní."

She squinted and glanced out of the corner of her eye. "I'm a what?"

"A female warrior. Part of the Fianna in Irish mythology." One eyebrow winged upward. "But since you've angered him, he'll be looking for ya. At least if the guards locate him, they'll detain him."

Jeanette banged a fist against her knee. Conlin made a valid point, and her assailant may desire vengeance. "He probably knows I'm staying at the Trident Hotel."

Conlin massaged his forehead. "Stay here tonight."

How many times in a day was she going to impose on his kindness? She shifted her position on the sofa with increasing restlessness and fidgeted her legs. "Are you sure?"

"You'll have plenty of privacy in the flat and we'll figure out how to proceed in the marra."

"Okay. I'm thankful for your generosity."

"No bother." Conlin stood and gestured with his hand. "I'll show you the room."

Jeanette arose to her feet, followed him down the hall, and outside the backdoor. He passed her the key, and her muscles eased a fraction.

"Shout if you need anything."

A smile budded and she tilted her head in consensus. She trusted Conlin and accepted him as an ally.

The next morning, Jeanette straggled out of the detached guestroom, rubbing her sore leg after kicking her attacker. Golden sunbeams pierced through the gray clouds, reflecting off the window of Conlin's backdoor, and straight into her eyes. Should she knock or waltz into his house?

Jeanette squared her shoulders and turned the doorknob. She opened the unlocked entrance, ambled through the hall, and into the kitchen. A lightness lifted her chest with a slight bounce on her toes at the sight of Conlin standing near the sink, wearing a gray sweater over a white-collared shirt and dark trousers. She tugged at the rolled hem of her flannel top.

Conlin turned from the stove, holding a kettle in his hand. "How did ya sleep?" His eyes darted toward her lips, and he raised his brows. "Feeling all right?"

Jeanette lifted her fingers and touched the tender, swollen tissue on her mouth. *Yikes.* She didn't examine it in the mirror before she exited the guestroom. She focused on fixing her hair and freshening up without toiletries. Thankfully, Tom left mouthwash behind and spared her the awkwardness of speaking with morning breath. "I slept fine, and I'll live."

Conlin gave a lone nod and grabbed three plates. "Grand weather for the day."

Saoirse strolled into the area from the hall. "Hiya." She rested her elbows on the wooden block island.

"Good morning." Jeanette smiled, cringing at the soreness of her bruise.

Saoirse said, "That's cat."

"It's bad?"

Jeanette pitched her gaze toward Conlin. He stepped closer, inspecting her face, and a hint of worry formed a slash between his eyebrows.

"Ya needed to ice it longer last night."

A rising heat crept along her chest and spread through the tips of her ears.

Conlin pulled out a cold pack from the freezer, wrapped it in a tea towel, and placed it in her hand.

"Not sure how much it'll help now," he said.

Jeanette slumped onto the stool beside Saoirse. "Did you have sweet dreams?"

A glint touched her eyes and a soft giggle escaped into the air. "Ah yeah, I dreamed about this fella—"

"Aren't ye eager to hear my ideas for today?" Conlin served Saoirse a plate of scrambled eggs, tomato, and potatoes. "I was t'inking about driving Jeanette to Dingle. If she agrees with the plan." He dipped his gaze toward her and passed a dish of seasoned fried spuds, fruit, and a bowl of Irish oatmeal.

Conlin outdid himself with the hospitality. His attentive nature after her attack, the concern for her safety, allowing her to stay overnight and now a breakfast catered to her dietary preferences.

She ran her fingertips along the surface of the tabletop, searching for the right words.

"Thank you for the offer to accompany me, and I appreciate everything you've done, but it's too much of an inconvenience."

"Don't worry yerself. All we're doing is taking a drive." Conlin folded his arms and hoisted a shoulder. "It'll be faster since I know the roads."

"Ah, please let's go together," Saoirse mumbled, chewing a slice of soda bread. "'Tis better than hanging around here all day."

"Sure, we'll stop by the Trident Hotel, pick up your hired car and belongings. So, when you find Thomas, you'll not need to return."

An empty feeling beside her heart rocked her on the seat and she gripped the table for balance, resting her chin on a fist to mask any noticeable reactions.

"Will we see Thomas?" Saoirse asked.

"I hope so," Jeanette said.

"I'll get dressed." Saoirse spilled tea on her pajamas, scooting the stool away from the counter and hurried down the hallway.

Conlin didn't flinch, and he kept his sight on Jeanette, observing her movements.

She squirmed under the weight of his stare, twisting a ringlet around her finger.

He moved closer and leaned forward. "If we don't locate Thomas, you're welcome to stay in the flat until you figure t'ings out."

Jeanette parted her aching lips, but no words came from her mouth, and she nodded in agreement. The more time they spent together, her fascination grew and with the simplest gestures toward her, she gained an interest in discovering everything about Conlin Murphy.

"Shall we leave in half an hour?"

"That'll be great." Today she might find Tom, or at least gain another clue about his current location. Jeanette tapped her finger against her lips and winced. She'd pray for Conlin and Saoirse safety, remaining in her company since they had already risked too much. If anything happened to them on account of her, she would never forgive herself.

EIGHT

Conlin chose a scenic route on their way to her hotel and pointed out historical sites to Jeanette, hoping he'd keep her mind off Thomas' whereabouts for a moment. He stopped on the corner of the street and gazed upward at the brick three-story urban tower house.

He glanced out the side of his eye at Jeanette and directed her attention to the building. "Maurice FitzGerald built Desmond Castle in 1500. It has a colorful history of serving as both a customhouse and a prison."

She stared off into the distance as loose wisps whirled around her face in the breeze, drawing his eyesight to the delicate curvature of her cheeks. He rolled his shoulders, loosening tight muscles, and removed his coat. "I figured you'd appreciate our historical society's restoration of the exterior façade—"

"Da, you're making a holy show of yourself." Saoirse wrinkled her nose and turned toward Jeanette. "Can't take him anywhere."

Conlin said, "G'wan so, slagging yer auld man."

Jeanette took her mobile out of her bag and snapped a photo of Desmond Castle, then spun around, extending her device at arm's length.

"Smile." She leaned close, reflecting their images, and pushed the button on the screen, clicking several pictures.

"What was that for?" Conlin edged rearward out of the frame.

A slow curl of her lips turned upward, and her facial features beamed. "Capturing a few memories of my first visit to Ireland and our time together." She ducked her chin and glanced at him from under her eyelashes.

Conlin stared at her for too long, attempting to sort out the pieces of his puzzling feelings about Jeanette. He shook his head and looked in the other direction.

"Yera, you'd want to forget an attack like last night," Saoirse said.

Jeanette hugged herself and pulled her jacket tighter around her waist. "I'm a little shaken by the incident, but I'll be okay." She flashed a reassuring smile at Saoirse.

Leave it to a teen to blurt out an unfiltered remark. Conlin didn't wish to pressure Jeanette, yet he needed to encourage her to take it up with the authorities. "We should still report the assault," he said.

She appeared distracted with her thoughts, or maybe she suffered a delayed response to the attack and didn't feel like talking about it. Conlin angled his neck to catch her attention. "How about if you're unable to locate Thomas, you'll come back and file a complaint?"

"All right, I promise," she said.

Conlin believed her regardless of their brief acquaintance. He always trusted Thomas even when their friendship became strained because of his dealings that enticed dangerous people to lurk around his home. He intended on helping him, but in the safest manner possible, for the sake of protecting Saoirse and Jeanette.

"Right then, let's continue our walk." Conlin led them on a short ramble through town toward the waterfront and stopped in front of the harbor. "There, she's a pure beauty." His eyes locked onto his sailboat. "A fine thing."

Jeanette visually searched the marina, and a blush darkened her skin. "Where?"

Conlin reached over her shoulder, pointing across the water. "The white-and-navy trim Bavaria 30 Cruiser."

"Oh, your boat." A peal of shaky laughter ripped free.

Did he imagine the relief in her tone? The thought of cruising in his sailboat with her swelled an expansive tide in his chest, but reality grounded him to the fact she was searching for Thomas and leaving soon, breaking the building tidal wave inside.

"He's always sailing off on his own," Saoirse said.

"Sometimes I have you by me side." Conlin slid his arm around Saoirse. A lump built in his throat and an ache settled into his heart. He wouldn't have his dear one beside him for much longer.

"Have you lived in Kinsale long?" Jeanette asked.

"A little over eight years ago we moved from Cork, I t'ink," Saoirse said.

"Yeah, you were near the age of seven." Conlin continued leading the way toward the end of the street at the quay. Water lapped against the docks, and he crammed a hand in his pocket, rattling the metal sailboat attached to his keys.

Jeanette angled her head to one side. "Where I live, in Moultonborough Bay, New Hampshire, my house overlooks a vast lake. You can walk a few feet from the back porch and stand at the water's edge," she said with a distant smile. "It was my grandparent's home and when the folks moved to Connecticut, they left it to me since Tom lives in Boston. Maybe he already told you."

He could not recall Thomas telling him too much about Jeanette, other than childhood stories, and even if he had mentioned it, Conlin wouldn't deny himself listening to her share where she lived or anything about her life. "We heard a lot about his expeditions."

She said, "I don't own a watercraft, but many times I've gone boating with neighbors, friends, and family. There's nothing like sailing on a warm summer day and drifting for a few hours to quiet yourself with the movement of the water."

"You talk like my dad about it."

Now he knew he had the right idea to invite Jeanette on his boat and set sail. She even appreciated the tranquility of floating adrift along the waves on a sunny afternoon until sunset, waiting for the rising moonlight to dance in ripples on the surface, creating magic.

Walking toward the entrance of the Trident Hotel, he opened and held the door for Jeanette. She almost bumped into the glass, glancing at her mobile for a second time during their stroll. Hair blew into her face, and she sighed. "I'll need at least forty minutes to change, pack and checkout."

"Sure. I'll fill the car with petrol and meet you at the entrance." He checked the current time on his watch. "Around ten o'clock?"

Jeanette dug into her bag, retrieved the keys, and handed them to him. "That's helpful, thanks." She flaunted a smile and left, taking quick strides.

Conlin's line of vision followed her steps toward the lifts. "Does she seem preoccupied with something other than locating Thomas and the incident last night?" He voiced his thoughts rather than expecting a response from Saoirse. He turned and headed through the car park, once Jeanette was out of sight.

"Probably her boyfriend. Like Jeanette needs to explain to him why she spent the night at another fella's house." She displayed a wicked grin.

Conlin stopped dead in his tracks, and a coldness swept through his body. He craned his neck to one side, stretching out the tight pinch, and cracked his knuckles. No need to tense up at the mention of a man in her life.

"She told you about him?" Conlin snapped his mouth shut. Exhibiting a blatant interest in Jeanette's personal affairs revealed a keen curiosity. He pushed the key fob, waiting for the beep to locate the hired car. Lights blinked on a red, two-door Opel Corsa.

"Ya think a woman like her is single?" She halted and placed a hand on her hip, arching a brow. "Da, even you'd date Jeanette." Saoirse shook her head, laughing.

Forced laughter juddered his throat and he playfully nudged her arm. "Gas one!"

She giggled and climbed into the passenger seat. Conlin stared off across the water, then sat in the driver's position. Two things unsettled him about her comment: his little girl showed signs of emotional maturity with her accurate assessment, and if circumstances were different, he wouldn't hesitate to ask Jeanette out on a date. Conlin blinked twice, putting on his prescription eyewear for his nearsightedness, and drove off.

At 10:25 a.m., they waited in the Corsa. Conlin drummed his fingertips atop the steering wheel and peered out the corner of his eye at Saoirse, bobbing her head, listening to music. He tapped her knee and gestured toward the lobby.

Conlin exited the vehicle, cruised inside, and skipped a step at the sight of Jeanette in her figure-fitting jeans, a striped-collared shirt under a tan twilled jacket with her hair wildly loose sweeping past the middle of her back.

A jolt zipped through his body as she waltzed closer with a sweet curve of her lips upward and everything in him hoped she intended it as a flirtatious look. Her eyes met his, sending an electrifying surge through his nerves as he felt her stare. He rolled his shoulders, loosening his muscles, and played it cool.

"All set to go."

Conlin reached for her large backpack-style suitcase. "'Tis your only bag?"

"I'm a simple gal." She winked and held onto her baggage.

Conlin assessed during the past couple of days, Jeanette was far from ordinary. Everything about her appeared complex and intriguing at the same time. Given more days with her, he would enjoy learning about the details of her life. The ridge of his backbone straightened and stiffened his neck. Moving aside, he pushed the glass doors and waited for Jeanette. They entered the car park and aimed for the Corsa.

Jeanette opened the passenger door and leaned inside the vehicle. She turned and looked at Saoirse in the backseat. "Aren't you sitting in the front with your father?"

"I assumed you'd want to discuss where you need to go, and I'll be listening to music."

Conlin glanced at Saoirse, and she ducked her chin, concentrating on her mobile to avoid eye contact. Sure, she'd like to see her auld man make a complete bollix of himself. He let go of a smirk accompanied by a light laugh at his daughter taking the mick out of him. Jeanette climbed inside, closed the door and he proceeded to the driver's seat.

"We're off then."

An hour and a half later, after leaving Kinsale, they arrived in Killarney. Saoirse leaned over the back of his seat from behind. "Da, can we stop for tea?"

"What do ya t'ink?" He side-eyed Jeanette.

"Yes, we should have lunch and I need Wi-Fi to search for the Saint Brendan's locations."

"There are many megalithic sites on the Dingle Peninsula." Conlin pulled into a parking spot along College Street. The busy main road through town provided plenty of diverse food selections and pubs.

Jeanette's thoughts already traveled onward, and Conlin figured it would be best to let her sort things out in her mind. He stepped out of the car and opened the passenger door for her and Saoirse. "Ciaran's Restaurant has vegan options on their menu."

Conlin glanced upward, appreciating the pleasing aesthetics of the border of flowers above the signage. He held the entrance open, and they entered the pub. When was the last time he left Kinsale for a day trip or took Saoirse on holiday?

He gave a quick nod to the lads at the bar and selected a table in the back corner. Conlin sat on the striped-cushioned bench beside Saoirse. A framed picture of The Dubliners hung behind him on the pale-yellow wall. Jeanette settled into a chair across from them and dropped her handbag next to her on an empty seat as a heavy breath escaped her lips.

Fixated on her device, a crease deepened between her eyes as she wound a curly strand of hair around her finger. She didn't even hear the server approach the table and ask for her order. Conlin reached and his fingertips grazed her forearm.

"Em, Jeanette."

"Huh, what?" She flicked her gaze upward, then shook her head and perused the menu. "Oh, yes. I'll have the falafel and tofu open sandwich and a black coffee. Thanks."

Saoirse reclined against the back cushion. "A burger and a cola, please."

Conlin collected the menus and handed them to the server. "The chicken wrap, a basket of chips for the table, and a cuppa cha, t'anks."

His gaze wandered toward Jeanette again, and he rubbed his jawline. "Let me know if I can help you decide on a location in Dingle or anything." A minute passed before she seemed to process and acknowledge his words.

"Mm-hmm, I will," she said in a soft, distant tone. Her eyelashes fluttered until their eyes locked, and a smile brightened her visage.

A balminess arose beneath his sweater, and he shifted on the bench, turning away. No point in getting caught up in Jeanette's admirable qualities; self-sufficient, determined, and not to mention her alluring facial features he could no longer ignore. God in heaven, he tried to deny his physical responses to her touch. The glances turned into lingering stares, and he longed to wander beyond her meadow-green gaze.

The waiter brought their meals with impeccable timing. Grand, he needed a distraction. A scratch tickled at the back of his mouth, causing him to down his water and choke.

"Are you okay?" Jeanette asked.

He coughed and cleared his throat. "Em... sure."

"I'm like morto for ya." Saoirse eyed him down with reddening cheeks and took a bite of her burger.

Conlin agreed with Saoirse's critiques about the peculiar behavior he developed since Jeanette arrived. Why did she have such a powerful effect on him? Best if he focused on helping her find out about Thomas' disappearance and nothing more.

What else could there be between them when she lived thousands of miles away? If he was honest with himself, Saoirse's comments about dating Jeanette caused a heavy feeling inside. Conlin focused on eating his food and hoped his mannerisms didn't expose his thoughts.

Jeanette remained quiet for at least ten minutes, and she continued studying several websites about Saint Brendan. Every so often, in-between internet pages loading, she grabbed a thick-cut chip from the large basket in the middle of the table. Conlin found it fascinating to watch the methodical process of her working.

His gaze bounced from Saoirse to Jeanette, staring at their phone screens. He didn't have the heart to tell them he had a feeling they were probably going to reach a dead end. Even if Thomas explored the megalithic sites, the chances of him still being in Dingle were slim. He left Kinsale weeks ago with a target on his back and he doubted Thomas hung around any of the locations on his map for an extended period.

Conlin assumed Jeanette came to the same conclusion. Yet in the two days he interacted with her, he had seen a rare hopefulness and faith. The kind that her parents lost and discouraged her from clinging to anymore.

Jeanette popped her head upright. "I think we should go to Kilmalkedar Church. The ruins might provide insight into Tom's journey."

Conlin nodded in agreement. "'Tis a good start and you'd know best, working in the same field where he would go next. Then we'll continue the drive around Slea Head."

A smile shadowed her mouth, and she lowered her lashes. Conlin witnessed the hope of finding Thomas slipping away. He didn't know how to encourage her when little convinced him she obtained a strong lead. Yet, her optimism, dedication to family, and overall tenacity inspired him, regardless of Thomas' request to keep her out of the situation, and Conlin believed if anyone had a chance of sorting everything out, Jeanette was the person to conquer the task.

NINE

At Kilmalkedar Church on the Dingle Peninsula, thick, gray clouds covered the sky, and a wind whipped through Conlin's wool coat. He stood outside the Corsa and shoved his hands in his pockets.

"Here we are," he said.

Saoirse and Jeanette exited the car. Conlin stared off in the opposite direction, overlooking the water. *Ah, the ocean breeze and air.* All the blessings in life surrounding him in one setting—his daughter, a symbolic site of faith, and the picturesque scenery of home. He glanced at Jeanette, managing her hair blowing in a gust.

Conlin pointed toward the church. "Follow the pathway."

"It's quiet for an attraction." Jeanette strolled alongside him and Saoirse.

"Late October's the off-season," he said.

"That'll help with the investigation on where Tom went after Kinsale."

"We'll wander around and allow you to use yer expertise."

Jeanette alternated her gaze between them and squared her shoulders. Hiking up a steep, grassy incline toward the church ruins, they viewed the surrounding area and the Atlantic waters extending beyond the horizon.

"The scenic view alone is worth the trip." Jeanette's hair encased her face like wild vines.

"'Tis a grand sight." Conlin stepped up behind Saoirse. The salt-infused ocean breeze stirred, and the taste of sea water settled onto his tongue. He closed his eyes for a moment, escaping into a daydream about sailing off on his boat. The melodic movement of the waves, a balance of following the flow and controlling the hull of a watercraft.

"I remember visiting during our summer holliers as a child." Saoirse wrapped her arm around his and he glanced at her, cracking a smile. Part of him tried to forget and he pushed those memories into the back of his mind. Reminiscing about the past was too painful and he missed sharing his life with someone.

"Ah listen, those were grand times." Conlin rubbed the top of Saoirse's head and she edged away from his grasp.

"Ye're messing up me hair."

"Oh, am I now?"

Laughter mingled between them and for a second it was like the old days, feeling the bond of family ties. A lightness filled his chest, realizing Saoirse was enjoying her visit for the first time in a while, and a genuine connection developed even though the circumstances earlier in the summer strained their relationship because of Kera's recent marriage.

He started to put it behind, focusing on the few moments he had with Saoirse, and it enabled him to feel the possibility of something more was in the near future. Maybe her assessments were correct, and he needed his own social life. Perhaps he could invite a woman to dinner. Had he met any women that caught his interest?

Conlin peered at Jeanette, already at work and examining the grounds. Raising a hand to her forehead, she shielded the glare of silver-gray clouds and scanned the terrain. She hiked farther uphill.

"Let's see if she's made any discoveries." Conlin wrapped his arm around Saoirse, and they walked up the sandstone trail.

Jeanette stood at an erected six-foot Ogham Stone outside the ruins of a 12th-century Romanesque church beside a graveyard. Using her fingertips, she rubbed the diagonal engravings on the uneven top and examined the symbols. She pulled a small notebook from the inside pocket of her jacket. A pencil hid between the pages, and she jotted down a couple of things, then pressed a blank sheet against the rock. Jeanette scribbled hard, transferring the imprint onto the page before tucking the writing utensil behind her ear. Then she photographed the etchings from every angle.

Saoirse strolled the grounds and Conlin took a few steps to join Jeanette. His presence didn't seem to disturb her work or phase her at all. "Interesting, yeah?"

"Yeah, I'd estimate this standing stone is from the 6th-century."

Conlin hooked his forefinger through a hole near the top of the rock. "Legends of Ogham stones remain today. Visitors come from around the world and pronounce their vows."

Jeanette stared him in the face, and he enjoyed having her full attention for the first time all day. For at least a minute, he stood gawking at her with a stupid grin. The slightest curve of her lips upward streamlined a surging heat across his chest and into his limbs. *Ya thunderin' eejit.*

"Em, followers of the lore believe an engaged couple stood on each side of the stone and pressed their fingers together in the center as a sign of binding nuptials." He slipped his finger through the opening. "People gathered and witnessed the ceremony."

His eyes locked onto Jeanette's and swept him into a crashing wave of the Celtic Sea. Forcing a long blink, he broke the visual contact. The coolness of her fingertip pressed against his warm flesh, awakening him from the trance.

"They touched their fingers?"

"Em, yeah…"

"What did the couple do next?"

The straightforward question, accompanied by the nearness of their bodies, commanded his attentiveness. A slight sheen on her lips emphasized the small pucker of her mouth and it took every ounce of willpower to hold himself back from indulging in a passionate kiss. Not here, not now, not in front of his daughter, where they spent holidays in the past.

Saoirse meandered in their direction. "Did ye discover something important?"

He shot a glance at Jeanette, and her smile grew as if his expression revealed his thoughts.

"Maybe I need more time to figure it out," she said.

Jerking his elbow, his finger slid from Jeanette's grasp. Again, a simple look twisted him up inside yet unraveled his fetters in the same moment.

He gulped the excessive saliva in his mouth. "Ye're willing to explore further with the possibility it might end in disappoint?"

"We never stumble upon anything significant in plain sight. It requires deep exploration to determine if you've found something of vital importance." Jeanette laid her palms against the standing stone.

"Even if nothing comes of it after you've invested all your efforts and emotions?"

"Without additional examination, and willingness to accept all experiences leads to the development of self-discovery, we'll miss opportunities. If every choice we make, whether sensible or foolish, helps us learn about ourselves, then it does not waste our altruism."

Conlin understood her underlying meaning. Did he dare continue the conversation and allow Saoirse to witness their verbose dalliance? A minute ago, he desired to kiss Jeanette and now, seconds later, he wanted so much more than a tender expression of physical intimacy. He had an overwhelming need to delve into the expanse of her mind and the depths of her heart.

Conlin placed his hands on the Ogham Stone. "Perhaps we'll uncover somet'ing essential in our venture—"

"You're doing it again, Da."

"What?"

Saoirse shook her head. "Ye're a holy show. I'm scarlet…" She pinned her arms across her chest and galumphed away.

Conlin turned toward Jeanette, and they erupted in laughter. "Ow." She pressed her lips tight and scrunched her nose.

He squinted and sucked in a breath through his teeth. "Still hurts?"

She nodded and tucked the bruised bottom corner of her mouth under her top lip. Conlin slid his palm below her chin, angling her face to get a better view. "The swelling has gone down a bit."

Her skin reddened and he felt the surge of heat in his hand. Good Lord, he hadn't seen her so closely, admiring her warm, ivory complexion and dusty rose-colored cheeks. Conlin lowered his arm and glanced in the opposite direction.

A middle-aged couple exited the church and walked toward them. "Aren't you a pair of sweet peaches?" the woman said in a Southern-American accent. "Newly engaged or recently wedded?"

"Em…"

"Oh, I didn't mean to intrude, sugar. I'm Sissy. We've been married for twenty-five years. Earl and I came here for our anniversary to renew our vows. Right, honey?" The man opened his mouth to speak but didn't get a word in as she continued, "I noticed the obvious affection you have for each other. And I know a lasting couple when I see one." She winked.

The sensation of a boat anchor piercing the surface of his chest and digging into his heart generated a natural resistance. Conlin stepped backward, creating a space away from Jeanette and the stone. "She's doing research."

Conlin threw an imploring look at Jeanette, and she interjected. "Yes, I'm an archaeologist studying the site to gain information about Saint Brendan's voyages."

Sissy's smile cracked the thick makeup on her face. "Y'all don't need to explain, but I have a feeling you've already found what you're looking for. You two have fun, toodles." She tugged on her husband's arm, and they waltzed downhill.

Saoirse traversed the pathway. "What was that woman going on about?"

"I'm not sure. Speaking utter ráiméis."

Jeanette asked, "What does that mean?"

"Nonsense," Saoirse said.

Jeanette's lips curved downward. "Oh, I see." She pivoted on the heels of her boots and trudged toward the church, entering the roofless ruins.

He didn't intend on hurting her feelings again and only spoke his honest opinion about the woman. It had nothing to do with her assessment of the extent of their relationship. Besides, there was no point in approaching Jeanette and convincing her otherwise. She needed to stay focused on finding Thomas, and his top priority remained to protect Saoirse. Even at the risk of forgoing any amorous ideas about Jeanette.

After she analyzed the alphabet stone inside the monastery, she worked her way through the remnants outside. Conlin and Saoirse kept silent while she studied the goblet-shaped sundial stone. Saoirse shivered and he put his arm around her, pulling her close.

Jeanette made a few *hmm* noises with a contemplative expression as she crouched and sketched an image of the sundial's semi-circular head. She stood and scribbled a few more things in her book before sticking it in the pocket of her jacket.

"Any indications that Thomas came here and where he might've gone next?" Conlin asked.

"It's peculiar. The markings and the holes are similar to other stones..." Jeanette's eyes widened, and her mouth opened, pulling in a loud intake of air before she spoke. "Conlin!"

"Wha—" A man shoved him into the rocky exterior of the church. The force pushed the breath from his chest. Saoirse gasped and ran over to him. He squeezed his eyelids tight and shook his head to refocus his mind. Blinking a few times, he cleared his vision.

The attacker stomped toward Jeanette. Her posture stiffened and she squared her shoulders. Conlin could not decide if she acted brave or reckless.

The gurrier grabbed her by the hair. "I wasn't finished with you last night."

Jeanette crumpled her face as he yanked her head backward. He slipped his hand around her jaw and pinched. "At least I left my mark." A scoffing laugh barreled out, examining the bruise on her mouth.

Conlin stepped forward, and Saoirse tightened her grip. He glanced at her watery eyes, pleading for him not to intervene. Sake! How did they get mixed up in it? Gently, he tapped Saoirse's hand and slid it down to her side. She shook her head and her expression revealed she didn't believe him capable of taking on the threatening man. Conlin crept closer and his boot squished in the mud.

The man darted a glare toward him. "Stay put." He pressed his palm hard against Jeanette's throat, and she winced with a whimper.

Jeanette took advantage of the man's distraction and kicked him in the leg. A muffled grunt escaped his lips, and he clutched his shin, releasing his grasp on Jeanette. She slipped away from his restraint and gathered close to them. They huddled together, making their way down the slope. The click of a loaded gun stopped them in their tracks.

"Hold it, you're not going anywhere."

Conlin spun around and stood in front of Saoirse. What an eejit for bringing her out here. He should've sent her to a friend's house for the day.

Jeanette peeked to her left and rotated, confronting the pistol pointed at her chest. A coldness streamed through his veins, watching from a helpless position. He was powerless to protect his daughter and Jeanette.

The man waved the handgun, directing them to line up against the wall. "There's no escaping this time."

"I'll give you the map." Jeanette's voice trembled.

"It's too late for that now. You're coming with me."

"Then please let them go. They're not involved."

"Shut up! I'm giving the orders." He grabbed Jeanette and bent her arm behind her back, pushing the barrel of his gun against her spine.

Jeanette discharged a grunted breath, and the man made a gruff noise with a hint of pleasure. "Not so tough anymore, are you?"

Conlin summoned every bit of self-control to refrain from charging after their assailant. What options did he have for an offensive strategy when they had a gun pointed at them and he remained in a defensive stance? The man inched her forward. If he took off with Jeanette and left them behind, he could at least take Saoirse and rush to the gardaí.

The gurrier shoved Jeanette, knocking her onward, and he turned, facing Conlin. "Let's go, you two." He motioned with his pistol for them to move ahead.

Heat flushed through his body, and his heart pounded, vibrating throughout his torso. Conlin held Saoirse's arm and guided her from behind. They took cautious steps in the direction of the hired car.

"Get in and drive." He aimed his handgun at Conlin, gesturing at Jeanette's rental.

"Ye're leaving your vehicle?"

"It's not mine." His lips twitched, revealing his stained teeth.

"I beg you, just take me." Jeanette tugged the man's arm.

He grabbed the collar of her shirt, opened the rear entry, and pushed her inside. "You're all collateral now."

The door slammed, and he scowled at Saoirse. "Move it."

He escorted Saoirse to the driver's side and her body trembled under his touch. She joined Jeanette in the back seat, and he climbed into the front of the vehicle.

Conlin started the engine. "Where are we off to, then?"

"Travel along R559. You're all taking a flight."

Everyone remained silent, yet the soundless tension reverberated in the compact car. Why would he force them onto a flight? A charter to the islands off the coast? Conlin put the automobile in drive and took off. If they went to Kerry Airport, security would stop a man carrying a weapon and travelers without passports. Perhaps they still had an opportunity to walk free from this nightmare.

TEN

"Turn left onto Slea Head Drive." The man directed Conlin in the vehicle.

Conlin glanced in the rearview mirror several times, checking on Saoirse. She huddled close to Jeanette. If the gouger hadn't threatened them at gunpoint, he would've blackened his eye. Saoirse's safety took precedence over everything and hopefully they'd gain an opportunity to get out of the situation alive.

Seven kilometers down the road, he nudged Conlin's shoulder. "Make a right, here."

Conlin followed his instructions and continued on Slea Head Drive. Nothing about the situation made sense. Why didn't the welthead tell him to drive to a specific airport when he already divulged information about sending them on a flight?

"Pull alongside the road."

Conlin held his breath for a moment and parked the car. Maybe they weren't flying anywhere, and he intended on shooting them in an open field. The chances of another automobile passing by were slim.

"Everyone out and don't try anything funny or you'll get a bullet in the back." The hardchaw shoved the pistol in his pocket. With any luck, he'd injure himself without the safety on.

They all exited the vehicle and Saoirse hurried to his side, hugging him close. Conlin gave her a reassuring pat on her back. Jeanette lobbed him a stunned look, then averted her gaze and grabbed her backpack. He didn't blame her for what happened. After all, he offered to drive to Dingle, and even if she reported her attack, there were others tracking Thomas.

The man stomped through the bushes. "Follow me." He climbed over a waist-high rock wall.

They wedged in the middle of the brush, hopped over the rocks and into the open terrain. Conlin stumbled a step at the sight of a private airplane a few meters away. His mouth went dry, losing the hope of an escape. Slogging through the grass, Conlin took mental note of the soft soil. The ground wasn't an ideal runway.

Another man stepped out from the other side of a white-and-blue-striped Cessna 340A plane. Conlin had flown in the aircraft as a passenger in the past. The piston-twin aircraft boasted the same safety standards as major airliners, yet any small jet taking off from a sod field wasn't a good idea. So much factored into the conditions for a successful lift into the air.

The large man grabbed Jeanette by the arm and swung her forward as they approached the medium-built pilot. "Hey Ace, I'll text the boss and let him know you're bringing him the Hillestad woman and the map."

"So, you finally succeeded at finishing your job assignment from weeks ago, eh, Harry?" Ace said.

"Some of us have more challenging tasks than flying planes around the world."

Ace scoffed and pulled down the airstairs. "Who are the other two?"

"Additional insurance in case she refuses to cooperate." Harry shoved Jeanette's shoulder and leered at Saoirse. "Besides, there's a special interest in this young lady."

Every muscle tensed in Conlin's body, his hands stiffened, and he curved his fingers. He lunged at Harry, grabbing his shirt into his fists, and yanked him close. "She's just a child." Conlin pressed his knuckles up against Harry's throat. Strained laughter howled through his choking.

An intense pressure slammed into Conlin's stomach, and he loosened his grasp on Harry. Conlin cringed and his muscles hardened, reacting to the force of a punch in the gut. He bent forward, holding his breath, and a cough caught in his chest.

"Dad!" Saoirse placed her forearm around his back.

"Get them out of my sight," Harry said in a raspy tone.

Saoirse's chin quivered, and tears clung to her lashes. "It'll be all right," he said in a steady yet labored voice and gave her a nod. She joined Jeanette at the foot of the two steps to board the four-seater aircraft.

Conlin pressed his palm against his midsection. A sickness churned, ready to erupt and a sour taste crept up in his esophagus. He swallowed the queasy feeling and hopped into the copilot position. Out of all the times he felt he failed as a father; this moment topped them all. He was unsuccessful at protecting Saoirse and now they were on their way to God knows where, escorted by violent people. At least that pathetic excuse for a human being, Harry, wasn't getting on the airplane. Although Ace might be the same or worse. All that mattered was his responsibility of guarding Saoirse and escaping from the disastrous, life-threatening situation.

Conlin glanced over his shoulder. Saoirse's eyelids remained shut, and she laid her head against Jeanette as she petted the length of her hair. His eyes stationed on Jeanette, and other than a shallow dip of a frown, she hid her concerns well. She appeared a tower of strength and strong-willed to the point of possible recklessness. Indeed, a banféinní.

The sensation of rushing blood coursed through his veins. Not once, but twice Jeanette put herself at risk, trying to keep him and Saoirse out of danger. Conlin took a sharp intake of air and exhaled hard through his mouth, looking in the opposite direction. In the short time they knew each other, they seemed to develop a nonverbal communication. He never shared that experience with anyone in his life. A dampness covered his palms and he swiped them against his pant leg.

Ace entered the cockpit. "Do you know what you're doing?"

Conlin adjusted his eyeglasses and put on a headset. "I piloted a Skyhawk with the auld man for years."

"All right, let's get going." Ace started the engines. First, the left propeller slowly spun, then the right.

"Are ya sure about taking off on soft turf?" Conlin doubted they'd achieve enough speed for lift because of the weight and drag.

Ace flashed him a pinched expression. "I've had the Cessna modified with a Robertson STOL kit for short-field takeoff and landings."

Both concern and fascination filled Conlin about the aircraft getting off the ground. "That includes the Fowler Flaps and improves takeoff?"

"Yeah. We'll get off the ground at seventy-five knots." Ace went through the checklist. "The pressurization safety valve's set, trim setting, auxiliary fuel pump, flaps, and now we're waiting on the oil to warm up."

The Cessna moved ahead and rounded at the far end, preparing for takeoff. Conlin cracked his knuckles and peeked over his shoulder at Saoirse. She hugged herself, staring out the window. He sighed and faced forward. Harry stomped off and drove away in Jeanette's hired car. What had these guys planned and where were they being taken next?

At least in the copilot position, he could watch the modern-engine monitors just in case a cylinder overheated or if they developed other issues that might arise piloting a private plane.

Ace adjusted his seatbelt, contacted air-traffic control and cleared their departure. "Okay, we're good to go. We'll accelerate up to about seventy-five knots and lift off."

Conlin kept his cool and rolled his neck. He no longer questioned the STOL conversion and the plane's capabilities of getting off the ground, but he would still pray for their safety.

"Here we go." Ace increased speed. "Thirty... sixty... seventy-five... now she'll fly."

Conlin's adrenaline spiked, his mind failing to catch up with everything going on as they headed into the unknown. The airplane elevated off the field and relief whooshed from Saoirse's mouth behind the pilot's seat. He glanced at her, giving a quick nod and a wink.

"Success," Ace said.

The wheels pulled inward, and they were clear. Golden-amber lights pierced through the steely colored clouds above the Atlantic in front of them and the aircraft climbed in elevation. Conlin's senses heightened, and a lightness filled his chest. The takeoff impressed him, and the view left him speechless. He hadn't flown with Dad in about ten years.

Conlin needed to stay alert and gather any information he could about where they were traveling. He pictured Thomas' map in his mind. Did Jeanette figure out any connection between Thomas' plans and Saint Brendan's tales of the promised land? She was going to mention something about the markings on the sundial before criminals forced them to leave at gunpoint. Perhaps they were being taken to Thomas and destined for the same doom, whatever that may be. He'd say a silent prayer and hope for a miracle.

Conlin shifted his torso in the gray leather copilot's seat. Eight hours into the flight without landing in Iceland or Greenland marked on Thomas' sketch, and Conlin assumed North America was next on the list of destinations, considering they needed a fuel stop soon. They flew at a comfortable altitude of twenty-seven thousand, the Cessna 340A could maintain.

So many things raced through his brain, yet he remained levelheaded and kept a neutral demeanor. Any other reaction would give Ace and the others involved leverage against them. With a nonchalant stretch, he peeped at Saoirse. Both she and Jeanette slept most of the flight. What else could they do?

For the first couple of hours, Jeanette wrote things in her notebook. He felt for her predicament and cared about Thomas' whereabouts, but now protecting Saoirse and returning home won the top place on his list of priorities. They needed to get out of this situation alive.

Half an hour later, the plane descended a few thousand feet. Tensions strained in an unnerving silence for the past several hours. None of them could guess what would come next or their fate. Flying over a large river extending from the Atlantic Ocean, Ace contacted the air-traffic-control tower. Conlin straightened his back in the seat, preparing for their descent and landing in Quebec City.

Jeanette nudged Ace's arm. "Excuse me."

"Don't bother me now," Ace said in a stern tone.

"It's about the plane."

"What?"

Jeanette leaned closer to the pilot. "Look."

Ace turned and Jeanette misted pepper-spray in his face. He yelped, covering his eyes. Jeanette forcefully swung her bag and knocked it against Ace's head. A thump boomed in the cockpit as his skull smacked into the window.

The weight of a rock dropped through Conlin's center, and his frame snapped straight, locking his joints in place. "What're ya doin'? How are we going to land?" His pulse throbbed and hammered at his throat.

"You told Ace you've piloted planes."

"Never on me own."

"You flew with Grandad all the time," Saoirse said.

"Landing is completely different." Conlin grunted, secured a firm grip on the yoke, and scanned the instruments.

Jeanette placed her hands on his arms from behind, bending close with her breath on his ear. "You can do this," she whispered. "I have faith in you." She leaned back and buckled her seatbelt.

Conlin sharply drew in a lungful of oxygen, leveling his shoulders, and pushed the control column forward. The nose of the plane dipped down, and he eased the wheel backward until they swooped up a bit. His stomach knotted and sweat pearled along his hairline. He had to manage it for the sake of their survival. *Jesus in heaven, protect us.*

Conlin followed the checklist and switched on both fuel-boost pumps. At the exact moment, he glanced at the number three, cylinder head temperature that ran high most of the flight and lost the left engine. A tightness constricted his windpipe and created difficulty breathing. They would never make it to the airport utilizing one engine. Yeah, he expected a full head-on assault from dark forces. His reflexes slowed and his movements became unfocused. Losing power, the plane drifted downward and into a foggy atmosphere.

"Watch out for the Ile d'Orleans Bridge," Jeanette said in an urgent yet calm tone.

At lightning speed, he turned the left boost pump back off and yanked the yoke too fast. The fuel gauges waved at him with the wild yawing of the aircraft. Saoirse released a tight breath, and a squeak escaped her lips.

Air deserted his lungs, and he didn't blink. Conlin heard the auld man in his head. *Keep it stable, don't throttle the engine, and ease into the steering control, lad.*

Clearing the bridge, Conlin brought the Cessna closer to the water, lowering the flaps and wheels. He slowed for the emergency forced landing, and a nerve twanged in his neck. The canal hadn't frozen across the entire waterway and lacked proper support for the touchdown of an aircraft, even a private plane. He aimed for the thickest blocks and widest patches of ice covering. His first solo landing and he had to cope without a solid runway or aid from air-traffic control.

Sixty-two… forty… twenty knots. The tires touched down, skidding on the slick top, and Conlin fought against the swing of the tail as he braked, sliding into the sway. Once the rubber wheels hit, he lost control and the plane skated along the river until it did a three-hundred-and-sixty-degree loop and the Cessna slowed, reaching a complete stop.

Nothing prepared him for the burden of that responsibility, and he rocked forward, deflating his torso. All at the same time, everyone let out a heavy sigh. He didn't even have a second to process what had transpired.

"Are ye all right?" Conlin swiveled toward them.

Saoirse nodded with an owlish blink. Jeanette placed an open palm on his biceps and swept her lashes upward, revealing a look of admiration.

"Well done," she said.

He inclined his head in recognition and his chest puffed out, knowing she was proud of him. Still and all, they weren't out of danger yet.

Conlin shook Ace's shoulder, stirring him from his blackout. He groaned, effin' and blindin' under his breath. A loud crackle of splitting ice thundered from below the plane.

"Hurry, get out." Conlin whipped off his seatbelt and turned toward Saoirse, fumbling to unfasten the belt, then threw the strap aside. Jeanette grabbed her bag and lowered the air steps.

"Take it handy as you exit." He tugged Ace's arm. "Let's go." Ace squeezed his red, swollen eyes tighter and groaned.

Conlin observed Jeanette treading outside on the frozen parts of the river. She held out her arms and reached for Saoirse.

"I'll help you," she said.

Conlin opened the door and tested his foot on the ice. Fractures in the surface splintered and he inched his way around the front of the plane to the opposite side. Jeanette took Saoirse by the hand and shuffled carefully toward the highway running parallel to the St. Lawrence River.

Stress fled from his sinews at the sight of them only feet away from safety. Conlin unlatched the pilot's side and Ace slumped forward, rolling halfway out.

"You're gonna have to climb out," Conlin said.

Ace slipped downward and placed an arm around his shoulder. "Go easy." Conlin moved closer to assist him and they took a couple of steps.

Straightening his body, Ace regained balance. Conlin supported his back to ensure he didn't fall. He watched Jeanette and Saoirse hop over the guardrail. Thank God, they made it to the road.

Ace's shoe squeaked and he tripped, pulling them both down onto the thin ice. A crevasse deepened and split apart, separating the frozen blocks. Like an earthquake rumbling beneath his feet, the surface cracked and engulfed them in a liquid space.

"Da!" Saoirse said.

The glacial temperatures speared his flesh, similar to a knife lancing his skin. Conlin gasped at the air and an icy inhalation burned his lungs. Ace gripped the back of his jacket and clawed him with his fingers. The load anchored them down and all he could think of was Saoirse watching him drown. Seconds felt like an eternity, struggling against the pressure.

"Grab my hands." Jeanette extended her arms.

Reaching out of the freezing river exerted his energy, yet she gained a firm clasp and pulled with all her might. The bulk of his wet clothes and the heaviness fought against her physical abilities. He focused on Saoirse and pushed his chest upward toward the solid wedge that Jeanette leaned against. The rubber soles of her boots squealed as she squatted and yanked him hard. He thrust his upper body from the water and threw his knee up onto the solidified ice. Out of breath and drained of any vigor, he heaved with one last great effort, rising above the surface, then rolled onto his side on the frozen slab.

Ace splashed with bobbing movements and rasping breaths. There was no way she could aid him on her own. Jeanette reached over and Conlin blocked her hand. "He'll pull you under." His teeth chattered, and he noticed Saoirse hugging herself and crying.

"We'll do it together." Jeanette shoved aside and fastened her hands onto Ace's forearm. He paddled and water filled his mouth. "We're helping you, calm down and try lifting up your body."

A constant chill quaked Conlin as he leaned forward and wrapped his forearms around Ace's body, lugging him upward. Using their combined strength, they tugged hard until he scampered out of the water, spitting fluid and coughing.

"Quick, before the ice breaks again." She beckoned him forward, draping his arm over her shoulder.

Ace dragged his legs and Conlin took hold, supporting him on the opposite side. The strain crumpled his torso, and he battled for a lungful of air to conquer the few steps to the highway. A serrated exhalation burst from his lungs, bending at the waist to lower Ace onto the guardrail and Jeanette ensured he gripped the edge.

Saoirse rushed to him and flung her arms around his soaked clothing. "Shh." He soothed her, petting the length of her hair, and she trembled in his arms.

Jeanette dug inside her backpack, removed a wool coat and draped it across Conlin's back. "It's the best I can do at the moment."

"T'anks, Banféinní." Conlin gripped her hand with a gentle squeeze.

"You're the one that landed the plane."

"You made sure Saoirse was safe—"

"But I've a feeling we better go now." Jeanette turned and removed her jacket, placing it over Ace's shoulder. "We need to make it across the street."

Conlin glanced behind, spotting a silver Jaguar XJ sedan. The car slowed down, flashed their hazard lights, and stopped at a traffic light.

Jeanette tapped Ace on an elbow. "Come on."

He said, "Get outta here while you still can."

She flicked her head upward and stared at Conlin. He gave her a single nod and she hopped over the rail.

"Are you certain that you will be okay?" Jeanette asked.

"Go!" Ace tossed her the jacket.

Jeanette slipped her arms through the sleeves and wrapped a hand around Conlin's hip. He had Saoirse on one side and Jeanette on the other for support.

An unexpected release of gratefulness surged through his limbs and for a second, he regained stamina. After everything that happened, they were safe, at least for a moment.

ELEVEN

Jeanette fought off exhaustion and they rushed across the busy Auf Dufferin-Montmorency Autoroute huddled together. Her body shuddered and her hamstrings burned, carrying the extra weight of Conlin hanging on her shoulder. They arrived at a sidewalk beyond the intersection and caught their breaths.

The major priority, after escaping their pursuers, was for Conlin to remove his clothes, dry off, and warm himself. He hobbled beside her as she supported him, tucking an arm around his hip. Water streamed from his curls, matted to his forehead, and dripped down his face. A tinge of blue outlined his lips and his skin appeared paler.

Passing Montmorency Falls on their right, Saoirse paused and struggled, holding the partially distributed weight of her dad. It was imperative for them to keep moving, yet they needed a break to process everything and Conlin's condition required immediate attention.

"Follow me." Jeanette picked up the pace and almost dragged Saoirse along. The tourist attraction would give them a chance to evade anyone trailing them and provide amenities to aid Conlin.

Crossing through the parking lot for Parc de la Chute, Montmorency, Jeanette dug into her bag and paid before they boarded a cable car. The three of them huddled together, keeping Conlin's internal temperature stable. A small crowd joined the trip to the top. After a couple of awkward stares, the people turned their consideration toward the view of the waterfall.

The doors glided open, and they toddled through the courtyard. Conlin managed the few stairs at the entrance for the country farmhouse style Le Manoir visitor center and they entered the building. Behind a line of patrons at an information desk, Jeanette viewed the signs and directed Conlin to the restrooms.

"Dry off and try to warm yourself." Jeanette opened her backpack and pulled out a towel. "We'll go to the gift shop and grab a change of clothes for you."

The hint of a smile wavered, and he staggered a step. With a heavy heart, she visually followed his footsteps until he rounded a corner. Reality set in about the death-defying acts that just transpired, and a fit of shivers coursed along her spine. For the sake of remaining positive about their unfortunate events, she stayed strong by surrendering her worries to prayer.

Jeanette linked her arm with Saoirse's. "How are you doing?"

She glanced up and tears bordered the rim of her eyes. "Middling. Do ya think me dad will be fine?"

Jeanette stared her square in the face. "Of course, once he's dried and changed." She reinforced the statement, offering an encouraging smile. "Let's find him something to wear."

About ten minutes later, Conlin met them in the corridor near the washrooms. He removed his eyeglasses and tousled his hair using the towel, yet his soaked garments still clung to his figure. Jeanette handed him a sack from the store, containing tourist garb, including socks, and only lacked a pair of underwear.

Jeanette said, "It was all they had, and Saoirse selected the sizes."

"'Tis dry clothing," he said in a hoarse tone and peeked at the items.

"You're grand, yeah?" Saoirse pinched her lips tight, and her chin trembled.

"Ah sure." Conlin's eyes glistened as his mouth twitched upward to one side and he placed a palm atop her head, giving her a pat. The set of her frame sagged downward, and Saoirse bobbed her head. "Have a cuppa and I will see you in a few minutes."

Jeanette untangled her hair, combing her fingertips through the strands. "We'll order you a hot drink."

Conlin settled an intense gaze on her that she had never seen and rested a hand on her arm. "Banféinní, the way you responded in a moment of crisis, I can't convey my gratitude..."

A tightness in her lungs constricted her breathing. "It's my fault. I involved you and Saoirse in Tom's mess. None of this would've happened—"

"I don't blame you. You're not responsible for their actions."

A heaviness expanded through her extremities, slipping from his caress, and she tucked her fingers into the pockets of her jeans. She refused to acknowledge his pardon for her involvement, and the role she played in triggering the onset of violence.

"We'll meet you in the café after you're dressed." She kept her voice steady. There was no way she'd accept any gratefulness when her family dragged them into the dangerous situation.

His eyelids lowered and he headed toward the restrooms to change his clothes. A quiver rippled over her flesh. Now she appeared cold and unfeeling, but she didn't deserve any appreciation or thanks.

They wandered into the café, ordered drinks, and sat at a table beside a window with a panorama of the cascade. Saoirse sipped on hot tea and Jeanette drank a cappuccino. The steamed almond milk warmed her insides, yet the caffeine did nothing to relax her nerves.

Conlin arrived wearing gray sweatpants, displaying the city name Quebec below a front pocket, a navy sweatshirt of Montmorency Falls and her towel draped behind his neck.

He crashed into the chair beside Saoirse. "T'anks again. I appreciate the socks most."

"Here's your tea." Saoirse pushed the cup closer to him.

Conlin gripped the mug, raising it in a salute, and winked. "Ye're my, dear one."

Now that they settled and felt safe for a moment, a knot tightened in Jeanette's stomach. The realization of everything that had happened hit her at once and her leg shook under the table, bouncing a knee up and down. A pang struck her middle and her insides pitted into coils. Jeanette needed to sort out what to do next. Finding Tom was no longer her top priority, protecting the Murphys and helping them return home took precedence. Jeanette stood from the table.

"Excuse me," she said.

Conlin flicked his lids upward from his drink and did a double take. "Feeling all right?"

She pressed a palm against her belly and pulled draughts through her nose. "Yeah, I'll just be a few minutes."

Jeanette stepped outside into the cool, crisp fall weather and moseyed toward the large circular fountain and sat on the stone edge. She stared off into the distance. Fairmont Le Château Frontenac towered on a hilltop within the walls of Old Quebec. The illuminated points of the turrets spiked the skyline, piercing the blue of twilight, and defined the structure's magnificence among the surrounding buildings.

Jeanette withdrew her phone and set her data usage for Canada. She connected to the hotel's online reservations, booking a standard studio for Conlin and Saoirse for two nights. It was the least she could do for them. She called a local taxi service and requested a pickup in half an hour.

"Madame, have you viewed the breathtaking falls?" a man said in a French-Canadian accent.

Jeanette acknowledged the stranger wearing a tweed sports jacket and tan trousers. "Thank you, but I'm not interested in a tour."

The semblance of a smile flickered. "Allow me to introduce myself. My name is Geron Leclerc, and I'm a colleague of Thomas Hillestad."

Her heart froze mid-beat, and she sucked in an icy breath. She eyeballed him and studied his expression. An overall look of superiority emitted from his entire demeanor and made her hesitate about listening to him, yet she required information about Tom.

"Shall we take a walk?" He extended his arm toward a path along the waterfall. "You are his sister, Jeanette Hillestad?"

"Yes." She stood, following his lead.

"Pleasure to make your acquaintance. Thomas told me much about you and your profession."

A deep-muscle shake jostled her. Would Tom tell this man details about her life? "Monsieur Leclerc, where is my brother?"

"Please, call me Geron." The smug slide of his mouth accentuated his mustache. "Unfortunate circumstances separated us after being pursued by disreputable people, eager to obtain our relic."

Was he the same man that tracked Tom and the artifacts in Kinsale? "You worked with my brother in Ireland?"

"Oui, we created a partnership in Hardanger, Norway."

They meandered the wet, wooden planks leading to a steep set of concrete stairs beside the roaring water surging over rocks. A mist doused her as she climbed the stairwell behind Geron. "What exactly did you find?"

He remained silent until they reached the last steps, directing them onto a suspension bridge across the falls. Geron turned, facing her as he avoided a group of tourists, pausing for selfies overlooking the almost 300-foot drop. He continued crossing, avoiding the crowd of people, and stopped in the middle. He laid his arms on the wood railing along a chest-high fence lined with steel spikes to protect the public from the perilous plunge. The observation point overlooked the St. Lawrence River, where they crash landed an hour ago.

"I'd like to discuss our findings with you and what I know of Thomas' disappearance. Perhaps in a quieter, less tumultuous setting."

She figured he had an ulterior motive and appeared untrustworthy. "We can talk here. I prefer the location."

Geron glanced both ways. The crowds dispersed and his dark eyes gleamed. "Take a closer look." A firm grasp latched onto the collar of her jacket, and he gathered the material into his fists. Yanking her upward, he shoved her forward and she balanced herself on the tips of her toes. He forced her against the steel, holding her chin inches above the spikes. The sound of the water growing louder echoed an evil laughter bellowing from below. Her heart pounded and her pulse raced at the velocity of the flowing falls.

"Accidents have occurred at Montmorency."

Jeanette pushed her shoulders backward. Geron rammed himself hard against her torso and repositioned her body, bending her forward. The points dug deeper into her sternum. She winced and looked in every direction, noting a few tourists lingering at the far end. If she yelled for help, there was no telling what he'd do or if he carried any weapons.

Geron spoke into her ear, his breath seeping through his clenched teeth and creeping along her neck. "Are you ready to listen to my instructions?"

Jeanette grunted through the pain and managed a strained reply. "Yes."

An immense pressure subsided as Geron stepped away and her chest slid against the railing until her feet were flat on the ground. Her limbs shook as her eyes fixated on the height of the drop. "What do you want from me?"

"Your full cooperation." He swiped a palm through his hair and slicked it back, composing himself. "I will give you the details when we meet later."

"Is it safe to assume the men who forced us here are working for you?" Her voice wavered and her nerves strung tight.

A cocked smirk emerged on his thin lips. "You're a bright woman, so don't do anything foolish. Our communications must stay confidential." He smoothed the wrinkles from the front of his shirt with his palms. "I'll continue watching you."

"Where and what time—"

"When I decide to contact you." He pivoted on his heel and exited through an access side street into the upper parking lot.

Jeanette slapped her hand against her breastbone and stumbled along the walkway. Whatever Tom's dealings were with Geron could've already cost him his life and hers, too. What a fool to value an artifact above his own wellbeing and others. At the end of the suspension bridge, she kicked a wood post. *Tom, when will you learn?* She clawed shaky fingers through her hair and tightened the elastic band. The situation became increasingly dire, and she must get them all out of danger.

TWELVE

Jeanette gripped the steel pole along the steps and descended from the at close range view of Montmorency Falls. Making her way to the front entry for the country style manor, numbness crept into her legs and her knees wobbled. Outside the Le Manoir entrance, Jeanette noticed Conlin and Saoirse looking in all directions until they spotted her staggering toward the fountain. She sucked in a deep breath and squared her shoulders, gaining composure to keep up the guise that nothing happened.

"Where did you go?" Conlin drew his eyebrows inward. The peach tint of his lips and the rosiness of his skin complimenting his complexion returned.

"I... I thought some fresh air and a short walk would help, but..."

Flashing their owl-like eyes and questioning expressions, she imagined her appearance resembled a drunkard partying all night.

"For a second I wondered if you left." Conlin held her luggage in his hands.

Jeanette shot a glance at Saoirse and shifted a teary gaze at Conlin. She swallowed the lump in her throat and shook her head. "I wouldn't, at least not without saying goodbye."

He squinted his eyes, searching her face and placed a reassuring hand on her shoulder. "Hold on, I'm only messing with ya."

"I feel responsible for everything, so a taxi's arriving to take you to the Fairmont Le Château Frontenac. I booked you a room for two nights."

"Aren't you coming?" Saoirse vocalized in a wavering tone.

"Tom and I caused enough problems. It's imperative for you to escape from this dangerous situation."

"'Tis best if we get through this together." Conlin gazed at the river and the wrinkles deepened at the bridge of his nose. "We survived out there working as a team and we'll all need to make a full report to the police." His fingers slid down the length of her arm and rested on her hand. The severity of the incident they endured seemed to hit him, and his torso caved inward.

"Sorry that I dumped the responsibility of landing a plane on you. It wasn't fair to demand so much of you." She grazed her front teeth along her lower lip and balked at the tenderness, forgetting about the bruise on her mouth.

"Ah, y'know yerself." Conlin gave her hand a gentle squeeze, then relaxed his handclasp. "Glory be to God."

"Here's the jo maxi," Saoirse said.

"Come with us."

Would he still want her to join them if he knew about her encounter with Geron and his threats? She should send them off on their own, but she lost the courage—staring into his vibrant bloodshot, blue eyes, damp loose curls brushing against his forehead, and heartfelt request, referring to them as a team.

"Okay." She collected her bag from him and flicked her eyelashes upward, meeting his gaze. "Hopefully I've made it clear that Saoirse's safety is important to me, too."

His lips pressed into a fine line, and he breathed deeper through his nose. "You've proven that already."

They walked toward the vehicle and climbed into the passenger seats. Jeanette said, "Fairmont Le Château Frontenac, s'il vous plaît." The driver exited the parking and drove several miles to the property in Old Quebec.

Saoirse stared out the window. "We're staying in a castle?"

"Not quite like the estates in the UK and Ireland, it resembles more of a French manor. The property is over a hundred-and-twenty-five years old with a rich history." Jeanette gazed at the pitched roofs and ornate towers emulating Gothic architecture, highlighted in a steely blue-gray ashlar stone and brick cladding main façade. The impressive construct remains a gem in the United Nations Educational, Scientific and Cultural Organization, World Heritage Site of Old City Quebec.

Saoirse sat in the middle and leaned close to her dad, resting her head against his biceps. "Have ya ever stayed at the hotel?"

Emotions welled in her throat, reflecting on the memories. "Many years ago, with my family." Jeanette hadn't visited Quebec since she was a teenager during the February festival when Tom took part in all the activities. "We attended the Winter Carnival in 2002, when I was about your age."

"Wow, that's before I was born."

Conlin leaned back, outstretching an arm, and grazed his fingertips along her jacket. "A really long time ago." He emphasized the words and curled his lips upward to one side.

Jeanette suppressed a laugh and scrunched her nose, guessing Conlin was at least a year older. She welcomed his humor and added it to her mental list of qualities she admired. No wonder he maintained a healthy balance of parenting and friendship with Saoirse.

The taxi drove through a porte-cochere and parked. A valet attendant opened the back door. "Bonjour, et bienvenue à Fairmont Le Château."

"Merci," Jeanette said.

They entered through the revolving glass doors and into the lobby. Jeanette glanced up at the rows of chandeliers hanging from blue crown molding and proceeded to the roped queue at the check-in desks.

A woman waved at them to approach. "Bonsoir," she said.

"Bonsoir."

The time change struck Jeanette, and an ache throbbed in her brain, triggering a migraine since it was going on eleven at night in Ireland.

In her current state of mind, she didn't even want to attempt speaking French. "Parlez-vous Anglais?"

"Oui, yes." The woman smiled. "What is your name, please?"

"Jeanette Hillestad."

The woman's eyes remained on the computer screen as her fingertips tapped the keyboard. "A studio suite for two nights?"

"Yes, thank you."

"May I get your credit card to secure the accommodations?"

Jeanette slid off her backpack and pulled out her wallet. She slouched and bent her elbows on the gold-plated counter. "How many beds are in the suite?"

"Two doubles and a sofa," the receptionist said.

Conlin placed his palm on her back. "There you go now, space for the three of us."

Jeanette stared into his eyes, a deeper blue than the St. Lawrence River. Unable to maintain visual contact, she looked down and twirled her tresses round a finger.

The woman passed her plastic key cards. "Room 1210, offering views of Old Quebec's architecture."

"Merci beaucoup," Jeanette said.

"Enjoy your stay."

The three of them turned and made their way toward the brass elevators between mahogany wall panels. Saoirse stopped as she spied a black-and-white canine lying next to the concierge desk. She kneeled and petted the animal. A smile sat loosely on her mouth, and she continued to stroke the fur. It was the first time she showed a joyful expression since the multiple incidents.

Saoirse stood and viewed the large photo and read the description of the dog displayed on an easel. "Her name is Daphnie. She's a Labrador and Bernese mix known as a St. Pierre breed." Her voice rose in excitement. Saoirse rubbed Daphnie's head a couple of times. "Da, can we get a dog like this one when we return home?"

"Em…"

Jeanette nudged Conlin's arm. "Looks like you're getting a new addition to the family."

Nervousness curtailed his laugh, and he massaged the back of his neck. "Here's the lift."

Walking the maroon carpet on the twelfth floor, they stopped in the middle of the hall and stood at the entrance to their suite. Jeanette swiped the smooth keycard through the slot until the lights flashed green and they stepped inside, greeted by a fresh scent of cleaners lingering in the air.

Conlin set his bag of wet clothes on the sofa and sighed as he slumped into a sitting position. He placed his elbows on his knees and lowered his head into his hands.

"Take a hot bath and rest." Jeanette dropped her backpack onto the floor. Conlin glanced up with sunken eyes and offered a single nod.

She asked, "Do you mind if I take Saoirse downstairs to the shops?"

"'Tis safe enough."

Jeanette looked at Saoirse. "Hey, want to go shopping?"

"Sure." She shifted her glance between them. "Da, how are ya?"

"Not too bad." Conlin dug in the souvenir sack beside him and pulled out his wallet, tugging at his credit card stuck in the damp leather slot.

Jeanette swatted her hand in the air. "My treat. It's the least I can do for all the trouble—"

"What are you on about?" Conlin's brow crinkled. "You don't need to pay for everything." He rose from the couch cushions and handed Saoirse the form of payment.

"Thanks a million." Saoirse stood on her tiptoes and kissed his cheek, then headed toward the door.

Conlin faced Jeanette and his stance raised a hyper-awareness of their proximity.

"You can stop blaming yerself now. What occurred in Dingle wasn't your fault." His rich tone sent a judder throughout her body, and she seemed to shrink under the weight of his stare.

The sincerity in his voice made her feel worse. Guilt by blood relation. If Tom hadn't got mixed up with Geron and his crew, leading them to Conlin's house, none of this would've occurred.

"Are we leaving now?" Saoirse bounced on her feet.

Jeanette found it difficult to tear her gaze away from Conlin. "Yes, we're all set."

Saoirse opened the door and Jeanette tripped backward into the wall. The seams of his lips curved up into a grin. She whirled on the ball of her foot, and they left.

The stores in the corridor beside the main lobby consisted of minimal clothing options for a teen, displaying several mature, classic-style garments and dressier eveningwear for sale. Jeanette glanced at Saoirse, and she scrunched her face with a disapproving headshake.

"Few choices for you, huh?" Jeanette said.

"I noticed loads of shops on the ride over here."

"Hmm, we told your dad we'd stay downstairs." She coiled a curly strand of hair around her finger. "You better text him."

Saoirse stared out the corner of her eye and a brow elevated in a slow arch. "His mobile's banjaxed now, ya know, after falling into the river."

"We'll call up to the room from the concierge."

Saoirse followed Jeanette to the front desk and sat on the cobalt area rug alongside Daphnie, the canine ambassador.

"Bonsoir, may we phone our guestroom, 1210?"

The attendant rang the room. "There's no answer."

Jeanette slouched onto the counter, then turned toward Saoirse. "He must be in the bathtub. We should go upstairs and wait."

"Ah, c'mon, it'll be fine. We're going across the street, and it's practically on the same property."

It seemed clear that Saoirse developed the masterful ability of persuasion. Jeanette figured she perfected the technique over the years to sway both parents. With a doe-eyed stare, she flitted her lashes and pet the dog. Jeanette imagined she always got her way. No surprise Saoirse liked her brother, since she possessed the power of influence that rivaled Tom's skillful level.

"You may leave an urgent message with an alert." The concierge suggested.

Against her better judgment, she agreed and left a priority voicemail. They exited at the back of the hotel, leading onto a boardwalk overlooking the St. Lawrence River. The reality set in that earlier they were in Ireland and now strolled Old Quebec—after being taken at gunpoint, forced on a flight to Canada, survived an emergency crash landing, suffered another threat to her life and Geron's guarantee he'd be watching. Her heart clambered up her throat and she looked in every direction. Jeanette needed to do everything in her power to keep Saoirse from harm.

THIRTEEN

An hour later, Jeanette and Saoirse returned to the suite, enjoying their girl time and getting to know each other better. They giggled swooshing the entry open and entered the room. Conlin whirled around, almost spilling a cup of tea in his hand.

"Where've ye been?" His voice strained and the teacup clanged as he set it onto the table.

The automatic closer slammed the door shut and Jeanette stiffened for a moment. "Didn't you get my message?" She noticed the illuminated notification blinking on the phone.

Conlin followed her line of vision toward the writing desk, staring at the red light, and scrubbed his hands over his face. "After a soak in the tub, I fell asleep on the sofa."

"Da, don't have a freaker. We went across the street; the clothes downstairs were dreadful."

Conlin's jaw tightened and the crease between his eyes deepened. "You agreed to stay inside the hotel." His gaze came back to her. "Something could've happened. Ya know those fellas are here, and they will not give up."

Sickness swirled in Jeanette's belly, figuring Conlin would be even more upset if he discovered she encountered Geron at

Montmorency Falls. "You're right. It was poor judgment on my part."

His facial muscles relaxed, and he stepped forward. "I've a feelin' you were swayed by a tactic I know all too well." Conlin shot a stern look at Saoirse.

"The shops are like straight outside the backstairs." Saoirse hid a smile and fluttered her eyelashes. "Ye want to see the dress?"

"G'wan." He dropped his shoulders and uttered a hushed laugh. "Heaven help the lad she marries."

Conlin edged nearer and fire crackled beneath the surface of her skin. Jeanette struggled to keep her thoughts focused, with him standing close and wearing nothing but a robe. She wriggled, overheating under her shirt, and his nearness lit a fuse of passion burning through her veins.

"Sorry, we should've gone our separate ways, leaving you free to get away from the disaster Tom and I brought on—"

"I'm not cross, only worried about Saoirse." He slipped his finger under her chin and tilted her head until their eyes met. "And you."

Jeanette's cheeks scorched as he slid an open palm along her face, encasing her jawline and his thumb brushed against the bruise on her lip. She quivered under his touch and leaned into the caress. The doorknob to the bathroom turned and she staggered backward. Quickly moving away, his fingertips grazed her flesh and his stare drilled into her for what felt like minutes, yet a mere second passed.

Saoirse stepped out in a black-and-white polka-a-dot baby doll dress and ebony leggings. "What do ye think?"

"Lovely, dear one," Conlin said.

"T'anks, Da." Saoirse turned toward Jeanette. "Change into your outfit."

"Okay, it won't take long." Avoiding eye contact, she grabbed her belongings and streamlined for the restroom.

Jeanette closed the door and locked it, taking a deep breath. She pressed her palms against the ledge of the marble counter and stared into the mirror. Her hair grew three times fuller than usual after Geron pushed her head into the misty cloud at Montmorency Falls. Goosebumps scattered across her flesh, thinking of the impending contact he promised.

Conlin was right. Geron had an opportunity to approach them at any point when they cruised the streets of Old Quebec. She didn't know what bothered her more, the thought of Geron watching her every move or her reaction to Conlin's touch.

After a quick shower, she slipped on the navy polyester, nylon, and spandex-blend dress she purchased in town. Jeanette used her comb to tame her unruly locks and had no choice but to air dry her hair without a diffuser attachment tool for the blow-dryer. She wrangled the massive curls and gathered the strands at her nape, pushing the total length over one shoulder. Since she wore cocktail attire, she applied rouge-blush and lipstick. When was the last time Brian took her out for dinner? Ah yes, she blew out a gusty exhale, remembering the work banquet in August. For Brian, it's always about business.

Jeanette exited the bathroom. "I'm all set."

Saoirse glanced up from her phone. "Ya look deadly."

"Thanks." Her field of vision roved toward Conlin. "Do you think it's too much?"

He flipped his head upward, dropping the hotel amenities binder into his lap and opened his mouth, but no sound came out. His eyes lowered down the entire length of her body and ricocheted back up until their eyes locked. A warmth spread up her neck and Jeanette slid her palms over the front of her dress.

"Not at all, you... em..." His gaze darted around the room, landing on her again and a garnet color splotched his face. "Ye look dolled up and raring to go."

"Aren't we going out to eat?" Saoirse asked.

"What am I supposed to wear?" Conlin tugged at the collar of the white velour robe and rendered a light laugh.

Saoirse rolled her eyeballs, angling her head to one side with a crooked grin. "Can't ya buy new duds downstairs?"

Conlin caved his torso inward. "Give me twenty minutes." He strolled into the bathroom.

Jeanette grabbed the bag containing Conlin's wet garments. "I'm taking your clothes to the front desk for laundry service. I will be back soon." Jeanette left the suite and headed downstairs.

Strolling out of the elevators in the main lobby, she brought Conlin's clothing to the concierge. "Can we please get these clothes laundered within twenty-four hours?"

"Oui, fill out this order form and we'll deliver them to your room."

Jeanette entered the information and handed the laundry to the worker. "Thank you."

"Bonsoir," a man said, standing uncomfortably close.

She whirled around and faced Geron. Jeanette froze, and her heart stuttered a beat. No location offered refuge from him. He could show up anytime, anywhere, when least expected, and now he was in the exact spot she stood with Saoirse an hour and a half ago.

"I'm delighted you dressed for the occasion." He placed a firm grip on her arm at the bend of her elbow and guided her toward the dining area. "Nice choice in accommodations."

Jeanette remained silent, and her tongue stuck to the roof of her mouth. Geron escorted her to the podium inside a restaurant and she stationed her fists on her hips. At least in a public setting, she'd be safe. On second thought, he didn't have a problem manhandling her at Montmorency Falls with witnesses present. The greeter grabbed menus, led them through a maze of dinette tables, and placed them beside a fireplace in the center of the room.

"Merci." Geron flashed a pasted-on grin. The usher nodded and returned to the entry post.

Jeanette accessed his niceties toward the unsuspecting and figured he possessed the skills to deceive anyone he aimed to manipulate. Did he use those strategies on Tom? Geron ignored Jeanette and perused the cocktail selection.

"Ready to order?" A server stepped forward.

Geron peered over the top of the menu and stared at Jeanette. "I'm buying."

A sickness churned in her stomach. She glanced at the man waiting for her response. "Flat water, please."

"Suit yourself." He shrugged a blasé shoulder. "A glass of Château La Coudraie, merci."

"Bien."

Jeanette gazed at the fire and shifted in her chair as Geron scrutinized her mannerisms. Her nerves twisted, and she fired a hard stare at him. "Where's my brother and why are you chasing us?"

Geron bent forward, his arm rested on the white tablecloth. "Your Viking heritage flows through your veins."

Jeanette pressed her backbone straight against the chair. "What do you know about my lineage?"

"More than you realize."

Did Geron research her ancestry? For certain, he gained more knowledge about her than she had acquired about him. A chill shimmied down her spine, and she trembled. The server swung by, set their drinks in front of them, and spun around in the other direction.

He lifted his glass. "Santé."

Geron kept his eyesight fixed on her, and an eerie sensation swept over her, thinking he involved Tom in something dangerous. The hairs on her forearms rose and she tucked her hands under her thighs.

Jeanette leveled her shoulders and tipped her chin higher. "Once again, where's Tom?"

"I don't know." Geron sat his drink down on a coaster and maintained visual contact. "He's placed himself in danger, hiding an unexamined artifact."

"What do you mean?"

"I explained earlier, we worked together and after our discovery in Ireland, Thomas disappeared."

Her mouth went dry and she sipped her water. "What did you find?"

"This is the Jeanette I heard about," he said.

Geron finished his drink and reached into the inside pocket of his brown leather sports jacket. He pulled out a small stack of photographs and stretched out his hand.

Jeanette retrieved the pictures and examined the snapshots of an excavation site. Her eyes roved over the images of a rectangular-shaped rock and carvings of the Futhark alphabet etched onto the surface. A breath caught in her chest for a few seconds at the sight of the same stone depicted in the drawing displayed in Jack's attic that she and Tom first saw when they were kids. With a gentle swipe, she brushed her thumb across Tom's image. *Fool.* A heaviness pressed against her heart.

"Thomas had the same expression when he unearthed the artifact in Hardanger, Norway."

"How do I know you didn't steal the relic and murder my brother?"

"Why would I inform you of my plans? Listen"—he leaned closer—"I believe we'll locate him and the stone, if we work together."

"If Tom disappeared in Dingle, why did you have us brought to North America?"

"I live in Quebec City and felt we should meet in person for a discussion. A few of my employees stayed behind in Kinsale to keep looking for Thomas."

She drummed her fingernails on the tabletop. "If you're interested in talking, why assault us, then order our abduction and threaten my life?"

Geron reclined and held open palms skyward. "I'm not responsible for all their actions. I instructed them to approach you and relay the message that I desire to discuss my findings with you."

"And your personal methods of brutality at Montmorency Falls?"

"At the moment, anger got the best of me. You injured my pilot and cost us an expensive plane."

Jeanette folded her arms across her chest. "Why do you believe Tom's in jeopardy holding onto an ancient stone?"

"Your brother didn't explain it to you?"

"No." Tom never included her in his risky escapades unless he found himself in trouble, and now it seemed he waited until it was too late.

"I'll divulge the information if you agree to work on my team."

"You'll tell me." Jeanette straightened her shoulders and braced her neck. "Otherwise, I'm going to the police and report that I suspect you're responsible for my brother's disappearance."

"I don't think so."

"Why?"

A snigger escaped from his mouth. "We want the same thing, to find Thomas and the artifact."

Jeanette massaged the lump in her esophagus and gulped her water. She didn't have much of a choice. He was one of the last people to have contact with Tom and might know more about his whereabouts than he disclosed. If she wanted answers about what happened in Ireland and details about their discoveries, cooperating was her only option to gain a solid lead on where Tom went after departing Dingle. Her upper body sloped downward and she sighed.

"What do you propose?"

Geron rested against the table, raising a brow. "Thomas kept a map. Have you seen it?"

"Yes, but it's nothing more than a sketch. It doesn't give any detailed information."

"I prefer to examine it." His tone evoked an order and the muscles in his face twitched. "There might be clues to aid us in our search for Thomas, and it'll prove your loyalty."

"I understand." Jeanette didn't believe a word he said. Even his characteristics conveyed the intent to harm and destroy.

She had to keep him away from Saoirse and Conlin, no matter the personal sacrifice. A sickness brewed in her abdomen. "When do we start?"

"Tomorrow." Geron sneered and raised his wineglass. "Welcome to the team."

FOURTEEN

At about a quarter after eight, Conlin finished purchasing new duds. Signs for restaurants in the hotel caught his attention and he ambled toward the end of the hall to make a dinner reservation. A bar with dimmed lighting and neon-blue trim for a display of drink selections reflected seating options in a mirror behind glass bottles. Conlin rounded the corner and scoped out the dining area. He spotted Jeanette at a table in the company of a man, and his body jolted.

What the... He scratched his scalp. A waiter cleared a plate of appetizers in front of her guest and nothing other than a drink was at her place setting. The person turned and flagged down the server. Conlin cocked his head back, recognizing the fella from Ireland.

Conlin observed the two of them chatting. When... how... Did she plan on meeting him? None of it made sense, and his mind whirled too fast to keep up with his thoughts. He wasn't aware Jeanette had ever met the man since he hadn't seen him around after he approached Saoirse. The joints in his fist burned and begged to let loose. No hasty moves. The last thing he needed was to get into a fight without a passport.

Best if he waited and approached Jeanette on her own. The last confrontation involving the gouger at his house caused an argument with Thomas and he left, never to be seen again. If Jeanette departed on poor terms and disappeared...

Conlin slapped an open palm against the shifting sensation beside his heart and massaged his chest. Jeanette stood from the table, nodded, and aimed for the exit. He searched in every direction and backtracked into the closest shop. Posing as a shopper, he picked up a candle and handled it, peering over his shoulder and watched the man leave the property.

Conlin stalled for a couple of minutes before exiting the store. He strode toward the bar entrance, and she ambled down the corridor, almost cruising right past him.

"What's the story?"

Jeanette halted and glanced up. "Conlin..." She fidgeted and twisted her hands together. "I dropped off your laundry and got distracted."

"A meeting is more than a mere distraction."

"Did you follow me?"

"Hold on now. I came downstairs to shop for clothes and thought we were all going to dinner." Heat spread up his neck and across his face. "Instead, you're dining with the man who's hunting for Thomas and was searching for relics in Ireland." Conlin tossed his arms heavenward.

"Yes, I can explain—"

"How could you sit there in his presence after all he's done to us and knowing he's likely responsible for yer brother's disappearance?"

Jeanette gripped the front of his sweatshirt and tugged, stretching the fabric. "Let's talk."

Conlin's limbs hardened at her assertive gesture and shadowed her down a spiral staircase. She yanked him toward a secluded corner beside a large potted plant, close enough for him to lean into the curves of her body. He rolled his shoulders, allowing cool air to flow under his collar.

"His name is Geron Leclerc. He's behind everything that's happened, and I don't trust him at all."

"Then why did ya join him for drinks?"

"That's what you think of me?" A wrinkle deepened in her brow and her eyelashes flew high.

Conlin shook his head. "I... I'm confused about what happened." He still needed to sort out his thoughts about Jeanette. Brave, tenacious, compassionate...

"Geron forcefully escorted me into the restaurant, and I remained in his presence to determine his motives."

"His intentions are obvious; he's using you to locate Thomas."

"Of course. He asked about the map too and threatened if I refuse to cooperate, he'll withhold specifics about his business dealings with Tom."

Conlin stared at her, and for the first time her eyes reflected a helplessness hid inside. Her body trembled against his and he slipped an arm behind her back. Ever since he met Jeanette he tried to assist and protect her yet failed like he had on several occasions with Kera and Saoirse. *You've bollixed up everything again.*

"The good news is Thomas must've evaded Geron and his men. I'm sure he's hiding out and safe now."

"Yes, Conlin." She cheered him on and bumped his biceps with an elbow as if he scored a winning goal for the Football Association of Ireland. "And if we find Tom first, we'll have leveraging power."

"I'll support you in any way possible, within reason, for the safety of Saoirse."

"We should've gone our separate ways earlier," she said in a serious tone, and her grin vanished. "It's best if we work on getting you home and, in the meantime, keep your distance from me."

A hollowness wafted through his chest. Jeanette lowered her eyelashes and Conlin raised her face by positioning a curled finger under her chin. Now he perceived the depth of her care for him and

Saoirse as a radiance shimmered in her eyes. An unnerving push of blood coursed throughout his body. If only he possessed the courage to confess, he cared for her, too.

"I appreciate yer concern for us, but I'm not going anywhere until you're safe from Geron."

"The risk is too great, and I can't allow you to jeopardize your safety for my family anymore—"

"Pardon, puis-je vous aider?" A hotel employee offered to assist them.

Conlin lurched and turned around. "Em, we're deciding where to eat."

"May I recommend Le Sam Bistro?" He extended an arm in the restaurant's direction.

Conlin craned his neck, visually following the recommendation and keeping a hand on Jeanette's lower back. "Grand, t'anks."

"Have a good evening," the man said.

Twisting in her direction, she sidestepped to the right and bumped into his torso. Lost in a jungle of her tresses, strands covered his face and caught in his stubble, sliding across his mouth. Her cheeks flushed and she nudged past him, avoiding eye contact.

Humor plucked at his lips, and he took a faulty footstep backward, knocking the potted plant. "We'll finish our discussion upstairs and figure t'ings out."

Inside the suite, Conlin set his shopping bag on the bed and plopped down beside it, pushing his hair back from his forehead. He peered at Saoirse, focused on her device. He had every intention of following through on his word, yet Geron posed a serious problem.

Jeanette dawdled in the doorway, settling a palm on her hip. "I apologize for causing so much trouble for the both of you."

"What's the matter?" Saoirse set her mobile aside. "Did ya find something to wear, Da?"

"Yeah, I'll go change." Conlin shifted his eyesight ahead. Every time he looked at Jeanette, he lost the nerve to admit he agreed with her suggestion to leave and allow her to continue on her own. Because her eyes contradicted her words and revealed that she wanted them to stay.

Conlin tugged the tags off his purchases, dressing in dark trousers, a black button-down shirt and matching suit jacket. He gawked at the longer stubble on his jawline, then rubbed the growth and shrugged. Facial hair was the least of his worries. At the restaurant, they'd need to devise a plan on how to handle things with Geron and begin the process of heading home.

He stepped out of the bog and joined Saoirse at the door. "Ready for supper?"

"I'm staying in for the night." Jeanette's fleeting look danced around the suite, and she altered her stance twice before placing a fist on her hip. "Enjoy some father-daughter bonding time—"

"But we bought our dresses for tonight," Saoirse said.

"Ah please, join us." Conlin held open the door and extended his arm to take her hand. "I'll buy you a nice vegan meal at Le Sam Bistro. I read the menu and they have buckwheat pasta stuffed with butternut squash."

"Thanks, it sounds wonderful."

Pushing his cleared plate of ravioli to the center of the table, Conlin reclined in the dining chair. He crossed his arms above his belly and sighed. "I'm full and knackered."

"It's strange to think we left Dingle this morning or yesterday, or however long ago?" Saoirse said.

Jeanette peeked at him and dragged her front teeth against her lower lip. "There's an Irish consulate in Montreal to apply for emergency travel documents."

Her expression revealed she continued blaming herself. How could he convince her otherwise?

"We're leaving?" Saoirse asked.

"We aren't on holiday." Conlin rested his napper against his palm and gripped a fistful of hair. "Yer ma is going to have it out with me when she finds out."

"She already knows."

"What did ya say?"

"That we left town on holiday."

Conlin huffed out a weighty exhale to release the stress of the day. "Don't fib to yer mother."

"Like tell her gougers forced us out of the country at gunpoint?" she said.

"I'll explain everyt'ing to her later."

"Yera, she texted pictures from their holliers in Cabo San Lucas."

"'Tis grand."

Jeanette finished the last bite of her meal and cleared her throat. "I reserved a car rental for pickup tomorrow and I'll drive you to the next destination. From there, you'll be able to catch a flight from Montreal to Ireland." Her voice trailed off with a slight hitch in her remark.

"You needn't sort it all out for us."

"Helping you is my primary concern."

The level of selflessness she demonstrated was unlike anyone he encountered in his life. Conlin propped his chin on a fist. "What about Geron? Ye'll be fine handling the situation by yerself?"

Her back elongated and she lifted her head higher. "There's no other choice. It's the only lead I have at the moment."

"Careful, he's dangerous."

Jeanette looped curls around her fingertip and shifted in her seat. Conlin had a feeling that Geron had shaken her up with more than verbal assaults and threats. Increased heat escalated behind his neck and he cracked his knuckles.

"Yer wan asking questions about Thomas?" Saoirse pushed her cheese pizza aside.

"He's in Quebec and demanded Jeanette work for him to learn information about Thomas."

"We have to help—"

"Ah, here. We're going home and that's the end of it." He used a firm, authoritative parental tone. Saoirse dropped her lower lip in a pout and slumped her posture in the chair. "Order afters. Something for us to share." He handed her the dessert menu.

Conlin looked at Jeanette. A sweet smile of fondness adorned her face. She possessed a calmness under pressure, a take charge, and no one told her otherwise attitude. A pure banféinní.

"I want to stay and help you." He made a rolling eye gesture toward Saoirse.

Jeanette dipped her gaze and flicked her lashes upward. "I know."

After eating Sablé Breton with a hint of smoked caramel and nuts lingering on his tongue, they sauntered down the hall from the lifts to their room. Saoirse rested her noggin on his arm and Jeanette walked close to him on the opposite side. A contentment filled him despite the circumstances that led them together in Quebec. Conlin swiped the keycard and opened the entry.

"Thank you for dinner." Jeanette placed a box of Saoirse's leftover pizza slices on the counter.

"'Tis the least I could do after you paid for the accommodation." Saoirse said, "I'm ready for bed."

"The ladies take the doubles and I'll sleep on the sofa."

"Please, make yourself comfortable after the physical stress you endured today." Jeanette grabbed her backpack and strolled toward the couch.

"Em, I'd like to be near the windows," Saoirse said.

Jeanette glanced at him, and he gave a single nod. Although now she would be in the bed beside him. His muscles tightened and he turned, pointing to the option closest to the sofa. "I'll choose this one, if you're fine with the arrangement."

Jeanette set her luggage on the floor and unzipped her bag. "Whatever's best for you."

Once again, her tone conveyed confidence, yet her body language opposed the certainty. His line of vision followed her as she gathered her night clothes, shuffled into the jacks, and shut the door.

"Do ya think she'll find Thomas if she works with Geron?"

"Sure she will. Don't worry yerself at all." He hoped Saoirse didn't detect any doubt in his voice. Jeanette could manage by herself, but agreeing to work with Geron troubled him more than he cared to admit.

Jeanette stepped out in a pair of plaid flannel pajamas and he bit back a smile. Did he prefer her wearing the slim-fitting dress, caressing her curves or casual pjs, or maybe...?

"The bathroom is available if anyone would like to change."

Saoirse hopped up, grabbed her shopping bag, and entered. Jeanette retrieved her mobile, a small notepad, and sat at the desk. She flipped on the lamp and tapped her finger on the screen of her device. Conlin picked up his phone, sim card and battery off the nightstand. He dried the pieces with a towel earlier and moisture lingered in the cracks. The damage seemed beyond repair. "I'll need to buy a mobile in the marra."

She oscillated between her screen and writing notes in an almost rhythmic motion. "Did you say something?" She didn't bother to look at him.

Conlin removed his black blazer and unbuttoned his shirt. "What's captured yer attention?"

"Just verifying information about travel documents." She swept her gaze upward from the notebook. "Good thing I booked the room for two nights. The embassy in Montreal opens on Monday." She peered at the handwritten page. "I wrote down the requirements for a new passport. Are any of these reasons applicable?"

"Do they list forced out of the country at gunpoint?" Conlin walked toward the desk, stood behind the chair, and leaned over her shoulder. Lavender mixed with sage swirled into his nose from her loose and wild hair as the curly strands brushed his neck, beckoning him closer. He blinked hard and stared at the blurred words.

"What do you think?" she asked.

"Em..."

"What are ye looking at?" Saoirse said.

Conlin straightened, stiffening his back and spun around. "The Irish Consulate website."

"Do ye need to use me mobile?"

"Jeanette's taking care of it." He glimpsed at the web page she studied showing a picture of a relic with runes markings on it, similar to the ones at Kilmalkedar.

"We'll finish up in the morning." Jeanette turned off her phone and closed her notebook. She stretched and glanced at the digital clock displaying 10:20 p.m. in green numbers. "Feels like 4:00 a.m."

Conlin overextended his arms above his head and yawned. "We should get some rest."

"Night." Saoirse crawled into the sheets on the sofa and covered herself with a fleece blanket.

"Sleep well, darling." Conlin cruised into the washroom.

He slipped into the sweatpants Jeanette bought him at Montmorency Falls and swigged a bit of mouthwash before heading to bed. When he traipsed out, they had already turned the lamps off except for the entry nightlight. Jeanette was asleep and swaddled in a comforter. He flipped the last switch, darkening the room and climbed onto the plush mattress.

A stream of city lights beamed through a corner window. Saoirse always kept the curtains parted at least a half inch at nighttime. He rolled on his other side, discovering Jeanette's gaze pinned on him before she squeezed her eyes shut and the thought of her staring at him triggered an involuntary smile. The moonlight outlined her figure, casting a silvery glow, and she looked angelic.

Lifting her lashes, her lips curved upward. "Goodnight."

"Night." He'd fall asleep thinking about Jeanette and knew she'd be in his dreams.

FIFTEEN

Jeanette tiptoed from the bathroom, waking before Saoirse and Conlin. She showered and dressed, leaving ample time for them to get ready as she prepared for her meeting with Geron. She didn't have the clarity of mind last night to study the findings Tom and the team uncovered in Norway. Instead, she emailed Tom's boss, Mr. Bonhoeffer, and updated him on her discoveries about the expedition.

Saoirse squeezed past, holding a bundle of clothing in her arms. "Hiya."

"Good morning."

Conlin rolled out of the sheets, placed his bare feet on the floor and scraped a palm over his face. The comforter slid from his back as he stood from the bed, shirtless and wearing sweatpants.

Jeanette remained motionless and opened her mouth, yet nothing came out. Her gaze meandered along his defined pectorals and abdominal muscles. He glanced up, wrinkling his brows, and she averted his stare. Why did she keep finding it difficult to concentrate around Conlin? Maybe because his blue eyes drew her in deeper than a body of water and with certain pronunciations of words, his accent crooned a sweeter tune than any too-ra-loo-ra-loo-ral Irish lullaby.

"Sleep well?" she asked.

"Can't complain." He tugged at the bedding, straightening the blankets. "Yerself?"

"Yeah, all things considered."

"You're meeting Geron the day, yeah?"

She picked up her handbag off the desk chair and dug out her notebook, flipping to the second page. "This afternoon at 12:30 in the park at Plaines d'Abraham."

"I'm coming with you."

Jeanette's lids trembled downward and she bit the inside of her mouth. "I appreciate the offer, but that's not a good idea."

"Without the authorities involved, you need to consider the dangers of walking into a situation where he has the upper hand. You've experienced firsthand the people working with him, and they have no problem using physical force."

Conlin presented another valid point and he didn't even know about the encounter at Montmorency Falls. She bumped a fist against her chin. "For your safety, please stay away."

"How about I watch from a distance and only intervene if an emergency arises?"

Jeanette searched his mien. The intensity of his stare revealed a genuine care, and the thought of him keeping watch raised her internal temperature. Managing her job, balancing everyday life, the challenging relationship with her parents and worrying about Tom while maintaining an image of perfection for Brian depleted her strength. Conlin expressing concern without negating her choices filled her with an inexplicable comfort only he provided. Although she'd never lead them into any more trouble.

"I've already subjected you and Saoirse—"

"She can wait in the suite."

"I'm not staying at the hotel by meself." Saoirse strolled across the room in jeans, a maroon sweater and her hair wrapped in a towel, piled atop of her head.

"Ya will if it means you'll be safe." He pointed his forefinger at her. She exaggerated an eye roll and dumped her pajamas on the sofa.

Conlin grabbed his robe and faced Jeanette. "There isn't much I can do against weapons, but I'm here if you need anything. I don't want ya to get hurt."

A lightness spread throughout her limbs, and she held a breath for a second. "Oh, the hotel delivered your clean laundry. I hung it on the hook beside the shower." He gave a sole nod and continued toward the bathroom.

Jeanette stared at the handwritten location for her meeting. Conlin's reassuring words permeated her heart yet reiterated the reason she declined the suggestion of him following. Remaining out of sight, but observing the appointment supplied a sense of peace and protected him from the potential use of a gun again. No, the risks outweighed the benefits and she would go alone. Jeanette had every intention of preventing Conlin from sustaining injuries, or worse, at any cost.

Her phone buzzed on the desk, causing a muscle twitch. She picked it up, peeked at Saoirse, and strode to the entry.

Jeanette exhaled aloud, then tapped the accept call image on the screen. "Hello Brian."

"I'm glad you answered." He paused, audibly breathing on the line. "You seemed upset during our last conversation."

"Sorry, but I have a lot going on and you ignored my letter—"

"Where are you now?"

"I made an emergency stop in Quebec," she said.

"What for?"

"Remember, I'm trying to locate my missing brother?"

"I think you might be in over your head. Let the experts pursue any leads."

"No," she said.

"Why? You're not a detective or on the police force."

"Listen." She kept a steady and firm pitch. "I'm collaborating with Tom's former colleague. Once I figure things out, I'll head home." She didn't believe for a second Tom and Geron had a partnership.

"You sound different."

"It's a stressful situation and pressuring me doesn't help."

Brian stayed silent for half a minute. "I'm concerned about all the traveling and how many days you've missed at work."

Just as she suspected, he had his own interests in mind and preferred she return to her job right away. Jeanette sighed. "All the stress is overwhelming."

"Then come back to New Hampshire for the sake of normalcy."

How could Brian assume she'd go along like nothing had changed when no one had seen Tom for almost a month? Jeanette rushed her response. "It's going to be a long day. I'll talk to you later."

"If you think that's best," he said in an uncertain tone.

"Thanks for understanding, bye." She pushed the end icon, stepped into the parlor room, and tossed her device onto the bed. Jeanette spotted Saoirse, surveying her every move.

"Was that yer boyfriend?"

A shaky laugh escaped under her breath. "Sort of. It's complicated right now."

Saoirse sat on the edge of the sofa, leaning forward, and her eyes beamed. "What's his name? Is he a flah, and are ye getting married?"

Jeanette hesitated about how much to divulge. "Well, I've dated Brian for a few years and I used this time apart to end the relationship, so we're definitely not planning a wedding."

"'Tisn't serious then, and there are plenty of other fellas." She shrugged a shoulder and set her phone on the couch. "Do ya like my dad?"

Jeanette sucked in a mouthful of air, and her heart plummeted into her belly. "Um, your father is great." She rubbed a palm against her pant leg. "And so are you."

Saoirse pursed her lips and squinted. "I mean, would you want him as yer fella?"

Her fingers fidgeted, uncoiling a ringlet, and she smoothed the ends of a few tresses. "Well, we just met."

"I've watched the two of you together," she said.

"What have you seen?"

"I'm not a child. I've been here the whole time and noticed the flirting and lingering looks between youse."

"Hopefully it hasn't made you feel uncomfortable."

"Not at all." She flashed a cheeky grin. "He's happier with you."

Maybe it didn't bother Saoirse, but the observations unsettled Jeanette. The kindness they showed Tom when he was their guest, and the tolerance Conlin revealed throughout every problem she led them into, created a connection she hoped would cement an extended friendship. How could there be anything more?

Conlin exited the bathroom in blue jeans and his laundered gray-acrylic pullover sweater. Jeanette glanced at him, feeling the powerful force of his gaze, stronger than the rushing water of Montmorency Falls, pouring over and hauling her into a whirlpool. An emptiness ensued beneath her heart and a fluttering circulated throughout her stomach.

A smile flickered across his face when he caught her expression. Jeanette distracted herself by gathering her handbag and tore off the front page of the hotel stationary.

Conlin clapped his hands and rubbed his palms together. "How about we get something to eat?"

Saoirse perked up and hopped off the couch. "I am fierce hungry."

He shifted his gaze toward Jeanette. "Are ya prepared to go?"

She straightened her back, squared her shoulders, and took a deep breath. "I'm ready."

Two hours later, after breakfast and visiting a local shop for Conlin to purchase a prepaid phone, they stood on the wooden planks at the rear entrance of the Fairmont. Jeanette checked her watch. "It's five past noon. I should go." She swiped at a thick, wavy strand of hair blowing into her face.

"And you're sure about going by yerself?"

She wasn't certain about anything. "Yeah."

Conlin gazed across the waterway, the wind whipping loose curls off his forehead. "I'll give you me mobile number, just in case." He extended a hand and Jeanette passed him the phone.

He typed in the digits under contacts and placed the device in her palm. "Take it handy, Banféinní."

A warmth flooded her body whenever he called her by the nickname, and she felt empowered that he thought of her as a warrior. "I'll see you soon." Jeanette swung around and walked the boardwalk in the direction of the city park.

The twenty-minute trek, including three-hundred steps parallel to the St. Lawrence River, refreshed her with a surge of energy. Golden autumn leaves and crimson-orange sugar maples lined the promenade. She enjoyed the icy air of the season and inhaled deep, taking long strides up an incline. The historical citadel sat perched atop a hill adjacent to the Plains of Abraham.

Jeanette searched in all directions and spotted Geron walking from outside the fortified walls. At least he didn't have any of the other guys accompanying him, and quite a few people strolled the pathways. Of course, a crowd never stopped him from using any means necessary to get what he desired.

"You arrived on time, wise decision," he said.

"I'm here for my brother."

"Oui, let's take a walk."

Jeanette followed his lead along a flat-stone walkway to a large center fountain. Geron motioned for her to join him on one of the several benches. He eased his back against the seat and crossed his legs. She sat beside him, as close to the opposite edge and removed Tom's sketched map, passing it to Geron.

He analyzed the paper, then placed it in his coat pocket. "Do you know what took place here?" he asked, looking out into the distance.

Jeanette surveyed the area, recalling her world history courses. "A battle, part of the Seven Years' War."

"Correct. In 1759, between the French and British Empires, a fight for dominance and world supremacy."

"Does this have anything to do with the stones discovered in Ireland and Norway?"

"An age-old pursuit, to possess and conquer."

"I'm struggling to make the connection."

"The exploration for new lands by earlier settlers all had the intention of claiming the territories for their own."

Jeanette nodded in agreement. "Right—"

"Yet prior to their arrivals, greater forces than the will of kings, queens, and armies directed certain groups of explorers. They submitted their lives to their gods and relied on spiritual guidance."

She was confused by the direction their conversation took. Weren't they discussing physical, historical artifacts? "So, you believe spirituality influenced their choices?"

"Madame, have you read the Bible, The Icelanders' Sagas and Native American Literature?"

"Yes, I've studied—"

"Then you understand the significance of their rituals." He kept steady eye contact. "I know for a fact the stones unlock an unearthly force." He jutted his chin and spoke in an arrogant manner.

A chill crept across her skin, and she shivered. "I'm surprised you'd make that claim. Most historians and archaeologists base their statements on firm data, my brother included."

"Even in our era of technological advances, we haven't gained the level of achievements the Celts, Vikings and Indigenous obtained."

Jeanette petted the length of her tresses. "What kind of accomplishments?"

"Tapping into the supernatural forces surrounding us." His lips curved upward to one side.

The sound of her heartbeat thumped in her ears and she swallowed hard. She lost the words to speak and snapped her mouth closed.

"Your response reveals you don't doubt me but have questions. Thomas had a similar reaction. I dare say it troubled him to the extent of abandoning the rest of our mission."

"Whatever supernatural event that happened caused him to flee?" She thumbed her lobe.

"Not quite. When the team unearthed the second stone in Kinsale, the energy of the relics grew when we brought them together."

Her finger slipped from her earlobe into a ringlet and she twisted the strands. "Can you assure me that my brother left Ireland unharmed?"

"We amicably parted ways. Now whatever occurred after he departed"—he tossed up open palms—"it's out of my hands."

"Why would he still be in jeopardy? Did your men continue following him?"

"The circumstances are more serious than you comprehend. Thomas retained the stone from Norway. The source of power is unstable. We need to contain the stones for further study and testing in a proper facility."

"They should undergo a systematic examination and kept in a museum—"

"I assure you; we're dealing with spiritual realms of divine origins."

Jeanette's body quaked and she wrapped her arms around her waist. Geron's cautionary tale didn't cause her alarm. Tom knew how to handle artifacts. It was the knowledge of his borderline obsession to find the ancient relic, since they were kids, that unnerved her and his declaration to discover the stone, even at the cost of his life, hummed in her head. Tom's disappearance from everything and everyone, including family, made her second-guess the theories about his vanishing.

"Things don't add up. Why would he disconnect himself from all contact?" Jeanette hunched forward, resting her elbows on her knees.

"It's best if we locate Thomas and the relic soon to ensure his safety. Plus, you'll both be contributing significantly to the archaeology world." His eyes narrowed. "Perhaps you know of somewhere your brother might seek refuge."

Jeanette pulled in a sharp breath through her nose and jolted. The one place and person they considered a home away from home...

"Any ideas?"

"Um, no, but I'll keep thinking." She'd never share any information about Tom or disclose his location.

Geron stood and turned on his heels, facing the St. Lawrence River. He stepped toward a sundial and Jeanette followed.

"It's almost November's first sunrise." He focused on the dial. "What—"

"Would you like to see the Celtic Stone we excavated in Ireland?" He tossed her the side-eye.

A ripple of goosebumps scattered over her skin. After viewing the images Geron shared at dinner last night of the artifact from Norway, she had been eager to analyze a relic in her hands. "Yes, I think it'd be helpful."

"Good. You should know what spiritual forces you're up against."

Jeanette managed a nod and her posture shrank. He shuffled through the fallen leaves scattered on the ground and she traipsed alongside.

"Where are we going?"

"Port of Quebec Marina."

SIXTEEN

Conlin crashed into a chair beside the writing desk. Jeanette had left over an hour ago and he hadn't heard from her yet. He rested his noggin in his palms, gripping a fistful of locks, and eyed the notebook she scribbled in last night. His gaze shifted back and forth. He didn't intend to pry, only protect. He thumbed through the palm-sized book and skimmed the information written on the first three pages—the Irish Embassy, a rental car reservation number, and meeting place. Right, she was at the Plains of Abraham. Conlin flipped onward and read the handwritten words:

How are the stones connected?

He witnessed Geron's aggressive tactics in his pursuit of possessions in Ireland. His intentions appeared self-serving, maybe evil. Conlin pushed his hair off his forehead, sighed, and reclined. Perhaps he should take a walk and get some fresh air. He stood and faced Saoirse, sitting on the couch, listening to music with earbuds.

She yanked one side out of her ear. "If ye're leaving, I wanna go."

"Stay in the room. I'm going for a stroll."

"Let me join ya."

Conlin didn't want to argue. "You shouldn't have even gone to Dingle."

"But I did, and I am here so." Saoirse tucked her lower lip under her front teeth and folded her arms over her chest. "Take me with you."

He motioned with his head and winked. "C'mon, darling."

Saoirse bounced from her seat and aimed for the door. Now it was best to wander in the opposite direction of the Plains of Abraham and avoid any trouble. He would pray for God's protection over Jeanette.

Conlin ordered take-away tea for them at the café downstairs and exited the Fairmont. At a slow pace, they ambled toward Terrace Dufferin and rode the funicular down to Basse-Ville. The charm of the obvious French-influenced architecture transported them into the ambiance of France, and they roamed along Rue du Petit-Champlain, the historical pedestrian corridor. They wandered in and out of three-story buildings with gabled roofs, dormer windows, and stacked chimneys—both enjoying their purchases of fudge, macaroons, and caramel popcorn.

Saoirse laughed and had a genuine smile. "T'anks, Da." She popped another sweet in her mouth.

Conlin chuckled under his breath. Although he told Saoirse they weren't on holiday, he appreciated their time alone and forgot about the chaos for a moment. "You're welcome, Cricket."

She halted and gawked at him. "Ya haven't called me that since I was a child."

True, he stopped using her nickname when she was seven, soon after Kera left. The feeling of family unity deserted their home and the father-daughter tie broke. He lost himself and her over the years. Too bad it took being forced against their will to another country while enduring life-and-death situations for them to bond.

He pulled his mobile from the rear pocket of his cacks, checked the time, and expelled a heavy breath. A quarter to three and still no messages from Jeanette.

"She'll be fine." Saoirse placed her hand on his arm.

Conlin gazed at her and nodded in consensus. "Let's wander this way." Conlin continued their hike toward the waterfront. Ships and tour boats lined the docks. A wind stirred, walking along the marina, and he buttoned his coat.

The yearning to set sail returned. "Maybe we can rent a yacht?"

"That'd be grand. We haven't been sailing together in ages."

Conlin dropped his shoulders. Work consumed his life in recent years, and Saoirse spent more time with Kera in Dublin. He needed to take advantage of these precious moments with Cricket when he still had the chance.

At a rental facility off the wharf, Conlin devoted thirty minutes to filling out papers, proving his capabilities of operating a boat. "I'm surprised after a deep freeze ye're open for business."

The sales representative said, "We don't close until the end of October. The unpredictable weather is common in Quebec and the marina is many kilometers from the shallower sections of the river. We're at the outlet of the Atlantic." The agent accompanied them down to the pier, reviewed emergency procedures, pointed out features on the watercraft and handed Conlin the keys.

"T'anks." He spent most of his life on the water and navigating yachts since he was a kid.

They boarded a white-and-navy striped 30ft Cobia 301 motorboat. The man untethered the ropes and gave him two thumbs up to proceed. A lightness extended throughout his limbs and he stepped from the stern into the cockpit. The Yamaha engine purred as he eased the throttle.

An hour and a half later, Conlin had cruised well beyond the harbor and into the open waters of the St. Lawrence River. Saoirse sat beside him, tying her hair in a bun as the wind whipped through the console. A sightseeing cruise approached, and he steered starboard to pass before an oncoming vessel, behind the ship, proceeded in the wrong direction instead of port side.

"Hang tight." The quick reaction stiffened his left shoulder.

At a high speed, Conlin swerved, turning the helm hard to avoid a collision. The motor flooded and the watercraft sputtered. He shifted the gear into the idle position and rode the waves. A huff of air expelled from his cheeks and he shook his head in a swift arc. "Are ya all right?"

"What happened?" Saoirse asked.

"A boat passed incorrectly." Conlin peered at the stalled vessel drifting along the waves. "Eejits."

Conlin hunched over the outboard. The plugs weren't wet, so if he let the engine sit for at least twenty minutes, all would be grand. The passing yacht floated closer, and he called out, "Ye need help?" He walked to the edge of the bow and raised a hand to his brow, blocking the sun peeking through the gray clouds.

Two men stared at him, then turned their attention to the person exiting the cabin. Geron stepped outside and Conlin's muscles tightened.

"What are you doing?" Geron asked his crew.

"We almost crashed into another boat." One man pointed and Geron's head followed the direction.

He straightened his posture and smirked. "Monsieur Murphy? You're a long way from home."

"Not by choice."

Geron said, "Out for an afternoon cruise on the St. Lawrence River?"

"Where's Ms. Hillestad?"

Geron gestured, waving his hand at a brawny man and directed him toward the cabin. He snapped his fingers at the other fella to tie the lines and connect the vessels. Trouble seemed to follow them everywhere, even when they tried to avoid it and he didn't like the situation. A man pulled the motorboats parallel, attaching them to the grab handle. He turned and glanced at Saoirse, standing behind him.

Cricket leaned closer and spoke in a shaky voice. "What should we do?"

"When I signal, untie the rope."

Geron kept his eyesight fixed on him, and the crewman escorted Jeanette outside. Conlin let out a huge breath, pressing a palm beside his heart.

"Conlin." Her pitch raised and she shifted her gaze toward Geron. "What's going on?"

Slowly turning his neck, he stared at Jeanette. "The fates have brought us together."

"You're not making any sense," she said.

"We cannot ignore signs of destiny, especially when they come at us head-on."

A shudder jostled Conlin, unable to deny the eerie truth that out of all the places, modes of transportation and people in Quebec, they almost collided with a boat carrying Jeanette onboard. He thought she met Geron at the Plains of Abraham and now she was on a sailboat on the St. Lawrence River. Did danger surround her wherever she went, or did she go looking for it? He believed her only intentions were to find her brother.

Geron shadowed her footsteps and blocked her path by extending his arm. "Consider the evidence I provided and what we discussed." Two of his crewmen advanced toward the bow. "Join us, s'il vous plaît."

A muscle ticked under the rim of his eye, and he disregarded his suggestion. "No thanks, our rental contract has almost expired." He turned and flicked his chin, motioning to Saoirse. She crouched down and yanked at the knots in the line.

Geron proceeded forward, stepped aboard their Cobia, and reached for Jeanette. She ignored him and jumped across the gap, landing with a steady foot on the deck.

Conlin leaned close enough to feel her against his arm. "You're fine, yeah?"

"Yes, I—"

"As you can see, it's been a civil visit. We conversed about Thomas and discussed mutual business interests. Nothing to hide when we're in plain view."

"I'd hardly call private quarters on a yacht a public setting."

"You found us."

Conlin rolled his shoulders and angled his neck, cracking his joints. Jeanette brushed a palm over the back of his hand and curled her fingers, giving him a gentle squeeze.

"We're ready to go. I have a lot of information to process after our discussion." She kept a constant, unintimidated focus on Geron. Did anything shake this woman?

"Then we part ways, bonne journée." Geron approached Saoirse, and she took a step back from the grab handle, securing the ties. "Mademoiselle, you are a descendant of pure Irish?" He offered a handshake.

Conlin rushed and moved in the middle of them, shielding Cricket. "Never talk or look at her again." He clenched his hands and his fists hankered to strike. "If ya even think of laying one finger on her, I swear to God—"

"Interesting, you trust in a spiritual entity."

"Please, let us leave now," Jeanette said.

Geron eyed her down, then spun on his heel and stepped onto his yacht. "Adieu."

Conlin wrenched the tethered lines free and returned to the cockpit. Saoirse trailed him and Jeanette remained at the bow until he started the engine. She walked along the deck and entered the center console. He opened the throttle with no choke, allowing as much air in as possible, and cranked the motor.

"Have a seat," Conlin said.

His eyesight focused ahead, navigating the watercraft in the marina's direction, and sped off before Geron got any other ideas.

At high speeds, the hull cut through the water and they cruised closer to their destination in record time.

Jeanette patted Saoirse on the knee and rose from the cushioned bench. She staggered toward him and swayed, smacking a palm against the window to regain balance. Her hair whirled in the wind, and curls extended like overgrown vines.

"Sorry you had to endure another encounter with Geron," Jeanette yelled over the rumble of the motor and whistling of the rushing air.

"Weird coincidence, I guess." He didn't believe in coincidences and hated agreeing with Geron that fate entangled them together. Conlin shifted his gaze between her and the St. Lawrence River. She remained quiet and sat down again. He slowed the speed of the boat and coasted into the dock.

In less than fifteen minutes, they disembarked the vessel and headed for the rental location. Jeanette checked behind them a few times, taking long strides.

"Everyt'ing okay or ye're worried about Geron following us?" Conlin asked.

"I'll tell you about it when we're settled in the hotel room," she said in a serious tone. "We should act quickly and get out of sight."

What other deals did Geron force her to accept? Part of him wanted to involve the authorities, regardless of Jeanette's decisions to hold off so she could gain information from Geron about Thomas. Did she actually think he'd be truthful? Still and all, he trusted Jeanette's choices and believed she'd never place Saoirse in danger, at least not on purpose.

In the refuge of their suite, Conlin followed behind Jeanette and Saoirse, letting the automatic door closer slam shut. Jeanette flinched and kept her back toward him, staring out the bay windows.

"So, are ya going to tell me about the meeting?" Conlin maintained a neutral voice.

"Da, she's not responsible for what just happened." Saoirse set her shopping bags on the counter near the entry.

"Sure, I know. We want to finish our conversation in privacy." He forced a smile and nodded to reassure her that the run-in didn't make him cross.

Cricket pressed her lips tight, lowered her lashes, and sat on the sofa. Bless, she already tuned into something on her device and used earbuds to block out their discussion. He preferred she didn't know the details about whatever Jeanette got mixed up in now.

Jeanette stayed silent and rummaged through her handbag. She pulled out a handful of photographs and an item wrapped in a linen cloth. Conlin fixed his gaze on the objects, then peeked at Saoirse from the side of his eye as she remained engrossed by her videos.

Jeanette handed him the pictures. "Geron showed me the photos last night. Snapshots of Tom from their expedition in Norway."

Conlin shuffled through a few prints. "Gain any extra clues from the images?"

She closed her eyelids for about half a minute. "It gives me hope that Tom's alive." Jeanette turned on her heels and paced around the room. "I have a theory, now that I've had a couple of conversations with Geron." Interlocking her hands behind her back, she continued, "It's unclear what arrangement Tom and Geron had, but it's evident their partnership dissolved and they didn't part on good terms. I believe Tom took off to an undisclosed location with the stone in the photos. Geron seems desperate to retrieve the relics and he thinks they have supernatural properties. He wants to bring the artifacts together to examine his hypothesis."

An unshakable sense of something ungodly scattered chills over his flesh. Plenty of mystical lore originated from Ireland, yet Jeanette explaining Geron's theories and intentions didn't settle right. "What do you think?"

Jeanette paused and looked him square in the face. "I'm glad you asked." She unfolded the wrapping around the object, displaying an oblong-shaped rock no bigger than a pocket-sized paperback book, with obvious carvings of eyes, a nose, and mouth etched onto the surface.

She passed over the item and a buzz tingled his flesh as he tightened his grip on the exterior, rubbing a thumb across the etchings. A type of impulse shock coursed through his veins and caused a burning sensation against his skin, yet there were no visible marks. He'd rather never learn whatever secrets the rocks contained, despite the curiosity rising inside.

"Did he give it to you?"

"Not exactly." She grazed her front teeth along her bruised bottom lip. "I'm going to examine the Celtic Stone because I believe Geron has an interest—"

"Do ya want him to keep following and threatening you?" Conlin arched a questioning eyebrow and set the relic on the desk.

"He asked me to investigate the piece on his yacht. I need more time to study the petroglyphs and determine the stone's origins."

"In other words, you stole it."

"Archaeologists pass many artifacts between researchers—"

"I get it, but we can't remain in yer company while Geron pursues you and his conquest to the extent of risking my daughter's life."

Jeanette dipped her chin and peered at him under half-moon eyes. "I'd never let anything happen to either of you. But you're right, and I understand the need to distance yourselves from me."

She didn't understand. It pained him to walk away from her and he wanted to help her find Thomas, but it seemed she ignored the fact she had as much interest in the mysterious stones as her brother. What was their obsession with the ancient relics? Conlin believed she cared about their safety, and her actions proved she had Saoirse's protection in mind when she made all her decisions, yet at the moment it appeared discovering the mysteries behind the artifacts meant more.

Did she think solving the mystery of the stones would reveal additional information about Thomas' disappearance? At least she agreed Cricket's welfare took precedence over anything else. Guarding her was more important than helping the Hillestad family, regardless of his growing attraction and care for Jeanette.

SEVENTEEN

Jeanette woke up late. She tossed and turned all night after a tense evening. Although they all agreed to order room service for dinner to avoid another possible encounter with Geron. Rubbing the sleep from her eyes, she dragged herself out of bed. The lamp on the nightstand lit the suite and she realized they had already left. She shuffled her feet toward the desk and read a note from Conlin, written on hotel stationery.

Meet us at the café when you're ready.

Jeanette grabbed her jeans, a thermal long sleeve shirt and a cable-knit sweater then headed into the bathroom. Staring at her reflection in the mirror, she combed her unruly locks and gathered her hair, securing an elastic band around the curls.

Yes, her messy mane caused daily annoyance. Yet today, the real frustration was Conlin's disappointment that she took the stone from Geron. Jeanette gazed into the glass until her image became a blur. More mysterious stones. How many existed in the world and what was their purpose? She paused, as if listening for an answer.

A sensation of an entity lured her, as if sleepwalking, out of the bathroom and toward her purse. Jeanette reached inside the bag, and her fingertips grazed the linen cloth wrapped around the stone. She gulped the knot building in her esophagus and an echoing heartbeat pounded against her chest, drumming in her ears. Retrieving the artifact, she unfolded the material and her eyes fixated on the rock. She shook her head, snapping out of her dreamlike state, and shoved the covered relic inside her bag.

Jeanette collected the last of her clothing items scattered on the hotel bed and put them into her backpack. She looked around the area to ensure she left nothing in the room. When she exited, the door slammed, and her shoulders jerked forward. She straightened her posture and continued down the hall toward the elevator to meet Conlin and Saoirse downstairs.

Strolling into the coffee bar, she spotted them at a table in the corner. She swallowed hard and sucked in a frigid breath. Conlin said less than a few words to her last night and left before she awakened. Jeanette surmised he was still unsupportive about her decision to confiscate the Celtic Stone. She scanned the restaurant and approached the dinette until his eyes locked her down—a steely blue stare pierced her, and she looked away.

Jeanette said, "I checked out and I'm on my way to the rental car agency a block away."

"Em, I found a bus online that'll take us from the city center to Montreal."

A knot doubled in her belly and a gurgle rumbled. Jeanette peeked at Saoirse, lowering her head and allowing loose strands of hair to drape across her view.

Forced to look directly at Conlin, her arms weighed heavy along her sides. "I know my choice seems contradictory, but I've made it a priority to find Tom and keep you both safe."

"You did yer best for us." He raked his fingers through his curls and lowered his gaze. "I need to continue protecting Saoirse and make our way home."

"I didn't mean for you to get so involved…"

"Ah, sure, Banféinní. Be grand," he said.

"I guess this is goodbye." Jeanette stumbled a step backward and her heart seemed to stop for a moment. She patted a flat palm against her breastbone.

Saoirse leaped from the chair and hugged her as if she were part of the Murphy clan. "Text me when you find Thomas." She leaned back and tilted her chin upward. "And don't let the gombeens get ya down."

A breathy laugh burst through the emotions building. "Take care of each other." Jeanette gave Saoirse's upper arm a light squeeze, then turned and hurried outside without looking at Conlin again.

The frosty air smacked her cheeks and she coughed to loosen the feeling of indigestion rising in her esophagus. Taking brisk steps, she walked to the car rental location on the opposite corner of the hotel property. She didn't even allow Conlin to speak another word before storming out the doors. After everything he had done and sacrificed, she did nothing but offer him a cold shoulder.

Jeanette inhaled fast and blew a calming breath from her lips. She would write him a letter explaining her choices after she found Tom and returned home. For now, she needed to get her head refocused on the task at hand. It was best if Conlin remained unaware of her theory that Geron entertained the idea of testing the supernatural abilities of the stones with Saoirse in mind. Leaving the artifact in his hands was too great of a risk, and she had to take the relic to keep her safe.

After paperwork and signing the hired automobile contract, she drove off the lot in a metallic-blue Nissan Versa. The forty-five-minute transaction distracted her from focusing on Conlin, but now, alone in the quiet of the car, her thoughts dwelled on the Murphys. Because of the change of plans, and no answered calls or email replies from Jack, she'd head south toward New Hampshire, following her gut instinct on Tom's whereabouts.

Driving outside of fortified Old Quebec, she glanced at her rearview window, spotting Geron's silver sedan behind her at the stoplight. A chill ran throughout her body and she quivered, expecting to drive farther than a few kilometers before he tracked her down. Jeanette gazed ahead and held her breath for thirty seconds. Horns honked and she joggled her head, staring at the green light. Geron's car moved into the next lane, accelerated, then sped past and cut in front, making a quick turn onto Avenue Honoré Mercier. She pulled alongside a curb and her line of vision followed the path of the vehicle.

Jeanette blinked twice at two people walking north on the opposite street. "Oh no," she whispered.

Geron seemed to have his sights on Conlin and Saoirse. She checked her mirrors, looked over her shoulder and entered traffic flow. Her grip tightened on the steering wheel and air whistled through her constricted windpipe.

Although she didn't know the city streets of Quebec, she made an immediate left, trying to make a calculated move and beat Geron by one block.

"Proceed to the route." The programmed GPS directions repeated multiple times.

"Shut up, Siri." Jeanette tapped the end function icon.

She turned right at a stop sign, then made another turn at the next block, and scouted the two of them a couple of feet up the road. Ignoring the no parking signs, she rolled the passenger window down and cruised up to their steady pace. "Conlin."

He did a double take, stepping off the curb, and Saoirse followed. "What are ya—"

"Hurry, get in." Jeanette pressed her foot on the brake pedal and hit the hazard lights. "I'll explain in a minute."

Saoirse hopped into the backseat and Conlin's mouth fell agape. "Hang on, we're taking the bus."

The blasting of car horns resounded through the city streets. A lengthy sigh escaped from his mouth as he rushed inside the vehicle and closed the door. Jeanette continued to inch along in the congestion. Her eyes darted from each mirror, checking for Geron's position. She noticed his Jaguar, in the center lane, about five vehicles behind.

"What's going on now?"

"Um..." She bit her lower lip. "I saw Geron following you."

"Maybe because you took the artifact."

"Right, he knows I have the Celtic Stone. So, it seems my assumptions are accurate and he's interested in—"

"Don't say it."

Jeanette cringed at the sound of Conlin grinding the enamel on his teeth. "If he has any intentions toward her, by God in heaven I'll—"

"I know... I know." Jeanette bounced in her seat. "I'm getting us out of here." She hooked a left at the traffic signal, exiting the busy main avenue, and took Route 125 across the St. Lawrence River in the direction of Montreal.

Saoirse stretched as far as the restraint allowed and slipped her hands over Conlin's shoulders. "Everything's fine and dandy, you'll see. Jeanette will sort it out."

Conlin pitched a narrow stare through crescent lids. "Sure, she will."

A painful pinch constricted her swallowing reflex. There were no words of affirmation, nothing she could say to encourage them or ensure their safety, but Lord help her, she'd do whatever needed to protect the Murphys.

Twenty minutes outside of Quebec City and sitting in silence, Saoirse leaned forward between the middle armrests. "No sign of Geron. We lost him, and now we can stay wit' Jeanette."

"Em, yeah..."

Jeanette didn't dare look at Conlin's expression. Understandably, Geron's pursuit disturbed him, and he was less than thrilled about being stuck with her longer than he intended.

Saoirse slid against the backseat, cool and collected, exhibiting an ease all teenagers possess, believing they're invincible. "How far is Montreal?"

"About a two-and-a-half-hour drive." Jeanette peeked in the rearview mirror.

"Wake me when we get there." She popped in her earbuds and closed her eyelids.

Jeanette longed for the simpler times in her youth. The kid showed amazing strength through the constant ordeals they encountered. "Saoirse's so strong and intuitive."

Conlin slouched in the reclined leatherette interior and crossed his arms. "She's young and inexperienced."

"I don't think so. She expressed a mature insightfulness during our talks."

"What kind of chats have ye had to draw that conclusion?"

Jeanette held in a laugh, tightening her lips. "Just girl talk."

"Ah sure, y'know her well, after a couple of days, and seeing her react with survival instincts to dangerous situations."

"It must've been a relief to part ways after all the traumatic events and finally protect your daughter from the real dangers of having conversations with me."

"She's at an impressionable age." Conlin exhaled and massaged his forehead. "During the time we've spent together, you've modeled a woman who places family above all, which is commendable. Except your actions are to the point of extreme risk, placing yerself and others in danger. Your determination to locate Thomas and learn about old stones is causing you to make impetuous decisions. Still an' all, yer compassion, and ambitions are inspiring yet appear misguided now."

"Wow, you have a running list of the things you despise about me?"

"They're attributes I admire in you."

The confession circled her, tightening a lasso around her heart, and a series of palpitations jerked against the reins. "Then... why worry if you think they are positive traits?"

"You've had life experiences cultivating your character into the woman ye're today. Cricket needs time to grow, develop, and mature. There's no need for her to take unnecessary chances for the sake of adventure or a t'rill. These incidents during the past few days might entice her to make some foolish mistakes."

"Sounds a little overprotective."

"You don't understand, you're not a parent."

The stabbing pain of his remark cut her deep. It wasn't intentional and Conlin didn't know he stomped into the territory of a delicate subject, yet it hurt all the same. A sickness swirled in her stomach and a cold sweat spread across her nape. The bitter truth lodged in her throat, making it difficult to ingest. She had no right to advise him on parenting when she lacked the knowledge, and he had done a superb job raising Saoirse.

"Once we're certain that Geron hasn't followed us, I'll leave you alone and promise my carelessness will no longer jeopardize your daughter's security."

The weight of his stare was a four-ton boulder bearing down on her. Out of the corner of her eye, she noticed his lips parted to speak, yet he remained silent. The fact he said nothing spoke loud and clear. For the first time, after years of going after Tom, she doubted her objectives and questioned herself on how far she would go to rescue her brother, if it put others in danger.

Ten minutes later, at the Quick Mart, they grabbed a few snacks and bottled waters. Conlin paid at the cashier and Saoirse followed, carrying two paper bags to the Nissan. Jeanette stood at the driver's side and they climbed inside the car. Everything that happened over the past week created a storm of confusion. The primary concern of finding Tom wasn't at the forefront of her mind at the moment. Conlin's comments about her characteristics he liked became clouded by his equal displeasure at her misdirected motives and her lack of parenting skills, however accurate, still stung.

He lowered the windows and asked, "Do ya want me to drive?"

"I'm fine, just distracted by my thoughts," she said.

"If you change yer mind..."

"Haven't we taken enough risks in the past twenty-four hours?" Saoirse said.

Conlin pulled a treat from a paper sack. "Here." He read the name and tossed it to Saoirse. "Eat a King Don."

Jeanette smiled at their sweet interactions and an ache developed, since she endangered them again. She opened a bottle and drank a mouthful of water, started the car, and entered the freeway. Gazing straight ahead, she struggled to concentrate on driving, and remained quiet, replaying their conversation in her mind.

Conlin was right in his assessment of her behavior. She went above and beyond the normal dedication to a family member, putting others in jeopardy because of her personal reasons for finding Tom. Now Geron entangled her in whatever he and Tom had going on in Norway and Ireland. Jeanette tucked her purse beside her hip as her body temperature spiked, and an itch crawled along her skin.

Fog haloed sycamore and black-maple trees, lining seemingly endless highway. Focused on driving provided the avoidance she sought to distract from certain truths about her family, Brian, and Conlin... A few rapid blinks cleared her muddled thoughts and realigned her priorities.

She pictured the sundial in the park at Plains of Abraham. How was Geron planning to test his theories? Did she jump to conclusions about him involving Saoirse in his plans? Maybe the stress of everything finally caught up with her and she needed to go home. Not until the Murphys were safe, and she located Tom so they could discover Geron's intentions with the stones. She tried to forget the artifacts, yet she envisioned the ancient relics and their carvings of symbols from Vikings and Irish Celts. What did they have in common, if anything at all?

"Ye're far away at the moment." Conlin offered her barbecue-flavored chips from an open bag. "Crisp? There's a vegan approved label on the package."

"No, thanks."

"If I said something harsh to ya, it's because—"

"Not at all. Your opinions are valid and you know what's best for your daughter." No point in getting into her theories about the stones or how he wounded her with his comment on a sensitive subject. "I've got a lot on my mind."

"Banféinní..." He extended his arm toward her, then paused, and lowered his hand onto his drink.

"We need some music," Saoirse said. "Tap the Bluetooth icon."

"Now you're in for it." Conlin chuckled under his breath and touched the picture.

"The playlist is pure fire and you like Fontaines D.C., Inhaler..."

"I do?"

Saoirse nudged an elbow against his biceps. "We both listen to Power of Dreams, The Frank and Walters—"

"They're class. And The Pogues are legends."

An exaggerated sigh bellowed from her chest, up her throat and out of her mouth. "We'll see what Jeanette t'inks about the song selections."

"Tom and I could never decide if The Clash or The Jam were better."

"The Clash," Conlin and Saoirse said in unison.

"I agree."

Good thing Saoirse diverted the conversation and selected a song by Fontaines D.C. Music had a way of drifting her off elsewhere. The melodies, lyrics, and tunes always evoked recollections about certain moments in her life when she replayed the songs years later. Now whenever she'd listen to the legendary Irish bands again, memories and emotions would stir, reflecting on her time with the Murphys.

What would Conlin and Saoirse remember of their stint with the Hillestad siblings? Trouble, chaos, putting their own family first and risking the lives of others with an insatiable curiosity for relics? A heavy weight pressed against her torso and a breath hitched in her chest. Better leave it all unspoken and push any feelings aside. She'd reserve the pent-up frustration for Tom and give him a verbal lashing. More than ever, she was confident he escaped from Geron with the stone he discovered in Norway. Geron revealed his scheming tactics, providing Jeanette an offensive position to discover the purpose of the stones and locate her brother.

EIGHTEEN

The music playlist ended when they arrived in the suburbs of
Montreal. At the sight of skyscrapers and the observation
wheel, La Grande roue de Montréal, visible in the distance, her
muscled relaxed. A new city and different environment that they
hadn't encountered Geron or his hired men.

"How about lunch?" Jeanette cringed at the question, assuming
Conlin wanted to get out of the situation. Better fix the blundering
remark. "Or I can drop you at your next destination."

"We'll join ya for tea." Conlin turned and faced Saoirse. "Please
give me your mobile to search for flights online."

"You're welcome to use mine for anything," Jeanette said.

Conlin twisted his torso toward the front, brushing her arm as
he settled straight into his seat. "Thank you, although Cricket can
spare a few minutes off her device." His striking eyes peered at her
and she focused her gaze on the road.

Saoirse asked, "Where're ya traveling? Any thoughts on where
Thomas might be now?"

Jeanette parted her lips to speak and glanced at Conlin. He
rolled a shoulder and stretched his neck to one side. On second
thought, best to keep her opinions to herself. "I'm still piecing
ideas together."

"Can we stay and help?"

Jeanette scrunched her face and hunched forward over the steering wheel, biting her lower lip. She didn't intend for the reply to sound like an invitation.

"The arrangements are to replace our passports and depart for Kinsale," Conlin said in a firm yet loving voice.

"But we're here and—"

"Saoirse, the plans haven't changed, and I'm done discussing it."

Folding her arms across her chest, she huffed and slammed her back against the seat. "The Bible says to carry each other's burdens."

An audible exhale escaped his mouth, and he pinched the bridge of his nose, massaging between his eyes. "True, and the scriptures also state a wise person sees danger and seeks refuge."

"It's sweet that you care, and you've already done so much." Jeanette glimpsed at Saoirse in the mirror.

She attentively raised her head. "Like what?"

"Well, you welcomed troublesome siblings into your home. You warned me about Geron, and even at significant cost, you traveled to Dingle."

"I guess..."

"And I consider you a friend. I've valued your positive attitude and the encouragement you've given me to continue my search for Tom."

"Sound." Saoirse smiled and her posture relaxed. "You're a dote."

"T'anks," he whispered, and flashed a wink.

A sudden release of tension loosened her nerves. Finally, she said the right words and felt at ease with Conlin again. A renewed hope of carrying on a friendship returned, and she inhaled a cleansing breath.

Two hours later, they finished lunch in downtown Montreal. Conlin spent most of the time researching information on obtaining emergency travel documents and flights to Ireland.

"Be right back." Saoirse stood from the wrap-around booth.

Conlin did a double take. "Where are ya hopping off to, Cricket?"

Saoirse angled her head downward, concealing the eruption of pink on her cheeks, and rolled her eyes. "Da, I'm going to the jacks." She flung her hair over her shoulder and traipsed away.

"Why do you call her Cricket?"

"A special childhood nickname. She was frightened of the Sí, fairy folk in Ireland, and sang little tunes, hoping the creatures would remain at a distance." He paused and stared at her with a mischievous cock of his eyebrow. "We consider crickets lucky and their singing keeps fairies away at night."

Jeanette propped an elbow on the table and rested her chin against a palm, mesmerized by the enchanting tale he told. She found it enjoyable listening to Conlin, gazing into his blue irises and his accent was easy on the ears.

"The feeling of security disappeared from our home and the term of endearment lost meaning." He lowered his eyelids and looked off across the room. "Something happened after her mother and I split..."

Jeanette didn't want to bring up painful memories. She hadn't figured out if he harbored romantic feelings for Kera and was bitter about the marriage or missed the idea of being a family. Better question was why did she care about the reasons? For both their sakes, she'd change the subject.

"Under more ideal conditions, I would like to revisit Ireland. The island is abounding in history, mythology, beautiful landscapes, and the people are hospitable." Jeanette's sight riveted on Conlin and a warmth spread throughout her body. "Well, the few I met."

"Hopefully, I've given ya a good impression of the Irish."

A magnetic intensity between them drew her closer. "A genuine representation that I'll never forget." She focused all her attention on the curve of his mouth and leaned forward, pressing a shoulder against his biceps. "You're supportive, kind, endearing..." What was she saying? She held a mouthful of air for a second.

"Am I, now?" Conlin inched close enough to feel his breath on her cheek.

In intimate proximity, he exuded the scent of the hotel's courtesy soap, infused with cedar and hints of amber, permeating her sense of smell. Her heart rate increased and heat swarmed under her clothing. Conlin caressed her jawline and rested a thumb against her chin. Jeanette's eyelids fluttered, then shut as she puckered her lips.

"Finished?" the server asked.

Jeanette's eyes popped open. She gasped as if they were twelve and caught hiding in the closet playing *Seven Minutes in Heaven*. Words jumbled on her tongue, attempting to process everything happening.

"Em, I t'ink we're done." Conlin craned his neck in the other direction.

The young man collected the dishes, extending his forearm and stacking the plates. Jeanette gawked and blinked a few times. Did she almost kiss Conlin? The thought set off a swooping sensation of a plane dive in her belly. *Get it together, girl.* She straightened her collar and smoothed the wrinkles in her shirt.

Conlin created a greater gap. "What did ya say before the interruption?"

"Um, I'd like to spend more time in Ireland." She dared to look at him and surrendered herself to his earnest gaze. "You know, to study ancient sites and search for relics."

"Sure." Conlin's tone sounded despondent.

Or did she misinterpret in hopes Conlin desired her to admit she wished to explore her emerging feelings for him?

Now was a good time for a disruption. "The brief survey of the ruins at Saint Brendan's Church intrigued me and the site revealed many fascinating petroglyphs to analyze."

"Right. You were going to tell me about something you discovered in Dingle."

"Oh yes, the runes carved in the stone have similarities—"

"Perhaps it's best you keep it to yerself." Conlin tipped his head sideways.

Jeanette followed his line of vision as Saoirse approached. "Where are we off to next?" she asked, typing on her phone and scooted beside him in the vinyl booth.

"Now I see why ya took so long, texting again."

"Never mind." Saoirse blew a loose strand from her forehead and flicked her stare upward.

"We're going to head-on." Conlin placed a hand around her shoulder. "The first stop of many, on our way home."

Saoirse said, "I doubt we'll get far this late in the day."

She was right, yet Jeanette refrained from getting involved in Conlin and Saoirse's disagreements. "What's number one on your itinerary?" She sipped her unsweetened green iced tea.

Conlin let out a heavy sigh and pushed curls off his forehead. "I need to file a police report."

Jeanette gulped her drink and chewed on the straw. "How much of the truth are you divulging?"

He ran his palm across his face, scratched the longer stubble along his jaw and expelled a gusty breath. "I'd prefer giving them all the information I have on Geron and the incidents." Conlin rested his arms on the tabletop and drummed his fingers against the surface.

"The problem is, I'm not sure what I know or if the authorities would believe my story." He kept his eyesight fixed on the table sugar as he rolled a piece of the torn sweetener packet between his thumb and forefinger. "I suppose I'll write that I misplaced our passports."

A sickness swirled in Jeanette's stomach. "Sorry for putting you in an uncomfortable position..."

"Are we staying with Jeanette?" Saoirse perked up and flashed a grin.

"The procedures will take time and I'll have to book lodging for the night." He peeped at her from the side. "Although we should let Jeanette continue her search for Thomas on her own."

Good thing the waiter interrupted their kiss. For a minute she lost herself, denying the fact Conlin remained anxious to get away from her and the circumstances. Maybe if she assisted him in expediting their trip home, they could part on pleasant terms and stay friends.

Jeanette typed into her map's app for the closest police department. "We'll go together, in case they require a witness." She finished her drink.

Conlin gave a single nod, tautening his lips. "I'll pay the bill."

They left the car parked on the street outside the restaurant and walked a couple of blocks to the station. Strolling up to the front desk, Conlin checked in. "Hello, we want to report our lost passports."

"Sign in here." The woman tapped a pen against an open binder. "Have a seat and someone will call your name soon."

"T'anks."

Conlin sat in the middle chair and Saoirse leaned against his arm. "Ma said she'd have cellular service for a few hours before she boards the cruise ship again, if we need anything."

"Ah great. What did she say about ya being out of the country?"

"She wasn't cross, just surprised you'd leave work for more than a day and she'd appreciate it if you discussed our travel plans in advance next time."

"If she allows a next time…" He stroked the top of her head. "When will they be back from their honeymoon?"

"Wednesday."

"She'll need to take a copy of your birth certificate to the Irish Embassy in Dublin."

"Mr. Murphy," a man called, standing behind a gray partition near a small cubicle.

They all reacted and joined him around the corner. "Good afternoon, I'm Officer McLachlan." He pulled up an extra chair and placed it at the metal-frame desk for Jeanette. "Reporting your misplaced identifications?"

"Correct."

The officer retrieved a packet of papers from a drawer. "Fill this out."

"It'll also take care of my daughter's, yeah?"

"The statement covers all passports involved in the incident, including your wife's."

"Em…" Conlin looked at her and stifled a smile.

She twiddled her fingers and bounced a knee. "Just a friend and here for support."

The man's expression remained uninterested. Saoirse reclined in her seat, making eye contact and she tightened her lips to hold in a giggle. Jeanette assumed she recalled their conversation yesterday morning about being interested in dating Conlin. Good thing Saoirse didn't observe her blatant display of affection for him in the restaurant.

Conlin finished filling out the papers, set down the pen and handed the report to Officer McLachlan. "What happens next?"

"Give me at least twenty minutes to type the deposition. I'll provide a copy for you to submit at the embassy. For now, continue waiting in the lobby." He stood and extended a handshake.

"How long does the process take? We must return to Ireland straight away."

"Depends on the case, and each consulate is different." He passed Conlin a checklist. "They'll want supporting verification, too."

"Officer, 'tis a matter of urgency." Conlin leaned his head against a palm and gathered a fistful of hair.

"I understand, but there's a process and it requires your patience."

Conlin rose from the seat and waved a hand for them to follow. In a single-file line, they marched into the waiting area. "I guess we're stuck in Montreal." He rubbed the back of his neck and slid into a chair.

"Don't give up hope." Jeanette sat beside him and placed her palm over his forearm, relaxing on the armrest.

He peeked at her face, then shifted his gaze toward her caress. She froze for a second and jerked her elbow backward as if his flesh was too hot to touch. Jeanette raised her eyelashes and their eyesight locked.

A sideways smile tugged upward at the corner of his mouth. "I appreciate the encouragement, but ya needn't stay. You've hung around long enough, and we've taken up too much of yer afternoon. I'm sure you'd rather be searching for Thomas and handling the relics."

A lifelessness lingered inside, the heaviness weighing her down, and her voice dropped low. "Conlin..."

"We're fine, right Cricket?" He nudged her arm and Saoirse lowered her chin, shrugging a nonchalant shoulder.

"I'm not leaving the two of you at a police station in a foreign country."

Conlin opened his mouth, "Jea—"

"I know you disagree with my choices, but your safety is a top priority. Let me help and I'll accompany you to the Irish Embassy tomorrow morning." She blew an exhausted breath and rose to her feet.

"That's a kind offer, but we'll be grand, y'know what I mean?"

She tucked her arms tighter against her midsection for balance with the waning strength in her legs. "I'm confident you can manage but—"

"Mr. Murphy," Officer McLachlan said.

Conlin jumped to his feet, strode across the room and the officer handed him the statement. "I also printed out additional instructions on acquiring an emergency travel document at the Irish Embassy."

"Thanks for yer assistance," Conlin said.

Officer McLachlan turned, then pivoted on his heel. "One more thing, if you're planning on staying at a hotel, most require travel papers and won't accept the police forms."

"Any suggestions?"

"Maybe rely on someone who hasn't lost their passport." He inclined his chin, gesturing toward Jeanette. "Good luck."

Saoirse got up and stepped close to her dad. "Where're we gonna sleep tonight?"

Conlin angled his head in Jeanette's direction. "All right, if ye're willin' to assist us again."

"Yes, I'm willing." She straightened her shoulders, took a deep breath, and checked the hour on her watch. "It's a quarter after three, so let's find accommodations for the night."

"We'll follow you." He outstretched his arm for Jeanette to lead the way.

They shadowed her and returned to the parked car. She unlocked the vehicle and Saoirse climbed inside. Jeanette set her handbag on the backseat and retrieved her phone. Conlin stood behind her on the curb. She whirled around and crashed into him, brushing her chest across his torso. Jeanette moved backward and bumped the door close. "Sorry. I'm trying to look up places to stay in the area."

Several awkward sidesteps commenced, equivalent to beginners learning the Cha-Cha until Conlin extended his arm and blocked her access to the driver's side.

"Em, I want to explain about earlier," he said.

"Of course." *For the love of all that's holy, please don't mention the missed kiss.* She rattled the car key in her hand.

Conlin squinted at the busy street, then refocused on her and cleared his throat. "Protecting Cricket is my primary concern, and you've understood the importance. Still an' all, when I heard Geron followed us, I took it out on you and—"

"No, you didn't, and your objectives are crystal clear. We've spent the past twenty-four hours working on getting you home, and I intend on upholding my promises." She reached for the door handle and Conlin grasped her hand.

"I'm certain ya will. The t'ings I blurt out in frustration are in response to meself." He released his handclasp and scraped a palm through his hair. "I should've let you leave Kinsale alone."

The unmistakable regret he expressed smacked her in the face and the sting of his honesty caused increased blinking. "Yeah, I'm a dangerous liability, and each second in my company is intolerable. Did I miss anything?"

"What are ya on about now?" Conlin shut his eyes and sighed. "I enjoy your companionship, and I'm finding it difficult to part ways, leaving you to take on everything yerself, although I know you're more than capable. Yer valor is commendable yet maddening at moments." Light laughter floated into the air, and he composed himself, deepening his gaze. "You are incredible, Jeanette, and if circumstances were different..." He moved and stepped back. "Ah, listen to me rambling."

The pounding of her heart vibrated through her torso, weakening her knees, and she leaned against the vehicle for stability. She didn't think it was possible to feel elation and devastation all at once. Street traffic, people passing on the sidewalk, mis-communicated words, near kisses—none of it mattered. Only now, this minute, existed for them to express their thoughts and feelings. *Say something, anything.* Jeanette opened her mouth and sucked in a mouthful of frosty air. Nothing.

"Maybe we should go?" Conlin backed farther apart and headed toward the passenger side of the car.

Jeanette stared down the road, and an emptiness ensued. All the sights and sounds returned, limiting her ability to process everything. How did she feel about Conlin? Great dad, caring, responsible, dependable, hard-working, and cute. Get real. The intense draw she experienced gazing at his facial features lured her into the bluest eyes she ever lost herself in, to the point of drowning. She shook her head, opened the door, and climbed inside.

No matter the circumstances of how she met Conlin, both he and Saoirse meant something more than the landlord of a room her brother rented or innocent bystanders. They formed an unbreakable connection, and in God's strength, she'd protect them to any extent, even personal sacrifice.

NINETEEN

Jeanette plugged in her phone for directions. "I found a property for us to stay tonight. I think we're in the clear and slipped under the radar." Maybe if she said it aloud, she'd believe it herself and stop thinking every other car looked like Geron's Jaguar.

A few kilometers outside of downtown Montreal, she turned into the parking lot for Chalet Beacon, stopped and kept the engine running. "Saoirse, can you hand me my purse?" Jeanette reached behind and she passed it from the backseat.

Conlin pressed his palm against the bag. "You don't need to continue paying for our accommodations."

"Yes, I do. It's my choices that landed us in this situation."

"You're not responsible—"

"I'll be right back," she said and patted his arm, then climbed out of the Nissan.

Ten minutes later, she opened the driver-side door. "We're all set." Jeanette drove to the end of the property and parked in front of a unit. She gathered her luggage and led them to an individual cottage, unlocking the door for room seven using a larger than necessary old-fashioned brass key. Conlin and Saoirse followed behind, carrying their shopping sacks of the clothing items they purchased in Quebec.

"There's a kitchenette, a double and two singles. I figured us gals will sleep in the smaller beds and you can have the full-size bed."

"Em, sure." He glanced around the space. "I spotted a market on the main street. I'll walk and pick up some fresh food."

"Sounds good. Oh, and—"

"Ya won't be wanting any animal products, no?" A playful grin plucked at the bend of his mouth.

Jeanette gave him a narrow-eyed look and bit back a laugh. "I was going to ask for bottled water." She joined him at the entry. "Watch your back."

"Right. Stay here, Cricket," Conlin said.

"I'm either cooped up in a car or hotel room." She rolled her eyes, twirled on her heel, and slid into a chair. "Whatever."

"She's safe. I'll refrain from saying anything that might influence her or cause impulsive behaviors."

His eyebrows drew to the center, and his smile twitched downward. "Tá brón orm. I'm sorry, that's not what I meant and, of course, she can spend time with you." He placed his palm over her hand. "I'll return soon." He stepped outside and glanced at her before he strolled through the lot.

Jeanette shut the door, took a deep breath, and flicked her gaze toward Saoirse. She lost her train of thought, spun on the ball of her foot and marched across the room. "I'm going to see if there're utensils in the kitchenette."

"Don't worry about Da." She swung her extended legs from the chair and hopped to her feet. "He'll always mollycoddle me."

"In this case, his reasons are valid." Jeanette opened her mouth, then clamped her teeth down and bit her tongue. She didn't want to say anything that would upset Conlin again. "And my opinions aren't worth much since I'm not a parent." She rotated in the opposite direction and checked the kitchen drawers, searching for cooking utensils.

"His rules are stricter than me mas."

"Dads are usually protective of their daughters. Tom could drive, date and move out sooner than my father allowed me."

"Did ya sneak out and meet boys secretly?" Her eyes widened and her tone elevated.

Jeanette peeked at Saoirse, and humor ruffled her lips. "No. Tom was the rebellious one, and I did everything my parents asked of me, but..."

"Wha'?"

"It's in the past and doesn't matter now." If she were honest, it still bothered her that Tom ignored Mom and Dad's wishes, yet always remained their golden boy. Even in the current situation, he gallivanted all over the globe and became entangled with dangerous people, but somehow, she was the crazy one making questionable decisions.

Jeanette didn't have time or energy to think about the discrepancies in their childhood and the outcomes. She blinked hard, clearing her reflections on family. For now, she needed to focus on finding Tom and keeping the Murphys from Geron's plans. Taking the Celtic Stone from him was a mistake, even if he had wicked intentions.

Conlin shoved his hands into the pockets of his jacket and sighed as he aimed for the major street. The events over the past couple of days replayed in his mind. Daily routines of going to work, making ends meet, spending quality time with Saoirse and enjoying the few precious moments on his boat drifted out of reach. Now his days consisted of split decisions in the face of danger, protecting his daughter, endless paperwork, complicated procedures to get home and all the while Jeanette made a definite impression on him...

Ah, Banféinní. How she frustrated and fascinated him with equal measurements. Conlin halted on the sidewalk of a busy intersection, shaking his head to clear all the distracting thoughts. Fuzzy ideas about her caused him to lose track of his senses. Standing at the entrance of the market, he surveyed the surroundings. Out of the corner of his eye, he spotted a parked vehicle on the adjacent street and felt he was being watched.

A tightness gripped his chest. They barely caught their breaths between Geron's pursuits. Another couple of days and he'd have Cricket safe on a plane back to Ireland. The tires screeched as the vehicle hooked a sharp turn into the car park across the road. It was safe to assume they spied him, and he ducked into the building.

A public location didn't guarantee his safety. These fellas had no problem threatening, assaulting, and abducting people in a crowd, if it served their purposes. Conlin collected a basket and perused the fresh produce aisle at the rear of the shop. He selected ingredients for a salad—spinach, a seedless English cucumber, radishes, and a bundle of asparagus for a side dish, checking over his shoulder every few seconds.

Keeping a watchful eye on the customers, Conlin hurried toward the neon sign on the wall for the meat section. Fish brine hung in the air and he inhaled deeply, savoring the scent as it reminded him of home. He examined the choices, picking up prepacked cuts of salmon. He would need to find an alternative main course for Jeanette.

"Stupid people make my job so easy."

Conlin's torso stiffened as he straightened his shoulders and peered at the man standing to his right. "Ace." He gave him a quick nod of acknowledgment before returning his attention to dinner options. "I'm surprised to see ya again." Conlin kept his cool and sorted through packages of plant-based protein.

"Geron will stop at nothing to achieve his conquests," Ace said in a gruff tone. "Why didn't you get out of the country when you had the chance?" He gave Conlin a disbelieving headshake. "Like I stated, brainless."

"Well, funny t'ing. I had to leave Ireland unexpectedly." He tossed down a wrapped block of tofu. "And they require passports to travel internationally."

"The least you could do is get your daughter under control."

He altered his rigid stance, placing more weight on one foot, and a spasm cinched his muscles. "What's that supposed to mean?"

"It means she's left a trail of all your locations, where you've eaten, stayed, and shopped, including photos," Ace said.

The confirmation that he was still a failure at parenting caved his chest inward. He should've thought about it and cautioned Saoirse to not share things online. "The news will devastate her when she learns that her innocent posts created an issue or worsened our situation," he said, more to himself than in response to Ace.

"Tell her to become a social media ghost."

"You're giving me advice on kids?"

"I have teenagers at home in Wisconsin."

Conlin rubbed his chin and moved aside for other shoppers. He never considered when they helped Ace in the St. Lawrence River that he had children. Did his family know what their dad did for a living? Maybe he needed to stop being so tough on himself and accept he was not the worst parent in the world. "You almost sound like ya care."

"Not really." Ace shrugged an indifferent shoulder. "However, you saved my life."

"So, you intend to spare our lives?"

"No. I'll give you a head start," he said in a flat voice. "Don't mess up this chance. Use common sense and get out of town." He turned on his heels, then spun around. "I'll do what I can for twenty-four hours"—he lifted a pointed finger—"but no promises. I'm not the only one tracking you." Ace pivoted, walked off, and left the shop.

A sudden hot to cold flushed through his veins. Conlin shook the feeling off, as a sense of urgency prompted him to leave and return to the inn. Grabbing the last ingredients for supper, he headed for the checkout.

Near the exit of the shop, he noticed a rack of clothing items—sportswear, sweatshirts, and t-shirts for the tourists. Conlin rummaged through the jackets, choosing a navy windbreaker along with a blue-and-red cap of the Montreal Canadiens ice hockey team. All right, he'd heed Ace's warnings. He slipped on the new attire and lowered the hat brim below his brows.

Emptying the handbasket, he loaded items onto the squealing conveyor belt and a market employee scanned the selections. "I'm buying the clothes, too." Conlin handed the cashier behind the counter two tags. After the last beep, he processed his credit card payment and helped bag the groceries. He gathered the sacks in his arms, grinned, and gave a nod.

Conlin exited the store, glancing in both directions. No sign of Ace, Geron or any of the others hot on their trail. He raised the paper bags up and balanced them close to his shoulders, hiding his profile. Cutting through the rear lot, he headed away from the main avenue and kept out of sight.

Conlin picked up the pace. Could he take Ace at his word and trust he wasn't a mere distraction while Geron made his move against Jeanette? He whispered a prayer and rushed back to the hotel room.

TWENTY

"Do you have any fun activities planned for when you get home?" Jeanette pushed a curl from her cheek and swiped a clean dish towel across the counter. Adult problems shouldn't burden a teenage girl, let alone life-and-death situations.

"The auld man is considering letting me attend a gig." Saoirse pressed flat palms together, under her chin in a prayerful gesture.

"Fontaines D.C.?"

"I'm excira, they're deadly." Saoirse bounced on her toes and her overall expression shined.

"You'll have the best time ever." If she delivered on her promises, Saoirse would return safely to Ireland and see her first live show. "You're aware I never wanted to involve your family in Tom's problems or expose you to dangerous people, right?" Jeanette stopped gathering dishes.

Saoirse dunked her chin in understanding. She tucked her elbows close to her sides and picked at the chipped black polish on her fingernails. "Em, I need to tell you somet'ing."

"Let's talk." Jeanette waved her toward the dinette and sat. "What's on your mind?"

"Earlier in the car..." Her eyelids lowered, staring at the floor.

Jeanette gave her a reassuring smile. "Don't rush and take it slow."

Saoirse looked her in the face, slipping her lower lip under her front teeth. She opened her mouth to speak, yet no sound came out. A loud knock at the door jolted Saoirse and she gripped the sides of the table. The reality of everything that transpired probably hit her hard and rocked her nerves.

"Must be your dad. We'll finish our chat later." The knocking increased and grew louder. She hustled to the entrance and checked the peephole. Conlin stood glancing over his shoulder, wearing his jacket collar up and a baseball cap.

Jeanette swung open the entrance. "That was quick." She eyed him up and down. "And you picked up more Canadian souvenirs."

Conlin stepped inside, carrying two sacks of groceries, and kicked the door closed. "'Tis a disguise, not mementos."

Jeanette moved aside, allowing him to enter the room. "Everything okay?"

Conlin gestured at Saoirse to come over and collect the bags. Then he angled his body closer, whispering in her ear, "I'll tell you in a bit."

Jeanette shuddered at the uneasiness in his tone and shut her eyes for a moment. Grabbing onto his wrist before he took another step, he spared a fleeting glance and she uttered, "Are we facing an immediate threat?"

"Maybe. They followed us." Conlin pressed his lips into a fine line and wrinkled his brow. He approached the ivory drapes and yanked them together in a sweeping movement. In an amateur sleuth style, he pulled the material back about an inch and peeked out the window.

An itch spread across her flesh, and she leaned against his hip. "Did you see Geron?"

Shifting his glance, he removed the hat and his jacket. "I ran into Ace. He'll give us a twenty-four-hour lead to get out of Montreal."

Jerking her head backward, loaded with questions, Conlin held a silencing finger in the air and she refrained from questioning him.

"Hold tight. Saoirse and I need to have a discussion." Lowering his voice deepened the Irish accent.

"I understand." If Ace knew where to find them and followed Conlin, then Geron must be in town too. Sickness stirred in her stomach, and she already lost her appetite.

Saoirse rummaged through the bags on the dinette. "What did ya get for dinner?" She broke into their inaudible conversation.

"Salmon." He dug into a sack, withdrew a package and read the wrapper. "And tempeh for you" Conlin flashed her a closed-lip grin.

"Thanks, I appreciate it." The weight of his stare lingered for a minute and she avoided looking at him.

He returned his attention to the food, unpacking the rest of the ingredients. "I also picked up rice, vegetables, a lemon for zest and a torte."

Conlin had perfected the parental technique of acting like everything was fine for the sake of protecting an impressionable teenager. Saoirse gathered the items, plonked them on the counter near the stove and yanked out her phone, typing at lightning speed.

He leaned close and snatched the device from her hands. "Not now, Cricket."

She tried to grab it, and he held it out of reach. "Da—"

"After supper. Go wash up."

"I'm not five," Saoirse mumbled and trudged toward the bathroom.

Jeanette flinched and fixed her eyesight on him. He rubbed his forehead and stared at the phone, swiping his thumb across the screen. "Did you take her phone away because of your run-in with Ace?"

Conlin crashed into a chair at the table and sighed. "Saoirse posted all the places we stopped on social media, and they found us by checking her pages."

"Oh, no." Jeanette stepped closer and placed a tender palm on his arm. "Saoirse's just being a typical teenager. She shouldn't have to worry about dangerous people searching for her profiles and tracking our locations."

"I feel terrible about taking her mobile without explaining."

"Now I've added an unnecessary strain on your relationship."

"'Tis my responsibility as a parent to think of any potential online concerns. I should've suggested she make her accounts private and turn off her location settings."

"Yeah, but the only real danger is staying with me." Jeanette turned away and slogged in the direction of her backpack on the foldable luggage rack. "I perpetuated the problem by keeping the Celtic Stone."

"I did something wrong." Saoirse dipped her chin toward her chest, petting the length of her hair.

"I'm accountable, Cricket. As yer father, I need to watch out for you."

"It's not the online posts." Focused on the floor, her pose rounded into a hunched shape. "I am sorry about that but..."

The stupid stones. Geron gave her his number. First opportunity available, she would call him and hand the relic over, if he promised to leave the Murphys alone. Jeanette searched her crossbody bag for his business card and dug, moving her belongings around until her fingers scraped the bottom. Adrenaline shot through her system, and she removed her items—wallet, keys, notepad...

"It's gone." The strain in her voice made it unrecognizable. "How's that possible?"

"I have it," Saoirse said in a shaky tone.

Jeanette stiffened and whirled in a half circle, addressing Saoirse. "Why?"

"I wanna help you."

"Is that what you wanted to tell me earlier when your dad was at the store?"

"Yeah." Saoirse twiddled her fingers, staring at her feet.

"What are ye talking about?" Conlin stood from the table and pushed loose curls off his brow. "Did you take something from Jeanette?"

Saoirse paused and looked at Conlin. "The stone."

Jeanette pressed a hand against her breastbone to alleviate the pain inside her chest. She viewed Conlin's reaction as his eyes widened and he stumbled a step, catching himself on the tabletop.

"For what purpose?" He gaped at Saoirse and wiped a palm across his chin.

She bowed her head and her dark hair draped over her cheeks. "I thought it'd be helpful if I studied it and discovered something."

Too many incidences spiraled out of control and Jeanette no longer had a firm grasp or focus on what she was doing. The whole thing was a fiasco, and everyone seemed to recognize she could not manage the situation or find Tom on her own. All her choices initiated one disaster after another and now a caring teenager got sucked into the catastrophe, leading to the consequences of a reprimanding from her dad.

Conlin's expression softened. "Ah sure, ya have a kind, generous heart, and I love that quality in you." His eyebrows drew inward. "Yet I still don't know what you hoped to accomplish. Jeanette's a professional and hasn't determined the origins or significance of the stone."

"It's true. You inadvertently placed yourself in danger by taking the artifact." A numbness in her legs weakened the joints in her knees and she slid into a tweed-upholstered chair until her rear hit the cushion.

Light went out in his eyes, and he offered an empty seat at the dinette to his daughter. "Sit down and talk to us."

Saoirse walked a few faltering steps to the table and claimed the chair. She reached into her shopping bag and removed the relic, placing it on the smooth surface. "Em..." She faltered, licked her lips, and refocused on Conlin. "I hoped to solve the meaning of the symbols, and then we could stay longer." Saoirse fastened her eyesight on the artifact, allowing the wrappings to slide off the oblong-shaped rock, exposing the obvious face carved into the antiquity.

"I recognized an engraved mark." She rotated the ancient object and revealed the image.

The sweet and clever girl cared about her and Tom in the same way she cherished the Murphy family. All her wrongdoings, including her error in judgement and the multiple incidents that played out since they met weighed on her like a millstone, dragging her heart toward the ground.

Conlin squinted at the petroglyph. "The Trinity Knot." He expelled an audible breath, rose to his feet, and pointed a finger, giving her direction. "T'anks for yer honesty. Now return the stone."

Saoirse stood and shuffled her feet to meet Jeanette. She dropped her lower lip into a perfect pout and lifted long, dark lashes, revealing an apologetic regard. "Sorry," she said, in a mousy tone.

"Apology accepted. Thank you for telling me." Jeanette retrieved the stone.

Folding his arms across his chest, he threw her a cutting glare, emphasizing his rigid stance. "You see how yer decisions influenced me daughter?"

"Da, it's not her fault."

"Hold your whist."

The icy stare froze her limbs for a second and a sinking sensation drained into her stomach. The unfortunate event entitled Conlin to blame her for all that happened because of her numerous mistakes and the terrible decision she made to take the Celtic Stone from Geron. What kind of person steals in front of a teenager? It didn't matter the reasons were to protect Saoirse, all they knew was she lured Geron to chase and torment them longer.

Heat rose from her neck and mushroomed behind her ears. "You're right." She dared to look at Conlin. His lips pressed tight into a slight grimace and a sickness crept up her esophagus. "I've created a colossal mess and—" She clamped a hand over her mouth and rushed into the bathroom.

"Jeanette," Conlin called out and outstretched an arm, grazing his fingertips against her shoulder.

She flung the door shut, fell to her knees on the cold floor, and leaned over the porcelain commode. Her heart rate increased as a cool sweat broke on her forehead and she closed her eyelids, ingesting excess saliva. Gripping the toilet rim, she slowed her breathing and waited until the sickness subsided.

Jeanette sat on the tile for about two minutes, staring at the blurred black-and-white checkered pattern as tears brimmed. Conlin revealed his genuine sentiments that he regretted meeting her the second she arrived at his home in Kinsale. At times she thought, no, hoped they developed a solid friendship. A hollowness ensued, twisting her from the inside out and unwinding all her tightly coiled feelings. Before this moment, she held herself together for the benefit of everyone involved and to model the belief they'd triumph.

What could she do to repair the damage? So much was at stake—their lives, Saoirse's safety, finding Tom, preserving artifacts, and Conlin...

His look of utter displeasure would perturb her forever. Would he forgive her for involving them and putting Saoirse at risk? Jeanette pushed herself off the ground and a shudder throttled her spine, wobbling her legs. She scrutinized her reflection in the mirror and brushed off damp curls stuck to her cheeks. Her shaking limbs tied up the messy tresses into a bun, and she swiped the wetness from under her eyes. No point in feeling sorry for herself since she caused the turmoil and sorting it out was her obligation. The voice in her head echoed repetitive words from Mom in the past.

Jeanette blinked a few times to clear her mind and breathed through the nausea still brewing in her belly, processing each problem to fix. First, sway Geron to leave the Murphys alone, guaranteeing their safety, then travel home, making one last stop on the way in her last-ditch effort to find Tom. If she failed, it proved her parents were right, but if she succeeded, she'd show Mom and Dad that Tom wasn't their only child to prevail in life.

She turned on the hot and cold faucets. At a tepid temperature, she splashed water on her face and patted droplets off her skin with a white-cotton towel. Whatever choices made up to this point, good or bad, right or wrong, she would correct the issues. There was no way she'd allow anything to happen to the Murphys. In God's miraculous power, she would attempt to restore the friendship between them all. A gentle knock broke her concentration.

"Jeanette?" Conlin spoke from behind the door. "We started preparing the meals."

She inhaled a calming breath, straightening her rumpled blue-plaid-flannel shirt, and gazed at herself a final time. Pivoting on the ball of her foot, she opened the door. "Just freshening up." She didn't dare stare him in the eye when she exited the bathroom.

"Em…" He rubbed the back of his neck and glanced across the room. "I apologize for overreacting again."

"Please, don't. You wouldn't even be here if it wasn't for Tom and me—"

"Ah, look here. I haven't made it easy for you." Conlin placed a soothing touch on her forearm and sighed. "I go into protective mode and lose me head. At least, that's how Saoirse describes my reactions."

Jeanette laid her palm over his hand. "I understand and want to relieve the additional pressure I've caused. Lord knows I don't possess any parental skills." She'd be a lousy mom. Perhaps Brian recognized her deficiencies in parenting and that was one reason he never discussed marriage.

"I'm certain you'll make a mighty fine mother."

A cold to hot prickle spread over her flesh. Jeanette spent more time speaking about parenthood and relationships with Conlin than the three years she dated Brian. She searched Conlin's appearance, wishing for additional lighting to view all the details of his facial expressions. Her gaze roved until landing on his eyes, staring deeper and losing herself in the dark abyss of his pupils. If she let go, maybe she'd fall and reach his soul.

The curve of his lips grew into a knowing smile. "What a day." Conlin altered his stance and slid from her grasp. "Can we chat again after dinner?"

"Of course, I'd like to continue our conversation."

"Grand." A growing grin creased the lines around his mouth, and he headed into the kitchenette.

The easiness of their interactions after the tense circumstances lifted her spirits, and her muscles loosened. He gave her the opportunity to mend the situation and she wouldn't ruin it again. The few moments alone with Conlin encouraged her and supplied a glimmer of hope. She vowed to do whatever was necessary to achieve the desired outcome and remain friends.

TWENTY-ONE

After dinner, they cleaned up the dishes and Conlin glimpsed at Saoirse resting on a single bed with her eyelids closed, listening to an audiobook. Jeanette sat on a gray-upholstered chair with her feet propped up on the coffee table, a notebook in one hand and mobile in the other.

Conlin finished organizing the information required for the emergency travel documents to present at the Irish Embassy in the marra. He peered at the digital clock on the nightstand, 10:40 p.m. illuminated in a glaring red and he squeezed his eyes tight as he pinched the bridge of his nose. Time flew by and he already missed the important conversation he wished to have with Saoirse about taking the stone without permission. It seemed evident she fell asleep, but he'd allow her to sleep rather than wake her to change her clothes. Although, she would probably carry-on the next day about it. He stood, turned the lamp off beside her bed, and blinked over to Jeanette.

Wavy strands slipped from a hair bun and hung along her cheeks limiting his view of her face. He blew a hard breath and stretched his arms toward the ceiling, releasing energy. Did he lose the chance to chat with her, too?

So very few opportunities to gaze into her hazel eyes and learn more about her life beyond a missing brother, relics, and threatening people pursuing them. Still and all, he didn't want to interrupt her study and work. Rummaging through his bag, he selected the knit pants Jeanette had purchased in Quebec and tossed his pajamas over a shoulder.

"I'm gonna change, then turn in." He popped a dry toothbrush into his mouth.

She stopped writing and glanced upward from the notepad. "Um, you and me, we..." Laughter rolled out on a breath. Jeanette dropped her feet onto the floor and set papers on the tabletop. "I was hoping we'd finish our talk." She pulled her knees inward, curling her legs on the seat cushion and her mien relaxed into a smile. "If you'd like to continue the discussion from earlier."

Heat ascended underneath his sweater, and he tugged the material away for air to flow around his body. The hairs on his nape raised on end and he removed his toothbrush. "'Tis best if we sort out a few t'ings."

Conlin laid his belongings on top of his bag, selected a chair, and sat beside Jeanette. For at least a minute, he remained silent, appreciating her facial features, and taking in the fine characteristics. She embodied all the beauty of the Emerald Isle, green eyes the color of endless rolling hills, untamed tresses like waves along the Wild Atlantic Way and her unpredictability reminiscent of winding curves with hairpin turns on Irish roads. Wait, what did he intend to discuss?

Conlin cleared his throat. "I want to explain meself and why I'm so overprotective of Saoirse."

Jeanette tucked her hands inside the sleeves of her sweatshirt and inched closer, intensifying her stare. He licked his lips and leaned against the cushioned armchair. "Years ago, when Saoirse was seven, on my first weekend alone as a single parent, we went out on me sailboat. We enjoyed a sunny August afternoon on the calm water in Kinsale and sailed along the coast to nearby Sandy Cove."

Conlin pictured it in his mind, as clear and poignant as if the events took place last week. Most days, he pushed the occurrence far from his thoughts and wished the incident had never transpired. He inhaled and exhaled through his mouth before continuing the story. "Dropping anchor near shore, we spent the day swimming and had a picnic. About an hour after tea and playing on the remote beach, I cleaned up so we could return to the boat. Saoirse was wading in knee-deep water and I turned me back, collecting our belongings in a trice, no longer."

Jeanette kept constant eye contact as she listened, resting her jawbone against a fist. Conlin gulped through the strain of contained grief, preparing for the most difficult part of recounting the tale.

"I spun around to check on her and she had disappeared. In a panic, I searched the area and ran into the water. Too many seconds passed, looking in every direction until I spotted her limp body, floating face down."

A gasp emerged from Jeanette's lips and her eyes shot open, shaking her head. "How scary. And you were all alone?"

"Yeah, I scooped Saoirse into my arms and hurried to the shoreline. She wasn't breathing, and I thought she was gone in that instant." He slouched and ran a clammy palm along his pant leg. "Positioning her rigid body on the sand, I began CPR but to no avail and it seemed unlikely I'd revive her, but I prayed without ceasing while delivering rescue breaths for two minutes. Then after chest compressions, I rolled her onto her side, and she coughed as fluid spurted from her mouth."

A quiver rippled through his torso as he glanced at Cricket asleep, secure, and tucked into a blanket. It didn't matter that it occurred ages ago. The accident would haunt him for the rest of his existence. Nothing he did or could do in the future would erase the experience or make up for his wrongdoing.

"I left everything and rushed her to the closest emergency room for an examination. T'ank God she was all right and the doctors kept her overnight for observation." Conlin scratched his nape and let out a pained rustle of air. "The reality of my failure as a parent settled in when a social worker from the Irish Child Protection Agency visited and questioned me during an inspection of every minor scratch or bruise on Saoirse. An accident, a neglectful moment, and lapse in judgment singled me out as an inadequate father. She almost died because of me."

Telling the story diminished his strength to the point of exhaustion. Conlin slumped forward in the chair, hoping to avoid the horror in Jeanette's eyes after listening to the details of his ultimate downfall. She must deem him an unfit parent. Jeanette had already witnessed his poor choices, and he failed again when Cricket accompanied them to Dingle. Being taken by gunpoint and exposure to multiple life-threatening situations did nothing to build confidence in his parenting skills.

"Oh Conlin, I can't even imagine how terrifying the ordeal must've been for you both." Jeanette curved her body closer, and slid an arm around him, massaging his back in a soothing circular motion. "I'm sure landing on the St. Lawrence River caused all those memories to resurface."

The tone of her voice, complimented by a gentle touch, comforted and calmed his nerves. Conlin lifted his gaze until their eyes coupled. Any doubts he experienced telling her about his struggles faded the second he observed her softhearted manner and steady eye connection. The nearness of her body triggered an unexpected release of tension in his muscles.

"Saoirse knows about the incident yet has no recollection of the occurrence and never developed a fear of water or anyt'ing." Conlin peeked at Cricket rolled up in her sheets and a lightness expanded in his lungs. "She's actually a strong swimmer."

"I'm not surprised by her resilience, and she trusts her father."

"Ah sure, although my mistake continues to have long-lasting repercussions."

"Did Kera's reaction emphasize the feelings of guilt, in addition to social workers questioning your parental abilities? I assume she didn't receive the news well."

He squinted at Jeanette from the corner of his eye. "I never told her about the accident. I called the auld man from the hospital to sort me out and haven't shared the shameful story with anyone else till now."

The second he confessed, she repositioned herself, getting nearer, and only chairs denied them a full embrace. He met her stare straight on, and leaned across the armchair, causing a hyper-alertness. Conlin envisioned tossing the accursed furniture aside and gathering her into his arms. He sagged in the seat and banged a fist against his thigh.

Jeanette angled her neck, bending her lips upward and more strands of hair slid alongside her cheekbones. "Thank you for entrusting me and sharing your traumatic experience."

Conlin caressed her forearm, and an electric jolt shot through his veins. "Ya deserved an explanation for my harsh responses toward you." Other reasons existed, though he lacked the courage to divulge the entire truth. The pleasure of her company, and the sensitivity she expressed gave him a feeling of contentment.

"You don't owe me anything. Your obligations are to protect Saoirse. She's your responsibility and main priority." A thoughtful expression compressed a wrinkle across her forehead. "It must be a difficult time for you already. Are you wondering how Kera's marriage affects your parental role in a blended family?"

"Frank, her husband, will be there as a father figure. Yet..." He unloaded a protracted exhale and his sight roved to Cricket. "'Tis hard to believe she's practically a grown woman."

"No one can replace you in her heart and your daughter knows she means the world to you."

"T'anks, you're kind."

If he said anymore, he'd be in jeopardy of admitting he spent their days together, dumping the liability on Jeanette to maintain an emotional and physical distance. Whenever he removed the barrier, an extreme awareness of her presence in his world awakened a desire to know all the specifics about her life.

Jeanette lowered her eyelashes, pulled away, and inched backward into the armchair. "I apologize for causing you extra worry and stress over her safety," she said in a quiet voice.

"You've protected Cricket on multiple occasions." Conlin stretched across the space between them and placed a delicate touch on her knee. "It wasn't my intention to make you feel worse and I revealed what happened because it's unfair that I've been holding ya accountable for Geron's actions. You have yer own concerns, too."

Despite the dangerous encounters surrounding Jeanette, she didn't cause, nor could she predict the vile deeds Geron planned. Conlin craned his neck to view her face. "And I've a feeling ya didn't take the stone out of curiosity."

She looked through the tops of her eyes and collapsed her shoulders. "I felt it was the right choice, but my decision worsened the situation."

"All we can do is attempt to make the best choices based on facts, experiences, and information while praying for guidance."

"That's good advice from someone who's so hard on himself about his parenting techniques."

A rapid haul of air filled his lungs and expanded his chest. If only God brought her into his life sooner... Conlin rubbed his nose and scraped a palm over his mouth. "How 'bout we stop blaming ourselves and I'll do better at not overreacting, given ye're willing to disclose everything, even if you think I won't like it?" He bent forward and a wee gap parted their bodies. "I'll place faith in ya, if you'll do the same for me."

"I believe in you more than you know." Jeanette clasped his hand, exhibiting an attentive regard. "And I'm grateful for your trust in me."

The brightness of her complexion sparked a flickering flame in his heart. All the chaotic thoughts and feelings stirring—horrific events best buried in the past, threats from Ace, Cricket taking the stone, and Jeanette's understanding words... The sensation of a wave crashing onto shore, dragging him under the tide overwhelmed him and he withdrew into his seat, raking his fingers through his hair. Better think of something else.

His gaze darted around the room, searching for a distraction, and he targeted the notebook Jeanette set on the table. "Any news on Thomas' whereabouts?"

She followed his line of vision and lunged forward, fumbling to collect the pages and she gathered them in her hands. "He might've gone to a close family friend's house in New Hampshire that Tom and I visited every summer during our childhood."

"Arctic Jack's cabin?"

"Yes." Jeanette clutched the notes close to her heart. "I tried to contact him, but he doesn't check his email and only uses a landline telephone."

Conlin figured she had refrained from providing the details. After all, he requested she keep him and Saoirse out of the loop. Although, that was before and now they were in the thick of it and made a promise. He appreciated her honoring his wishes, yet the crease between her eyebrows revealed the burden became too great. Not to mention Saoirse sharing their locations on social media and removing the artifact from Jeanette exacerbated her predicament.

"Did you discover anything else about the stones?"

Jerking her head back, she eyeballed him with an incredulous stare. "I've respected your boundaries and kept my findings as confidential information."

"Ní scéal rúin é ó tá a fhios ag triúr é. An Irish Gaelic proverb, *'It is not a secret after three people know it'*. And if ya want to tell me..."

"Interesting saying. I like it." Her contemplative demeanor brought an upward tilt to her mouth when she spoke.

Conlin adored the smile he brought to her face and quivered inside, thinking about the sadness he caused her a few hours ago. Jeanette's grin faded, yet a glow lightened her skin, and she grabbed the notepad.

In a frenzy, her gaze widened, and she drew a quick design. "Conlin, you're brilliant."

"Well..." He suppressed a smirk. Chances were slim of her using the term beyond the common phrase, but he enjoyed hearing her say it and a pleasant warmness distributed throughout his chest.

"Triquetra." She jumped from her seat and showed him the sketch of the Celtic symbol. The triangular shape of three interlaced arcs. "When you referred to three people knowing a secret, I remembered the importance of three, and Saoirse pointing out the etching in the relic has prompted a theory."

Conlin hadn't confessed his interest piqued when Jeanette first shared Thomas' letter that included a reference to Saint Brendan and led them to Dingle. He quelled the fascination in order to keep them safe and out of danger. Truth be told, he and Cricket became involved the instant they welcomed him into their house. Now all they endured and overcame... A teenager perceived they were in it together.

"What's yer hypothesis?" Conlin rose to his feet and peered over her shoulder, examining the drawing.

Jeanette tapped a fingertip against her chin and raised a brow. "I'd rather examine the other stone before any speculation."

"Let me guess, the magic number is three?"

"At least symbolic."

"In what way?" he asked.

"Spiritual."

"The Trinity Knot, representing the Father, Son, and Holy Spirit?"

Jeanette nodded, tapping a ballpoint pen in the center of her drawing. "Sheloshah, three in Hebrew, means harmony, new life, and completeness. The Valknut, a similar design, appears on many runestones from during the Viking Age, and some archaeologists presume the image signifies life, death and rebirth."

"Go on."

"Carvings symbolizing lifecycles, spirituality, deities represented in different cultures, and rituals..." She paced the area, swinging her arms as if she were stimulating ideas. "The number appears significant, yet there's only two stones Geron mentioned."

"Geron believes the artifacts are supernatural, yeah?"

"He claims the stone's abilities increase when they're brought together, but he can't test the theory without possessing both stones."

"So, the actual stones contain a type of power?"

"Or they act as vessels, drawing energy from greater sources. I'd need to study the relics." She tossed her notes down, holding her palms heavenward and shrugged.

Conlin coiled his fingers over her wrist before she twisted away. "'Tis getting more difficult to leave by the second." He instinctively lured her nearer, reacting to a protective nature. "Knowing what yer up against."

Jeanette leveled her frame in his grasp and winched a stubborn chin. "I can take care of myself."

"Well enough, and others, Banféinní. Doesn't mean you need to go it alone." He wrapped his arms around her waist, welcoming her into a hug. She rotated inward and encased him in a tight embrace. The closeness of their bodies sent a shock through his nerves.

"I'm here for you." He spoke into her hair and cuddled her closer.

At least two minutes passed as their limbs remained interlocked and he treasured the friendship they had developed. He'd hold her all night, if she allowed, cradling her in comfort that she wasn't on her own and could count on him as a dependable friend. Who was he fooling? Conlin found solace in her company and conversations. Jeanette listened, cared, and understood him in a way no one else had in his lifetime. The feel of her in his hands, clinging against him, increased a sense of certainty. A mutual respect and equality existed, deepening every moment they were together.

TWENTY-TWO

Jeanette kept her eyelids sealed, losing herself in their embrace. She laid her head against the nook of his arm and chest. The rising and falling of his torso put her in a hypnotic trance—a boat adrift at sea, ready to surrender, no longer navigating through the wild waves of his rhythmic breathing and tugging her into the undertow, leaving her shipwrecked.

Yes, she aspired a friendship with Conlin and her muscles softened now he clarified his viewpoint on their dangerous circumstances. She relaxed, allowing the fact to sink in that he didn't blame her, even though she wasn't without faults. The serenity of their prolonged hug emphasized their connection, strengthening each passing second, and she knew what she must do—leave.

Jeanette opened her eyes, slackening her limbs, and inched backward. She tilted her neck upward at the same time Conlin angled his chin down. In a brief, exquisite moment, her mouth brushed alongside his bottom lip. The feathery caress kindled a dormant necessity for someone to listen, value, and accept her as a true partner. No, not anyone; Conlin.

Succumbing to an overwhelming instinct, she pressed her puckered lips against his lower lip-line. A sweet spot between the crevasse of his chin and curve of his mouth. Jeanette froze. Did she just make another desperate attempt to kiss Conlin?

He leaned closer and awkwardly pecked above the arches of her upper lip, right below her nose. All her senses heightened, inhaling Rose 31 lotion from the Fairmont, blended with white tea, shea butter and bergamot.

Conlin glided his fingertips along the middle groove of her back until settling at her nape, and he cupped his palms behind her ears, angling her head to meet his gaze. "Let's try again," he whispered so close she breathed in peppermint toothpaste.

The gentleness of smooth skin stroked the edge of her lips as his stubble scraped her jaw, sending a rippling tingle over her flesh, and the banging of her heartbeat buffeted her eardrums.

Conlin secured the fullness of his lips on her mouth. Slow, melodic motion worked into a dizzying dance. An Irish jig or reel? It didn't matter. She lost herself in his tender touch, in sync with every movement. Fueled by passionate synergy as their kiss deepened, and they clung to each other.

A vibration rolled up her spine, shuddering her body and constricting her tendons. Jeanette squeezed her eyelids tighter, savoring the physical contact and sensations. Another reverberating pulse tore her from their dreamlike embrace. The wicked phone in her jeans buzzed, awakening her like a hateful alarm clock and robbing her of the sweetest dream.

Jeanette stiffened her shoulders and stepped rearward into the chair. Her eyelashes flicked up and Conlin stared at her with a wild intensity. His blue irises a vibrant shade of the sky after thunderstorm clouds clear and reveal a sunny afternoon.

She'd ruminate over his deep gaze all night. Remembering *that* look forever and their fervor kiss exposed more than they intended to show. Nothing would be the same between them.

Jeanette's fingers fumbled with the denim material, yanking the device from her pocket. She swiped the screen and glanced at Conlin. "I wasn't expecting..." Skimming the text, a knot constricted her throat and she blinked, clearing her vision to verify the message.

"An update about Thomas?" Conlin asked.

A pressure built inside her chest, and she staggered a step. "Um, no."

"Yer man?"

"Who?"

"Saoirse told me about yer fella." Conlin kneaded the back of his neck and expelled a gusty exhalation. "Never mind. I have no right to ask."

"It's a fair question." She grazed her front teeth along her lower lip and the taste of him still lingered in her mouth. The feeling of an instant freefall tripped out a frantic heartbeat and her knees buckled.

Weaving a hand into her hair, she tugged and straightened a few strands. "Brian and I—"

"Em, 'tis late and I'm knackered." Conlin grabbed his clothes and eyed her cornerwise. "We'll chat the marra." He held his toothbrush clenched in his jaw and headed toward the bathroom.

Jeanette kept him in her line of vision until he disappeared behind the door. A mix of words, reactions, misunderstandings, heavenly kisses jumbled in her mind and twisted her emotions. And now... Refocused on the phone screen, she read Geron's messages.

I know where you are and that you've stolen my stone.
There's no point in running and Thomas can't hide forever.

She shivered. They should've left after Ace confronted Conlin at the store. Jeanette flung herself into the cushioned armchair and pressed her brow against her palms. Ten minutes ago, she planned on leaving after the Murphy clan settled their paperwork at the Irish Embassy and booked a flight to Ireland. Now, the thought of going separate ways at this point shattered her heart and fractured her soul.

Why did she indulge in a momentary act of intimacy with Conlin when his departure was inevitable? Jeanette shut her eyelids and massaged her temples and her ribs descended in a turbulent exhale. Oh, she'd never regret the experience. A flutter swooshed in her belly thinking about their kiss, and she was ready to do it again.

Conlin stepped into the room and Jeanette sprang upright as if he had read her thoughts. Her cheeks singed as he cruised past her shirtless, wearing only sweatpants, and dumped his bag beside the bed. Did she misinterpret his level of interest? No way could he deny the fervency displayed during their embrace, and he only became uncomfortable after he inquired about Brian. Was Geron intent on ruining every aspect of their lives?

"The text message wasn't from Brian."

Conlin gave her a side glance, pulled back the sheets and climbed into bed. "No matter, night." He turned out the light on the nightstand.

"Good night," she whispered. Numbness scattered across her limbs, and she slid farther down the seat. She fluttered her lashes, clearing her watery vision, breathing through the heartache, and prayed through the pain.

A few minutes of meditation on God's promises realigned her focus and plans. Jeanette gathered her belongings, dragging heavy footsteps toward the restroom, and changed into her pajamas. She required a good night's rest and the hope of a new day.

Jeanette sat in the rental car with the motor running at 5:00 a.m. in the parking lot of Chalet Beacon. Five hours of sleep didn't revitalize or make her feel refreshed; she felt worse. Did she have a choice? Geron's threats redirected her plans and actions.

An early morning rainfall streamed down the windshield. The tiredness strained her eyesight and emphasized the grogginess in her brain. Jeanette shook the sleepiness from her head, then inhaled and exhaled deeply through her nose. Half asleep, she created a mental list of priorities for the day—drive to Jack's, evade Geron, contact Mr. Bonhoeffer and above all put Conlin out of her mind. Simple enough, yeah right...

God, why did they meet at the worst possible time? Tom missing for weeks, relic hunters willing to kill for ancient stones hot on their trail, plus Brian complicated matters and meanwhile, her affection deepened for Conlin. Everything seemed like an epic disaster in her life, yet she created most of the problems with Geron, Brian, and Conlin because of her attempts to fix each situation that in reality were beyond her control.

Jeanette picked up her phone, scrolled the contacts list, tapped Brian's number and clicked on the speaker as it rang three times. She peeked at the clock on the dashboard. He always woke up at 5:30 a.m. on weekdays for a jog before work.

"Good morning. You're up before seven?" Brian asked.

"I'm driving to Jack's today," she said.

"It's about time you came home."

Her grip tightened on the steering wheel. She didn't want to forgo searching for Tom or desert Conlin and Saoirse. "If Tom isn't at the cabin, I'll have no choice but to rely on the authorities."

"Smart girl. You've come to your senses."

She already regretted calling him and his remarks goaded a harsh sigh. Every comment he made undermined her choices. "You never understood me at all."

"What are you talking about? I've known you for five years."

"Exactly, and you don't believe in me."

"Meaning?"

"I'm a banféinní." Jeanette used a sharpened and confident tone.

"Now you're speaking gibberish." His laughter was low and caustic. "No wonder you always sleep-in late."

A hardening of her stomach generated an onset of nausea, and she clutched her belly. Brian wasn't the only person remaining willfully ignorant of the truth. She was aware for a while that their relationship didn't work, yet she maintained the guise, hoping the longer they stayed together, he'd appreciate and accept her in entirety. "At least you know I'm not a morning person."

"For sure," he said in a muffled voice. "Got a sweatshirt on and taking off for my morning run now."

"Okay."

"See you soon." Brian smooched the microphone and hung up.

Jeanette cringed and hit a fingertip against the end call button. She tried. No, she didn't, but reiterating their breakup during a phone conversation after explaining her decision in a note rubbed salt into the wound. Although, she also left a poor excuse in a letter on the table for Conlin and Saoirse without saying goodbye. Jeanette grunted aloud and curled her fingers into fists to keep herself from honking the horn.

She needed a strong espresso if she was to function and travel on the road for half the day. Jeanette straightened her posture, selected *Hateful* by The Clash, in her iTunes music library, and cranked up the volume. Driving the open highway always cleared her thinking. She shifted the gear in drive and left. *Don't look back. They're better off now you're gone.*

Green traffic lights reflected off the rain soaked, desolate city streets. At least the storm moved on and the weather application forecasted partial sunny skies for the day. She drove east on Sherbrooke Street and turned into the driveway for a Tim Horton's coffee shop.

Jeanette coasted past the entrance and squinted at the sign posted. They didn't open till 7:00 a.m. and the lousy store hours validated the reason she slept past seven in the morning. A groan seeped through her pinched lips. She parked in a space, staring at the blue, orange, and light-yellow colors of dawn. Did Conlin awaken and read her letter?

A queasiness stirred in her stomach, and she lowered the glass on the driver's door, inhaling a lungful of fresh air. The lack of sleep and bodily demand for caffeine intensified her headache. She closed her eyelids, picturing Conlin's fleeting glance before he went to bed. He inundated her thoughts, imagining his brows drawn inward and a down-turned mouth while reading her note. How could she leave without a single word, realizing she'd never see him again? Oh, those lips and eyes...

Jeanette shook her head and raised a flat palm against her warm forehead. What was the big deal? They only shared a kiss. In the core of her soul, she knew it was so much more and she still walked away depriving herself of looking at his face one last time before proceeding on their own paths. She flitted her eyelashes to clear unshed tears.

Maybe she wasn't a banféinní and failed at representing the warrior Conlin dubbed her in Kinsale. Departing before a final farewell seemed like a coward's move. Too late, she must forget the Murphys and push them from her thoughts. She entered Jack's address into her maps for directions and verified it was seven kilometers to Autoroute 10.

The entire journey proved Brian was correct, along with her parent's judgments of her lacking abilities to help anyone and her conduct supported their assessments. All she wanted to achieve—find Tom, rescue him out of the mess he made, and protect the Murphys ended in additional hardships. Might as well give up on her goals and admit defeat before making the situation worse, but she refused, knowing the seriousness of Tom's predicament.

Jeanette lengthened her arms overhead, and interlinked her fingers for a deeper stretch, prior to placing her hands on the wheel. She put the car in drive and exited the parking area. The automatic doors locked, and Jeanette pressed her foot on the brake. Checking in both directions, she flipped on her left blinker and raised the sole of her boot off the pad. In a split second, the Nissan accelerated before she could touch the pedal.

With quick reflexes, she changed into the center lane and swerved, speeding uncontrollably at 65 mph. Her heart rate increased velocity and adrenaline shot through her body. She pushed the foot brake to the floor and nothing happened to decelerate the vehicle.

Jeanette bulleted through a red light and veered from an oncoming car, clipping the curb. She gripped the emergency handbrake and pulled upward, turning the tires in the opposite direction of the curve in the road. The Nissan skidded on the sleek surface of the street, slowing the automobile to 35 mph.

In an instant, she lost control again, drove onto the sidewalk, and crashed into a hedge bush. The vehicle rolled until the front slammed into a concrete pole, and the impact forced the car to a full stop.

Jeanette lurched forward, knocking her forehead on glass at the same moment the airbag deployed, shoving her back into the seat. A fiery sensation blazed across her skin and the power of a battering ram smashed against her chest. Weakness spread throughout her torso and she swayed, feeling faint and slumped onto the passenger side.

TWENTY-THREE

Conlin gasped for air as his eyelids flashed open, and a cold sweat broke across his brow. He sprang upright on the mattress, blinking several times, and adjusted his vision in the dark. A burning scorched his chest, and a bead of perspiration ran down the middle of his torso. Wet hair stuck to his forehead and he pressed his palms on the follicles, pushing the locks away from his face. A bright glow from the clock illuminated 7:16 a.m., and he glanced at Cricket asleep in bed.

He squeezed his head, applying pressure as a migraine surfaced. The images in his mind didn't appear as dreams or nightmares, and the mental pictures seemed to relay a prophetic event. Recollection of his visions faded, and the details became unclear.

Conlin flipped on the light switch and flinched at the brightness. He looked around, noticing Jeanette and her stuff had vanished. Jumping out of bed, he hurried toward the jacks. His ligaments cramped and he groaned, searching the area. Just like that, she up and disappeared from their lives. A pang of emptiness lingered beside his heart, and he stumbled into a chair next to the bench. Why would she leave without a word?

Leaning forward, he rested his elbows on his thighs and laid his napper in his hands. Faint whispers came from behind the front door in the walkway. "What the—"

Conlin hopped up and stood close to the drapes, scratching the stubble along his jawline. Their quiet voices made it difficult to sort out the conversation—something about Geron, Thomas and the stones. A narrow opening of the curtains next to the wall allowed him to peer through the window and scope out the situation.

The golden rays of sunshine peeked through thick, gray clouds as Conlin squinted and gawked at the people standing beside the entrance. There was no sign of Geron, and he didn't recognize the men. Ace warned them and provided a little less than a twenty-four-hour lead, yet they neglected to vacate the property when given the chance. Was Jeanette's disappearance connected to Geron's absence? *God, keep her safe.*

A loud beep rang from the alarm clock, set for 7:30 a.m. Conlin sucked in a hard intake of air and rushed to the nightstand. Knocking his knee on the center table, he swore under his breath and lunged across the mattress on his stomach. He smacked the top button, turning off the electronic device. Rolling onto his back, he massaged his leg to relieve the throbbing ache in his kneecap.

"Da, what're—"

"Shh." Conlin sat upright and gestured with a thumb at the entry. "Gougers are lurking outside."

Saoirse rubbed the sleep from her eyes and glimpsed at the space. "Where's Jeanette?"

"I don't know."

"Did ya have a row last night?"

Conlin quelled a bittersweet smile, picturing Jeanette's puckered lips and inviting gaze. "The complete opposite."

"I'll wet the tea."

"Did ya hear me about the gits waiting for us?"

Indifference bounced her shoulders. "They can wait."

"Hurry and get dressed." Conlin coughed over a contained laugh.

She spun in the other direction, grabbed her clothing, and proceeded to the bog. Conlin gathered his belongings and checked his mobile. No messages from Jeanette and so many unanswered questions, although the current scenario didn't allow him time to dwell on the unknown.

Less than thirty minutes later, dressed and ready to go, they packed their luggage. Conlin pressed his back flat against the wall and peered through the corner of the curtain, spying on the people loitering in the same location. He banged a fist on his thigh, thinking of their limited options for exiting the cottage.

He'd need to devise a clever plan of escape, reminiscent of a program on the telly. Maybe they could climb out a rear window or dress in disguises for a non-confrontational getaway. Conlin hadn't sized them up, but he aimed to prevent getting into a scrap with two gurriers. However, he would do whatever was necessary to keep his daughter safe.

He scratched his chin and skimmed the room for ideas. Saoirse stopped texting and peered up from the screen, narrowing her eyes. She must've recalled his failed attempt to defeat Harry in Dingle and his lack of protection landed them stranded in a foreign country.

"Don't lose the head," Saoirse said.

"Lost faith in the auld man?"

She exaggerated an eye roll, picked up the hotel telephone, and pushed a button. Her smile broadened, coiling the cord around a finger, and she gave him a confident nod. "Hiya, I'm in cottage number seven and need help. Two men have been standing outside me door for over an hour." She shifted her shoulders and bobbed her head, as if listening to music.

Conlin observed her with fascination. Everyone recognized how self-sufficient, skillful, intuitive, and grownup she had become, even him, yet she'd always be his little girl, his Cricket.

Saoirse continued talking on the phone. "Yeah, okay. That'd be grand, t'anks." She hung up and a grin stretched across her face. "Problem solved." She swiped her palms together, highlighting her finished accomplishment. "The manager's taking care of it and sending a security guard."

Drawing in a deep breath, his lungs expanded to their fullest. "You've done me proud."

She was beyond fine, past surviving, and he trusted Cricket would thrive in all aspects of life. The concerns for her well-being never stemmed from doubting her capabilities. It developed from a lack of belief in his own abilities. Impostor syndrome and overprotective reactions grew out of control as a result of his own shortcomings.

Conlin collected the rest of their bits and pieces, checking for forgotten items, until he spotted an envelope on the tabletop. He moseyed over, picked up the hotel stationary, and gaped at the familiar handwriting of his name scrawled in the center. A note from Jeanette seemed to confirm his intuition that she had made a conscious decision to depart before he awakened, denying him a chance to see her face and say goodbye. The weight of an anchor dropped on his chest and his heart sank.

"The hardchaws left," Saoirse said.

Conlin pressed his thumbs against the letter, folded the envelope twice and stuffed it in a pocket of his trousers. "Right, we go now."

He collected the bags and ambled toward the doorway. The paper crinkled with every movement and the unread words begged for him to discover Jeanette's reasons for leaving before saying bye.

Conlin gripped the handle, cracked open the door and surveyed the car park. A hardy breath left him at the sight of the hired vehicle gone and the visual confirmation that she headed on dragged his shoulders downward.

Saoirse squeezed close behind and leaned on his arm. "Where're we going?"

"The lobby." Conlin stepped outdoors and motioned for Cricket to follow.

The bright sun illuminated the glaring reality of never seeing Jeanette's eyes light up whenever they confided in each other, or hear her laugh, and worse, not ever kiss her again. A sudden weakness extended through his limbs.

Hurrying along the pathway leading to the main entrance, Conlin peeked over his shoulder and checked that no one tracked them. An automatic glass entry at the foyer slid open, welcoming their arrival and he aimed for the front desk.

"I'll wait at the café for brekkie," Cricket said.

"Hold on."

Stop the knee-jerk reactions. Since Kera granted her ample freedom, he needed to allow her more independence or jeopardize reducing their visits together and risk becoming *that* parent. The kind kids left when they came of age and never drop in on nor stay in contact. He wanted the right balance of enacting healthy boundaries and trusting her judgment. The best way to achieve a lasting relationship required action. Continuing to tell Cricket he believed in her choices while hovering didn't convey the correct message, and the frustration he caused was driving her away.

"See ya in a minute." He nodded and flashed a wink.

Saoirse grabbed his arm with a thoughtful expression. "I'll choose seats and get settled. Care for a cup of cha?"

"Order me a coffee instead of tea."

She cocked her neck backward and eyeballed his appearance. "You must feel wrecked this morning."

"Off with ya." He grinned as she turned and walked across the hall into the eating area.

Conlin pivoted on his heel and approached the concierge. He set his bags on the tile floor and rested his elbows against the oak-wood counter. "Hello."

The desk agent glanced up from her computer screen. "Hi." She gawked and her cheeks reddened. "Pardon, Monsieur. How may I assist you?"

"We're checking out of room number seven." Conlin placed the key onto the desk.

"Of course." She stared before refocusing on the monitor and tapped her fingertips on the keyboard. "You're all set and there are no other charges." The receptionist dipped her chin toward her collarbone and ogled at him beneath her lashes. "Anything else for you today?"

"We'll need a taxi to the Irish Embassy in about an hour."

"Yes, I can arrange that service." She ran the tip of her pen along her lips.

"Grand, t'anks. I'll be at the restaurant."

"Well, I take a break in fifteen minutes." Straightening her posture, her tone perked up, and she swiped her palms along the material of her shirt.

"Em..." He cleared his throat, seeking the kindest and easiest avoidance of the encounter.

"Da, I selected our seats over here." Cricket strolled up from behind and yanked on his sleeve. He looked at her, setting a palm on her shoulder and gave her a light squeeze to express his thankfulness. Second instance, the day that her quick and clever thinking sorted out potential issues.

"I appreciate the call for a taxicab. We're going to have breakfast so," Conlin said.

"You're welcome. On behalf of Chalet Beacon, we hope you enjoyed your stay," the woman said.

Conlin held up five fingers as a goodbye gesture, then turned to follow Saoirse. "I owe you one," he whispered.

"It's always awkward watching women flirt with you."

"I wasn't aware it happens on a regular basis."

Saoirse halted and stared him down. "'Tis a surprise no woman's shifted ya in a while."

He suppressed a chuckle since she was unaware of Jeanette kissing him last night. Heat flared up his neck and across his face, pondering on the passion they shared.

"You really should consider dating," she said.

When was she going to accept, he wasn't interested in troubling himself about going on dates? At least, not when his work schedule left few opportunities for hanging out with his daughter and sailing. Conlin eased into the chair and the letter in his pocket crunched as he sat down at the dinette.

The note wouldn't permit him to deny his interest in Jeanette. He was willing to create room in his life and share it with her. What was he thinking? She had already departed, lived in another country, and he would never see her again.

How careless he acted after their tender moment... no wonder she took off without a word. He gripped the hot coffee cup, focusing on the dark liquid, trying to decide if he wanted cream and sugar. Conlin massaged the sharp pain in his right temple and sipped his drink to alleviate the feeling of light-headedness. If he struggled to make basic decisions, how could he sort out his thoughts about Jeanette?

"I assure you; it'll be forever and a day before I rush into a relationship again." Conlin took a large gulp of coffee, hoping to wash down the knot in his throat.

"What about Jeanette?"

The ache in his heart intensified at the mention of her name. "Cricket—"

"Two full Canadian breakfasts?" the server said, holding a tray, waiting to set the dishes on the table.

Saoirse nodded. "Brill, thanks."

"Thank you," Conlin said.

He settled his eyesight on the plates brimming with eggs, rashers, fried potatoes, toasted bread, and French toast. Thankfully, they'd be busy eating, and he could avoid answering Saoirse's questions about Jeanette.

An hour later, after they finished their breakfast, Conlin and Saoirse sat on a bench in the lobby at Chalet Beacon. The rich scent of Canadian maple syrup wafted through the air, underlining the French toast that put him over the top and he leaned back, relieving the fullness in his belly. They definitely wouldn't need to eat until supper.

Conlin's breath eased out his mouth, shopping online for a transatlantic flight. All the airlines flying from Montreal offered fourteen plus hours and stops on the way to Ireland. The only nonstop options available departed from the USA.

"Any luck?" Saoirse stared out the glass entrance, waiting for their ride.

"There're direct flights from Boston, Massachusetts," he said.

"Jeanette lives near there."

He glimpsed out of the corner of his eye and crossed his arms over his chest. "She lives in New Hampshire. Besides, she's long gone, and on her way to Jack's house."

"And I'm sure if you call her—"

"Give over! We're never going to see Jeanette again." Saying the words aloud plunged a mast into his heart.

Saoirse flinched with watery eyes and a quivering chin. On rare occasions, he raised his voice to reestablish authority, yet a dullness spread throughout his body. Anything but, not tears accompanied by a frown. He averted his gaze—convinced she held a type of superpower, and if he looked directly at her during an emotional eruption, he'd chance falling under her hypnotic spell. Fathers seemed more susceptible to their daughter's sentimental reactions.

Mastering the parental skill of a neutral response took years of practice and even then, he risked an oncoming storm of every emotion unleashed at once if he neglected to quell her hurt feelings in a timely manner. At any minute now, she'd reveal her next tactic.

"Now I understand why Ma left. You never take any risks," Saoirse said with a tongue that could shear a sheep. She huffed and turned away, offering him a cold shoulder.

A hard verbal blow walloped his gut as she decided on initiating escalation, another arsenal in her teenager's emotive toolkit. Combative techniques allowed her to test how far she could push before he or her mother either caved or enforced their authoritative power.

How he responded to her hurtful remark determined the next level of drama she would perform. Choosing the path of a peacemaker achieved an effective resolution for calming her down, emphasizing his maturity and reestablishing their father-daughter bond.

"You're right. When it comes to protecting you, I'll never risk your safety." Conlin laid a gentle palm on her knee. "We've been through a great deal over the past few days and you've handled it well, but there's a lot I'm factoring into my decisions."

She rolled her shoulders inward and slouched, lowering her eyelashes. "Sorry for what I said about Ma. I didn't mean it."

"Ah, sure, dearest. We split when you were young and it was too much for you to process your feelings during the separation. Now that ye're older, you've gained a perspective on the breakup." He stared into the eyes of her mother. "And Kera's better off with Frank."

Saoirse tilted her head, and her smile curved upward to one side. "Maybe you'll be better off with someone else, too?"

"We'll see." A nervous laugh found its way out.

"I'm just t'inking about yer happiness." She wrinkled her nose, curled her upper lip, and scrunched her facial features. He mimicked her expression and laughter erupted between them.

"You fill my life with joy." Conlin slipped his arm around her neck, tugging her closer and she leaned, resting her noggin against his biceps. "Should we go home and take a proper holiday on the boat?" He gave her a loving pat on the back.

Saoirse avidly nodded in agreement. "Yer the best, Da."

"Ah, yer me pride and delight." He nudged her arm.

His chest swelled, pulling in a lungful of air and he sat taller, now that they made a little progress. Both of them realized they had each other's greatest concerns in mind, and he admitted he had been holding onto her too tightly, suppressing her growth to blossom into adulthood. He needed to let go and entrust God with the protection of his daughter. If he learned anything from the drowning accident and recent events, control was an illusion.

Saoirse proved on many occasions, this morning alone, how capable she was at handling things fine on her own. Still and all, changes would take time, requiring mutual effort required while he eased his grip, and she honored boundaries.

Conlin released a tight breath through his lips. Saoirse loved and respected him, regardless of his imperfections, realizing it was okay for parents to mess up too. When he admitted his mistakes and apologized, it seemed their relationship strengthened because of honesty. More than accepting responsibility, he recognized she wanted him to hear and listen to her as a young adult, not as daddy's girl.

"Here's the jo maxi." Saoirse stood and picked up her bag.

Conlin glanced out the window at the taxi parked in front of the property and collected their things, following Cricket to the curb.

"Where to, monsieur?" the driver asked.

"The Irish Embassy." Conlin opened the passenger access for Cricket, and they slid into the backseat.

The cabdriver started the meter. "It's about ten blocks away."

At last, the distances weren't so extreme. Everything seemed closer—the embassy, airport, home, and his relationship with Saoirse. Except Jeanette. The vastness between them grew as the car drove farther down the street. Leaving behind faint traces of their days together yet deepening the impression she made in his life.

Rare feelings of planning a future with a partner stirred inside and Conlin struggled to remain composed. He hadn't experienced ideals of deep friendship blooming into something more with a woman in a while, and the budding emotions caused him to break a sweat.

Jeanette appeared emotionally unscathed, bolting after he divulged his shortcomings, and sharing a kiss. Maybe she regretted their moment of intimacy and didn't want to look him in the face again. Either way, she was miles away, creating a greater divide and he had to know the truth. Conlin leaned forward and brushed his fingertips along the edge of the letter. His pulse increased as his clammy hands gripped the paper.

The driver pulled alongside the entrance gate for the Irish Embassy and stopped, pressing a button on the meter that displayed the total fare in red. Jeanette's note would have to wait till later. Conlin removed his wallet, selected a credit card, then processed the payment in the machine and they exited the taxi.

"T'anks," Conlin said and closed the door.

He viewed the road, his thoughts as congested as the traffic maneuvering in and out of street lanes. Heaving a chest full of air through his nose, he tried to clear his mind of Jeanette. The only option now was to continue with their separate lives, like they had never met.

TWENTY-FOUR

Jeanette sat on the sidewalk and blinked, clearing her blurry vision. She rubbed her left temple and squinted at the flashing lights atop the patrol car. Crossing one arm over her chest, she readjusted an ice pack the police officer provided from her first aid kit.

"Then what happened?" Officer Mallard wrote in her incident log.

"Um, I braked and lost control of the vehicle."

The woman paused, looked up, and pointed her pen at the streets. "The roads are slick and it's easy to spin out."

"Right, although I suspect the operating system wasn't working, like someone hacked into the computer. I've read the cases are rare but have occurred."

Officer Mallard gawped and raised a brow. "Do you think there was malicious intent, and somebody caused the accident by tampering with your vehicle's instruments?"

"Yeah, it sounds farfetched..." Jeanette shook her head and cringed at the sound of the tow truck hooking up the totaled Nissan. "But it's a complicated situation."

The officer closed her notebook and passed Jeanette a card. "Here's the station's contact information, and I included the case number at the top. Call if there's anything else you want added to your report."

"Thank you."

"Are you sure you don't require any further medical treatment or a ride anywhere?"

"I am fine, thanks. The rental car company is dropping off a new vehicle in the next half an hour."

"All right, Ms. Hillestad, don't hesitate to reach out for additional assistance." Officer Mallard tipped the front of her hat and left.

Jeanette moved the cold compress to her forehead and shut her eyelids, blocking traffic noise as she replayed the crash in her mind. If Geron attempted to hurt her again, then Conlin and Saoirse might be in danger, too. A chill shot from head to toe, and she shuddered. *God, please protect them from harm.*

Fifteen minutes later, a driver arrived, delivering a replacement and the representative of the agency had her sign a new contract after snapping photos of the police statement. He handed her keys for a Honda CR-V and drove off with a co-worker. A message popped up from Saoirse and her heart sank as she clicked the notification to read the text.

The screeching of brakes stopping alongside the curb distracted her, and she glanced up, viewing Geron's familiar sedan. Tension pinched a nerve, stiffening her neck as the passenger door opened and he exited the Jaguar. Jeanette inhaled, holding her breath for a second, and she clutched the hidden Celtic Stone tighter inside her bag. Dressed in an overcoat, with his dark hair slicked back, he approached her, standing on the pavement beside the Honda.

She raised her chin and looked him square in the face. "You look disappointed that I survived the crash."

"Nonsense. You agreed to work for me with an understanding I'm in charge and you'll do whatever I request," Geron said.

"You're mistaken. You have no authority over me."

"Madame, I already explained, the incomprehensible supernatural forces involved, and that people have been manipulating you from the beginning."

"I'm not intimidated by you."

"I am aware of your impulsive behavior and hasty choices make you a key player in our plans." He arched a deliberate eyebrow. "We're counting on your continuous irrational reactions to fulfill my purposes."

She levied a glare at him and stiffened her posture. "I'm done listening to your deranged ideas."

"You are not in a position to decide what happens next."

"Then if I return the artifact, will you quit following my brother and the Murphys?"

"The problem with your proposal is you have a job to finish." Geron folded his arms and angled his chin downward. "For now, keep and study the relics."

"What are your expectations?"

"Find Thomas and bring the stones to a specified location."

"And if I refuse?"

A sneer yanked at his cheek, and he clasped his hands together. "Mr. Murphy and his daughter will never arrive at their destination in Ireland."

Her body tensed at his threat, and her pulse increased. "Why can't you leave them alone? They have nothing to do with the artifacts or the deal we made."

"Because they're important to you and threatening their safety pressures you to carry out all my demands."

Yes, Conlin and Saoirse meant more to her than she thought possible, and her care for them seemed apparent to everyone. Did Conlin know? An empty feeling surrounded her heart. "If I do what you ask, will you stop pursuing the Murphys?"

"Forty-eight hours." Geron pivoted on the heel of his Oxford shoe "I'll be in touch." He entered his Jaguar and the car drove west on Sherbrooke Street.

Jeanette clenched her jaw, holding in the sickness churning in her stomach. The pain worsened by the minute, intensifying her headache. No matter how she tried to distance Conlin and Saoirse from the dangers, Geron pulled them back into the situation.

She hunched forward and laid her forehead against her palms. "Lord, I pray Conlin got an emergency passport and found a flight home…" Jeanette flung her head upward, remembering Saoirse's message, and flinched at the discomfort. She looked at her phone screen and viewed the text.

We need your help. Please meet us at the Irish Embassy.

Upstairs at the Irish Embassy, Conlin and Saoirse stood in line for replacement passports. He gripped the completed forms and rocked backward on his heels, tapping his fingers on the papers. "It'll all work out, and I've selected a flight to book once we're approved for travel." He turned toward Cricket and gave her a reassuring single nod.

Saoirse picked at her thumbnail and glanced over her shoulder at least five times in the past three minutes. She caught him observing her behavior.

"We're cool, yeah?" she said, and a nervous laugh ended in a sputter. "Like how I handled everything at the hotel?"

Conlin cracked a smile, tilting his chin in acknowledgement. She was quick thinking and demonstrated maturity through the chaos during their recent experiences. He figured she would ask permission to attend a Fontaines D.C. gig, and he recognized she was ready. Despite having to accept she was no longer his little singing Cricket, the time had come for him to release her into the world, to a certain extent, always keeping a watchful eye on her since he could not deny his protective nature.

Arching an inquisitive eyebrow, he crossed his arms. "What are ya—"

"Are you okay?" Jeanette rushed up behind Saoirse and placed a hand on her back.

Conlin jolted at the sudden sound of her voice. His heart skipped a beat when he lifted his gaze and saw her standing beside Cricket. His mind reeled, searching for answers. Why did she go prior to saying goodbye and then show up again? Did the letter explain her temporary absence and that she had planned on returning? A mixture of perplexity and curiosity stirred his thoughts, trying to figure out her actions.

Scratching his scalp, he shifted his stance and gaped at Saoirse. She didn't seem bewildered by Jeanette's reappearance. Ah, he should've known. "Em, did ya want to tell me something?"

Saoirse hunched and displayed a hesitant grin. "So, yeah, I texted Jeanette..."

"What happened?" Jeanette asked.

Conlin cleared his throat and turned his torso toward Jeanette. The last time he looked into her eyes, he cuddled her in his arms and kissed her lips. A warmth crept across his chest and he pushed the sleeves of his sweater to his elbows. "Let's just say unwelcome visitors arrived at our door early in the morning, but we sorted it out."

Jeanette pressed a palm over her heart. "Thank God you're both safe."

A line inscribed into the space above her nose, and he felt the load of her burdens bearing down on his shoulders. Jeanette bore all the responsibility, and he knew at her arrival she would endure their problems on top of everything else. "I hope we didn't inconvenience you."

"Never. I'm here whenever you need me."

Summoning all of his might and strength, he restrained himself from grabbing her into a close embrace without surrender. Until *this* moment, he didn't realize the immeasurable extent of how much he needed Jeanette. The revelation comforted and unnerved him, twisting his feelings into a bowline knot. All the things he desired to profess to her last night and lost the courage when the idea of another man sharing a life with her crushed him inside, thinking he missed the chance and now...

"Jeanette—"

"Da, it's our turn."

Conlin shook his head and blinked to refocus. "Right." He strolled over to window thirteen with Jeanette and Saoirse on each side. After they finalized their requests and finished at the embassy, they'd go separate ways again. Regardless of their limited time together, he would cherish every second.

"How can I help you today?" the clerk asked.

"I misplaced our passports." Conlin slid the forms across the desk. "I included a duplicate of the police report we filed."

The woman examined the papers. "If you're both requesting an ETD, emergency travel document, we require a photocopy of the minor's birth certificate."

"Her mother is on holiday and will scan a copy when she returns home on Wednesday." They remained silent while the clerk inspected the application.

"When does your flight depart from the USA?" she said.

"On Friday from Boston, Massachusetts."

She added the information to the form and returned her attention to the computer screen. "What's the name and address of the accommodations prior to your departure?"

Eejit. He forgot to book a hotel before submitting the request. Conlin fixed his eyesight on the plain white wall behind a row of desks. Maybe they could finish the procedure if he stepped aside and secured a reservation online.

"Do we have a place to stay?" Saoirse whispered.

Jeanette squeezed beside him, nudging against his biceps, and leaned on the counter. Her curls brushed his cheek and facial muscles tightened, holding in a sneeze as stray strands tickled his face.

"Hello, I'm Ms. Hillestad and they're staying at my residence in New Hampshire." She placed her passport on the countertop and the clerk opened her identification, then keyed in the information.

Jeanette turned, and he studied the details of her features, visually connecting light freckles, creating a constellation across the bridge of her nose.

"Did I overstep any boundaries?" she asked.

"Yer timing's impeccable and you're magnificent."

She gazed at him under fluttering eyelids and flaunted a coquettish smile. Heat crackled beneath his skin and singed up the back of his neck. Whenever she flashed a flirtatious look at him, he fell into a daydream about sailing off with her to a secluded island. He stared into her endless green eyes, reflecting his future, yet a hardness clenched his stomach, grounding him in reality and he forced the thoughts from his mind.

"Mr. Murphy, sign on the line." The representative pointed at the document. "Complete the process at the Irish Consulate in Boston on Thursday, November 4th in the morning at 11:15."

Conlin picked up the pen tethered to a chain and Jeanette stepped backward, giving him room. He paused and glanced at her sidelong. "You're certain about us staying at your house and driving to the airport?"

"I'll do anything for you," she said in an unwavering tone and without hesitation.

She meant it and he believed her more than anyone who had given him their word. The corners of his mouth twitched, containing his gratification, and he concentrated on the paper. Although, one detail kept nagging him—why did she leave while they were asleep and before they discussed...? Conlin massaged his forehead, refocused, and signed his name.

"Miss Murphy, please stand on the yellow line." The clerk motioned at Saoirse, and in an instant, snapped a picture. "You're next." She waved Conlin over to the marker and after a quick flash from the camera, the photo session ended.

The office worker concluded the transaction in five minutes. She selected a business card and wrote the specifics for their appointment on the backside. "Here's the location of the consulate in Boston and your ETD to cross the border into the United States. We authorized your daughter to travel using the same document." She handed him the passport style booklet.

Conlin gave a single nod to the clerk, then faced Jeanette and Saoirse, outstretching a hand. "I guess we're set to go."

Cricket leaned near and elbowed his rib. "Good thing I contacted Jeanette."

He wrapped an arm around her shoulder and tugged her into a side hug. "I'm aimless without you."

Exiting the office, they walked down a corridor to the lifts. Cricket led the way, and Jeanette slowed her steps as he caught up to her pace. Conlin grasped her wrist and reeled her toward him. "I appreciate you coming back." He loosened his grip and gulped. "Ya know, responding to Saoirse and helping us."

A wholeness filled him, reflecting on the sacrifices she made. Jeanette proved in so many ways to be a person of integrity, and her actions spoke louder than words. No chance of denying how special she had become to him and each passing moment they spent together would drive the painstaking truth that he'd have to let her go and resume his life in Kinsale.

She rested her eyes on him, expressing absolute resolve. "You can always count on me." Jeanette skipped her gaze to Saoirse. "Both of you."

With total certainty, she was the most dependable person he knew, and trusted her promises. "You must've been halfway to Jack's before returning to Montreal."

"I never left the city."

"What changed your plans?" She might have explained it in her letter and his question revealed he never read it.

"We need to talk." The tone of her voice conveyed a serious discussion, beyond the sentiments about kisses, notes, leaving and showing up again.

"Sure, we'll have a chat in the car."

One side of her lips kicked up her cheek, yet her shoulders seemed to drop, and he had never seen her drained of vitality. Her pallid complexion hinted something else transpired between last night when they talked, embraced, shifted, and now.

TWENTY-FIVE

Jeanette unlocked the new rental car in the parking lot at the Irish Embassy and flashed a reassuring smile at Saoirse. "How about riding in the front for a change?"

"Coola Boola."

Jeanette tossed her the keys. "Choose a music playlist."

Her expression lit up, and she twirled around before climbing into the Honda. "I'm glad you came back."

"Me too."

"Evading Geron by getting a replacement car?" Conlin elbowed her in the ribs.

She yanked his sleeve and motioned to follow her behind the white Honda CR-V. "Wasn't sure if you'd want Saoirse hearing our conversation."

"After everything we've endured, I t'ink she can handle it." He opened the rear door and tossed in their bags. "Did ya have another encounter with Geron?"

"He gave me a warning to locate Tom and deliver the stones." Jeanette took long and deliberate breaths through her nose. "And somehow, he caused me to crash by hacking into my vehicle's operating system."

Conlin's eyebrows drew inward, and he stepped closer with a searching stare. "Are you injured?"

"A little sore and a bump on the head." She pointed to the injury on her forehead and the closeness of their bodies caused her to quiver.

"Ah, Banféinní…" He caressed her face, lovingly swiping a cheek.

Conlin's fingers trailed along her jawline, and his thumb rested on the edge of her chin. He tilted her head backward and his hand roved to her nape, kissing the bruise below her hairline. Every nerve in her body reacted to his touch, aching to feel the fullness of his mouth on her lips again.

"Why did you leave?" His breath brushed the tip of her nose.

Jeanette released a soft sigh, and her eyelashes fluttered. "Didn't you read my letter?"

"I want ya to tell me." The urgency of his voice emphasized the Irish brogue.

"You're in danger because of me, and I can't let anything happen to you."

Conlin gripped her and gently shook her shoulders. "Get it through your skull; we're in this together." Listening to him speak, the lilt entranced her with his constant drop of *h* in words beginning with *th*.

Jeanette froze and fixated on the blazing-blue flame ignited in his irises. The heat radiating from his gaze burned all barriers, weakening her knees and she softened in his arms. No longer willing to fight her feelings anymore, she surrendered, accepting that she required Conlin by her side. They made each other stronger, complimenting their strengths, and compensating the weaknesses, creating a powerful alliance.

"I thought we agreed last night," he said.

The bump on her head, fatigue, Geron's threats, and now reunited with Conlin all muddled her senses. "Well… it's settled today that we're staying together."

His palms glided down her arms, and he clasped her hands. Their fingers interlaced, emitting a warmth, and forging another level of intimacy. Conlin inched closer, his torso pressed against her chest, and he deepened their handclasp. Passion surged from every gaze, the brush of his skin on her flesh, their meaningful and unforgettable kiss asserting the need for a partnership, connecting two souls in a way she never experienced.

Conlin slanted his neck sideways, exposing his throat in line with her lips, and she pecked his Adam's apple. A low moan rumbled from his larynx and he relaxed his grasp, then gathered her into a hug, burying his face in her hair. A couple of seconds later, he stepped rearward and his magnetism lured her nearer to him once more, and she rested her head against his collarbone.

He massaged, then squeezed her deltoid muscles, signaling they needed to leave, and shut the tailgate. "Should we set out on the road?"

Three minutes standing outside the car ended too soon, hoping for a lifetime of togetherness. How could she let go of him and say goodbye on a future date? Part of the reason she left a note was to avoid looking at him and hide the surmounting emotions inside.

A swelling lump in her throat strained her voice. "Yeah."

"Are ya feeling all right to drive?"

Jeanette squinted at the pain from her headache. "I'd appreciate a break from driving."

Conlin's mouth curled upward at the corners, draping his arm around her and escorted her to the passenger side. "No trouble at all." He opened the door and did a double take at Saoirse, sitting in the backseat.

"Aren't ya riding in the front?" Conlin asked.

"Changed me mind." Saoirse revealed a knowing look and an approving smile—the kind shared between girls when they wish for a friend's happy outcome with *the* guy.

"Besides, I'm safer here if ye're driving." She teased her dad and pulled the door closed.

Laughter tore out of him, gesturing at Saoirse. "Always slagging me off." He spun about and walked to the other side of the vehicle.

Jeanette squelched a grin and entered the Honda. An inexplicable contentment lifted her spirit. Although she still needed to find Tom, study the stones and handle Geron's looming threats, they understood a power existed by staying together.

Conlin hopped in the driver's position, slipped on a pair of eyeglasses, and started the engine. Jeanette plugged her device into the USB connector and set it in a holder on the dashboard. "You can use my phone for directions." She tapped the maps icon as Conlin stared at the screen and a text from Brian popped up.

Let me know when you arrive at Jack's house.

She swiped upward, removing the notification, and caught a glimpse of Conlin. A brick dropped through her center, and he gawked at her for a second, then turned away. Yeah, he had seen the message. Random communications from Geron and Brian blindsided them whenever they bonded, yet there were no excuses for not making her intentions clear to both men.

"Prior to departing for Ireland, I wrote him a letter, explaining the relationship is over for me, but he's refusing to accept it."

Conlin gripped the gearshift and remained silent. She laid her palm on his hand. "Otherwise, I wouldn't have kissed you."

A high-pitched squeal arose from the backseat. She imagined Saoirse watching the drama unfold like a reality TV show. Sure, the spectacle involved her dad, but Jeanette felt confident Saoirse understood she wouldn't do anything to hurt or mislead her father. After all, Saoirse seemed to recognize the extent of Jeanette's affection for Conlin before she knew herself.

Conlin breathed aloud, staring out the windshield, then leaned forward, retrieving an envelope from his pocket and passed her the unopened note. "Try expressing yerself in person next time, so there'll be no confusion." He put the car in reverse and Saoirse gave him a reassuring pat on the shoulder.

And in a world of instant messaging, their blissful moment ended. Jeanette crunched the paper in her hand, emulating the crushing force in her heart. She held tears at bay and turned in the opposite direction. The painful truth plunged a knife into her core.

Jeanette avoided tough discussions, and the challenge escalated whenever it involved people closest to her. She preferred written communications to choose her words wisely and escape the other person's reactions.

Brian never listened to her anyway. Jeanette clutched her midsection, thinking about their phone conversation earlier and how he brushed off everything she said. If they had sat down for a serious talk before leaving, he might've attempted to talk her out of breaking up and delayed her search for Tom. She shut her eyelids to shun the emotional consequences of contemplating that if she stayed home, she wouldn't have met the Murphys.

For once, she appreciated Siri's incessant voice navigating the route. Conlin entered the QC-10E, Autoroute Bonaventure and drove across Pont Champlain Bridge over the St. Lawrence River. So many wonderful and awful things happened in Montreal. A coldness prickled her skin, reflecting on the precarious events that took place in Quebec and how they remained in constant danger.

Right, what was she doing getting caught up in Conlin's entrancing gaze and colloquial language when she had an ominous deadline? If she focused on the relics, she could push Conlin from her mind, but she didn't want to and discovered it was impossible now that he infiltrated her heart too.

Jeanette reclined, hugging herself, and gazed out the window, watching the autumn colors blend into a golden blur. With heavy lids, she pictured the Trinity Knot, its intersecting lines, and the importance of three. What did it mean for the mysterious stones?

Jeanette awakened to the warmth and comfort of a palm resting on her shoulder. Inhaling a deep, satisfying breath, she rotated over and met Conlin's gaze.

"Howrya feeling?" His gentle tone and softened expression lightened the weight on her chest. "You've slept for two hours."

Blinking a few extra times, she cleared her vision and sat upright, tying her hair into a bun. "A little better." She viewed the surroundings. "Where are we?"

"Derby. I stopped for petrol and Saoirse is inside the market purchasing drinks."

"We're close to the border."

He shifted in his seat, removed his hand from her body and took off his eyeglasses. She already missed his touch. "I'm sorry I left a note." Jeanette pushed her messy tresses away from her face and turned toward him. "I lacked the courage to say bye when I wanted to stay..."

"I understand an Irish goodbye and we never expected..." He rubbed the stubble along his chin and a smile budded. "The pleasant surprise of us meeting."

"Isn't that how all the best relationships begin?"

"A serendipitous encounter." Conlin angled his chin downward, arching a thoughtful eyebrow as his fingers curved around her forearm, placing her hand against his heart. "We'll never say a final farewell, always slán go fóill, bye for now and a promise to see each other soon."

A lightness lifted her chest, hoping to keep Conlin and Saoirse in her life in any capacity. Whether continuing a deepening friendship or distant communications as casual acquaintances, yet she desired more.

Saoirse opened the back door and leaned forward, passing her a bottled water. "Howya, Jeanette?"

Conlin released his grip, and she grabbed the bottle. "Fine, and thanks for the drink."

"Did he set t'ings right with you?" She shifted a glance between them. "I told him he needs to learn how to talk to women."

"Enough buzzin' wit' me." He playfully poked her arm.

Jeanette repressed a laugh and looked Conlin directly in the eyes. "I think we're good."

"Grand, altogether," he said.

"Ready to switch places and select your top road-trip tunes?" She gestured for Saoirse to trade spots.

Jeanette jumped into the driver's seat. Saoirse joined her in the front and Conlin sat in the back. Everyone buckled their seatbelts, and she drove onto I-91, following the signs for the U.S. Customs and Border Protection at Derby Line, Vermont.

After a few minutes and waiting behind six cars, Jeanette arrived at the port of entry, slowing to a stop. Conlin passed her their emergency travel documents, and she lowered the windows, handing all their passport information to the officer.

The woman examined their identifications. "Where are you coming from and what's the nature of your trip?"

"We stayed in Montreal during our vacation and we're going to my house in Moultonborough Bay, New Hampshire before they depart for Ireland on Friday." If she volunteered more details, perhaps they'd avoid additional questions or worse, a vehicle inspection.

The officer glanced at Jeanette, then peered through the windows at Conlin and Saoirse. "Are you bringing anything back into the country?"

"No." A prickly sensation covered Jeanette's skin, considering the Celtic Stone. She shoved her bag lower, between her seat and the door. Thank God the agent didn't inquire about cultural property. All their lives were at stake and she could not risk border control confiscating the artifact.

The woman stared at Jeanette for a few seconds. "Any purchased goods, such as tobacco, alcohol, fruits, or vegetables?"

"We bought a few clothing items and souvenirs."

The officer stepped inside and processed their information. Jeanette fidgeted and rapped her fingertips on the steering wheel. If Tom was at Jack's house, she'd wallop him for everything his careless actions caused.

Conlin stretched forward and tapped her back. "Be grand."

"Of course, it's just the usual trouble Tom creates. Four years ago, I convinced the U.S. Embassy in Ecuador to declare his diplomatic immunity during our Tayos Caves expedition."

Within two minutes, border protection cleared them for entry. "You're all set."

"Thanks." Jeanette retrieved their documents and drove past the gate as a collective sigh echoed in the car.

"There ya go, now." Conlin patted both Saoirse and her on their arms, then reclined in the backseat. "Another step closer to getting us home."

Words trembled on her tongue, piling in the back of her mouth, and a forceful swallow worked the remarks into her throat. She needed consolation from Conlin, the one person understanding of her predicament, yet she refused to place him in a difficult quandary of assuming responsibility for her conflicting emotions, struggling to watch them return to Ireland.

She turned to the next best source of comfort whenever traveling on the open road. "Let's crank up the music."

Jeanette shuffled a playlist on Saoirse's device. The player selected an indie dream-pop song, exemplifying the shoegaze genre with reverberating ethereal female vocals. She mused on the pristine singing, contrasting distorted guitars, and reminisced about her favorite bands in the '90s, sharing a similar sound. The lyrics resonated a specific meaning:

I still want you to stay,
Even when you're turning away.
We don't need to feel alone,
Weighing on my heart like a stone...

The entire tune spoke to her emotions, their circumstances, and the melody carried her off to a distant place. Music communicated feelings when speaking failed to convey her state of mind and summed up her moods. Saoirse understood songs in the same way.

"Who's the band? I'm adding them to my iTunes library." Something for Jeanette to evoke memories of the Murphys after they returned home. She observed Saoirse sinking into her seat, and her cheeks reddened. Maybe she considered Jeanette too old for listening to the same bands.

"Me mucking about with GarageBand." She mocked herself in a low tone.

"You're fantastic!" Jeanette reached over and bumped her softly, encouraging Saoirse.

"Bleedin' brilliant," Conlin said.

"Go way outta that." Saoirse laughed and a streak of color crossed her cheekbones.

Jeanette peeked at Conlin in the rearview mirror. "Your daughter's talented."

"She didn't get it from me."

"Wha'? You sing and play guitar," Saoirse said.

Conlin shrugged a laid-back shoulder. "In the church choir."

"I'm talking about yer rock band, One and The Endless."

"Oh, really?" Jeanette emphasized her words as her interest continued to escalate. "I'd love to hear those tracks."

Saoirse picked up her device and scrolled through the songs. "*In the River Lee* is on a playlist."

Jeanette bounced in her seat, unable to contain her enthusiasm. "Yes, please." She sneaked a quick look at his reaction. A hand covered his face, and he groaned, slouching in the backseat.

She longed for all the details in Conlin's life and desired more of him—the Irish slang, clever comments, charming demeanor, and caring nature. She wished they'd stay and harking back to the verses in Saoirse's song; it weighed on her heart like a stone. Jeanette faced the continuous dilemma of Conlin returning to Ireland without a promise of seeing him again.

TWENTY-SIX

Cruising along I-91, Jeanette drove the interchange at St. Johnsbury onto Interstate 93 toward the White Mountains. A banner of crimson, purple, golden-yellow, and fiery orange stretched across Franconia in the distance, crossing over the Connecticut River. Hiking trails, visiting covered bridges, eating cider donuts, going apple-picking, and riding the Cog Railway embodied autumn in New Hampshire's White Mountains.

A hollowness spread from her chest and throughout her body, passing state Route 302 to Sugar Hill. Jeanette could almost taste the rich New Hampshire syrup dripping from a stack of Polly's fluffy pancakes. The feelings of youthful innocence rushed over her with the force of a flume. Summers she and Tom helped Jack at his general store while he shared stories about his dad working with Grandpa Les at The Glen House added richness to her life.

In minutes, Jeanette would learn if Tom sought refuge at Jack's cabin and prove the accuracy of her assumptions. Of course, she considered the possibilities of being wrong in her assessments. Her headache intensified and she cringed at the pain. Skipping lunch didn't help her recovery and heightened the sickness brewing in her belly.

At 4:30 p.m., Conlin dozed in the backseat. Saoirse gazed out the window after hearing two hours of her favorite bands, including her dad's original punk rock track, *In the River Lee*, and giving her a language lesson in basic Irish phrases. Jeanette selected her 1990s music playlist, enhancing the seasonal ambiance and appeasing her nostalgia, listening to the Red House Painters' song *Have You Forgotten?*—stirring memories of the innocence of childhood. A bittersweet smile built, reminiscing and she exited the freeway, traveling along the Littleton Route 116 toward Whitefield.

"The scenery is just as Thomas described it to us," Saoirse said.

Yes, Tom spoke in an eloquent prose and acquired the gift of storytelling he undoubtedly learned from Jack. A prickle on her skin crept across her face and she twitched her nose. "New Hampshire exudes an awe-inspiring charm reflected in outdoor elements of nature, similar to the enchantment Ireland possesses."

"'Tis a stunning view with the diversity of colored trees," Conlin said in a sleepy tone, stretching his arms overhead.

Jeanette followed familiar curves on the mountainous drive and gripped the steering wheel tighter. A few miles farther, she made a left onto the private unpaved lane, Old East Road.

"How's it going?" Conlin leaned close and his breath brushed her nape.

"I'm okay..."

At the top of an incline, the slate-color roof of Jack's log home came into sight, perched among a landscape of red-sugar maples, pine trees nuzzled in a panorama of snowy mountain peaks. The gravel driveway looped around a grass planter, and she parked beside Jack's silver Jeep. No sign of Tom's car unless he stored it in the garage.

Jeanette turned off the engine and rested her hand on the gearshift, staring off into sun rays beaming through the glaring gray clouds. The moment of truth arrived, and for the first time, she lost the energy to handle the stress of Tom's actions alone.

"No matter the outcome, we're here for you," Conlin said as if he read her mind and had an intuitive awareness of her thoughts.

His comforting words, accompanied by the warmth of physical contact on her shoulder, shot a surge of electricity through her body and a new sense of encouragement boosted her strength, providing the hope she required.

They exited the CR-V, walking to the main ingress, and stood together, staring at the door. The soothing caress of Conlin's nurturing touch on her hand calmed her nervous tensions. Jeanette rang the doorbell, biting her lower lip as he flashed a reassuring wink and tightened their handclasp.

She experienced no other person's presence deeper than the support Conlin provided. In every defined line on his face, furrowed brow, and tensed posture, he reflected her expression, sharing her burdens, exemplifying the power of three. Standing beside her, he unified the alliance and interlaced their fingers. A minute passed and still no answer. Saoirse knocked on the glass and a light brightened the porch.

"Hello," Jack called out from behind the entrance, and he unlocked the deadbolt.

"It's Jeanette." She bounced on her toes like a giddy eleven-year-old.

Jack swung the doorway open, displaying a wide grin. "As I live and breathe, Love has arrived."

Jeanette stepped forward into Jack's embrace, the same bear hug she lost herself in as a kid, and closed her eyelids, inhaling the familiar aroma of sandalwood mixed with Grey Flannel cologne.

"You were expecting me?" She spoke into his navy, cable-knit sweater and tilted backward, searching the room. "Is Tom here?"

His eyebrows drew inward. "No."

Her heart sank and she slouched, angling her head downward. Conlin and Saoirse stepped forward and each placed a palm on her back. Their company made all the difference, processing the harsh news together. She didn't think Tom would go to Mom and Dad's. Where else would he seek refuge if he was in trouble?

"Please, come inside." Jack ushered them into the open concept design with vaulted ceilings and shut the door. "Who are your friends?"

"Conlin Murphy and my daughter, Saoirse." He held out a handshake. "Pleasure to meet ya."

"Welcome, make yourselves at home." Jack shook Conlin's hand and extended his arm toward the living room.

Saoirse moved closer and a glint brightened her eyes. "Thomas shared many stories about yer adventures."

Jack laughed, shaking his head. "The way Tommy tells a tale, I'm sure he embellished."

Jeanette patted Jack's forearm. "He learned from the best." A painful chuckle caught in her throat. Everyone closest to Tom appreciated his aggrandized storytelling. "Any ideas where he might've gone?"

"Heritage Trail. He left an hour ago."

Jeanette smacked a palm against her breastbone as a lightness spread throughout her limbs and a gusty breath escaped her lips. "Thank God, he's here."

Conlin drew her into a brief hug and rubbed her biceps. "'Tis grand. The brother's safe."

Jack tugged at his white beard and squinted behind his silver wire-frame glasses. "Aw Love, I told him to let you know he was staying for an extended visit. Although I'm not surprised, it's just like Tommy." He strolled into the kitchen.

"Yes, his predictable behavior..." Jeanette blew a calming breath to soothe her edginess and headache. Conlin escorted her to a stool at the island counter and stood behind, resting a palm on her shoulder. Saoirse followed and sat beside her in one of the four chairs.

Jack asked, "Can I offer you a drink? Tea, coffee, water, hot cocoa..."

The information about Tom processed in her mind, and she released a thankful exhalation. Finally, after weeks of wondering if he was alive, harrowing events, piecing together the whereabouts of his hideout, traveling to multiple countries and another continent, they found him, even though they still needed to deal with Geron.

"I'll have cocoa," Saoirse said.

"Conlin, Love, a glass of apple wine?" Jack presented a bottle on the granite tabletop. "Tommy bought it from a local winery."

"That'll be fine, t'anks," Conlin said.

"Nothing for me." Vino sounded nice and would relax her nerves, yet nausea swirled in her stomach thinking of their narrow escapes and how they remained on the run while Tom visited wineries without a care in the world. Her muscles tightened and she clenched her jaw.

Jack uncorked the bottle and poured two goblets. "Are you sure you won't join us, Love?"

"Yeah, I'm tired and have a headache," she said, and a smile wavered. "Just spending time here brings me joy."

Jack's eyes twinkled, and he cleared his throat. "Let me get a hot chocolate for the young lady and we'll all chat."

The front entry flung open. Tom stepped inside the house and his gaze bounced between them all. Jeanette pulled in a sharp intake of air and held a bottled breath for a second before exhaling.

He dropped his rucksack on the floor. "Did I miss something good?" His cheeky grin widened, flashing his white, straight teeth.

Jeanette huffed, crossed her arms over her chest and rolled her eyeballs. Typical Tom, downplaying a serious situation.

Saoirse hopped from her seat. "I'm glad yer safe." She stared up at him and a rose color crowned her cheeks.

"Sirsh, I wasn't aware you were coming to New Hampshire." He tapped her head. "It's nice to see you here."

Saoirse lifted her chin, facing Tom. "We had no choice, t'anks to you."

Jeanette clasped her hands, resisting the temptation to clap and cheer for Saoirse's impressive bravado. Given enough time around Tom the charm wore off for everyone. She observed Conlin hiding a chortle behind the wineglass.

Tom ambled toward the kitchen and extended a handshake to Conlin. "Good to see you, my friend."

He accepted the offer. "How're things, lad?"

"Great, couldn't be better." Tom patted his arm. He spun around, strolling past her chair, messing her curls and continued to the sink. "Hey Nettie, what brings you all out to Jack's house?"

She groaned, slapped her palms onto the counter, and launched upward to her feet. "Are you joking? We've been searching for you."

Tom paid little attention and filled a water bottle. "I know. Another rescue mission." Tom flashed a smirk and looked at Jack for validation.

A stern countenance pressed Jack's lips into a fine line. "You need to take this seriously."

Tom moseyed over to Jeanette and pulled her into a side hug. "I appreciate the gesture, but why did you travel to Kinsale? I left weeks ago."

"And disappeared." She bent away from his sweaty shirt, scrunching her face.

"I always go off the grid after an expedition."

"How can you act flippant about everything?" Years of suppressing her frustration bubbled to a volcanic eruption, flinging her hands skyward. "You're in trouble and put us all in danger because of your obsession with the stones."

"Net, why are you upset?"

"Don't pretend to be naïve." She pointed a stiff finger at his throat, and he took a step backward. "We all trusted you. The Murphys welcomed you into their home." Her voice raised an octave and squeaked. "They forced us onto a private plane at gunpoint to Quebec, and we risked our lives making an emergency landing on the St. Lawrence River. We've endured attacks, threats and I was in a car accident this morning, courtesy of your co-workers." A tightness pinched her esophagus, breathing through the ache.

A pained look torqued his mouth downward. "I... I get it and I'm sorry." He crashed into a dining chair across from her, combing his fingers through his hair. "What can I do to set it right?"

"Take responsibility for your actions."

Tom winched himself from his seat and approached Conlin. "I apologize for the things you've suffered on account of my choices." Conlin gave him a simple nod, and he peeked at Saoirse. "Please forgive me, Sirsh. I'd hate for anything horrible to happen to you."

"You're a bleedin' dope ya," she drawled in a strong Dublin accent.

Lighthearted laughter barreled out of him, inclining his head in consensus. "You got me."

Jeanette blinked a few extra times to clear her watery vision. The interaction between Tom and Saoirse reminded her of their own teasing when they were kids. Of course, Tom still had his moments of acting childish.

He returned his attention to her with pleading eyes. "Ha nåde."

"I'll think about it." Jeanette folded her arms and arched an eyebrow, figuring he would invoke Grandma's teachings.

"What does that mean?" Saoirse scrunched her face.

"It's the Norwegian word for mercy," Tom said. "Grandma Rodena created the family tradition of using the phrase whenever an offense caused grief to someone, requiring the offender to request forgiveness and rejecting the plea wasn't an option, at least not when she stood between us, accentuating her tall, strong stature. After accepting the settlement, she sealed the agreement with an offering of our favorite buttery Kringla cookies."

"The only other time Tom pleaded nåde was when the authorities almost arrested us at the Chiquihuite Caves in

Mexico," Jeanette said. "This situation goes beyond a mistake or a poor decision. Lives are on the line."

"Grandma would consider it applicable to this situation."

Yes, Grandma would agree and insist on having mercy. Theatrical groaning strained the sinews in her neck. "Oh, all right." She curved her fingers into a fist and socked him in the arm harder than a playful jest. "And you owe me a cookie."

"Splendid." Jack set a cup of cocoa on a coaster for Saoirse. "I've refereed Love and Tommy since they were children." He winked and served a platter of assorted vegetables, crackers, and a variety of cheeses.

"Why do ya call her Love?" Saoirse sipped her hot chocolate.

"It's her name, Jeanette LaVonne."

Saoirse shrugged, wrinkling her nose, and popped a marshmallow into her mouth. "Not much of a story."

"She's here for the stories." Jeanette bit into a flakey cracker.

"Ah, I see." Jack hunched his posture, supporting his elbows on the countertop. "Well, I've always called her by first and middle name. When Tommy was little, he heard it as Jeanette *Love on* instead of LaVonne."

"Until the age of nine." Jeanette peered over her shoulder, waiting for the kettle to brew herbal tea. They all laughed, and Tom flicked a gaze upward.

"My wife, Geneva, thought the term was so sweet that she adopted the nickname Love for Jeanette. After she passed, I continued referring to her as Love." Jack's voice faltered. "How did I do? I haven't told any stories in a while. They've heard all my tales."

"Nice one!" Saoirse said.

"You never fail, Jack. I'm heading upstairs for a shower," Tom said.

Jeanette dunked a tea sachet in heated water. "Wait, we need to discuss Geron, the stones, and—"

"I know and we will, after dinner."

"We were going to my house."

Tom paused and scratched his head. "It'll be late."

Jack leaned against the mocha-color sofa. "You're all welcome to sleep here tonight. I've plenty of space."

Tom stopped at the bottom of the steps. "You figure it out." He climbed halfway up the staircase and halted. "Conlin, there's a guestroom with two full-sized beds."

Jeanette directed her attention to Conlin and observed his reaction. "What do you think?"

"Em, you've been through a lot and should take it easy. You'll keep at it, but at least you won't need to drive."

Again, he considered her needs and feelings first. Reflecting on his thoughtful gestures and expressions warmed her insides. "I was wondering what's best for you and Saoirse."

"As usual, livin' up to yer nickname, Love."

Jeanette angled her chin downward, hiding her stare behind her lowered eyelashes, and a warming sensation flourished throughout her core.

"Seriously, you're my OTP, the one true pairing." Saoirse snapped her arms straight, bending her wrists out and pushing her hands downward. "Yiz better make it happen, or I'm going to die."

A lightness lifted her heart, sharing Saoirse's belief, hoping everything would work out for them to explore the prospects of a romantic relationship. Jeanette's gaze darted toward him, and he glanced across the room.

"Ah..." Conlin stalled the conversation. He curved his torso and faced Saoirse, widening his eyes. "Is that so?"

Saoirse flipped her hair, and a quiet laugh shuddered her body. "We're staying, yeah? I'll get the bags." She hurried out of the doorway.

Conlin finished the rest of his drink in one gulp and set the glass on the counter. "Em, I'll help Cricket and grab your handbag."

"Great, thanks."

He aimed for the door and spun around on the heel of his shoe. "How're ya feeling about the brother?"

"We found him safe and sound."

"God is good." Conlin raised palms heavenward and walked outside.

Indeed, she thanked God for protecting Tom and keeping them all alive. However, besides herself, Lord only knew how muddled her emotions became when she discovered he remained sheltered and escaped distressing incidents while they endured the consequences of his poor judgment.

Jeanette preferred dwelling on the awkward and delightful moment with Conlin after Saoirse's comment.

Daydreaming about their future sounded better than studying stones and facing the aftereffects of Geron's involvement. At least the worst was over for the evening and nothing else could go wrong. She'd enjoy the company, supper, family, deciphering relics, a good night's rest in the serene White Mountains and sweet dreams of being the one true pairing with Conlin.

TWENTY-SEVEN

Tom trudged downstairs with messy towel-dried hair, looking the same as he did in his teens. Jeanette placed a hand over her heart, placating the expanding feeling in her chest. He drove her crazy, like siblings and all family members do to each other. No matter how many times he continued to drag her into his fiascoes, she would show up for him in any way he needed. Although this time the situation was different. Tom crossed the line when his careless conduct involved innocent people, and she felt stronger about protecting the Murphys than running to her brother's rescue.

Tom strolled across the room and glanced in her direction. "You're still upset?"

"It's been thirty minutes and the seriousness of our conditions extends beyond dangers we've encountered in the past. So, yeah, I'm irritated."

He stood in front of her and placed his palms on her shoulders, staring her square in the face. "I understand, and we'll work it out. There's nothing to worry about, I promise."

Jack clapped his hands together to break the tension in the room. "Let's plan supper and I'll go shopping." He perused the kitchen cabinets, jotting down ingredients on a grocery list, and pulled out the crock pot. "I'll start the vegetable stock and run to the store."

Jeanette hopped from the dining chair, eager to avoid another confrontation with Tom. "Please allow me to prepare it, then you can get going."

"I will assist you." Conlin rose from a barstool and leaned against the countertop.

"That'd be nice, thanks."

"Wonderful." Jack washed and wiped his hands on a dish towel.

Tom ran his fingers through his damp hair from root to tip into a purposeful, untidy style. "I'll ride into town with you."

"I'd enjoy tagging along, too." Saoirse sprang from the sofa and peeked at her dad.

"I'm happy to entertain more company," Jack said.

Conlin said, "G'wan so."

"Thanks, Da." She sashayed toward the entry and slipped on her combat boots.

Jack grabbed his keys. "Don't worry, we'll be back soon." Tom and Saoirse followed behind, closing the door.

Jeanette flashed a quick look at Conlin and gathered various vegetables. "Are you able to peel potatoes?"

"You're questioning if an Irishman named Murphy can handle peeling spuds?" Conlin tilted his chin toward his collarbone, gazing at her from the tops of his eyes. "It's our nickname."

Jeanette laughed and tied an apron around her waist. "This reminds me of when we were at your house."

He joined her in the kitchen. "Seems forever ago." His voice trailed off and sounded distant.

She shouldn't have mentioned Kinsale and figured he longed for home. "Sorry for the extended stay in America and the slow process of returning to Ireland."

"We've done our best." Conlin nudged her arm and smiled. "You've made it easier to forget everything I'd usually miss."

Her mouth twitched, attempting to suppress a grin, yet she failed and peered out of the corner of her eye. "And you're making it harder to watch you leave."

Conlin cocked his head to the side and moved close enough for her to lean into a kiss. She resisted the urge, since reality hit too soon during the last intimate moment they shared. It wouldn't be fair to him, after explaining her recent breakup with Brian. Sentimentalities ran high, convoluting a mix of excitement and chaos. Could she even trust her judgment? Jeanette had little success with romantic relationships, and they didn't get off to the greatest start—Tom causing trouble, her talking to Geron, taking the Celtic Stone, leaving a note and taking off...

Jeanette stared at carrots on the cutting board. Feelings for Conlin persisted, burrowing deep and no matter how she tried curbing emotions, her foolish heart prevailed. Great, now she'd have Steve Perry's song stuck in her head. Yep, a 1980s rock ballad summed up her love life.

"Lost in thought?"

"No, thinking of a song."

"Happens to me often. How does it go?"

"You'll know the lyrics. It's by One and The Endless." She tapped a finger on her lips, recalling the melody and sang, "The way you bend me, breaking my heart... I'm in pieces and sinking in the River Lee..."

"Deadly tune." Conlin chuckled under his breath, elbowing her in good humor. "After the day, you're mighty craic altogether."

Heat from the crock pot and his flirting increased her internal temperature. "Despite all the challenges, we always have great fun. The craic was ninety."

Conlin angled his face toward her and raised a brow. "Saoirse's teaching you the slang?"

"How am I doing?"

"Keep working on it."

Laughter rang out across the space, and they finished preparing the veggies. "I'll check on it in forty-five minutes." She set the dial to simmer.

"Sit on the couch and relax." Jeanette removed her apron and left the kitchen. "I'm going to search for something upstairs and make the beds in the guestroom." She turned at the foot of the steps.

Conlin crossed his arms over his chest and bewilderment whittled into his mien. "Do you ever stop? I haven't seen you take a break once, and it wouldn't surprise me if ya work through the night."

He did see and notice every detail about her. The awareness triggered a physical reaction, and her belly became a sinking stone. "I like to manage my responsibilities and assure it gets completed."

"Ye're not alone in figuring out the lot and there're people who want to assist you."

"Oh right, Tom has done a great job so far resolving the issue." She refrained from mentioning Brian's lack of support.

"He might've discovered something about the stones. Ye haven't discussed the matter, and he doesn't seem worried."

Jeanette stretched her backbone to its full length and lost her footing on the steps. "It's easy for him to remain calm about the situation when he's been stopping by wineries, taking nature walks, and avoiding the problems he created."

"Sounds as if you lack confidence in him, or do I detect a hint of jealousy?"

She gripped the railing tighter, feeling an itchiness crawl across her skin. "Me, jealous of my younger brother?" Jeanette discharged a grumbled exhalation and glanced away. "Ridiculous..."

He bowed his head to view her face. "'Tisn't the first time I noticed."

"If you want to hear the truth, our parents, friends, colleagues, all praise Tom for everything. You name it and Tom's the number one guy, regardless of the cost to anyone else or if I've bailed him out of jams." She pulled in a taxing breath. "And if that wasn't enough, I am labeled the dramatic, too sensitive, controlling and overbearing sister." A rough grunt reverberated in her throat. "Tom's smart, funny and I love him. After all, he is my brother. But sometimes..." Slumping onto the banister, her hair bun flopped against her forehead.

"You're tired of being the responsible sibling, since it's expected of you, without so much of a thanks, and Thomas' carefree lifestyle is simply whimsical to everyone when he's acting the maggot."

"Yes!" She flung her head upward and flinched, tilting backward an inch. "You're the first to understand what I'm saying."

"I know a t'ing or two about family."

"How do you cope having so many siblings?"

"It requires a lot of patience and living in a different county helps. At gatherings I just nod and grin."

"If only it were that simple."

"C'mere, it'll all be grand." Conlin inched closer and placed his palm over her hand, resting on the handrail. "Now"—he gazed into her eyes—"what can I do for you?"

When was the last time someone asked about her needs? A tremble dispersed through her limbs. "Will you help me look for a book in the attic?"

"Whatever you need." He brushed tresses from her brow and swiped a gentle thumb across the bump on her forehead.

Jeanette lowered her eyelashes and tugged the hair tie holding her bun, allowing curls to fall free before heading up the steps. Conlin followed behind her upstairs. Climbing the last of two staircases, Jeanette dragged her heavy feet until they reached the attic door. A coolness rippled along her flesh as she twisted the doorknob and flipped on the light switch. She adjusted her vision and blinked, noting the few changes in the room.

Jack cleared most of the clutter and removed special furniture pieces. A garment rack of Geneva's memorable clothing items hung on display, and an additional floor lamp provided more lighting to illuminate the space. Jeanette observed the new Victorian style medallion-print wallpaper in natural hues. The musty odor mingled with a fresh-cut apple fragrance diffuser.

Conlin sauntered the perimeter, analyzing watercolor paintings of New Hampshire's Rye Beach, Mount Washington, and Lake Winnipesaukee hanging on the walls. "Excellent artwork. Why hide 'em in here?"

Twiddling her thumbs, her eyesight fixed on the floorboards, and she peeked at Conlin through flittering lashes. "By request of the artist."

He squinted and leaned closer to the signature in the right corner. "J.L. Hillestad." Conlin shot a glance, widening his eyes. "You?"

Jeanette slinked down and curved her shoulders inward. "The framed painting of Jack's house, above the fireplace downstairs, was a gift and the only one displayed for others to view."

"I enjoy learning more about yer life and all the aspects of who ya are."

Jeanette grazed her teeth against her lip and her gaze darted to the opposite end of the room until settling on a familiar sketch. She jolted and proceeded toward the drawing. "Here it is."

"The book?"

"The artifact that started it all." Picking up the frame, she stared at the inciting image and a chill bulleted through her spine. Seemed only yesterday she and Tom snuck into the attic and discovered the relic. Now he had the actual stone on the premises.

Conlin moved beside her and peered at the picture. "Interesting similarities to the Celtic Stone and obvious differences."

"All the stones share a likeness in design, etchings of their gods, and some have symbols representing specific provisions the land supplied."

He walked toward an oak bookshelf and browsed the hardcovers. "Em, here's a title, *The Mysterious Stones of the Ancients.*"

Jeanette positioned the framed picture on the bronze cabriole-leg cabinet and crouched, opening the glass doors. "It might be useful, but we're looking for a type of scrapbook." She retrieved a juniper-green photo album, opened the ring binder, and perused the pages. "The book contains photographs, documentations and written notes from my great-grandfather, Sjur Hillestad."

Conlin finished searching the shelves and joined her, leaning over her shoulder. "We need the blue photo album, documenting their expeditions in Norway." She flipped another page, seeing a picture and an inscription scribbled on the opposite side. "Looks similar to the linear script I read in Dingle. The entire book records their journey in Ireland."

"Perhaps it has information about the Celtic Stone?"

"Maybe, we'll bring it downstairs with us." Before closing the book, a phrase copied in Irish caught her attention. "There's an axiom etched into a rock, like the one we stood at on the peninsula. I'll try to pronounce it correctly, iss-too-mu-graw."

Conlin's entire demeanor expressed ardor as he advanced closer and licked his lips. "Is tú mo ghrá, you are my love."

Jeanette inhaled deeply and a quiver ran along her frame. The thumping of her heartbeat vibrated throughout her torso. Yes, he only repeated and translated the words, yet for him to look her straight in the face and speak in a bold, affirming tone, transported her back to when they interlocked their fingers in the hole of the Ogham Stone while he explained the ritual of professing a vow.

Best to play it cool and refrain from taking his comment as a literal declaration of his feelings. But what if she blew her opportunity to express how she felt about him? *Don't wimp out.* "Conlin, I want to say, you are..." His eyes locked her into place, and she lost the nerve. "Helpful."

Real smooth. An awkward laugh skidded through her throat, and she skimmed the room. "I mean, the translation, our conversations, the support, everything..."

He lowered his gaze, slackening his stance and dropped his shoulders. "No bother," he said in a lower pitch than normal.

Jeanette turned away, bearing an ache in her core, and gathered the books. "Tom probably grabbed the scrapbook."

She headed for the exit, and he followed behind, switching the lights off before closing the door. Stopping at a reading nook on the second floor, she arranged the books on a periwinkle pillow-top bench next to a window overlooking a valley of maple, birch, and evergreen trees.

"I'm going to put fresh sheets on the beds." Jeanette opened the linen closet and selected a stack of bedding sets. She shut the cabinets and Conlin stepped forward, pressing the linens against her stomach. He scooped the heap from her arms and the brush of his hand across her waist sent an electric surge outward from her middle.

"Since ya find me useful."

"You're more than a helper to me, so much more, and I believe you know..."

His sight roamed her features, and lines bunched over the bridge of his nose. "There's a mutual fondness between us." He shut his eyelids for a minute, blowing an audible breath from his mouth. "I'm trying to stay practical."

"About your feelings or the circumstances?"

"All of it, the situation. 'Tis impossible to remain sensible, concerning matters of the heart."

A weightlessness dispersed within her body and an adrenaline rush quickened her pulse. He confessed she touched his heart, and the delicate subject required the right words. Jeanette twirled a lock around her finger.

"Maintaining a long-distance friendship makes sense, but I'm an idealist, and hope we'll deepen our relationship because I want you in my everyday life." She emphasized the certainty in her tone before losing courage, then pivoted on her foot, evading his response, and aimed for the guestroom.

Okay, she admitted it, and now he knew her feelings. She peeped over her shoulder at him standing in the hall, clutching the bedding in his hands and staring past her. Jeanette stepped into the bedroom and focused on a framed cross-stitched inspirational quote hanging on the wall.

For love is as strong as death. Song of Songs 8:6.

Jack and Geneva's marriage modeled a sacrificial love shown through actions, a true partnership of equal esteem and an unbreakable union, beyond mortality. Jeanette prayed for years to experience the same devotion in a relationship and believed she found it with Conlin.

"How'd we work it out?"

Jeanette spun in his direction, and he braced a forearm on the doorframe. She took a few faltering steps and collected the sheets, dumping them on the first bed. "I-I don't know." The building emotions cracked her voice. "I will make the effort; whatever it takes to not lose our chance to see all we could be together."

A sudden weakness spread throughout her extremities, and she expelled a burst of air after holding her breath. At times, he ogled at her with an intense longing in his eyes, as if he desired to run off together to a secluded destination. The mixed signals may have arisen from her own fantasies. No, she wasn't delusional about their intimate moments. Even if they had denied themselves a kiss, a powerful connection existed and neither of them possessed the strength to break the bond.

"Em, sure, we'll take it slow and see how t'ings progress. I need to go home, get settled back into the daily routine, ensure Saoirse doesn't suffer psychological trauma from the events, and explain the mess to her mother." He scraped a hand over his mouth and released a stout exhale. "God, give me strength."

Jeanette snatched the sheets off the pile and slipped the fitted corner over the mattress. "Yeah, sounds sensible." Her tone changed to quiet, uncertain, and almost unrecognizable. "Keeping our heads without the risk of losing our hearts." All her feelings were best expressed in writing and why she always left a note. Her foolish heart didn't heed the warning.

TWENTY-EIGHT

Conlin placed the comforter on a chair adjacent to the dresser with a sudden weakening and feeling the need to sit. Jeanette embodied passion, and he extinguished her fire. No person ever spoke to him in that way, with blatant honesty and vulnerability, revealing complete trust. The boldness of her confession caught him off guard, and he struggled to process his feelings. He grabbed the flannel material, pulling on the opposite corner and assessed her receptiveness as she hid behind her tresses.

"If there's a better solution for us, y'know what I mean?" he said.

"I understand."

Once again, she didn't comprehend. How could she when he kept his sentiments concealed? It took every ounce of restraint to hold back from showing her by yanking her into his arms and kissing her madly. He couldn't surrender his heart now, when emotions were difficult to sort out. They needed time apart, differentiating the rush of adrenaline, excitement, and the thrill of it all without entangling themselves in a whirlwind romance. He desired a long-lasting relationship and realized she did too.

They formed a deep bond, anam cara—a soul friend, beyond sentimental foolishness. He aspired to build and continue strengthening that part of their rapport before delving into obvious natural desires.

Conlin reached across to tuck the fabric under the mattress and swept his palm against the backside of her hand. She froze, glancing up, and the whole of his being yearned to convince her without words. Even his fingers craved to touch and grasp her in his hands.

"I've got it," she said.

Conlin moved back and grabbed a flat sheet off the stack. He pivoted on his heel and bumped into Jeanette at the edge of the bed. She clutched the iron bedframe for balance, and he instinctively reacted by wrapping his arms around her waistline. Pressing their bodies together, he anchored his sight on her and she gasped, lifting her chin upward.

An inch from her, he gulped the saliva filling his mouth and his gaze wandered across her features. Her shiny lips slightly parted and her eyelids drew shut. Perspiration broke on his hairline, hovering close enough to feel the brush of her skin against his, sparking an inferno. A hotness engulfed him, and his muscles tensed as the banging of his heartbeat ached for relief.

He jerked his head backward and straightened, hauling in a harsh intake of air. His heavy limbs slid from her hips, and he staggered two steps, slipping on the hardwood floor, and smacked his ankle against the bedpost.

An incredulous stare widened her eyes. "What's wrong?"

Conlin scrunched his face and put a fist against his pursed lips to hold in a slew of curse words. "Em…" Bending his knee, he hoisted his foot and tilted forward, rubbing his heel. "Knocked meself against the bed."

"Can I do anything to help?" She advanced toward him and reached out her hand.

He erected his posture and outstretched his arm to maintain a distance. "I'll just wait for the feeling to subside."

"For a minute, I thought you wanted to kiss me again." A deep rose color crept up her neck and spread outward to her ears.

Lord knows he fought and wrestled with the constant urge. He treasured their heartfelt kiss and the moments they embraced. Right now, he struggled to repress his bodily response to her and growing attraction. *Stop thinking about it.* Perhaps if they had abstained from shifting last night, their emotions wouldn't have heightened, yet the thought of never kissing Jeanette... His heart sank, pondering their actions on whether they should've denied themselves a kiss. No, he'd always cherish the intimacy they shared, even if it meant suffering the repercussions of heartbreak.

"Better not get carried away," he said.

She upraised her chin and stroked her neck, then patted her breastbone. "It's fine. I believe more than physical chemistry exists between us."

Conlin flickered his eyelids, despising himself for hurting her feelings on too many occasions. If he hugged and comforted her, ensuring everything would work out, then maybe she'd be receptive to his quandary. Yet consoling her wasn't an option, at least not while they were standing beside the bed.

"Banféinní—"

The timer buzzed on the crock pot downstairs. She twisted a curl round her finger and darted a glance. "Please finish putting the sheets on the beds, and I'll check on the broth."

"Sure t'ing."

She hesitated in the doorway, gave a clipped nod, and walked out of the bedroom. Conlin's head rolled forward, and he sighed aloud. His reply to her declarations about a hope for their future and exploring their progressing relationship crushed her, just as he did in several instances with Kera and Saoirse. He massaged the burning sensation in his chest. He'd prove to Jeanette he prayed for the same things she did and given time, they would flourish into the ultimate one true pairing.

Twenty minutes later, Conlin joined Jeanette downstairs and stood at the bottom step. The awkwardness lingered in silence, and he wanted to kick himself for ruining the remaining days they had left together. She poured two cups of tea and set them on the table in the main room near the fireplace.

"There's a cup for you." Sitting in a chair, she propped her feet onto an ottoman, sipped her drink, and placed the mug on a coaster. She hugged herself, wrapping her sweater tighter around her torso and rubbed her arms.

"T'anks for the cuppa." He ambled across the middle of the living area and peeked at her out of the corner of his eye. She ignored him and refrained from making visual contact.

If he contemplated his replies before blurting comments about getting back to a life prior to meeting her, then maybe he would be sitting beside her, holding her close and keeping her warm.

"A bit of a chill in here." His remark covered a literal and figurative meaning, considering the dropping temperature and Jeanette freezing him out. Conlin set his drink on the center table and scanned the area. "I'll collect wood and get a fire started."

Trudging toward the entrance, he gripped the knob and the door swung open, almost striking his nose. Thomas and Saoirse entered, carrying firewood in their arms.

She blew a bubble with her chewing-gum and dumped a pile of sticks in his hands. "Howya?"

"Ah, y'know yerself."

Examining his expression, she peered behind him and raised an eyebrow. "What did ya say now?"

Cricket picked up on the dynamics and tensities between him and Jeanette. He opened his mouth to speak and backed from the door.

Thomas wedged in the center of them, balancing five logs and squinted at Conlin. "Everything okay?"

"Middling." Conlin followed him to the hearth and positioned the sticks into a woodpile. He peeked at Jeanette, and she dodged the line of his sight. A heaviness sagged in his soul, knowing his hurtful words caused her sadness and discomfort. Even Saoirse recognized he had been a complete eejit again.

"Hey Nettie, remember The Village Shoppe we visited as kids?" Thomas poked her biceps to gain her attention. "I bought your favorite vegan tiramisu fudge."

Jeanette angled her head, focusing on the flickering flames, and he assumed she escaped far away from him in her thoughts. If only she would allow him another chance to explain he wanted her to fill all the days of his life.

"Anything the matter?" Thomas said.

"Oh, it's nothing. I'm tired," she said.

Why was she cross with him? He didn't reject her or say the suggestion of them having a future together was an unrealistic, romantic notion, although someone needed to sacrifice more than the other to make it work. And Jeanette declared she would do whatever was necessary to realize the depths of their feelings.

"Where's Jack?" she asked.

"Grabbing the groceries, I'll go help." Thomas hurried out the door.

Conlin grazed his nape and glimpsed at the ceiling. He made a hames of it and had to do or say something to repair the broken connection. The silent treatment became unbearable, and she crucified his heart. Saoirse unloaded a sack in the kitchen, and he moved near Jeanette.

"Tá brón orm." He drew closer and kneeled beside the armchair. Her mannerisms reflected his same intermixed emotions. "I'm sorry," he whispered and placed a palm on her forearm, resting on the cushion. "You must know I want—"

Thomas burst through the front entry. "Guess who arrived right after us?" Jack followed behind a man, holding a briefcase and an overnight carrier.

"Jeannie." He set the bags on the floor next to a coat rack and strode over to Jeanette.

Conlin climbed to his feet and stepped aside. Her gaze bounced from him to the other fella wearing a three-piece-suit.

The dark-haired man lurked beside the seat with stiff movements, to keep his pressed clothes from wrinkling, and touched her shoulder. "Babe, it's good to see you."

"Brian, what are you doing here? I already explained that I'd be home in a couple of days."

"When you never responded to my texts or voicemail, I figured you'd rather see me instead." He coiled his fingers into a tight, possessive latch on her hand, pulling upward and kissing the inside of her wrist. "You must've missed me."

Conlin cringed as his gut churned and he diverted his stare, turning away to avoid an up close and personal viewing of whatever was going on between them. Strolling toward Cricket, he joined her at the kitchen counter and elbowed her gently in the ribs. "Well, that puts the kibosh on me chances of being part of your OTP."

Saoirse flicked her head upward and peeped over a shoulder, scouting the degree of his dilemma. "'Tisn't the end. Don't give up." She patted his biceps and walked to the sofa. "Can I meet yer man?"

Jeanette did a double take and stood, addressing Cricket. "Of course, Saoirse and Conlin Murphy." She fixed her eyesight on him during the introduction, and he welcomed her attention. "Please allow me to introduce—"

"Brian Adler, nice meeting you." He jutted his hand forward, underscoring an arrogant pose.

Conlin considered the offer for half a minute before receiving his handshake. "How're you?"

"Good and thanks for keeping an eye on my Jeannie." Brian hooked an arm around her waist.

Conlin craned his neck and inhaled a calming breath to ease rising strife. "She's quite capable of taking care of herself. In fact, she saved us from things going arseways more than once." He caught her reaction as she dipped her chin, hiding a smile.

"That's my girl." Brian gushed in a condescending tone and pulled her tighter into a side hug.

Conlin curved his hands into fists, then uncoiled his fingers, jamming them inside his pockets to keep from knocking the smirk off his face. He felt more aggression toward Brian than Geron at the moment.

Brian petted Jeanette's hair, flattening the lovely fullness of her curls. "It's noticeable that you've been through a lot. Turn in early." He sneered and visually scrutinized her. "You look worn out, and you're expected at work by the end of next week."

Jeanette stretched her torso, avoiding his touch. "Tom and I have research to finish tonight. Please, excuse me." She slipped out from under his clasp, and her detectible annoyance with Brian seemed to exceed the letdown she experienced from him half an hour ago. "Saoirse, want to help me in the kitchen?" Cricket nodded and followed Jeanette.

"Jeannie, be a dear and make my usual drink," Brian hollered across the room.

Great, now he was stuck having to chat with him. Conlin cracked his knuckles and loosened his clenched jaw. "Jeanette mentioned ye work together."

Brian scoffed. "She's a curator of antiquities. I'm vice-chair on the board of trustees for several New England historical societies. I oversee the organization for multiple locations, so we're affiliated in the same field, but far from co-workers."

"I see, her position requires a higher education."

Brian eyeballed him up and down. "So, how are things in Glocca Morra? Are you able to make a decent living?"

"Ah, sure. When I'm not out chasing leprechauns for their pots of gold, I am the director of operations at Inland Fisheries Ireland."

"Here's your scotch sour." Jeanette passed him an old-fashioned glass.

He shot a nasty glare at Conlin, then turned and faced Jeanette. "Did you squeeze fresh lemon?"

"I always do."

Brian pecked her cheek and Jeanette stiffened her upper body. She looked in the opposite direction until her gaze settled on him and Conlin found himself in the comfort of familiarity, an infinite green of abundant land in her eyes... home.

Her cheeks darkened to the shade of a pink rose. "Tá brón orm."

Her Irish apology enhanced her temperament, yet she had nothing to justify when she was the one being honest and risking everything.

"Why do you keep speaking double Dutch?" Brian said.

"Tá sé mahogany gas pipes." She fought against laughing, tautening her mouth.

Ah, there she was, the woman after his own heart. Teasing Brian with the meaningless saying, combining Irish and English that phonetically sounds like Irish to someone who doesn't speak the language. They'd be mighty grand altogether. Plenty of obstacles remained, although he trusted they could overcome anything after all they achieved as a pair. Conlin was a bleedin' gombeen for passing up a chance to kiss Jeanette upstairs and never again would he forfeit the gift.

"Cute. Is that supposed to be Gaelic?" Brian said in a flat tone.

"Irish," she said.

Brian downed his liquor and shoved the glass in her hands. "Get me another scotch. I'm washing up before supper."

No wonder she avoided conversations with Brian in person or even on the phone. Why did she tolerate his blatant insults? It appeared she was aware of his conduct since she ended the relationship, but the muppet couldn't take a hint.

The glow of her complexion dimmed, and he wished more than anything to be alone with her and talk. She side-eyed Brian in the hallway, entering the bog and reverted her attentiveness to Conlin. "What would you like?"

He'd like to escort Brian out of the house by force and stand beside her, confessing he guarded his heart in fear of losing her. Now, another man competed for her affections, and his thoughts became as clear as Waterford Crystal. "Em—"

"A beverage or appetizer?"

He rubbed the stubble along his jaw. "Don't trouble yerself. I'm here for you."

They stared at each other like time ceased and the world stopped spinning. He stepped closer to her side, placing a palm on her back, leaning beside her ear. "Go deo, forever."

Her body jolted, then she eased into his caress, angling her head and he lost himself in a wilderness of curls. The brush of her against his flesh stoked a fire in his heart and drew him nearer. If only they had gone to her house instead...

The twisting of a doorknob alerted Conlin, and he stepped backward, creating a space, before Brian returned. He preferred not to cause anymore difficulties for Jeanette since she had enough to manage, regardless of his feelings.

Jeanette's face appeared to shine, and her lashes flew high, revealing the whites of her eyes as if he shared his best kept secret. The lingering gaze pierced his soul and seared his heart, urging him to run out the front door together, hop in the car and take a drive all night long.

"Hey babe, where's my drink?" Brian saw Jeanette holding the empty glass. He glowered at Conlin and moved behind her in a predatory stance, ready to mark his territory.

"I'm going to see how Cricket's doing." Conlin gestured toward Saoirse and spun on his foot. He exhaled aloud, releasing the pressure built up in his chest, and an overwhelming thankfulness for their reconnection surfaced.

Now if only she severed the noose Brian tied around her, strangling her exquisite qualities. In the past two hours, every test of self-control thrown at him required God's supernatural power to endure temptations, trusting he'd overcome adversity and never suffer beyond what he could bear in Christ's strength. He valued Jeanette's judgment and wouldn't overstep or intervene, despite the pain of watching Brian grope and talk down to her.

How did a strong, vivacious, clever woman settle for Brian and his insolence? He had no right to judge and didn't know their past or how it was in the beginning. Still and all, he witnessed what they had become and based on Brian's treatment of her, somewhere during their relationship she seemed to allow him to believe he dominated her actions. Conlin stopped dead in his tracks in the center of the room, recalling his harsh remarks when they first met in Kinsale and moments in Quebec. A few occasions crossed his mind when he blamed her for events out of their control. Sure, she made mistakes and so did he. Moving forward, he would ensure to be mindful of his words and treat Jeanette like she deserved, proving all that she meant to him—the most important person in his life, equal to Cricket.

TWENTY-NINE

Conlin moseyed toward the kitchen and joined Thomas, leaning against the counter. "What's up, lad?"

He welcomed Conlin, tipping his head upward. "Hey, I appreciate everything you've done for me and watching out for Nettie. It wasn't my intention for any of you to be put in danger."

Did anyone know Jeanette? He had few opportunities to protect her, and she managed fine on her own, even succeeding at aiding him and Cricket through their challenges. They wouldn't have got this far without her support and commitment to their established friendship.

"I resolved little. 'Tis yer sister that deserves the credit. At this point, we've mostly been hiding out, and avoiding Geron. And I realize you intended on leading him away from us."

"Thanks." Thomas gave him a pat on the shoulder. "You're a trustworthy person and I can count on you." He lifted a wineglass in a thankful gesture. "Sirsh told me how you flew a plane and made an emergency landing on the river in Quebec. Wicked intense."

"I did my best." Conlin offered a single nod and spotted Jeanette striding across the room. She nudged in the middle of him and Thomas, resting her elbows on the countertop.

"How's dinner coming along? Need any assistance?" she asked.

Jack waved a dismissive hand. "I've got it taken care of. It's about done, maybe another five minutes."

A mix of spices, vegetable stock, pumpkin pie air-freshener, and Jeanette's rosemary scented shampoo filled his senses. The entire vibe of the kitchen area and the surrounding company generated an impression of comfort—a true picture of comradery and family.

Until Brian approached Jeanette from behind, pressing his body close, and placed his hands on her shoulders. A queasiness stirred in Conlin's stomach, and the feeling of serenity disappeared.

Cricket whooshed by carrying a stack of plates, and he spun around. "Let me help." He'd do anything to avoid Brian patronizing and pawing Jeanette. His actions reflected a lack of respect, and she deserved better.

Everyone gathered at the dining table. Sure enough, Brian sat across from him, and he would have to focus on eating his meal to prevent interaction.

"Enjoy." Jeanette placed a basket of fresh cut bread in the center of the tabletop. She moved her eyes in a slow arc, settling on him for a second before her rapt attention hopped between the others and landed on her brother. "I'm grateful we're all together."

Thomas raised his glass for a salute. "I'll drink to that, cheers."

The group said in unison, "Cheers!"

Jack positioned a ladle inside a large pot beside his place setting. He picked up a white ceramic bowl and scooped a helping into the dish, passing it to his right. "For Saoirse, please."

Conlin handed the hot stew to Cricket, and Jack filled another helping, giving it to Brian for Jeanette. "Gentlemen, help yourselves."

Jack's traditions reminded him of his family and cultural customs in Ireland. Conlin observed Saoirse's relaxed appearance and her face glowed. She needed this time in the White Mountains, a type of retreat. The peaceful moment faded when he caught sight of Brian. Conlin eased the stiffness in his jaw a fraction before taking a bite of his food. It was going to be a long night.

They finished their supper after suffering through Brian's nonstop discussions about work and Conlin made forced conversation whenever he thought it was necessary. He preferred to eat in silence, rather than hear Brian speak.

The gob on him and words spewing from Brian's mouth sounded all too familiar. Often, his chats with Kera during their years together centered on his job, since it validated his self-worth, or at least he believed that skewed thinking for most of his life. He enjoyed his career, applying his best efforts, yet discovered value in all aspects of living, and esteemed the recent progress made in his relationships with Cricket and Jeanette.

Brian turned toward Jack and wiped his hands on a napkin. "Thanks for accommodating my unannounced arrival."

"Not a problem. I always welcome Jeanette's friends into my home."

"She's been out of town for too long and has obligations at work. There's also an important fundraiser coming up next week."

"I'm sure you missed her companionship," Jack said.

"I don't need to tell her... she already knows." Brian nudged her arm. She sank into the seat and blotches of red erupted on her cheeks.

Conlin gulped his water to wash the bitter taste from his mouth. Jeanette adjusted her torso, leaning away from Brian and her gaze pinged to him. He didn't know how much longer he could take watching her suffer. His upper body hunched forward with an overall cumbersome feeling, and he slanted his head to the side, offering a thin-lipped smile.

Jack stood from his seat, clapped, and rubbed his palms together. "Who's ready for the dessert Saoirse selected?"

Cricket popped up, grabbed both their plates, and strolled into the kitchen. Conlin rose from his chair and collected a couple of dishes since he reached his limit with Brian.

"We'll pass on the desserts. We have a lot of catching up to do." He tugged Jeanette's sleeve and smirked.

She grunted aloud and yanked her arm from his grip. "You never listen to me." Her tone elevated. Everyone stopped in their tracks and remained quiet. Brian expanded his eyelids wide, and his mouth hung suspended. He took stock of her, blinking a few extra times.

anymore?" Jeanette moved her hands in a quick motion, back and forth between them, indicating their relationship.

"Sweetie, we'll go discuss it privately." He fumed through gnashed teeth.

"Later." Fire glittered in her eyes. "Tom and I have crucial work to finish."

"Well, if it's more important than us..." He guzzled the last shot of his watered-down scotch sour and slammed the glass on the table.

Jack carried in a round serving dish and Cricket followed, bringing the small plates. "Everything's better with pie."

"I agree. It looks delicious." Thomas brought in porcelain cups and the coffee pot on a tray.

The rigidity in her frame dissolved, and her body shrank. Conlin wished he could sit beside her, give her a consoling hug, and be the listener she needed. Above her eyeline he saw the shallow dip of a frown, and he hoped his expression conveyed all he was thinking. The slow blink and gradual curve of her lips communicated that she knew.

Brian shifted and relaxed into his seat. Poor fella, Conlin almost felt bad for him. Almost. He wouldn't want to be on the receiving end of Jeanette's displeasure and a breakup conversation. He already experienced the flip side and the emotional complexities of discussing the hopeful prospect of a relationship. A lightness uplifted his chest with the assurance of building a future together instead of going their separate ways.

After a double portion of warm, maple-pecan pie and coffee, Conlin reclined in his chair. He rested a palm on Cricket's shoulder. "We should get settled in our room."

"Da, I'm not tired."

Conlin gestured with an eye roll, signaling toward Brian. "I'm sure we're leaving early in the marra."

He tossed a questioning look to Jeanette for confirmation.

Nodding at his comment, her appearance brightened. "Good idea. It's about a two-hour drive to Moultonborough and there are a couple of stops I think you'll like on the way to my place."

"Excira!" Cricket said.

Brian cleared his throat and stepped closer to Jeanette. "They're staying at your house?"

"Yes, they need to be in Boston for a flight on Friday." She squared her shoulders and the cords in her neck were on prime display.

"Then, shouldn't they stay with Tom?"

Jeanette tossed a hand heavenward. "No, I signed an affidavit at the Irish Embassy, verifying they are my guests, and I'd take responsibility for their timely departure to Ireland." She turned her attention to Saoirse and Conlin. "Plus, they're my friends and I enjoy their company."

Brian glowered at Conlin and loosened his tie. "Fine, whatever. I was just thinking of what's easiest for everyone."

He looked in the opposite direction and scoped out the surrounding space. Conlin understood Brian's predicament, and it seemed apparent that Jeanette never told him they already slept in the same bedroom more than once. Jeanette proved through her actions there was never a need to worry about any indiscretions. Even if Brian was aware of an inevitable breakup in his future, he imagined the difficulty of watching Jeanette leave with another fella.

In fairness, he hoped to steer clear of seeing Brian escort Jeanette into a room alone. Although she explained her intentions and expressed her feelings, he had trouble trusting Brian. Conlin would be man enough to admit the problem originated from his own insecurities and not Jeanette's trustworthiness.

Cricket grabbed her handbags. "Night everyone."

Conlin observed Jeanette's movements collecting plates. Curls fell forward, brushing against her cheeks, as she sneaked a peek at him, and her lips twitched into a slight pucker. A yearning to cuddle her overcame him and he turned away, spotting Brian's pointed glare.

"Have a good night." Conlin directed Cricket upstairs. "We're the second guestroom on the left, and the bog is on the right." He ran a palm along the wood railing, climbing the staircase and fought the urge to behold Jeanette before reaching the top.

Saoirse opened the door and dropped her bag on the floor. Last time he was in the bedroom, he held Jeanette in his arms, and missed his opportunity to kiss her again, before Brian arrived. Principles kept him from indulging in the idea of kissing Jeanette, while her ex remained delusional about their fate and stayed under the same roof. Waiting proved the biggest test for him to overcome.

Conlin crashed onto the bed closest to the doorway and Saoirse selected the other near the window. He scrubbed his palms over his face and massaged his brow, relieving the pressure building in his skull.

"What do ya think of Brian?" Cricket flipped her locks to one side.

He squinted at her and breathed a laugh through his mouth. "Ye're codding me." She had to be pulling his leg. "He's a bit self-obsessed and disrespectful toward Jeanette."

"Ah, she can do better." She grinned and tilted her head, braiding her hair. "Like me dad."

Conlin flopped backward onto the mattress, crossing his hands over his chest and released a gusty exhale. "Jeanette told me that she wants our relationship to progress beyond a friendship."

"Yup the sesh!"

Inside the deepest part of his heart, he shared Cricket's excitement, yet he'd continue to protect himself and remain realistic about obstructions along their path. "I told her we need to settle into the daily routine at home and we'd see how things go." He peeked at her reaction out of the corner of his eye.

She slouched her shoulders and scrunched her face, crinkling her nose. "Isn't a romantic reply, but she knows you don't express yerself well. Y'know what I mean?"

"Ah sure, ye both realize I'm clumsy wit' expressing my emotions."

Fatigue weighed him down and a heaviness spread into his limbs. They couldn't work it all out tonight or even prior to their departure on Friday. Soon he would be home, in a different country, miles from Jeanette. The thought caused a shrinking sensation near his heart.

"Ye're already more than friends. Everything else will sort itself." She gathered her nightclothes and shuffled to the door.

Strange, chatting with his daughter about the struggles of adult relations and challenges. At least she didn't seem bothered by the fact her auld man appeared less experienced than a teenage boy. Perhaps she had a similar experience with Kera and Frank's courtship. He tried to imagine how she felt about her separated parents fumbling through the courting process alongside their sixteen-year-old. Conlin sat upright on the bed with a hunched posture. "Ya probably won't be asking me for dating advice."

"You're too hard on yerself. I still have a thing or two to learn from ya."

He shifted on the mattress, rubbed his nape, and looked her in the eye. "You are ready to date now, yeah?"

Laying a hand on his shoulder, she arched an eyebrow. "So are you."

Cricket turned and exited, traipsing across the hall into the bathroom. Conlin rose to his feet, stretched his arms overhead and shut the door. He changed into his sweatpants and a t-shirt from Montreal, noticing it was about time to do the washing. Gathering an armload of his and Cricket's clothing, he skimmed the space for any missed laundry. His eyesight focused on the far wall, and he read the framed Bible verse.

For love is as strong as death. Song of Songs 8:6.

If the events over the past few days taught him anything about life and love it was to embrace every moment as a gift, forgive fast, learn from failures, and never let the chance to tell someone how you feel slip away because things can change in a second.

THIRTY

Jeanette settled into the downstairs master bedroom and unpacked her pajamas, along with an outfit, for the next day. Jack vacated the space after Geneva passed away and only allowed her to occupy the main bedroom. At least the arrangement kept Brian in the farthest location inside the house, upstairs and at the end of the hallway. She paused and ejected a tight-lipped huff, throwing a hand skyward. Really, did he have to show up unannounced? And right when she and Conlin...

No, it was her fault Brian arrived, since she ignored his last three messages. Conlin assessed her issue precisely when he called her out on leaving notes instead of having conversations. Was it any wonder he hesitated about developing their relationship? After what he witnessed between her and Brian, he must have felt relieved that he dodged a bullet.

What was the point of dwelling on it now? Time to finish Tom's latest excavation debacle and analyze the stones so they could conclude their business with Geron. Jeanette grabbed her crossbody bag and retrieved the Celtic Stone. She exited the bedroom, catching sight of Conlin ambling downstairs, carrying an armload of clothes.

"Sorry for interrupting, just doing the washing," Conlin said.

Jack and Tom looked up from a stack of books, research papers, and maps scattered across the center table in front of the fire.

"No worries. The utility room is around the corner on the left. Don't hesitate to ask for anything you need," Jack said.

"T'anks."

Conlin slowed his steps as he saw her standing beside the sliding barn-door entrance for the laundry. She set the linen wrapped stone on a cabinet in the hall and smoothed a lock of her hair, straightening the curl.

Stopping under the hallway light, she stared into his striking eyes, infiltrating her soul. "Are you comfortable in your guestroom?"

"'Tis grand." He lowered his gaze to the clothes piled in his hands.

"Glad to hear." Jeanette slid the door open, and they walked inside. "I'm staying in the bedroom down here." She motioned toward the master suite. "It'll be strange sleeping alone, after all the nights we spent together."

Conlin set the garments on top of the dryer and raised an inquisitive brow as a one-sided smile plucked at his lips. She ratcheted her spine, reacting to her blundering remark that sounded like an invitation, and she turned away from him. Jeanette pushed the start button on the machine and recoiled, sealing her eyelids.

He leaned close behind, bowing over her shoulder, and spoke near her ear. "Ya needn't feel uneasy with me."

Her lashes beat softly, and she inhaled a breath of fresh air—his understanding tone, caring nature, the physical and emotional nearness. Her muscles loosened and she angled toward him, pressing her forehead against his collarbone.

Conlin outstretched his arms and drew her closer into a hug. Welcoming a full embrace, she twisted her torso until their bodies aligned and he enclosed her in a heartfelt cuddle. She clung tighter to his waist, and he pulled her into a snugger grip. *Don't let go.*

All the chaotic events of the day abandoned her body as if he absorbed her burdens. She trusted Conlin with all the fiber of her being and accepted his suggestion to exercise patience, waiting for their relationship to develop at a distance.

She kept her eyes shut, drifting off to a faraway place lulled by the drumming of his heartbeat, lavender detergent wafting in the air, overall exhaustion, and a bump on the head. Every part of her relaxed as he supported her weight. He rubbed her lower back and gave her a gentle squeeze. "You've been through a lot. I should take you to bed."

An agreeable moan juddered in her throat and his limbs tensed as he straightened his posture. She felt too exhausted and comfortable to read into his comment. Either way, she relished the sentiment and a warmth surged beneath her sweater. She imagined lying on his chest and his rhythmic breathing lulling her to sleep. Cozy in their embrace, a long sigh escaped her mouth. "No need to feel uneasy with me."

Conlin loosened his grip and tilted his neck to view her eyes. "I know, so I know."

The rushing water stopped filling the washer, and he inched backward, allowing his palms to glide alongside her hips before letting go. His touch titillated every nerve and a tingling rippled across her flesh. Jeanette quivered and stepped aside for him to add his laundry into the machine.

"Tom, Jack and I will be in the main room. You're welcome to join us." She moved at a slow pace, glancing at him sidelong and nudged a laid-back shrug. "I mean, we're examining old relics..."

"Em, yeah, I'm waiting for the washing, all the same."

"Okay, see you in a few." She dawdled in the doorway and flashed a smile before walking away.

A full smile cramped her cheeks and there was a skip in her step as she collected the Celtic Stone. The first encounter, following the outpouring of her romantic aspirations and the unexpected arrival of Brian, didn't involve a serious discussion. Their interaction remained balanced while they sorted out difficult circumstances and challenging talks in non-confrontational, drama-free ways. A sudden giddiness enlivened her mood with their ability to keep things mellow after her obviously hurt feelings, when Conlin appeared uninterested about cultivating a long-distance relationship and the spectacle Brian created during dinner.

Jeanette strolled into the work zone Tom set up in the living space and placed the wrapped relic in the center of his investigation. "Tell me what you know."

Tom tilted his head upward, flinching as his eyes shifted between her and the artifact. He rested his palms on the ledge of the table and hovered over the protected stone. "Did you take it from the archaeology team?"

Jeanette folded her arms across her chest and grazed her teeth against her lower lip, noticing Conlin wandering into the living area. The memory of his disapproval of her initial decision to keep and inspect the stone still lingered in her mind. "Geron demanded we examine the relics and meet him in the next forty-eight hours."

Conlin leaned against the settee, staring at her painting of Jack's house above the fireplace. He caught her gazing at him, and his grin grew, deepening his laugh lines. A sensitivity covered her skin, and she massaged her forearm.

Tom tossed her a pair of vinyl disposable gloves. "Let's get to work." He removed the covering from the Celtic Stone, and his hypnotic stare riveted on it. "When we were excavating at a Norse magnate's residence in Hardanger, Norway, we unearthed sacrifice offerings of jewelry, tools, weapons, and the Vanir Stone." Wielding delicate precision, he lifted the relic off the table and passed it to Jeanette.

A subtle burning sensation flowed through her fingertips and tightened her joints. She shuddered and raised the rectangular-shaped artifact eye level, analyzing the carvings on the guesstimated four-inches long, five-inches wide and sixty-four-millimeters deep relic. "A female and male figure, facing each other." Jeanette squinted, rotating the object as she inspected the markings of a wildcat and boar. "The goddess Freyja and her brother Freyr?"

Tom nodded and rubbed his chin. "Possibly 9th-century, sacrificial stones to praise their gods while taking part in rituals. Once the deities favored the tribe, they believed women became fertile, the land produced plentiful crops, and then buried the stones, giving thanks to the gods of nature. The patterns of lines, engraved in the Vanir Stone, suggest the Norse used it in blót ceremonies." He bowed forward and drew attention to the design. "Notice the symbol for the sun and how it's aligned with the top of the life tree."

Jeanette scrutinized the other etchings on the rock. Eihwaz, the thirteenth rune of Elder Futhark, symbolizing the yew tree, Yggdrasil representing life and death with the unique geometrical shape of a pillar connecting two ends. Her eyesight roved upward, and she studied the details. "If you're speculating a date between 800–860 A.D., during the Viking Age, it's possible the stones represented cycles of life like the three arcs of Triquetra on the Celtic Stone, exemplifying the domains of earth—sea and sky, or elements of fire, land and water."

Jeanette returned the Vanir Stone beside the Celtic relic and slanted her head to one side. "Conlin pointed out the significance of the Father, Son, Holy Spirit triunity. After examining the engraved face, accompanied by a willow tree, the images probably depict the Celt and Druid god Esus."

"Interesting. Likely related to the Celts idol worship of sun deities." His gaze alternated from the artifacts to her, and he spoke under his breath. "The concept of balance between life and death in nature?"

She cupped an elbow in her palm and supported her chin with a fist. "How did Geron get involved, and why does he believe the stones have supernatural powers?"

"I'll put on the kettle," Conlin peeped at her before walking toward the kitchen. She offered a single wave of appreciation and lounged against a cushion on the sofa.

Jack got up and followed him. "Please, allow me to assist you."

Tom assessed the stones, massaging his forehead, and relinquished a hefty exhale. "After I obtained a seventy-two-hour permit to excavate the location in Hardanger, I contacted my boss, Simon Bonhoeffer and updated our progress. In less than twenty-four hours another team of archaeologists arrived, led by Geron, and he claimed the Norwegian Directorate for Civil Protection instructed him to supervise our work."

"Let me guess, he took over the worksite and you became his assistant." Just as she suspected, Geron's story he told her at the Fairmont in Quebec left out major details and their acquaintance wasn't the partnership that he described.

"They limited my choices." He slouched and grunted, running a palm through his messy hairstyle. "I gathered a few pieces and the Vanir Stone, fleeing the country."

"Then, he referenced your map and followed you to Ireland."

He shifted a narrow-eyed glance. "I can't figure out how Geron knew about Great-Grandad's chart?"

"At dinner, he claimed during your excavation, he lost track of you after uncovering the Celtic Stone."

Tom scrunched his nose and wrinkled his upper lip. "You dined with him?"

Heat rose from her neck, spreading across her face. "Funny, I agreed after he threatened me." She threw a sofa pillow at him. "I was attempting to protect everyone involved and find out information about your disappearance."

"Hey, I'm joking. It's what we do."

"Not now. We're in serious trouble. This time is different and the lives of people I care deeply about are in jeopardy."

"Message received loud and clear." Tom lowered his eyelids and frowned. "You know I didn't mean any harm."

"Yeah, well, after discovering you're alive and vacationing at Jack's while we've been on the run, I can't decide if I want to hug or hit you."

"You already punched me."

She glared at him, shaking a fist, and he raised his arms, surrendering. "Okay, okay, you can punch me again."

"No, I'm too tired and you couldn't foresee what would happen. But maybe later."

Jeanette understood Tom benefited from lighthearted humor to manage the stress of trials and his blunders. She guessed he either ignored Geron's nefarious intentions or didn't want to face the truth. Stressful situations often required a level of escapism, especially when tackling intangible ideas and objects. Even she sought avoidance in the precious moments with Conlin and although it presented its own difficulties, she found solace in his company, regardless of their current relationship status.

Conlin nudged her biceps and she swiveled, gazing into his irises as he offered her a mug. "Thanks," she said in a quiet voice. The comforting caress of his palm on her back and the hot drink flooded warmth throughout her body.

Jack brought in the teapot, and cups, setting the tray on an end stand. He reclined in the chair beside the fire, shifted in his seat, and bent forward, positioning his elbows on his knees. "We must establish the importance of the stones and if there's a correlation."

Jeanette bundled a fistful of her hair, gathered the curls, and tied loose strands in a bun. She believed everyone's collective ideas and additional input would improve their chances of determining the original purposes for the archaeological finds. "Have you observed a reaction bringing the two stones together?"

"I've only experienced the personal effects of physically handling the Vanir Stone." A contemplative look rumpled his features, and she bit the inside of her cheek. It appeared Tom sensed a similar heat emitting from the relic like she did a few minutes ago.

"We're of Scandinavian descent. Perhaps there's a link between us and the stones." She stood, set her cup down and tapped her forefinger against her chin. Did the Celtic Stone have an effect on Conlin?

Jeanette looked at him, transfixed on the artifact, and guessed he felt some kind of response. She pivoted on her foot and took a few paces, then retraced her steps beside the fireplace. "Geron inquired about the Murphy's ancestry. Any strange sensitivities when you touch the stone?" Tom and Jack followed her attentiveness and the three of them stared at Conlin.

"Em, a bit of an odd feeling, similar to a mild electrical shock." Conlin rotated his shoulders and sipped his tea, glancing away.

Jeanette read his observable mannerisms, understanding the antiquities unnerved him and triggered his overprotective retort to Saoirse taking the relic to explore. Discovering the truth was imperative, if they were ever going to break free of Geron and his threats.

"If Geron theorizes the stones are somehow"—she summoned words with a sweeping gesture of her hands—"supernaturally charged by progenies of the tribes that fashioned the ceremonial artifacts, how would he test his hypothesis?"

"You will not like the answer." Tom altered his stance and cleared his throat. "At the excavation site, we unearthed animal and human skeletal remains."

A sudden chill froze her to the core and the room remained silent. No, Geron wouldn't... Yes, he proved they did not limit their threats to mere injuries, and he intended to use any tactics deemed necessary to test the stones, including murder.

"What purpose would it serve beyond a blatant attempt at killing another human? Does he hope to gain money, control, or prestige? Because if he continues to act out his deranged behaviors all he'll receive is jail time." Jeanette blew a loose curl off her forehead and slumped against the couch.

Conlin set his teacup on the tray and spoke in a low tone. "Geron hopes to hold the power of life and death in his hands."

"Exactly." Tom's brightened expression went ashen, and he addressed Jack. "Anything in Great-Grandad Sjur's scrapbooks about the stones and supernatural events?"

Jack knocked a knuckle on the Norway expedition annals. "The only mention in the book about ancient Norse mythology connecting life and death is Bifröst." He pointed to the tree of life etched on the Vanir Stone. "So, unless Mr. Leclerc believes in folklore and plans on crossing the Rainbow Bridge, his intentions are unclear."

"Without further observation and examination of the relics and knowledge of each culture's rituals, I'm finding it difficult to make a connection between Celt and Norse mythology." Jeanette twirled a curl and tucked the strand inside her clip. She caught Conlin watching her fuss with unmanageable tresses and a smile built, recognizing she captured his attention, even if for a moment.

He stared off to a far corner of the room and addressed Tom. "Sounds like different interpretations of our One True God. Maybe Geron missed details during his studies or is unaware of the direct spiritual access provided by the living God."

"Valid assessment." Tom's eyebrows furrowed, then released as he scratched his jawline. "The ritual practices of the ancients took place in pre-Christian times. Though, the Israelites performed ceremonial offerings to Yahweh, including animal sacrifices. In modern Christianity, experiencing the supernatural manifestation of the Holy Spirit requires personal faith in Jesus, and I have a feeling Geron expects to discover something more tangible. He doesn't want to connect with a god, he wants to become one."

"I t'ink I've seen the movie." Conlin rolled his eyeballs upward.

Jack chortled and pulled at his silvery-white beard. "Regardless of his philosophies, we can't allow Geron to test any of his theories. The artifacts must remain in a secured location, and you should get the authorities involved right away. He's endangered all of you and it's essential we thwart his plans."

"Has Geron accumulated stones from other ancient civilizations?" Her mouth went dry, and she gulped. Was he aware of the Mystery Stone?

Jeanette and Tom exchanged knowing looks. "He's amassing relics from around the globe. Are you concerned about the stone at your historical society?"

A coolness flowed through her limbs, and she rose to her feet, moving closer toward the fireplace. She leaned against the solid timber mantelpiece above the hearth. "I can't shake the feeling he recruited me for that reason." Jeanette peered at the time, 11:17 p.m., displayed on the clock and blinked her heavy lids.

"We've done all we can in a couple of hours." Jack cleaned up the cups and carried the tray into the kitchen.

"Right, and we'd need hours of extensive study on the artifacts before presenting any valid data." She released an abrupt swoosh of air and sagged her torso. "We accomplished the most important things, removing the stones from Geron's possession and hindering him from collecting anymore."

"I'll contact Mr. Bonhoeffer and update him on our progress." Tom wrapped the Celtic and Vanir relics in linen cloth, gathering them in his grip. "Nettie, talk to Brian about securing the Mystery Stone."

"I will in the morning. It isn't on display at the moment and kept in our storage facility."

"Good." Tom pressed his lips tight, lowering his chin. "Thanks for assisting me with everything. I know I've put you all in danger, but I'm going to correct the situation."

"Fair enough, lad." Conlin gave him a single nod. "Night." He faced her and the dawning of a smile ruffled his lips.

He strolled into the laundry room before she could reply, and a tightness gripped her chest. If she followed his advice to inform the authorities in Kinsale, or even in Montreal, they could have avoided all the dangerous coercions, and Geron would be under investigation right now. She banged a fist against her thigh. Brian advised the same course of action, for his own beneficial reasons, yet it still would have resulted in resolving the problem.

"Have a restful sleep, everyone." Jack headed upstairs.

"Good night," Tom and Jeanette said in unison.

"Hey, Net…"

Tom held the relics in his palms and the wonderment of a child on Christmas morning glinted in his eyes. After his lifelong pursuit, he held the coveted treasure in his hands. The corner of her mouth tugged up to one side. Although he caused too much trouble, she shared in the celebration of him accomplishing his goal.

"Congratulations."

"Thank you." He stared at the artifacts. "I couldn't have done it without you."

The moment didn't last long, and her heart sank to the ground. Conlin and Saoirse weighed heavily on her mind and the unnecessary hardships they endured because of her brother's dreams. His words drove a dagger into her, emphasizing the role she played in perpetuating the chaotic circumstances. The dilemma of letting go of Conlin for the sake of allowing him peace, stability, and a fading memory of the Hillestad siblings plagued her entire existence. Fatigue, overwhelming emotions, and a headache settled in, stressing the need for sleep.

THIRTY-ONE

Jeanette turned off the kitchen and entry lights. Tom sorted the books and papers on the table. Did she make it clear enough that she wouldn't clean up any of his future messes? "What's next on your agenda?"

"I'm continuing the exploration of the archaeology sites I discovered in Ireland."

She clenched her jaw and her stomach hardened. The news of him working at locations she wanted to revisit, closer to Conlin and where she left her heart, stripped her nerves bare. Jeanette repressed swelling emotions and breathed through the pain. "Great, now swear to keep out of trouble."

"I'll try, but I can't make any guarantees." He shrugged, flashing a mischievous grin.

"At least don't involve me or the Murphys again."

His smirk faded into dismay, and he set the artifacts in a protective case. "I wouldn't and never intended on it. The minute I realized Geron followed me to steal the Vanir Stone, I left their home, hoping to protect them. In the final conversation Conlin and I had, before going into hiding, I discouraged him from looking for me, and requested he deter anyone else searching, including you."

Conlin shared the identical bit of information when he showed her the map he found at his house. She massaged her temple at the hairline next to her bump and flinched. "If you didn't want help, then why did you write and send me a Saint Brendan quote? How does his tale factor into the Celtic Stone?"

Tom squished his eyebrows inward and scratched his scalp as if solving a riddle. "They're unrelated. The Dingle Peninsula sites, and Saint Brendan's voyages are part of the new fieldwork. I sent the letter to let you know I was safe and thought you'd appreciate a reference to the legend."

Jeanette curved her fingers into fists and dug her nails into her skin. She squeezed her eyes shut and suppressed a scream rumbling in her throat. Her eyelids flashed open, and she released a tension-filled groan. "Mr. Bonhoeffer emailed me about your disappearance, and I thought the note provided clues to find you."

"My boss?" Tom's head cocked back slightly, and he crinkled his nose. "Nettie, I don't always need you to rescue me—"

"Nope, I can't hear anymore tonight." She held out an extended arm and stopped him from moving toward her. "I understand you didn't intend to put people in danger, but it's all too much to process at the moment."

"Okay." His torso caved inward, and he collected the stones inside a briefcase. "See you in the morning." He slogged his way up the staircase.

"Everything grand?" Conlin approached and slid a hand over her shoulder.

Jeanette blew out a burst of air. "I was wrong, and you were right. I shouldn't have gotten involved." She angled her head toward him. "Following false leads to the Dingle Peninsula resulted in one disaster after another."

"None of the terrible events were yer fault and it was out of your control."

"But if I hadn't gone searching for Tom—"

"We wouldn't have met. And I'll never regret knowing you." His ardent declaration blazed in his irises. "Ah, sure, the stressful circumstances challenged us, but it's over now."

A stabbing ache spread through her chest. How much of it was over— running from Geron, deciphering ancient relics, or any prospects for them as romantic partners? "Yeah, and Friday's the end of our time together."

The downward point of his brows, deepened wrinkles at the bridge of his nose. "We aren't ending things and we'll be seeing each other in a little while."

A flutter swirled in her belly, and she shuffled a footstep forward, making strong eye contact. "What about returning to your daily routine?"

"'Tisn't much of a life unless you're in it now."

Between the words he professed and their intensifying closeness, she found it difficult to ignore the demands from her heart to spend the rest of her days with Conlin Murphy. But how when the Atlantic Ocean kept them at a distance? Jeanette fixed her sight on him, gazing long and hard, seeking to connect with his soul. Verbal expressions failed to convey the depths of her feelings. She wished to kiss and embrace him, never letting go.

Conlin closed his eyelids for half a minute and ran fingers through his hair. "Ah, when ya look at me like *that*, Banféinní." He scraped a palm over his mouth, containing his voracious appetite.

Her stare lowered down his neck, across his collarbone, and roved along the noticeable definition of muscles through his t-shirt. Recalling him shirtless, her line of vision followed the concealed hairline below his bellybutton until reaching...

Jeanette glanced at the fireplace as a mild pain quivered in her chest and she hugged herself. The dying embers of yellow-orange flames and blue sparks flickered, burning low. "One of us should put the fire out."

"Aye." He walked toward the hearth and grabbed a fire iron. "'Tis hot in here." Conlin dipped an eyelid in the slightest suggestion of a wink, and the hint of a smile curved a corner of his mouth.

Indeed, the temperature increased to the extent of considering a cool shower before bed. "The heat's definitely rising."

He poked at the logs till red glowing flares blackened and smoldered into charred wood, darkening the space. Smoke and ashes rose up the chimney, leaving a crisp, sweet scent from the burned cedar.

Conlin replaced the tool and leaned on the flagstone inglenook. The outline of his shadowy figure created an afterimage, and she blinked a few times. She tucked her hands into the rear pockets of her jeans and inched backward to refrain from rushing into his arms.

"You're too far away." Conlin extended his arm.

"Soon the distance will be greater than I can endure."

"C'mere, there's plenty to sort out and we'll figure out a way."

A different, yet nevertheless serious, danger existed, accepting an invitation into his embrace. Did she possess the willpower to refuse him or herself a comforting hug? Not to mention the genuine struggle of yearning for his kisses whenever they cuddled and she gnawed the inside of her cheek, fighting the urge.

She reached out, brushing her fingertips against his, and he gently tugged until she was an inch from his body. The deliberate space he created reiterated his obvious stance of guarding themselves from the overpowering waves of passion crashing over them and getting carried off into the undercurrent.

Conlin pressed their interlocked fingers near his heart. "Here, you know I'd be wanting to hold ya throughout the night."

The pounding of his chest against her hand accompanying a fervent gaze imparted the feelings he kept hidden inside. All the endearing sentiments he spoke deepened her affections for him and, although tempted to surrender herself to him in entirety, she appreciated his dedication to maintaining physical boundaries. A lump swelled in her throat, constricting her speech. What could she say without spoiling the moment?

Best to sleep on it, allowing a peaceful slumber to slow down her impulses and emotional reactions.

"It's late and we should get some rest. Almost unbelievable after a day of revelations, car accidents, crossing borders, studying ancient relics, outpouring of emotions, and Brian showing up." Snapping her jaw shut, she grazed her front teeth along the edge of her lip. Why did she mention Brian?

All too quickly, Conlin let her slide from his grasp, and she swayed off balance. Although Conlin accepted that she broke off the attachment, the fact her ex-boyfriend slept upstairs while they declared their regard for each other and planned their future seemed like poor timing.

"Sure, the brother's safe, and we're free of Geron. We'll enjoy the marra, just the three of us." An aura of anticipation and expectancy brightened his features.

"Yes, and I'm thankful for every second we spend together." At last, an opportunity for them to have moments alone without the concerns of life-and-death scenarios. A lifting sensation diminished her burdens, and she inched backward. "Sweet dreams."

"Oíche mhaith," he said good night in Irish and wandered toward the staircase.

Jeanette tore her gaze from him and ambled to the master bedroom. She peeked over a shoulder, catching sight of him at the top of the steps before entering his room. Conlin's encouragement embedded hope into her core and provided a positive outlook on tomorrow for them to relish each other's company in the picturesque setting of autumn in New Hampshire.

Jeanette woke up at six o'clock in the morning and made a dent in her schedule. After baking, she showered and dressed in her most comfortable pair of Levi's jeans and a pine-green blouse. She grabbed a comb off the nightstand to tackle her untamed mane. Standing at the full-length mirror, she managed the tumbleweed atop her head, and saturated the strands with a frizz-free spray.

An aggressive knock on the entry echoed throughout the room, and she peered at the wall clock, displaying the current time of 8:30 a.m. "Come in."

Brian entered and closed the door behind as she viewed him through the reflective glass. "Sleep well?"

"Not really. I waited for you." He moved nearer and stood beside her in the mirror. "We agreed to finish our talk."

"Tom and I worked till almost midnight."

He scrutinized her appearance. "I can see you're tired. Still, we need to discuss your inappropriate outburst at dinner—"

Jeanette slammed her comb onto the fixture next to the bed and glared at him. "My behavior? The entire evening you patronized me in front of friends and family, like you always do..."

He blinked slowly, stumbling rearward into a chair and rubbed his forehead. "Is this about that Irish guy?"

It seemed Brian witnessed the bond she shared with Conlin. But it wasn't about her feelings for another man since their relationship ended way before she met Conlin. He just refused to accept it.

"Look Brian." She laid a hand on his shoulder. "I'll never live up to your expectations, despite all my efforts, and struggling to make us work as a couple." She exhaled aloud and sat adjacent from him on the wood bedframe. "We want different things in life."

He hunched, sinking into the seat, and a host of emotions crisscrossed over his face. "You're breaking up with me?"

"Sorry, I should've talked to you instead of leaving a letter."

"I assumed you wanted a break during your search for Tom..."

"No, it wasn't a quick decision. I've thought about it for a while."

Brian jolted to attention, jumping to his feet and straightened his shoulders, jutting his chin. "Right, you've been restricting my talents. I need someone more supportive and tuned into my needs." His voice rose and strained as if he had food lodged in his throat. "There's a woman out there more suitable for me."

She expected him to lash out, and it was best to allow him a moment to digest the news. Jeanette maintained a neutral tone to circumvent an argument. "Absolutely, she'll be the person you deserve."

His jaw clenched, and his facial features twitched. "Then I guess there's nothing left to say but goodbye."

"Bye, Brian."

He smoothed his palms over the front of his pressed white shirt, tucked into his khaki slacks, and turned on his heel, storming out of the room. Part of her felt sorry for him, yet the awareness of freedom fulfilled her as she took a deep breath. A breakup at the start of her day should've caused a different reaction, except she spent the early hours musing on Conlin's promises about being together. She finished fixing her hair and exited the bedroom. Lured by the scent of a dark, smokey-roast coffee brewing, she aimed for the kitchen area.

Jack lined up vintage stainless-steel mugs along the counter. "Good morning, Love. I see you made your grandmother's lefse."

Jeanette zipped past him, pulling the carafe from the brewer, and filled a cup, passing the pot to Jack. "The process is relaxing, and I thought it'd be a nice treat for everyone."

"Your baking is a delightful indulgence." Jack put the decanter on the warmer. "It seems you had a busy start to the day." He pulled dishes from the cupboard. "Five settings? I spotted Mr. Adler departing in a hurry."

Jeanette shifted her glance and blew on her coffee. "Yeah, Brian's not joining us… ever again."

"That explains why he ignored me and rushed out the door."

"Sorry for causing all the drama at your house."

He chuckled and shook his head. "Nonsense, you're the last person I'd consider dramatic. However, your brother is a different story."

She missed Jack's company and spending summers in the scenic White Mountains. Complete joy overwhelmed her, wishing they could extend their visit and indulge in a three-week retreat. For now, she would continue to daydream about getaways and vacations.

"Howya?" Saoirse trotted down the stairs in a cheerful mood.

"Morning. Was the guestroom satisfactory?" Jack asked.

"Best sleep I've had in days."

Jeanette leaned on the ledge of the counter. "I'm sure it was nice to have a proper bed instead of a sofa-sleeper." She sipped her steaming brew. "Can I make you a cup of tea, coffee, or hot chocolate?"

Saoirse pursed her lips and scrunched her nose like she had a sour taste on her tongue. "Em, American tea's poxy."

Jack filled the remaining mugs on a tray. "The cocoa's much better." He winked, setting milk and sugar on the tabletop.

"Da would fancy a coffee. He was in and out of bed most of the night."

"That's a shame." Jack held a serving dish loaded with scrambled eggs and sausage links.

The knowledge of Conlin experiencing a restless sleep deflated her limbs. Was it something she said, or did that caused him to feel unsettled? She poured a bowl of granola, topped it with oat-milk and snatched a banana on the way to the dining area. Jack served a platter of toast in the center, and Saoirse chose a piece.

"T'anks." She chewed a slice of bread.

"Smells wonderful." Conlin jogged downstairs, wearing dark-denim pants and the black button-front he purchased at the Fairmont, layering a white t-shirt.

His face appeared bright and refreshed. She hadn't seen him donning shorter stubble since they first met in Kinsale. Jeanette didn't recognize any signs of sleep deprivation other than the redness in his eyes.

Conlin chose a full mug and nestled in the chair beside Jeanette. He eyed her and whispered, "You are lookin' lovely, as always."

A buzzing vibrated throughout her body, and she hid behind the rim of her cup. The flirting escalated to all the clichéd, cutesy compliments, but she didn't care that it bordered on silly and sweet. "I noticed you entering the room looking as handsome as ever."

Conlin's lips curved upward, discovering she had checked him out and he inched nearer, closing the gap between their seats. He reached across the eating table and scooped a portion of eggs onto his plate. "T'anks Jack, for the mighty tucker."

"Try Love's Norwegian lefse," Jack said.

Conlin angled his head toward her, arching a brow. "Ya needed one more thing to do, yeah?"

"Well, I made the mixture with the potatoes we prepared yesterday. It's my grandma's potato-flatbread recipe sprinkled with sugar and seasonal spices."

He picked up a rolled, brown speckled lefse and passed the plate to Saoirse. Jeanette watched him bite into the buttered flatbread and dry washed her hands.

Conlin nodded and chewed in rhythm as a grin grew. "Fair dues to you."

"Delicious," Saoirse said.

Jeanette beamed and finished her coffee. "We'll take a few for the road." She rested a palm on his biceps, offering a reassuring gesture. "Did you have a lousy night?"

"I was t'inking about our conversation and the stones..."

"Do you need anything? Maybe a listener to relieve your worries and stress?"

"'Tis appreciated." Caressing her cheek, he spoke in an emotion-rich voice. "Praying helped, and I'm content being here with you."

The steps rumbled as Tom rushed downstairs. "Nettie, I emailed Simon Bonhoeffer and he suggested we collect all three relics and examine them together." He leaned over the table and selected a piece of lefse. "Did you speak to Brian this morning?"

All heads turned in her direction, and she scanned each face until focusing on Conlin. "I talked to him, but not about the Mystery Stone."

He gave her a knowing glance and laid an open hand against her back, rubbing in a soothing, circular motion. A simple touch, unwound her coiled nerves, and she felt at ease for the first time in days.

"Let's get moving straightaway since we know what Geron's likely planning," Tom said.

"Brian's on his way to work."

"He left? We need—"

"I'll take care of it." Jeanette sighed and folded her arms across her chest. Just perfect, she had to ask for a favor right after their awkward breakup. Could another member of the board secure the museum piece?

Tom ate a slice of lefse. "Tastes like Grandma's, except you added cinnamon." He bumped her arm and grinned. "I prefer it."

"All right, I'll call Brian." Jeanette stood from the table and stacked her dishes.

Conlin clasped his hand over hers, removing the bowl and mug from her hands. "Cricket and I are off to pack."

"We'll leave in an hour," she said.

Tom tugged her sleeve and bent his posture, reminiscent of the embarrassed six-year-old asking for her assistance to help tie his shoelaces. "Are we good?"

"We're good."

With a quick pivot on her heel, she walked outside onto the raised deck overlooking a valley of endless trees and relaxed on a cushioned wicker chair. The views in New Hampshire revived her senses—the outdoor beauty of mountains, lakes, a rocky coastline, and quaint historical towns. Gray clouds haloed the snow-capped peak of Mount Washington in the distance and a soft drizzle brightened the multi-colored foliage.

Cold air cleansed her lungs as she inhaled pine and a sweet, woodsy scent. Everything seemed renewed, a fresh start—the beginning of a relationship with Conlin, Tom accepting responsibility for his actions, and liberation from catering to everyone else's needs while sacrificing her own.

THIRTY-TWO

Twenty minutes later, Jeanette ambled inside and walked through the living area toward the kitchen. After a few dropped calls, she successfully left a voicemail for Brian, waiting for the delivery of several sent texts. It took six attempts to remember Jack's code before entering the correct password. The service in Franconia and the Lakes Region of New Hampshire was always spotty and required a Wi-Fi connection.

Tom placed dishes in the drying rack and turned toward her. He slanted his torso onto the granite counter and drummed his fingers to the same beat as his jittering foot tap on the floor. "What did Brian say?"

"No answer, but I left him a detailed message."

Tom slapped a palm over his heart and closed his eyelids for a second. "I'm certain he'll take care of it and protect the stone."

"So, you're set, right? No more interaction or trouble with Geron?" She leaned on the countertop, slumping her shoulders.

"What else is he capable of doing when we have the three stones? And Simon assured me he'd contact the authorities."

A breath escaped her mouth, releasing a week's worth of tensions. Were they really free, and she had awakened from the nightmare? Pressing flat palms together, she touched her steepled fingers to her lips in thanksgiving for God's answered prayers. A joyful tremble coursed through her sinews, and she shivered.

A lightness raised her on tiptoe and she did a drumroll, banging her fingertips on the counter as reality settled in her mind. "Yes!" She propelled herself backward off the ledge and wiggled her hips in a victory dance, singing the 1990s song, *I'm Free.* Tom joined her in the celebration and sang along.

"Woo-hoo, we did it." He gave her a double high-five and began dancing Kid 'N' Play style, the '90s hip-hop version of the Charleston, their go-to celebratory response to anything.

"Ah-huh, that's right." She spun around, moving her arms and body in a circular motion.

Conlin stood at the bottom of the staircase, broadening his grin. "Keep celebrating yer freedom."

She laughed and waltzed toward him. "Oh, I'm definitely embracing it."

"I see that. Look at you and Thomas there happy out dancing."

"We have our moments." She glimpsed Tom, extending an arm in front and the other behind his head, making sprinkler movements. One of his earliest signature dance moves, since he never mastered the Roger Rabbit steps or the Reebok. Laughter spurted from her mouth, watching him let loose. Jeanette enjoyed having fun with Tom, when things were peaceful, and he listened to her advice on evading crises.

Saoirse came down the stairs. "All packed and ready."

Jack entered the house carrying a watering can, sniffling and wiping his nose with a handkerchief. "Darn allergies." He stuffed the cloth in his pocket and settled in the chair closest to the fire. "Hopefully, you have time for another story before you leave."

He wasn't fooling anyone, using the old allergy excuse. "Perfect timing. I need to finish packing and judging by the length of his usual stories, I'll see you in about an hour." The heartache of saying goodbye to Jack was almost unbearable.

Jeanette strolled into the living room and caught the conclusion of Jack's tales about his grandfather and Great-Grandpa Sjur in Ireland, listening to his soothing yet energetic voice as he weaved a story of grandeur. The story reminded her that she needed to visit him in the White Mountains more often and she would promise to return next summer.

Tom moseyed downstairs, toting a silver case and his travel duffel bag. A bittersweet feeling swept over her as he set his belongings beside the coatrack. The stones would finally be out of their lives, yet after months of limited communications and his disappearing act, he'd likely embark on another expedition again.

"What's that look?" he asked.

She carried her backpack to the entry and laid the soft suitcase down, rolling her sore shoulder from the car accident. "You're sure you can manage the rest on your own?"

"Yes. I'm staying here for lunch and will wait for confirmation from my boss about where to meet him with the stones." Tom put a hand atop her head. "Now, keep out of trouble." He rubbed her scalp, messing up her hair.

"Hey!" She smoothed the frizzy strands and huffed. It was the first time in days she used styling tools and products for a refined look. She glanced at Conlin chatting with Saoirse and Jack. A warmness spread up her neck, sweeping across her face and she subdued a smile.

"Oh, I see."

"What?" She darted her gaze to a far corner of the room and looped a curl around her finger.

"Mm-hm, you're blushing."

"Thomas Alfred don't even start..." Jeanette pressed a palm against her cheek. Okay, so everyone knew, big deal. She had nothing to hide.

"Drive safe and have a great time."

She angled her chin downward and deliberately raised an eyebrow, studying his expression. "No sarcastic remarks or teasing?"

"Nope." He slid his arm over her shoulder and pulled her into a side hug. "He's a good guy."

She fixed her eyesight on Conlin and spoke in a certain, unwavering tone. "Without a doubt."

"All right, enough of the sentimental stuff." Tom playfully shoved her aside.

Everyone gathered at the front door. "Take it easy." Tom extended a handshake to Conlin, and they shook hands.

"You do the same, lad." Conlin picked up his belongings and her backpack.

"See ya, Sirsh." Tom gently tugged her braid.

"Slán."

"An absolute delight getting to know the both of you," Jack said.

"T'anks for your hospitality." Conlin stepped outside and Saoirse followed behind.

"Just a second." Jeanette tossed him the keys. She faced Jack and his glasses magnifying glistening eyes.

"Don't stay away too long, Love." He pecked her cheek.

A lump caught in her throat and tears brimmed, blurring her vision. "I'll be back before you know it." Quelling the ache building inside, she forced a smile and redirected her attention, avoiding a tearful goodbye.

"Be careful." She pointed a finger at Tom, reminding him of the possible consequences for his actions.

"Always."

"Ha! I'll believe that when I see it." Jeanette rushed to the Honda as the drizzle turned into a steady rain. Taking a final glance, she waved at them, then hurried into the vehicle.

"Text you later," Tom called out and entered the cabin.

Driving south on Interstate 93, after a walk and lunch in the town of Lincoln, Jeanette exited toward the Lakes Region on Route 3. Passing the sign for the waterfront village of Meredith, she peeked at her phone screen. No messages from Brian or Tom. She trusted it meant all went according to their plans.

"Yer far away and quiet," Conlin said.

"I'm a little tired."

"And maybe a bit preoccupied thinking about the relics?"

A warmth swelled behind her nape, setting the tips of her ears ablaze. Mentally she noted that once again he understood and accepted her in entirety. "We're approaching the original site of the Mystery Stone." Jeanette headed east and drove in the direction of Meredith.

"In 1872, workers for Seneca A. Ladd. found the artifact along the shore of Lake Winnipesaukee buried in clay sediment." She drew their attention to the large body of water on their left. "He believed the egg-shaped, mylonite carved object to be of Native American origins because of the several petroglyphs etched on the stone, including a face, canoe, teepee, an ear of corn and other symbols. Ladd kept the stone in his possession for years until his death and in 1927, his daughter donated it to the New Hampshire Historical Society."

"Where you work, yeah?" Conlin rolled his sleeves as the clouds cleared and the sun shined at a temperature of 54 degrees Fahrenheit, creating the perfect autumn day.

Jeanette nodded and turned left onto Daniel Webster Highway. "I've cataloged a few other items in relation to the artifact, yet the investigations lead to more questions. Researchers and archaeologists' findings are inconclusive. Documents circulate about the item being a Native American agreement between tribes, others speculate it's of Picts or Inuit roots."

She entered a parking lot facing the docks and chose a space overlooking the water. Wind created whitecaps on the lake, and she lowered the windows. The restaurants were already closed for the season and made it an ideal time for locals to enjoy the town without crowds.

"Another popular theory is that the entire story about the stone was part of a hoax," Jeanette said, "since further examination suggests the use of power tools and dates it during the 19th-century. Either way, the Mystery Stone continues to be mystifying."

"Are there mythological or supernatural elements tied to the artifact like the Vanir and Celtic Stones?" Conlin asked.

"We haven't linked any mystical aspects because the origins are unclear." Jeanette stared at the north edge of the lake, close to the location where the people discovered the stone. "Assertions surfaced that it's a thunderstone or a lodestone but without identification of the creator or the stones intended function, the artifact remains a fascinating exhibit piece."

"Ireland's the land of myths. Still an' all, New Hampshire has plenty of its own tales."

"Wait till you hear our ghost stories."

"Wicked." Saoirse leaned forward from the backseat.

"I've had enough talk of relics, rituals, and apparitions. Visions plagued me mind all night and I'm relieved we no longer have any of the stones." Conlin rubbed his chin, shifting in his seat to find a more comfortable position. "In fairness, the precautions you've taken seem sufficient, and from what ya shared, the Mystery Stone doesn't appear relevant to Geron's supposed plans."

"I agree and can't wait to spend a quiet evening together. Tomorrow's open for anything and on Thursday we'll tour the historic sites in Boston, after the appointment at the consulate. Then Friday..." Jeanette's words jumbled on her tongue, and she couldn't bring herself to say they were traveling home, emphasizing the painful reality that their time remained limited.

Conlin curled his fingers over her hand and encouraged her with a joyous appearance, brightening his face. "We'll have the best days."

Around 4:30 p.m. they strolled along the brick walkway at Mill Falls Marketplace, and visited the bookstore, Innisfree, named after an islet in County Sligo, Ireland. Finishing their ice cream, they stopped and posed in front of a 40-foot waterfall for another photo opportunity. Jeanette cherished every moment and captured the memories in any way possible. Conlin walked in the middle of Saoirse and her, hanging his arms across both of them as they returned to the Honda. The day turned out better than expected and she believed the worst was in the past, entrusting God to help her overcome the challenges she would encounter after his departure on Friday.

The sun set on Lake Winnipesaukee and twinkling light sparkled on the surface like dancing fireflies. Inside the car, a sense of peace and fulfillment surrounded her, feeling that everything was secure. Jeanette replaced her phone in the holder, keeping it off for two hours, and powered on the device. She started the engine and multiple notifications displayed on her screen—messages from Tom, Brian, and the historical society director.

"Is there a problem?" Conlin asked.

"I'm not sure."

She clicked on Tom's voicemail, playing it on the vehicle's speakers. "Hey Nettie, sorry for interrupting your afternoon but I'm unable to get a hold of Brian. Please verify he protected the Mystery Stone."

"Doesn't sound too bad," Conlin said.

Jeanette tapped on Tom's first text and read it aloud. "I'm driving to your work now and will update you soon." Nothing too difficult for him to handle. She continued reading, scrolling to the next communication. "Still no news on the artifact." Her posture shrank with the onset of an emptiness in the pit of her stomach.

"Check Brian's messages. Perhaps his response clarifies the situation."

"Right, he states it's taken care of, but doesn't mention the stone."

They listened to the final voicemail from the historical society, requesting for her to come into work and resolve the misunderstanding. All the serenity slipped away, and she stared across the water, longing for the ideas she planned for the rest of their time together.

"Go and sort t'ings out," Conlin said.

"I'll drop you off at my house first. It's only twenty minutes from here, on the eastern shores of the lake."

"How far is yer work?"

"A little less than an hour."

"It'll take too long. Let's drive there now." Conlin patted her on the arm. "'Tis fine. Probably a lack of communication and nothing more."

His level of support and partnership surpassed any relationship she experienced. An expansion filled her chest and her nerves loosened. Jeanette replied to everyone, informing them she was on her way.

She gazed at Conlin, and her muscles relaxed. "I'm glad you are coming."

Conlin raised his hand to her cheek and caressed her jawline. "There's no other place I'd rather be."

"I called it, ye're the OTP," Saoirse said.

Conlin and Jeanette angled their heads at the same second, looking at her through the middle space between the seats and she donned a confident grin. Jeanette beheld him, and he reflected her sentiments in his gleaming irises. She returned to a forward position and gripped the steering wheel. The sooner she completed the business at her work, they could finish enjoying quality time together and forget about the stones.

Forty-five minutes later, Jeanette still hadn't received an update from anyone. *No need to panic, no news is good news.* She took exit 14 off I-93 and turned onto North State Street. At the end of the road, she made a right into the lot behind the granite building.

Jeanette parked near the accessible ramp and employee entrance. She surveyed the dark area, spotting Brian's red Fiat 124 Spider Abarth, and an unfamiliar black SUV in the far corner spaces. Nothing out of the ordinary for out-of-town visitors to use their parking after hours to avoid paying for meters on Main Street.

"I don't see Tom, but Brian's car is here." She opened her door and twisted her torso to exit. "Be right back."

Conlin grasped her wrist with a heartening caress, closing in on her personal space, and imparted his devotion. "I'll keep an eye out for you."

Bowing her neck in appreciation, Jeanette tapped his hand, pressing her lips tight to curtail emotions, and stepped outside. She crept ahead, taking cautious steps and searched in all directions. A shadowy figure rounded the corner from Park Street at the same instant a vibration rumbled on her backside, quickening her pulse. A quiver crawled up her spine, fumbling to pull the phone from her pocket, and she skimmed through Tom's text.

I'm here.

Jeanette did a double take at the person rushing toward her, holding in a breath until she recognized Tom, and a gusty sigh escaped her lips. She met him under the building's floodlights. "What's going on? I thought you had it all under control."

"The whole situation is strange. It felt unsettling, waiting at Jack's without a reply from my supervisor or Brian."

Jeanette swallowed the dryness in her cottonmouth. "Let's just check on the relic."

Tom agreed, ducking his head and followed her up the walkway. Jeanette typed in her identification code on the keypad and waited for green lights to flash. She tugged the handle, and someone pushed from the inside. Inhaling a sharp intake of air, she backed into Tom, and he stabilized her balance.

The entry opened, and Brian appeared in the doorway. "What are you doing here?"

Her knees weakened, and Tom placed a hand on her shoulder. She could guess he was relieved, too. "Neither of us received confirmation about the Mystery Stone."

Brian said, "It's settled—"

"Oui." The door widened and Geron stood behind Brian. "The artifact is where it belongs, in my possession."

Tom yanked Jeanette backward and she froze like an object on display in the museum. Geron stepped forward, pushing Brian in the open air with a forceful bump against his shoulder, allowing the door to close. Jeanette peered at the CR-V rental and observed Conlin exiting the vehicle. Her heart sank, and she closed her eyes for a few seconds. Why didn't he stay inside or better yet drive off?

"I told you I'd be in touch," Geron said.

"You know Mr. Leclerc?" Brian asked.

"How could you give him the stone, Brian?" She flashed him a stern glare.

His mouth fell agape at her wrongful accusations, judging him before he had a fair trial. "Mr. Bonhoeffer instructed me to meet Mr. Leclerc and grant him access to the Mystery Stone."

"Simon?" Jeanette looked at her brother, and she blinked a few extra times, clearing the spots obstructing her vision.

Tom ran a palm through his hair and staggered, grasping the handrailing. "No way... he wouldn't..."

Geron sneered, and a bark of laughter burst forth. "Didn't I warn you in Quebec about your lack of understanding and the individuals involved?"

Now he exposed the true culprit; Simon Bonhoeffer orchestrated the events from the beginning. The dullness in Tom's eyes and slackened facial muscles revealed his state of shock. Although Jeanette believed they still had a chance to negotiate since Geron didn't have the other two stones.

"Did I miss something here?" Brian asked.

"You've served your purpose." Geron shoved him, knocking him into Jeanette. "Leave, before I change my mind."

She tilted close to Brian's ear, hiding behind a curtain of her hair, and whispered, "Call the police."

His torso stiffened, and color leeched from his complexion. "Sorry."

She eyed him and offered a sole nod. Brian wasn't at fault. None of them were, and they had all been pawns in Simon's plans. He hurried down the ramp and her line of vision followed him until he made it to his car. At least one of them escaped.

Jeanette fixed her eyesight on Conlin, and he leaned his body against the hood of the Honda, observing their interactions. Too bad she didn't have the power of telepathy for sharing her thoughts with Conlin. Panic struck her paralyzed and her stomach pitted into tight coils, realizing she must act on impulse if they were going to achieve a getaway.

"Conlin, take off!" An increased heart rate shot adrenaline into her bloodstream, and she whirled around, clutching the silver canister containing the Mystery Stone in Geron's hand. "Run, Tom," she yelled, straining her voice.

Screeching tires echoed throughout the lot and Jeanette tried to pry the container out of Geron's clasp. He tightened his grip, knocking her with the force of a soccer player on an opposing team, and she tripped on the heel of her boot, falling onto her rear. Jeanette winced, shaking her head and grimaced at Geron.

"Get up, and don't try my patience again," he said.

Placing her palms on the cool cement, she pushed herself from the ground and rose to her feet. Conlin advanced forward, and Tom waited at the bottom of the ramp. Why did they ignore her suggestions and stay? The Toyota RAV4 parked behind her rental, blocking their escape, and Harry escorted Tom through the lot to his vehicle on the street.

"We have unfinished business. Remember, we're making a significant contribution to the archaeology community and restoring order in our sects."

Jeanette squinted and glanced at him sidelong. Their assumptions that heritage factored into their connection with the stones seemed accurate. Tom and Harry returned to deliver the aluminum briefcase containing the Vanir and Celtic Stones. A muscular man stood near Conlin beside the driver's side of the Honda. What chance did they have against Geron and his crew? His people outnumbered them, carried weapons, and left her with no choice but to plead for the Murphy's release.

Jeanette paused and held out a stiff, extended arm, halting Geron in his tracks. "There's no reason to involve them." She gestured at the CR-V. "You've acquired the stones and we're working together."

Geron glared, scrutinizing her expression, and pushed her forearm out of the way, walking past her. "Mr. Hillestad, and the stones are coming with us."

Jeanette remained still and her entire being drew in a breath of expectancy. Thank God, it seemed Geron granted her request and obtained all he demanded. A mouthful of air burst out and deflated her ballooned cheeks.

He paused at the back-passenger side of her car and grasped the handle, opening the door as pure scorn spread over his face. "Bring the girl."

"No!" Conlin and Jeanette said in unison.

Saoirse scooted to the far end where her dad stood and hopped out of the vehicle. The brawny guy blocked her path. Conlin charged at the man, crashing against his torso, and budged his stance maybe a quarter of an inch. The harasser retaliated and slammed Conlin against the Honda. Jeanette clamped a palm over her lips, glancing in every direction. What could she do when they all required help?

Geron and Harry disregarded their outcries and they loaded into the RAV4. Protecting Saoirse gained precedence over anything else, and Jeanette hustled to join them. Conlin rushed in front of the vehicle, avoiding the third aggressor, and reached for Saoirse at the backside. The man trudged behind the car and blocked him, creating a barrier between Conlin and Saoirse.

Tom clasped her hand and he looked directly at Conlin. "I promise to protect her; they won't lay a finger on her."

Geron rolled down the window and commanded the man standing outside. "Enough John, everyone in the car, now."

Wild hysteria filled Conlin's eyes. Clenching his jaw, every facial muscle tightened. Jeanette gripped his biceps, grounding him in the security of her support, and placed a palm against his chest. His heart pounded, watching Saoirse entering the Toyota's backseat and he lurched forward, flinching at the door slamming shut.

She would switch places with Saoirse in a second. "We'll do whatever it takes."

Conlin gaped at his daughter in the car, curving his fingers over hers and gently squeezed. "I know, so."

"Hurry, let's follow them." She patted him and they hastened to the Honda as the RAV4 exited the lot.

Jeanette sped out of the parking and tailed the Toyota through the streets of Concord on Route 13. She wanted to comfort and encourage Conlin to hold on to faith that God would protect Saoirse. Yet, her intense focus on tracking the SUV kept her silent, giving him a quiet moment to process his thoughts and feelings.

Ten minutes later, a text notification flashed on the screen, and she peeked at the name. "Tom sent a message. Please read it."

He jolted in his seat and snatched the phone. "Saoirse's okay." Emotions strained his voice and he choked. "Meet us at the ancient site in Salem, New Hampshire."

Conlin set her device into the cradle, sighed, and massaged his jaw. "Do you know the location?"

"Divinity Hill." She felt the weight of his gaze, awaiting details and reassurance nothing would happen to his daughter. "It's an area of stone structures from an ancient civilization. About an hour away."

Jeanette called the authorities and provided specifics about what occurred, the people involved and where they intended to assemble. With multiple calls alerting the police, she trusted the officers would be waiting for them upon arrival.

Conlin exhaled hard and slid down in the seat, crossing his arms over his chest as he stared out the window. She didn't dare mention the alleged rituals performed in the prehistoric period. Prayer and her knowledge of the landmark were their best hope.

THIRTY-THREE

Conlin clutched his midsection and reclined against the headrest, keeping his mind focused on diligent prayers for protecting of Cricket. The trust he developed in God, Jeanette, and Thomas assisted him in overcoming the feelings of powerlessness.

Every few minutes, Jeanette laid a calming touch on his arm, and he covered her hand with his palm, letting her know he appreciated the supportive gesture. Even in silence, she provided emotional strength, and he conveyed his care for her through his caress.

Conlin figured she split her thoughts between deciphering Geron's intentions and blaming herself for everything that transpired. However, he took responsibility for Cricket and another missed opportunity to stay at Jeanette's house, yet the burden eased during the past week when he realized events and actions of others were neither of their faults nor anything they could foresee.

At 9:57 p.m., Jeanette clicked on an interior light, keeping her eyes on the road, and reached for her bag behind the seat. "Here." She placed the satchel in his lap. "We're almost there, so grab my pepper-spray, and eat a protein bar."

"I don't have an appetite."

"You'll need the energy."

"I suppose..." He dug through her items and pulled out two bars, handing her one, too. Conlin ripped open the package and bit into the chewy mix of seeds, nuts, and berries. A sickness stirred in his stomach, thinking about his baby girl, and he grabbed a bottle of water from the cupholder to wash down the nausea. He unhooked the handheld pepper-spray attached to a key chain hanging on the zipper of her purse and tucked it in his shirt pocket.

"Ten minutes at the most." Jeanette swept the perspiration from his brow with her thumb and ran her fingers through his hair. The touch of her hand relieved pressure, and he breathed through an increasing headache.

The entire ride, he pushed his fears aside and the vivid images in his mind about human sacrifices from their discussion last night that plagued him with disturbing visions. A coldness rippled throughout his body, and he cracked his knuckles, bouncing a knee. Glancing at the temperature displayed on the dashboard, 38 degrees Fahrenheit, Conlin shivered.

Jeanette drove into a car park, and he spotted the Toyota Rav4, but no police. His pulse increased and he gripped the handle, preparing for a quick exit. She stopped and he flung open the door.

Grabbing his forearm, she yanked on his sleeve. "Wait, we can't make any hasty decisions."

He blinked over at her, and his breath rushed out on a grunt, understanding the plan required calculated actions. Of course, they needed to factor in being outnumbered and confronting armed men. Conlin scrubbed his palms over his face, exhaling through his mouth.

"My Cricket..." He held his head in his hands and applied pressure to his skull, relieving the pain.

"I know, and we're going to rescue her now." She grasped and rubbed his shoulder, making direct eye contact. "Trust me."

"I do and will follow yer lead."

"Let's get Saoirse." She hopped out of the car and waved him over to join her at a gap in the ground's perimeter fence.

In the darkness, he could only see a couple of inches in front of him and Jeanette's silhouette. They trudged through waist-high weeds and the smell of livestock circulated in the damp air. A humming sound grew louder, and his internal responses fluctuated from chills to hot flashes.

"Watch your step," Jeanette said in a low tone, trampling over fallen foliage.

At the exact moment, he tripped on undergrowth and bumped into her. He gained his footing and steadied her before she fell. A high-pitched warbling echoed in the sky and Conlin flinched, searching in all directions. "What the—"

"Alpacas shriek when they're excited or sense danger."

Keep calm. Cricket needs you. Conlin shadowed her up an incline into a thicket of trees. Jeanette must've known the layout of the grounds, and his assurance grew with each confident step they took. Hidden out of sight and in the woodlands, she flipped on the flashlight function of her mobile.

"A trail ahead on the left loops around to an astronomical viewing platform." Jeanette extended her device in front of her and picked up the pace, leading the way to a marked footpath.

A prickle crept along his arms, and dampness spread across his chest. His joints stiffened, restraining the urge to sprint and he maintained a speed walk to reach the observation hub.

Jeanette crouched and skulked behind a short rock wall, peering at the gathering. Conlin mimicked her movements and leaned against her backside as she paused, kneeling on the dry leaves covering the ground.

Tiki torches surrounded the enclosed monoliths similar to the rock structures in Ireland, several feet below the hilltop. Palpitations quaked throughout his torso as he surveyed the vicinity. "Where is she?" His voice wavered, keeping his emotions under control.

"Beside Tom, near the Oracle Chamber." Jeanette pointed and he peered above her, pressing against her body.

"Glory be to God." He rested his head on hers and blew a gusty breath. They arrived prior to any sick acts Geron intended to perform. Now he needed to get Cricket out of there before they started their rituals.

Jeanette angled her neck toward him, aligning their faces and touching foreheads. "I'm impressed by your self-control. It shows incredible strength and patience to keep from rushing over to her." She tilted her chin upward and kissed his lips.

A lighthearted feeling expanded in his chest, knowing the confidence she had in his actions, and he regained vitality. "'Tis belief in God and you."

Leaning backward, she turned and directed his attention to Saoirse. "You raised a tough girl. Look at her solid stance, confronting the unknown without crying or panicking, and even if she becomes hysterical, she possesses an undeniable strength."

Conlin stared at Cricket in the firelight, and drew in a big, settling breath. "Ah, she's bleedin' fantastic."

"Because she knows her dad is coming, and he'll do anything to protect his daughter." She brushed a hand along his jawline and his appreciation for her deepened every second they spent together.

Conlin felt blessed with two of the fiercest women in his life and a fullness satisfied his soul. Jeanette reverted her focus to the group standing in strategic positions and his eyesight remained on Cricket.

"What're ya planning?" he asked.

She tapped a fist against her thigh. "Geron's preparing for an ancient ceremony. I'm waiting here till I figure out a strategy. If you want to move near Saoirse and approach the Oracle Chamber from behind, it's a good opportunity to save her when the crew's busy."

"I agree." Conlin stood and she rose to her feet.

"I'll hide beside the Grooved Table to hear the details." She dug in her pocket and tossed him the car keys. "Leave whenever it's possible."

"I'm not leaving you."

Jeanette gazed at him and stretched her lips into a closed-lip smile. "Tom will stay, and the police are on their way."

Conlin caressed her cheek, wishing he could be in two places at once. "Promise you'll be careful, Banféinní."

"Cricket is waiting for you."

He gave her a single nod and pivoted on his heel, heading in the opposite direction. The fact Jeanette didn't assure him she'd take precautions led him to believe her tactics involved placing herself in danger, and he prayed she knew what she was doing.

Conlin hunched and dashed into the shadows downhill, hiding in the profile of a tree trunk. He stole a quick look at Jeanette, tiptoeing across the open area toward the large, stone slab, and exhaled hard through his nose. At least for now, she was safe.

Treading a short distance, he approached an exit for the rocky formation and crept inside. In the blackness, he inched his back along the craggy wall and followed the echo of Geron barking orders. As he rounded a corner to the left, fire-lit torches illuminated a passageway through an opening in the ceiling. Conlin peeked out of the entrance and saw Thomas closest to the ruins. Cricket remained beside him, and another person was on her opposite side. She was so close he could almost grab her and leg it.

He crouched, selected a pebble in the dirt, and maneuvered in a position to reach Thomas. Conlin scoped out the rest of Geron's crew. John was on guard by a lower gate at the bottom of the hill. Harry unloaded and carried objects from a crate while Geron skimmed through the pages of a book.

Pressing his backside against the stacked rocks, he outstretched his arm, aimed, and threw the nugget, striking Thomas below the earlobe on his neck. He swiped his fingers across his skin and glanced over to his left, glimpsing Conlin hidden in the crevasse. Thomas motioned for him to move backward.

He hid in the tunnel and waited near the entrance, yet his patience wore thin. After a couple of minutes, feeling like half an hour, he peered outside and checked the situation. Clever lad, Thomas and Cricket traded places. Now she was three feet away. He inhaled a deep, cleansing breath and swallowed the pinch in his throat.

"Psst," Conlin whispered, cupping his hand to amplify the sound loud enough for her to hear.

Cricket flipped her hair over a shoulder, angling her chin to the left and spotted him peeping between a split in the rocks. She shuffled her boots along the gravel, inching toward him and still facing forward. Conlin took inventory of the surrounding area, ensuring nobody noticed their attempted escape. Geron stayed distracted, organizing his ritual.

His body twitched as she moved closer, and he wiped the beading sweat off his forehead with a sleeve. Another few inches and he could reach and pull her to safety. He dried his clammy palms on his trousers, preparing to grab a hold of her and slink into the darkness.

The pounding of his heart, her shoes dragging across dirt, and voices in the background, all intensified. Conlin reached his trembling fingers outward, brushing the fabric of her jacket, and she stretched her arm, touching his fingertips. He caught his Cricket.

Conlin gripped her wrist and a sudden weightlessness spread through his limbs at her touch. Swiftly, he tugged Cricket inside the stone shelter and into a protective hug. A rush of feelings flooded his mind and core, yet one emotion overwhelmed him—gratefulness. *Praise Jesus.* He squeezed her tighter.

"Da—" she said in a muffled voice, pressing her face against his biceps.

Conlin leaned backward and created enough space to examine her appearance. "Are ya hurt?" He inspected her expression in the dim light. "They didn't harm ya at all?"

"I'm fine. Thomas was wit' me the entire time."

Relief swelled in his airways, and he blew the stress away, hugging her again. "We need to hurry. Follow me." He took her hand and guided her through the corridor. "Take it handy, 'tis darker round the corner."

They hurried along the tunnel, backtracking Conlin's entry route through the exit. Before stepping outside, he halted, and Cricket paused behind him as he scanned the terrain. "All clear." He waved for her to continue onward.

Conlin and Cricket pressed their bodies against the piled rocks, staying out of the light. The extent of his strategic planning didn't go further than retracing the trail he and Jeanette traveled. Still and all, a sense of accomplishment renewed his resolution. He looked at her beaming appearance and for the first time in years he perceived the pride she possessed for her auld man. Even in the realm of danger, contentment washed over him and soon he'd have her to safety. Around the last corner, before trekking uphill to the astrological viewpoint, he turned and Ace blocked their route, crossing his arms in a rigid pose.

Conlin froze and wrapped a firm grip on Cricket's shoulder, pulling her closer. "Move out of me way—"

"Or else what?" Ace flashed a pistol under his jacket, secured in a hip holster.

"Why are ye willing to commit murder?"

"It pays well."

A sour taste filled his mouth. "You'll even shoot a kid?" His grasp tightened on Cricket. "What if someone put your children in danger?"

"I told you before, I'd never be stupid enough to allow anything to happen to them."

"Too many things are out of our control. We can't protect them from everything, and all we can do is have faith in God's sovereignty."

"How desperate and pathetic." He rolled his eyes and laughed. "It's pitiful to witness a father failing to protect his family. I wonder how your beliefs would've held up if you had arrived to find your daughter dead."

A hitch caught in his chest at the mention of a horrific scene. Trusting in God was the foundation of his convictions, especially when confronting tragedies. Conlin noticed a shadowy figure creeping from behind the pillared rocks to the right of Ace and in the blink of an eye, Thomas struck the vagus nerve on the side of his neck. Ace dropped to his knees and blacked out.

Thomas stooped, checked Ace's pulse, and removed the gun from his holster. "Where's Nettie?"

"Waiting up the hill," Conlin said.

"Good, lead the way."

Saoirse held onto his hand, and Thomas tailed close as they rushed alongside hedges concealing their movements. The hope of getting them all out of there moved his footsteps faster. Shuffling through wet leaves, they climbed the short incline. Another few feet and they'd be on the other side of the fence, where Jeanette waited.

Conlin passed between two trees, approaching the marker for site thirty-one, closer to Jeanette. A jolt of adrenaline surged through his veins, believing everything would be grand, and now all four of them could escape together.

"Nice try," Harry said.

Conlin stopped in his tracks, shielding Cricket with his body, and she nuzzled against him. Thomas defended her at the backside. Harry aimed his weapon at them and climbed over the chained-off section of ruins. Geron waltzed in their direction and joined him at his side.

"Where are you going? You can't leave before our ceremony." Geron's mouth curved into a sneer. "We need the blót offering of a child."

"Enough of this craziness," Thomas said in a shaky voice.

Conlin's heartbeat skipped, and a dizziness swayed his balance. Cricket pressed her head against his spine. "You'll have to go through me first."

Geron nodded with a glaring squint. "I'd have no qualms eradicating you, Monsieur Murphy." He peered at Harry and waved for him to proceed. "Do whatever is needed and prepare the girl."

"Stop!" Jeanette jumped off the edge of a boulder, next to the flat-stone table. "I'm offering myself as the sacrifice."

Conlin's heart thrashed to break out, rattling in his chest, and lurched him forward. In the deepest part of his soul, he speculated she always planned to take Cricket's place. Jeanette revealed the clear evidence when she withheld details about her reasons for taking the Celtic Stone in Quebec, Divinity Hill's history, and the ancient culture's rituals, pirouetting around a straight answer like a trained ballerina. Yet he should be the one sacrificing himself.

Geron gawked at her silhouette in the torchlight. "Interesting proposal."

Thomas stepped forward. "Nettie, don't—"

"Shut up." Harry grabbed the back of his collar and shook him hard.

Jeanette advanced at a steady gait. "Blood from a descendant of the Vikings seems appropriate on Óðinsdagur during Gormánuður."

Thomas leaned close and whispered, "The first celebration of slaughter month, a winter feast held in honor of Freyr." He checked his watch. "It's almost midnight, Odin's Day, Wednesday."

"It's not a surprise you'd know about ancient festivals. We've prepared for the Celtic ceremonial Cross-Quarter Day, Samhain."

Geron's movement mimicked a viper ready to strike its prey. "However, I'm intrigued by the idea of a willing martyr."

"Then let's discuss the ritualistic preparations," she said in a level and emboldened tone.

Jeanette's hair blew to one side in the wind, and she brushed loose strands from her cheek. The oil-lamp flames fanning behind her emphasized her confident pose. She appeared unshaken and empowered by a divine spirit. The attention her presence and knowledge commanded deserved respect that even Geron couldn't ignore.

Geron gestured for Thomas to stand beside him. "Monsieur Hillestad will assist us with the formalities."

No wonder Thomas depended on Jeanette to bail him out of trouble. Her reliability was unmatchable, and Conlin felt certain everyone in her life counted on her to show up, despite the personal consequences she endured. She already sacrificed much in their short time together and had proven she'd always be there for them. A quality he admired in her and he would never demand or take advantage of her loyal devotion.

"Do you want me to dispose of these two in the woods?" Harry turned and sneered. "After you watch your girlfriend bleed to death."

Conlin stiffened his torso, and Cricket gathered the material of his shirt in her fists. He swiped a palm over his eyes, clearing the visions from his mind of a hooded figure raising a knife above a person and triggered his nightmares. Either way, the two most precious people to him had become targets and selected as blood offerings.

"Forget the Murphys for now." Geron pointed at Ace trudging uphill and rubbing his noggin. "Three times you've allowed them to escape and failed me. Monitor them until Mr. Bonhoeffer arrives and he'll decide their fate."

Conlin knew nothing about the Simon Bonhoeffer fella, but maybe he was more reasonable than Geron if Thomas worked with him for years, remaining unaware of his evil schemes.

Harry shoved his shoulder hard. "I'll gain pleasure from tying up your woman, making sure she revels in it, since I'm the last man that'll touch her before she dies."

Conlin choked back the need to spit excessive saliva filling in his mouth, tightening his clenched jaw. He stared forward, ignoring the filthy beast and denied him the satisfaction of reacting to his remarks. Harry stomped away, roaring out obnoxious laughter.

What could he do to save Jeanette other than pray for divine intervention? The biblical verse displayed in Jack's guestroom repeated in his head. *For love is as strong as death.* God's perfect gifts never failed, and he clung to his beliefs about scriptural promises being fulfilled.

"Sit down." Ace directed them toward a bench behind a chain-link fence above the sacrificial table. "You'll have front row seats to the event."

Conlin wrapped his arm around Cricket, and they huddled close together in the cold, damp air. At least Jeanette wasn't alone and had Thomas at her side. Conlin sighed, thinking about how she'd need to trust her brother for the first time.

THIRTY-FOUR

During the witching hour, a little after 3:30 a.m. brightness from the silvery moon gleamed through passing gray clouds. Jeanette's limbs weighed her down, slowing her movements as time ticked into the early morning, and Geron kept everyone busy preparing for the ritual.

Jeanette affixed her gaze on Conlin, sensing the weight of his stare. She believed even in the darkness and his limited view that he never took his eyesight off her. She experienced Conlin's reactions to danger on several occasions and was confident he prayed for her now. Comfort and a peacefulness spilled over her, regardless of confronting her martyrdom.

Everyone probably assumed she concocted an elaborate escape plan, yet the situation went well beyond anything she dealt with in the past. The fact she and Tom only theorized ideas about the stones and their original function didn't provide her any kind of leverage.

Geron left her alone to anticipate her impending demise and demanded she give her full cooperation to Mr. Bonhoeffer at his arrival. Tom glanced upward from his task of attaching the Vanir and Celtic Stones onto a two-pronged metal scepter. She followed his line of vision to Simon Bonhoeffer, hiking uphill through the monolithic-rock structures and his silver-white hair shimmered in the firelight.

Jeanette stepped closer and listened to their conversation. Perhaps she'd learn more about Simon's intentions toward the Murphys and if there was a way for them to escape.

Simon aimed his footsteps at Tom, outstretching an arm and laid a hand on his shoulder. "How does it feel to have reached your goal?"

Tom scrunched his facial features, presenting a defiant down-turned mouth, and glared at Simon. "None of your vile plans are part of my ambitions and you're a disgrace to the field of archaeology."

"You stated during your interview with the board you'd do anything to discover the mysterious stones around the world and determine their importance. It's why I selected you for the expedition in Norway. Because of your arrogance and impulsive behaviors, you were the perfect candidate. Not to mention, you had done extensive research on the relics."

"There's a difference between being overzealous about examining excavated artifacts and committing murder for the sake of testing a farfetched hypothesis."

"We have a willing participant." Simon jerked his chin upward, acknowledging her decision. "Your sister understands the meaning of taking one for the team."

"Only because Geron wanted to kill a child," Tom said through gritted teeth and curved his hands into fists.

Simon swatted the air, brushing off facts like annoying insects. "Experimenting with all the possibilities requires a thorough assessment of the stone's potential." He turned, then spun on his heel, and addressed Tom again. "I'm disappointed with your lack of knowledge and the honor given to the chosen sacrifice. The ancient cultures valued life and, because of their belief in an afterlife, they never interpreted the sacrifices as killing a person.

We're handling relics forged for blood offering and in order to reveal the true powers contained, we must present lifeblood."

"I'm aware of those primordial beliefs and your disturbing philosophies. Besides, you're blatantly disregarding the truth. There isn't anything sacred about these stones or Divinity Hill."

"Typical response from someone who turns a blind eye to the obvious supernatural activity around us at all times."

"What kind of phenomenon are you expecting?"

Simon peeked at his watch. "You'll see at sunrise." He departed and joined Geron.

They met each other's questioning look, and his expression revealed he was thinking the same thing. It appeared Geron and Simon intermixed worshipping rituals of early civilizations to cover all possible ceremonial practices.

She crept nearer and stood beside Tom. "When I met Geron at the Plains of Abraham, he mentioned the Seven Years' War representing power and control. The Norse seers and Celtic Druids used blood to foretell the future. Geron and Simon made specific references to sunrise, which coincides with the celebration of new life—"

"Of course, if they believe the stones act as vessels and harness an energy source, then their experiments will fail."

"You're certain nothing will happen?"

"They're attempting to prove the ultimate dichotomy of science and the supernatural coexisting in the cosmos." Tom inclined his head sideways and rubbed his neck. "It's all human constructs."

"How do you explain the strange feelings whenever we touch the Vanir Stone?"

"Charged or magnetic particles," he said in a pragmatic tone.

"Conlin's visions and dreams?"

"All in his mind."

"Or there's validity in individual experiences with the supernatural realms that's ignored and written off as myths."

"Nettie, you honestly expect their reconstruction of prehistoric behavior and ceremonial practices to produce results?"

"I guess we'll find out soon enough…" She shivered and glimpsed at the Grooved Table. Tom set a soft palm on her shoulder.

"All that matters now is stopping them from performing their ritual. So, what's your strategy?"

Jeanette peered into the dark, vast landscape and she flicked a gaze heavenward at the faint twinkling of stars burning light years away. A shrinking sensation engulfed her, realizing the smallness of her existence in the universe. Nevertheless, a fullness overwhelmed her with an equal revelation that her presence held significance at this specific point in time. Because if she served no purpose, then what was the reason if it all meant nothing?

"Conceding is my plan." She set her sights on Conlin and the surmounting ache in her heart consumed any other feelings. "Promise me that no matter what happens, you'll ensure Conlin, and Saoirse are safe."

He gently shook her arm as if to awaken her from a nightmare. "We can't allow them to—"

She pulled away and made direct eye contact. "Assure me you'll make it your priority."

Tom blinked a few extra times and wrinkles cut across his forehead. "Net, I…" He raked his fingers through his hair and expelled a breath from his cheeks.

"Promise, Tom." Her molars bore down on the inside of her mouth. Couldn't he follow through on one thing she asked? After all, she was surrendering herself to protect everyone else.

"A last-minute squabble between siblings before our transcendent event?" Simon interrupted their conversation.

In an act of desperation, Tom confronted Mr. Bonhoeffer. "Please, spare my sister and allow the Murphys to leave." He grasped the fabric of Simon's coat. "We've worked together in the office for years. I'm part of your field crew and I've been to your house for dinner... I'll do whatever—"

"Calm down, Thomas." He patted the back of his shoulder. "You still don't comprehend the privilege you've received, witnessing a ground-breaking method for collecting observable data by reenacting and interpreting ancient practices."

Geron stood on a mound beside a crude, carved circle with a hole in the center, wearing a hooded robe and holding the stones affixed to a mace. "Monsieur Hillestad, finish positioning the Asherah poles."

The constant illumination of a vibrant life in Tom's eyes flickered and the disconcerting circumstances extinguished the light. Tom dipped his chin as his torso caved inward and he focused on the ground, trudging uphill to meet Geron. A heaviness pressed upon her chest and her breathing became shallow, watching her brother follow their orders.

"Ms. Hillestad, do you have any suggestions before we begin the ceremony?" Mr. Bonhoeffer said.

Jeanette redirected his attention, pointing a shaky finger at the Murphys. "Let them go."

He squinted at Tom, tightening the lines on the outside of his eyes and considered her request. "All right, they are free to exit the grounds."

A sudden lightness spread throughout her limbs, wishing to hug, kiss, and gaze into Conlin's eyes before he left or better yet, join them in their freedom.

"But first, we need to prepare the offering." Simon waved a raised arm and summoned Harry. "Escort Ms. Hillestad to the sacrificial table."

The split second of joy she experienced regarding the Murphy's release drained from her body. If they didn't leave soon, the final images imprinted in their minds would be her bound to a stone and bleeding to death.

Harry grabbed and yanked her forearm. "Finally." He pulled her along piles of dried leaves to the Grooved Table. He tugged at her sleeves, swung her around, removing her outerwear, and tossed the jacket into the bushes. "Payback time. I've waited for this moment since our first encounter in Kinsale."

Jeanette swallowed an astute remark sprouting on her tongue. It wouldn't help anyone if she antagonized Harry. He shoved her backward onto the hard surface of the flat rock and she banged her skull. An instant pain shot through her brain, and she squeezed her lids shut.

Laughter rumbled from Harry's belly and rolled upward out of his mouth. He rummaged through a duffle bag, and removed bindings, then began securing her legs at the ankles. Leaning across her chest, he intentionally brushed against her breasts and gripped her wrists, lifting them overhead. She gulped the nausea rising in her esophagus as his sweaty midsection hung inches from her nose, and she rotated the other way, gasping for fresh air.

Rough ties scraped her skin as he bound the rope around her arms and drove a metal stake into wet soil. Harry pushed himself back from the rock, removing the pressure, and a lungful of alleviation dispelled.

He moved to the top of the stone and pounded the spike harder, using the heel of his boot. Each hammer dug deeper into her flesh, and she winced at the burning sensation. Jeanette flattened her lips, suppressing her grunts of pain. She peeked through a cracked eyelid. Tom positioned the pronged rod into a carved circle on the ground.

Geron retrieved a dagger, offering it to Tom in his open palms. "You'll have the role of slaughtering the sacrifice."

Tom's complexion became chalky white, and he gawked at the blade. "I'm not taking part in your demented plans."

"Your boss requires it. Otherwise, you'll be responsible for multiple deaths," Geron said. "Better to have your own family's blood on your hands."

Going quiet, Tom shifted a vacant stare toward Conlin and Saoirse. He slouched into a sagging posture and took the knife from Geron.

"Careful, I excavated the blade from an unearthed temple in Israel."

Tom held the decorated dagger, and a dullness veiled his appearance. At the moment, Jeanette felt the burden of her brother's plight, more than her own. Dying had to be easier than killing. Facing death should've terrified her, yet a calmness relaxed her muscles, knowing God was in control. Having her fate carried out by her brother seemed tolerable over Geron, or one of his men looming above her with a knife. How would Tom cope with being the person carrying out her execution? What would he tell Mom and Dad?

Tom made a straight line for Jeanette. The angle of his stance cast a shadow across his face. He didn't look like himself, and she beat her eyelashes for a second to clear the image from her mind. Although it helped the situation if he remained unrecognizable.

"Nettie," he whispered. "I'm so sorry for everything."

She peered at him and could see the boy from his youth. "Not quite the games we played growing up, huh?"

"A simpler, innocent age of digging in the yard, searching for artifacts, hiking trails and examining our environments in wonderment." A wet film glazed his eyes, and a crease deepened at the bridge of his nose.

The compressing mass of his words, recounting their childhood equated to the four-ton rock they fastened her on, and she struggled to catch her breath. The exact moment when their relationship changed eluded her at present. She lost the opportunity to say the things she intended to tell him over the years and held as much responsibility as Tom for the outcome of his decisions.

A soreness developed in her throat, suppressing feelings. "I love you, brother."

The muscles around his mouth twitched, keeping his emotions under control. "You'll always be my hero…"

A surge jolted her heart with the sudden awareness she had been a fool and blinded by her imaginary competitions. Knots coiled in her belly, and she turned her head in the opposite direction.

"We're on a tight schedule and are ready for the sacrifice." Simon held a single staff with the Mystery Stone attached by the always puzzling, drilled holes through the top and bottom. "I'll return in five minutes and enter the Oracle Chamber after positioning the rod at the fallen monolith, where the sun rises over the equator."

Jeanette craned her neck to view the stone. Even with her life at stake, curiosity grew about the relic's capabilities. It was intentional that she distracted herself to avoid looking or thinking about Conlin as their short-lived relationship settled into the deepest part of her heart and soul.

"Say your goodbyes." Simon walked along the trail, beyond the astrological viewing spot.

She sought solace from God and the deliverance provided for whoever has faith in biblical promises. She meditated on a memorized verse in the Bible, Isaiah 41:10:

Don't be afraid, for I am with you. Don't be dismayed, for I am your God. I will strengthen you. Yes, I will help you.

Jeanette needed Conlin to hold her hand through the darkest hour and provide comfort as she passed on from this world into the next. She dared to look at him and catch a glimpse of his face for the last time. Yet, she knew it was best for him and Saoirse to go now. Tears burned at the border of her eyes, and she chewed on the inside of her lip to refrain from crying. She gulped and uttered his name in a hoarse tone. "Conlin…"

He lunged forward and slumped his defeated posture against the barrier, hooking his fingers through the zig-zag pattern of the fence. "Jeanette!" The sound of emotions straining his voice crushed her and she was already dying inside.

THIRTY-FIVE

Conlin dragged his fingers along the steel-wire fence and coldness triggered goosebumps on his flesh. He grabbed a fistful of hair, staring at Jeanette tied to a rock and awaiting her death. How did their situation worsen and go so bleedin' wrong? The erratic thoughts of possibilities to save her oscillated in his mind.

Mr. Bonhoeffer stopped, stepped closer, and looked at him. "You're free to leave now."

"Why are ye committing this atrocity?"

Mr. Bonhoeffer pointed at Jeanette. "She understands and bargained her life to secure your freedom. Don't desecrate her sacrificial deed by provoking my anger and forcing me to take action against you." After a couple of steps, he made an about-face. "Oh, I've also taken care of the police. They're aware of our archaeologists working on the property and that any phone calls received are from a disgruntled employee falsifying reports of an incident occurring." He flashed a smirk and waved. "Goodbye, Mr. Murphy."

A tightness balled in his chest, darting his gaze between Jeanette and Saoirse. There was no way he would risk Cricket's life again, yet he refused to abandon Jeanette and allow her to die. Conlin inhaled deep, closing his eyelids and exhaled aloud, releasing the painful decision.

"Let me make the choice easy for you; take your daughter and go," Ace said. "There's nothing you can do to rescue your girlfriend."

Conlin's pulse throbbed in his neck and the torment crumpled his spine. The line of his sight drifted to Jeanette stretched out on the sacrificial altar one last time before he spun around and denied himself a final farewell. Cricket gaped at him and shook her head in protest of leaving Jeanette to suffer for the sake of their safety.

He gripped her hand, giving her a slight squeeze and a wink. The tension in her handclasp loosened, and she seemed to understand he intended to devise a scheme. They aimed for the trail toward the car park.

"The first smart choice you've made," Ace said.

Conlin paused, glancing over his shoulder. "Yeah, too bad you're determined to stay a right eejit."

He secured his grasp on Cricket and steered her into the darkness of the trees. His heart rate increased, and a perspiration broke on his hairline. She lit the route using her mobile and he followed the sound of the alpacas.

Barreling ahead, they arrived at the hired vehicle a few minutes later. Conlin fumbled in his pockets for the keys. "Okay, dear one"—he unlocked the Honda and opened a door—"keep trying to get cellular service and contact the police."

Cricket climbed inside the vehicle and stared him in the face. "You believe I can manage it, yeah?"

"I know, so. You've proven you're a fierce, clever young woman altogether."

"T'anks." She smiled and gave him a hug. "I also snapped like a few pictures and recorded a video."

"Ah, ye're massive." He pulled the pepper-spray from his coat and passed it to Cricket. "Here, just in case."

"Da..."

Conlin glanced at her weary, glassy eyes and patted her hand. "Be grand! See you soon." He shut the door and double-timed it out of there.

Sprinting along the familiar path, Conlin returned to the same location at the astrological outlook point, providing an eagle's eye view. *God, I hope I'm not too late.*

Conlin stood observing everyone's position. A huge breath escaped his lips, confirming Jeanette was still alive and her brother lingered beside clutching the knife. Did Thomas create a plan? Conlin couldn't wait and find out.

Searching in every direction, he verified John loitered at the lower entry gate; there was no sign of Mr. Bonhoeffer or Ace and Harry stood near the altar. Geron chanted in an ancient language beside the Vanir and Celtic Stones perched on the staff. Pyres burned on each side among the oil lamps, reminding him of the Old Testament book 1 Kings when Elijah challenged the prophets of Baal on Mount Carmel. Conlin's faith in God provided them with an equal likelihood of obtaining the same victory.

Creating a diversion presented the best option available. Conlin scuttled through the trees toward the backside of the barrier and chose a strategic spot above Harry. He crouched and gathered different sizes of rocks off the ground—pebbles shoved in one pocket, and a handful of gravel to throw in someone's face if needed. Conlin brushed his thumb over the smooth surface of three oval-shaped stones and stuffed them in his coat. Then, he armed himself with larger rocks in both hands.

At close range, Conlin chucked the first rock at Harry and missed his intended target, knocking him on the shoulder. Exercising his quick reflexes, Conlin ducked out of sight as Harry skimmed the surrounding area and massaged his arm. He capitalized on his Irish hurling skills and took another shot, aiming for Harry's noggin. The rock smacked behind his eye between the forehead and ear. The blow of the impact knocked him out.

Geron ignored Harry, slumped on the ground and continued reading from a book. Thomas appeared to recognize a moment of opportunity and charged at Geron. He lunged and tackled him with enough force for Geron to lose balance and stumble into the rocky structures.

"It's over, Geron." Thomas tossed the dagger aside in the bushes and withdrew Ace's gun, pointing the weapon at him.

John ran uphill, and Thomas fired the pistol, giving them a warning shot. Harry sat upright, swiping blood from the rim of his eye. In the middle of chaotic movements, Geron rummaged through the shrubbery and retrieved the blade.

Conlin looked at Jeanette and she wriggled her hips, yanking on the rope bindings around her wrists. He found his moment to set her free. "I'm coming for ya, Jeanette," he muttered, and retraced his steps.

At a steady jog, he followed a path to the entrance of the enclosed area. As he rounded the corner of the fence, a striking force like a hurley stick belted him in the gut and he staggered backward pinning a palm on his waist. Sickness swirled in his abdomen and a stinging inflamed the skin across his stomach. He doubled over and coughed, clasping onto the bordering chain for support.

"That's for calling me an idiot." Ace threw the thick branch he used to strike him on the ground. "Good luck surviving with your stupidity. I'm outta here." He turned away and left, trudging downhill.

Conlin shut his lids tight, clearing his vision and focused on Jeanette. Geron pursued her and raised the blade in both his hands. Time seemed to slow, keeping him from moving fast enough to reach Jeanette. Geron advanced and stood over her body. Adrenaline shot through his system, and he rushed into the entry. In every cell of his being, he believed Jeanette would survive.

THIRTY-SIX

Jeanette's heart raced, and the pounding echoed in her ears, vibrating throughout her body. A devilish gleam shined in Geron's irises as he leaned forward in his hooded cloak, resembling a raven's swooping attack. He positioned himself to stab the approximate fourteen-inch renovated, ancient blade into her side with the obvious intention of hitting an artery or major vein.

She hauled in a harsh intake of air and closed her lids. An image of Conlin flashed before her eyes, and she dwelled on the *Song of Songs* biblical verse. *For love is as strong as death*. Her lashes flickered to clear her eyesight. Geron plunged the dagger and struck her body.

"No!" Conlin said.

Jeanette's eyelids flitted open, and he tackled Geron after the blade grazed her rib cage. She sucked in a sharp breath, filling her lungs to capacity. Geron clutched the knife as he fell against a half-crumbled stonework and wrestled Conlin. Her thoughts teetered between a stinging pain and frenzied events taking place in a rapid succession.

Geron shoved Conlin off him and in an instant thrust the entire length of the blade below her ribs at a slant. She held in a gasp until he withdrew the dagger at full strength, and she expelled a breathy grunt. Conlin grabbed a handful of Geron's robe, tossed him aside and he dropped onto a leaf pile. He scampered toward the stony pulpit and Tom pointed the gun at him.

"Drop the weapon and move away from the staff," Tom said.

The prickling of thousands of needles spread across her torso, and a tingle streamlined through her nerves. Numbness dispersed throughout her limbs, and she surrendered to a lengthy blink. She peeked at Conlin through the fringe of her eyelashes for confirmation that she didn't imagine him here. He stayed and made his own sacrifices.

"Conlin," she moaned in a raspy voice.

"Shh, save yer strength." Removing his coat, he peeled off the button-down top, layering his t-shirt. He pressed the bundled material against her wound and applied pressure with one hand. Jeanette groaned and he caressed her forehead with his palm before brushing his lips across her hairline. "Sorry if I hurt ya."

"How's Nettie?" Tom yelled, holding Harry, Geron and John at gunpoint.

"She'll be fine."

Conlin reached for her bindings and yanked. Each tug and jerk aggravated her stab wounds. He hustled and kicked the anchor out of the dirt, untying the knots. The coolness of his touch on her wrists relieved the rope burns. Bending closer, he slid his forearms underneath her frame and curled his biceps, scooping her into his arms. He secured a firm clasp behind her thighs and backbone to support her weight. She curved toward his chest and an acute stinging returned, increasing difficulty of breathing. Wet soil, perspiration and a metallic odor circulated in the air.

Conlin carried her to shelter at the astronomical viewing structure, strode up the ramp of the platform and laid her onto wooden planks. Jeanette's vision doubled and blurred as she focused on him, ignoring the lack of energy to move. Kneeling beside her, he examined the seeping cuts and searched over her attire. He grasped the front placket of her shirt and tugged the sheer fabric, popping buttons, ripping down the middle. He slid the blouse off her shoulders, exposing a camisole, and removed the top, tying the material around her midriff to act as a tourniquet.

The intermixed sensation of his warm caress and the bitter cold fluctuated her body temperature, triggering internal shivers. Conlin grabbed his coat and covered her torso. She glanced at his blood-stained hands and the splotches on his white t-shirt. "Where's Saoirse? Is she safe?"

"Yeah, thanks to you." Conlin brushed his fingers against her cheek. "She's in the car calling the police."

A ball of emotions clogged her throat, and she inhaled deeply through her nose. The rapid intake of oxygen sparked a scorching ache, and her lips twitched, containing the pain. He pulled back the coat and checked to see if the wrappings had staunched her bleeding. The clothes absorbed blood loss, but the lacerations continued weeping.

"Texting Cricket now and letting her know we need a medic." Conlin heaved himself up and tugged his phone from a rear pocket.

The voices arguing below grew louder and Jeanette viewed the fog layered, cobalt-blue sky of civil dawn. "Tom needs my help." She shifted her waist and winced at the pinching near her rib cage.

"Stay and rest. I'll handle it."

Jeanette's range of vision followed Conlin rushing down the ramp to meet Tom. She tightened her abdominal muscles, struggling to sit upright and held her breath to suppress the constant jabbing behind her ribs. She pulled herself up using the wood railing and wobbled, experiencing a whirling in her head. Keeping Conlin's shirt bundled on her wound like a bandage, and her blouse tied to keep it in place, she was reconciled to putting an end to Mr. Bonhoeffer's schemes.

The wind snuck in through the open collar of Conlin's oversized coat and she trembled. Any movement and each staggered step stressed the need for medical treatment. At the bottom of the boardwalk, she shuffled her boots along the grimy leaves and peered through her hazy sight. Conlin stood at the entry for the enclosed ruins, assessing the situation.

"What are you thinking—"

"You put the heart crossways in me." He did a double take and pressed a palm on his chest.

"Didn't mean to startle you."

Conlin shook his head and slipped his hand behind, curving his fingers below her underarm to reinforce her stability. "I'd be in shock if ya rested, Banféinní."

Sparse laughter shuddered out of her, and she recoiled at the discomfort on her side. Jeanette shored her leaning frame on Conlin, and he drew her into a harboring embrace. All at once she became stronger and weaker, a complete balance of their centered relationship.

"Thomas has them held at gunpoint and Geron isn't surrendering." He intensified his stare. "I prefer you steer clear of him."

Jeanette understood Conlin's thought process and nodded in agreement. "Please make sure Tom keeps away from the stones. The sun's rising and I have a feeling something's going to happen."

"You're correct, it's time." Mr. Bonhoeffer strolled along the path, returning from the sunrise ruins. "Ms. Hillestad, you survived the ritual?" Simon halted and shifted his glance between them. "And for some reason, Mr. Murphy stuck around." He shrugged half-heartedly and spoke in a flat tone. "Observe the power of the stones. The Mystery Stone is in perfect position and in alignment with Stonehenge." Simon ambled beyond the gated area and joined Geron.

The moment of truth arrived, and a series of spluttering palpitations overwhelmed her. She swayed and Conlin supported her entire weight since the injuries rendered her useless. Now, Tom might suffer because she always needed to rescue him out of every circumstance and take control of a situation. "Conlin…" She motioned to Tom.

He dipped his chin in concession and guided her to the knee-high rock wall bordering the astronomical viewing platform. Conlin lowered her into a sitting position, easing the pressure on her wounds. His hand slid from her back, and he held an arm out, ensuring she remained stable. "It'll only take a minute." A smile flickered on his face, and he trotted toward Tom.

Jeanette angled her torso, relieving the ache of her deep cuts as a tingling set into her fingers and toes. Focusing on the interaction between the men gathered at the staff, a pulsating twinge spread across her midsection, and a migraine thumped in her brain. While Tom and Simon argued, Conlin kept motioning for him to step away from the mace and follow him out of the enclosure. Jeanette huffed out a peeved breath and placed a soft palm against her waist, disturbing her puncture wounds. She would witness a genuine miracle if Tom listened for once.

Pressing her hand against the craggy rocks, she fought to her feet and staggered along the fence. At the entrance, she blinked a few extra times to clear the imprint of bright firelight from her vision. Exhausted after walking a few feet, she gripped a fencepost and propped herself up from falling. Geron continued chanting, alternating between the extinct language of Pictish and Old Norse. Simon pointed at the skyline and Jeanette glanced over her shoulder, watching a glorious moment of when the sun splits the horizon line, melding an amber-orange color and a metallic-blue sky. She flung her hair from her view and remained entranced by its beauty.

Tom inched backward, aiming the gun at Harry and John. Conlin directed him by the shoulder. "Time to go, lad."

"The cops are on their way now." Tom spoke directly to Simon. "You're going to get arrested, or worse."

She appreciated Tom's dilemma because of their close working relationship, and she figured he felt the ultimate deception yet wanted to spare Mr. Bonhoeffer. Jeanette's heart rate increased as Conlin and Tom approached her at the gated entrance.

Tom dashed ahead until he reached her and laid a palm on her shoulder. "Shouldn't you be lying down?"

"Then who'd watch out for you?" she said.

He rolled his eyes and flicked his chin upward, acknowledging Conlin. "It's been a team effort."

A dizziness swarmed in her head, and she fell against Conlin's chest. The firmness of his muscles sustained her in a protective embrace and in the safety of his arms, her body went limp.

"We need to get her to a hospital." Conlin's voice sounded muffled and echoed in her ears, as if submerged underwater.

"Right, we can finally get out of here," Tom said.

Her brother stared at the stones, kneading his chest and she recognized the difficulty of leaving behind his life's work. Jeanette reached for his hand, craning her neck to see his face, and caught his eye. "You fulfilled your dream and found the stones. Now you need to let them go."

Tom tore his gaze from the relics and tucked the pistol into his coat pocket. "Yeah, I know."

"You'll sort it out later, lad," Conlin said.

Gliding his fingers through her tangled tendrils, he wrapped his arm around her, and she trembled in his grip. Torn on whether she wanted him to carry her again or tough it out and walk with his support, she shuffled the soles of her boots along the trail.

Conlin leaned close and asked, "Are ya sure you'll be all right walking to the car?"

"You have nothing to prove. You're the one who survived a human sacrifice," Tom said.

Did she? Everything after the incident seemed surreal and otherworldly. The thoughts caused a vibrating sensation throughout her nerves.

Conlin whispered, "Go deo, mo banféinní."

Her eyelids shut, lulled by his voice and the promise of his words that she'd forever be his warrior. They meandered the footpath, taking careful steps in the direction of the parking lot.

About a hundred feet from the astronomical platform near the mace Simon positioned, the sun peeked over the V-shaped notch in the fallen sunrise rock and streaming light ignited the Mystery Stone. The sunshine illuminated the stone and appeared to pass through the quartzite, creating a type of light beam.

A stream of sunrays connected to the strategically placed staff beside Geron, holding the Vanir and Celtic Stones, causing them to glow in a similar fashion to the Mystery Stone. The rays missed all three of them by inches, charting a course of sunbeams, and they shared a unified gasp.

"Avoid looking directly at the sunlight," Jeanette said.

Tom asked, "What's happening now?"

"'Tis something I feel we shouldn't know," Conlin said.

Harry stood in the pathway of sunbeams and stared into the brightness. He screamed, slapped his palms over his eyes and took off running in hysterics until he tripped downhill. After John witnessed the effects of sunrays passing through the stones, he rushed out of the gated ruins area, exiting Divinity Hill.

"They refused to listen and performed tests without enough research," Tom said. "It's time to put a stop to it all."

Jeanette reached to stop him and quailed at the throbbing on her side. "You can't—"

"I'm taking responsibility for my actions." Tom crouched below the sunlight and made his way into the enclosed area.

"The lad will be fine." Conlin drew her inward, holding her close against his chest.

She laid her head close to his heartbeat, closing her eyelids. What could she do in her current condition? Jeanette peeked at her brother entering the fenced site. As the sun continued to rise, the rays linking the stones ceased, and the glowing solar energized relics appeared activated.

"Come on, it's too dangerous out here. You'll get injured," Tom yelled at Mr. Bonhoeffer and Geron.

The same would happen to Tom if he didn't move away from the sun fueled stones. But God provided a greater supernatural force, and she prayed, "Lord, demonstrate your supremacy and let them know *You* are God."

"Amen." Conlin spoke into her hair.

He led her toward a dirt hub, designated for the other trails into the woods behind the astronomical platform and removed three palm-sized rocks from his pocket that he collected. Conlin bent and placed the oval stacking stones on the ground. "Our altar, representing the Holy Trinity and the power of three."

Clouds loomed, blocking the sunshine and a rolling thunder moved in from the east. Tom looked in every direction and tugged on Simon's sleeve. "Let's go. We're in the middle of a thunderstorm." He ignored the warning and Tom made haste to join them under the shelter of the astronomical platform.

"They refuse to listen," Tom said.

"You did everything possible," she said.

Purple hues brightened the sky. Lightning forked, and a main strike hit the staff holding the Vanir and Celtic Stones in Geron's hand. The rod juddered and he secured his grasp, grounding him in place. A secondary bolt of electricity traveled through him with a violent jerk, and the current of a side-splash split a tree in half, setting it on fire.

Flames arose from the torches, pyres, and trees, engulfing the entire fenced area. She squinted at the sight of firestorms consuming everything in its track and Mr. Bonhoeffer seeking an escape route. Despite Geron and Simon trying to kill her, among their other crimes, she found it difficult to watch the events unfold.

The hovering cumulonimbus clouds opened and revealed a bluish-white flash. A perfect sphere of ball lightning, the size of a grapefruit, hovered four feet off the ground with a slight horizontal movement. Humming grew from the orb as the size enlarged and the luminosity intensified, making it impossible to analyze. Fuzzy edges expanded, increasing the globe in diameter, until a booming sound exploded, and the ground quaked beneath their feet. The rare manifestation vanished.

Another thunderbolt collided with Geron, projecting him through the air about thirty feet away until he landed on a boulder. They all kept silent fixed in locked positions teetering on the edge of fascination and fear. High winds circulated, creating a tornado in the woods and it swelled, sweeping across Divinity Hill.

In the distance, Mr. Bonhoeffer sprinted downhill, and he flailed his extremities, fleeing from the flames, licking his legs. Then he stopped, tumbled, and dropped onto the ground, rolling around. Jeanette hunkered down between Conlin and Tom. Thank God, Saoirse waited in the car. She gripped Conlin tighter as weakness and severe fatigue overtook her senses. Was there any way to escape the storm?

In a split second, a torrential shower brought in a downpour and doused the fire. Little withstood the forces ripping through Divinity Hill. Anything in its path met ultimate destruction. Did the three stones Conlin set in the center of the woods survive its wrath? Her sight retraced the trail where he set them on the ground. The rocks remained in a perfect stack, untouched, and served as a memorial for God's provisions.

Conlin linked up with her train of vision and witnessed the same display. "Memorial stones," he said. "Similar to the twelve stones of remembrance Joshua placed along the Jordan in the Bible, commemorating the mighty acts of God."

Perhaps she and Tom would never deduce the ancient culture's original purposes and intent of the mysterious stones. Yet, in her anthropology studies, a universal human construct in the past and presence centers on remembering cultural traditions and respecting spiritual beliefs.

Pillars of smoke arose, and a team of firefighters sprinted up the slope. Two of them got down on their knees beside Mr. Bonhoeffer and attended to his medical needs. Three others charged ahead carrying a firehose and sprayed the remaining flames. The entire phenomenon felt like an out-of-body experience and the chaotic occurrences transpired in slow motion.

A paramedic dashed toward them and said, "A young lady told us there's an injured woman here?"

"She has multiple stab wounds." Carefully, Conlin positioned her to meet the medic.

A coldness extended over her appendages and for the past thirty-minutes the pain subsided. She felt nothing and maybe that should have been a cause for alarm, yet her mind dwelled on the transcendental incidents they encountered. One thing she knew for certain—they'd never forget Divinity Hill, the bewildering Mystery Stone, and the mighty acts of God.

THIRTY-SEVEN

The rain ended about the same time the nightmare ceased and Conlin would never stop praising God for keeping everyone safe. A release of tension fled his body now that Jeanette was receiving medical treatment. Although he remained on guard with an intuitive alertness, after all the harrowing ordeals and the sudden phenomena they witnessed. Conlin braced Jeanette, holding her steady as a paramedic checked her wounds.

"There's blood loss, but it appears you staunched the flow, and we'll examine the injury more thoroughly once you're in the ambulance." The medical attendant took hold of Jeanette at the bend of her elbow.

Conlin slipped his hand into hers and laced their fingers together. "I'm here for you."

"Hey, I'll join you in the parking lot," Thomas jogged in the direction of the firefighters, putting out the last of the flames burning the trees.

At a cautious pace, they passed the visitor center and arrived at the car park. Red and blue lights flashed atop the local and state police vehicles. Conlin's eyeline darted toward the Honda and his muscles relaxed at the sight of Saoirse standing beside the vehicle.

Conlin and Jeanette stood at the backside entry of the ambulance. The medics reacted with immediate attention and pulled out a gurney. Jeanette clutched his hand before letting go and she settled onto the stretcher. His sleepy gaze slunk between them, and his legs threatened to give way. Everything they underwent became entrenched in his joints and produced a heaviness in his appendages.

Cricket traversed the lot, drawing nearer and his heart lifted. He outstretched an arm and she crashed into his torso. Conlin patted her noggin and she edged away with a visual sweep of his condition.

"There's blood on yer shirt." Fret wove her eyebrows and underlined the dark circles round her eyes.

"'Tis Jeanette that's injured," he said.

"She's fine and dandy, yeah?"

"Sure, she'll be grand."

An ache swelled inside his core, watching the emergency medical technicians quickly responding. Conlin and Saoirse fumbled in reverse, giving them space to work. He concentrated on Jeanette to secure nonverbal communication while the medics loaded her into the truck. One removed his coat that she wore, then cut the layered shirts posing as bandages to disinfect her cuts, and the other started an intravenous drip-feed. The whole thing happened in a rapid procession and denied him a chance to express anything to Jeanette. Doors slammed shut and he flinched at the sound.

"We're transporting her to Parkland Hospital." The paramedic scampered into the passenger's side before departing.

The glare of the lights signaled an immediate departure and his eyesight rocketed in pursuit of the vehicle until they drove out of view. The gravity of Jeanette's injuries crushed every part of him, and Cricket laid a hand on his biceps. Wearing only a t-shirt for the past hour, the fine hairs on his nape lifted on end and the frigid temperatures burrowed into his bones.

"We'll see her soon," she said.

Drawing in a brisk pull of wind into his lungs, Conlin ducked his chin in agreement. Medics bustled to treat Harry, and rushed Mr. Bonhoeffer into a second ambulance, then sped out of the lot. Amid the chaos, the owner of the private facility, Divinity Hill, spoke to law enforcement.

"The guards arrived right when the pilot fella came running out of the woods." Cricket hugged herself in the brutal cold weather.

"Ya saved the day." He bundled her close as his chest expanded, hauling in a deep, gratifying breath. The scent of charred trees and wet asphalt mixed with a copper metal aroma that lingered in the surroundings.

Thomas approached, holding the swaddled artifacts. "How's Nettie?" He aimed his regard at the relics. "I'm putting the stones in the car."

"The paramedics took her to Parkland Hospital." Tautening his fingers into a fist, Conlin slackened his unsettled hands and shoved them into his pockets.

Saoirse skittered ahead, popped the boot and Thomas laid the relics between their bags, protecting them in a secure placement. Conlin watched from under his brow, then stared out into the middle-distance. Even covered, the stones gave him an eerie feeling. It would've been better if they left the supernatural objects behind rather than pack them in the vehicle.

"The firefighters removed all three stones from the staffs. They're still burning hot," Thomas said.

Conlin didn't concern himself with the ancient rocks. Time seemed to pass too slowly, and he wished to leave the godforsaken place. "The only t'ing that matters to me right now is arriving at the intensive care unit and being there for yer sister."

His shoulders drooped and he lowered into a slumping posture. "Of course, let's get going."

"Excuse me." An officer strolled over, holding a clipboard. "You'll need to answer some questions related to the incident that took place here."

In a receptive manner, he presented a handshake. "Yes, I'm Thomas Hillestad. Ms.—"

"Adelaide Dallas." She glanced at him for a few seconds before acknowledging the offer.

"Lovely name and a pleasure to make your acquaintance." Thomas lifted his torso to underscore his physique.

"Thank you, my mother's a *Guys and Dolls* fan. Frank Sinatra's song in the movie version is her favorite, you know…" She stated the comment as common knowledge that no other singer topped Ol' Blue Eyes' performance. "Anyway, call me Officer Dallas."

"I'm willing to cooperate in any way required. But would it be all right if I drive my friends to Parkland Hospital first and check on my sister?"

"She's the stab wound victim?"

"Yes ma'am, I mean Officer Dallas."

The officer hid a grin behind the top of her clipboard, curbing the laughter in her inflection as she spoke to Thomas. "I'll provide an escort to the hospital and then I expect you to come into the station." She pulled a card from her shirt pocket, jotted down the information, and turned to Conlin. "Here's the case number and my direct line. Contact me later with your statement."

"T'anks for accommodating us." He stuck the info in his wallet.

"No problem." Officer Dallas clicked the top of her pen and spun on her heel. "Follow me."

"Okay, I'm right behind you."

Without a response, she continued across the parking spaces towing Thomas' gaze after her. Conlin and Cricket exchanged knowing looks. "Nice one, lad." He patted his shoulder.

"Do you think she's interested?"

"Yeah, in your statement for her report."

Thomas sighed and slapped a flat palm near his heart. "Harsh."

They hopped into the Honda and Thomas drove up behind Officer Dallas' police car, exiting Divinity Hill. Severe fatigue settled into Conlin's brain, and he focused on Jeanette's recovery to keep from thinking about the nightmare she endured. Still and all, he thanked God for the miracle that they all survived.

Seven hours after the events at the Neolithic site and five of sitting on thinly padded furniture in the ER lobby, they waited for Jeanette. Conlin scrubbed his palms over his face, feeling like he drank an entire bottle of Jameson Irish Whiskey. Fluorescent lights aggravated his headache, and he squeezed his lids shut, anticipating the next update. Hand sanitizer wafted in the air whenever people hit up the antibacterial dispenser during a choir of coughs and sneezes.

Cricket dozed off a few times in the chair beside him, and now she sipped watery hot chocolate. They ate the lefse Jeanette packed earlier and Conlin changed out of his blood-stained clothes into a clean, long-sleeved striped t-shirt. He grabbed a fresh outfit for Jeanette and quivered inside, trying to push the disturbing occurrences from his mind. Two hours had passed since a nurse told them an x-ray technician took her in for a scan and they were waiting for the results.

"Da..." Cricket nudged him with her elbow.

"Thanks for sticking around for so long. I bet you're ready to leave," she said in a raspy voice.

"Banféinní." He launched himself upward from the seat and reached out for her, escorting her to a chair. "What did the doctors say?"

"The images showed no internal damage to arteries or the thoracoepigastric vein. They said it's a miracle the puncture wound missed my large intestine and, thankfully, I don't need surgery."

She waved off the suggestion to sit and instead stepped closer, leaning against his frame. Conlin was in favor of her seeking comfort in their closeness, and he wrapped his hand around her shoulder, luring her into an embrace on the opposite side of her injuries.

Conlin tilted nearer and kissed her forehead at the hairline. "How're ya feelin'?"

"Weak, tired, sore…" Jeanette wriggled under his touch and elongated her backbone.

He loosened his grip. "You're in a lot of pain, yeah?"

"Not at the moment. They gave me painkillers, a tetanus shot, thirteen stitches here"—she pointed below her ribs—"and Steri-Strip bandages for the graze."

The lack of physical and mental energy sagged his posture, listening to the degree of her medical procedures. Could he have done something more or acted sooner to prevent her attack? None of the horrific incidents should've occurred, yet the truth was he did everything possible. Even if he felt it wasn't enough, he refused to begin the vicious cycle of self-blame for years again, like Cricket's drowning accident. "I'll never be able to articulate my deepest gratitude for protecting Saoirse and the sacrifices you made for all of us. You've been through so much, and I—"

"We went through it together." Jeanette stared deep into his eyes with dilated pupils.

Her words struck the center of his heart and rooted in his soul. Although they lost precious moments alone at her house and enjoying points of interests for a sense of normalcy, the hardships brought them closer than any dinner date and small talk could ever achieve. However, he desired to experience the joy of chatting over a meal, staring across the table at her as she revealed intimate details of her deepest thoughts and feelings.

Cricket tossed a paper cup in the trash, rose to her feet, and laid a gentle palm on her arm. "Thanks a mill, for everything…"

Jeanette said, "Your actions were heroic, and you're a remarkable young woman. You have a strength that inspires me."

"And you've shown me the importance of family and putting others before yerself."

Contentment boosted his chest and a warmth spread throughout his body. "I grabbed ya clean duds." He picked up the folded clothing items off the chair and passed them to Jeanette.

In a playful fashion, she modeled the oversized hospital housecoat. "That was thoughtful of you." On her tiptoes, she puckered her lips and pecked his cheek. "I'll change and meet you outside."

Taking slow, deliberate movements, she did an about-face, and he figured her pain level was greater than she expressed to spare them a worrying outlook. Jeanette was always mindful of presenting an encouraging disposition, demonstrating a hopefulness for the impossible and bleak circumstances. She entered the jacks, and they exited the clinic.

Five minutes later, he parked in the loading and unloading zone, clicking on the hazard lights. Jeanette shambled through the automatic sliding doors, sporting a messy updo hairstyle, leggings, and a sweatshirt. The sight of her triggered a series of spluttering heartbeats and he hopped outside the automobile, hurrying to help her inside.

He crossed to the opposite side and adjusted his eyeglasses. "Em, Thomas is still at the police station. I sent him a text that we're leaving now." Conlin glanced at his wristwatch. "It's 4:38 p.m. We'll get food on our way."

"Quality. I'm starving," Cricket said.

Conlin drove off, exiting the car park and steered right onto Main Street. A few blocks down the road, he opted for an American '50s diner, pulled into an empty parking spot, and turned off the engine. "What would ye be wanting to eat?"

Jeanette reclined and curled her knees upward onto the seat. "A cup of vegetable soup's sufficient."

"A hamburger, fries, and a chocolate milkshake," Saoirse said.

"Cricket, your mobile, please. I'll place an online order." Conlin reached for her device, selected their choices off the menu and submitted the orders.

Jeanette peeked at her phone. "The battery's drained. Should we text Tom and check if he wants something?"

"Thomas messaged around t'ree o'clock, letting us know he and Officer Adelaide Dallas were having a late lunch."

"Oh, good…"

He glanced at Jeanette, struggling to achieve a comfortable position. It appeared she fought more than bodily discomfort. Did she want to talk about what transpired at Divinity Hill? He settled on pushing the episode in the back of his mind, yet he would discuss things if she felt it was helpful.

Conlin laid a palm over her hand. "If ya want to chat about anything…"

"I know." Jeanette rotated her head toward him and cracked a smile. "I'm exhausted and trying to process everything that happened."

"Ah sure, listen, you suffered a traumatic ordeal, and we all have our own way of coping."

"You're right."

The phone buzzed, notifying him the food was ready for pickup. "Cricket and I will grab the order."

A few minutes later, they returned and sorted out the meals. Conlin set his burger aside, waiting for when Thomas took over as driver. Jeanette nibbled on a roll that came with her soup, and he wished to make her more comfortable, although the best thing for her was a restful kip.

He drove twelve miles to the police station and braked to a stop in the fifteen-minute zone. Thomas waited on the front steps outside and waved. He waltzed to the driver's side and Conlin moved into the backseat, joining Saoirse.

"How are you doing?" Thomas pointed his question at Jeanette.

"Fine, I guess," she said in a despondent voice. "But hey, I survived a human sacrifice."

"Sounds like a bad reality TV show."

"If only…"

The listlessness of her tone troubled Conlin, and a desire to cuddle her close overwhelmed him. An ingrained image of the stabbing replayed in his thoughts. The emotions congested his throat, considering how he almost lost her at the hands of malicious people.

He removed his glasses, massaging the bridge of his nose, and attempted to forget by staying in the moment. She escaped and he resolved to focus on his blessings. His gaze bounced from Jeanette to Cricket, and a wholeness satiated his heart. Conlin subdued the rising emotions, swallowing a large gulp of his coffee, and ate his burger for sustenance to push him through the remaining hours before bedtime.

Thomas headed south on Interstate 93 toward Boston. "We can wait to discuss the facts of our case. The only information at this point is they've set bail at 375,000 dollars for Ace and Harry after his medical treatment. They released John at an amount of 250,000."

Thomas sipped his coffee from the police station. "They took Simon to Mass General and have a guard in his room. The judge posted his bail at 500,000 dollars once he's treated for his burns and discharged." Thomas gripped the steering wheel tighter. "Geron's presumed dead, considering my eyewitness account of the injuries he sustained and his missing body."

A moment of silence hung in the air, and Conlin guessed they all wondered about his disappearance. Better not ask questions and leave it unknown.

Thomas peeked at him in the rearview mirror. "Dally"—he cleared his throat—"Officer Dallas said you can give your statements once you're settled at the hotel."

Jeanette stirred in her seat, angling her head and maintained a shaky connection. "Where are you staying?"

"My bad, Nettie," Thomas explained. "I wanted to organize everything, so you didn't need to bother making arrangements."

"Great, thanks." The break in her voice rattled him clear to his marrow, and he opened his mouth to speak.

Thomas continued, "They're booked at the airport for two nights before their flight departs on Friday and you'll stay at my place." Satisfaction displayed across his mouth.

"Good plan." She rolled her neck, shrinking away from their visual contact.

The lad meant well and wasn't aware of the extent of the deepening bond they shared. Perhaps the separation would prepare them for the major parting on Friday. Conlin tossed his half-eaten burger in the paper bag and a tightness gripped his stomach. Nothing could ease the difficulty of creating a greater physical distance between him and Jeanette.

At a quarter to seven, Thomas exited on Hotel Drive, looping alongside Logan International Airport. Conlin strained his weary eyeballs and stared out the window at downtown Boston on the waterfront. The bright lights danced on ripples and blurred into a rainbow of colors on the water's surface.

Thomas drove into an entrance for the Hilton Hotel and stopped in the entranceway near a sign for registration. He leaped outside and opened the rear to retrieve their bags. Saoirse joined him and Conlin greeted Jeanette on the other side of the Honda.

He intended to deter her from moving too much, but she already stepped her foot on the ground. "I was coming here to help ya." She curved her fingers around his forearm, and he reached behind, supporting her balance.

A wind whirled loose tresses along her cheeks, and she peeked through the fringe of her lashes, stirring the heat of his blood. He hoped to gain a wee moment alone together, allowing him seconds to say… What did he want to say? More than he should, and he'd rather hold her, expressing his feelings through actions—run her a hot bath, tuck her into bed and lay beside her for the night. He brushed his fingertips along her jawline, and she adhered to his touch, lured by a magnetic force.

"Banféinní—"

"Here are directions to the consulate using the T, our public transit." Thomas approached them, passing him a slip of paper.

"Grand, I appreciate it." Out of all his blunders, this was his worst.

Saoirse grabbed Thomas' sleeve and motioned for him to follow her inside the hotel. "Um, Sirsh and I will check in since the reservations are under my name." Thomas faced her and they strolled through the revolving doors.

Now the lad understood, thanks to Cricket stalling the ball. Conlin entwined their fingers. "C'mere to me." He ushered her to a walkway beside the entrance, out of public view.

They stood close enough for him to feel her against his chest, and he stroked her chin with his thumb.

"Ah, I want to look after you tonight."

"I wish you would." Her piercing gaze crumbled his restraint.

In a swift movement, he cupped his palms on her face, and pressed his lips to hers with complete fervor, expressing through his caress how much she meant to him. He drove his fingers along the curvature of her jaw, reaching behind her neck, and ensnared a fistful of hair. Heat escalated between them, increasing the intensity of their kiss.

A shudder rattled her stability, and she pushed harder against his frame. Her silky moan skyrocketed an adrenaline rush through his body, readying him to lose himself within her. He inched apart, enveloping his mouth over the soft fullness of her lower lip, and gently tugged upward for a slow release.

The hum of a song trilled in her throat as she nestled into the crevasse between his chest and underarm. His heart hammered, vibrating across his torso, and he fondled the length of her hair. "I only be letting ya go, so you'll rest."

"Please, hold me longer," she mumbled into his shirt, and he embraced her tighter.

The sum of his being aspired to delay his departure, reserve another room for them, and carry her off upstairs, yet for her health and creating a solid relationship, he submitted their future to the Lord. Conlin sidled backward, gradually parting and the span felt greater than an ocean separating them. "Maybe we could skip the sightseeing after our appointment at the consulate and just enjoy each other's company."

"Whatever works for you and Saoirse." Jeanette dabbed a finger under her eyelashes, catching an unshed tear and her watery eyes stressed the inevitable reality awaiting them in less than forty-eight hours. The ache was already on the verge of unbearable.

Conlin reinforced her footsteps and guided her to the car. Thomas and Cricket waited beside the Honda, both biting back grins as they swapped glances. Did she tell him about the hope of them being her one true pairing?

"Here are your keys." Thomas passed him two plastic cards.

"'Tisn't necessary to pay for all of our expenses," Conlin said.

"The Murphys showed me true Irish hospitality in Kinsale and genuine friendship." Thomas extended a handshake.

Conlin accepted, and Thomas yanked him into a hug, patting him on the back. "Take care, bro."

"You too, lad."

Thomas made a turnabout and snagged Cricket's jacket. "Sirsh—"

"Yer actually saying goodbye?" She crossed her arms and focused on kicking a rock across the pavement.

"Nah, catch you later." Thomas slanted his neck to view her countenance.

"Visiting us again, yeah?"

"Absolutely, I love Ireland. I've scheduled another trip there soon to finish my research and planned an excavation."

Conlin noticed Jeanette slinking downward, and she braced herself against the car window. He guessed Thomas' plans struck her hard, accompanied by her exhaustion. The news of Thomas revisiting before Jeanette was a serious letdown. Nothing like challenging trials to test and strengthen their relationship.

Thomas did a double take, witnessing Jeanette's restlessness. "Let's call it a night. We all require a peaceful sleep." He rested a palm on her shoulder. "Ready to leave, Nettie?"

She tipped her head once and swung toward the CR-V. Conlin assisted her into the Honda and held her hand, ignoring the cruelty of time until the loaded ticks forced him to admit defeat. "Send me a text when you're in bed."

"All right." Her pallid complexion brightened to an amber glow, and affection emerged from her lips, curving the corners upward. "See you tomorrow."

Cricket flung her arms around Thomas. "Bye, ya dope." They erupted in laughter, and he strode a few steps to the driver's spot.

Conlin shut the door and careened away from the vehicle. Thomas drove out of the lot, beyond his field of vision, and left him robbed of breath. Air whistled through his teeth as a breeze mingled the scents of saltwater and a strong odor of sea life.

Cricket gripped his wrist and they proceeded through the glass doors, entering the Hilton. At least Jeanette would finally sleep and have an opportunity to recuperate after all she had endured. The rigidity of his sinews loosened, praying for her recovery, and he would sleep well with the assurance of seeing her tomorrow. A completeness raised his spirits, despite the state of affairs, and he felt positive they'd be together in God's perfect timing.

THIRTY-EIGHT

Jeanette rotated onto her right side and groaned, squeezing her eyelids tighter. Each move intensified the discomfort of her abrasions. Hair masked her eyes and she swiped strands away, blinking several times to clear her blurred vision. Desperate for a drink, her tongue cleaved to the roof of her mouth, and she smacked her lips.

Inching near the end of the mattress, she reached for her iPhone and winced at the stinging sensation of pricking needles across her waist. She peeked at the phone screen and a grumble vibrated in her throat. Dead. Oh yeah, she forgot to charge her device when she arrived at Tom's house.

Jeanette grabbed the extra pillow beside her and muffled a screech. Conlin wanted her to text him, but she went to sleep and sent nothing. When he made the request, the inflection in his tone revealed a desire to say good night in person like they had the past five evenings, and since change of plans denied them the chance, he was happy enough to accept digital communications. But the little energy she mustered last night allowed her to shower, drag herself into bed, and pass out right away. He would understand, yet she wished they had talked after their powerful kiss. The thumping of her heartbeat increased, thinking about him and his touch.

A renewed optimism strengthened at the actuality of seeing him and Saoirse soon. She slid out of the sheets and stood, flinching as she stretched her torso upright. Jeanette lifted her flannel pajama top and inspected her wounds. Reddish-brown spots seeped through the gauze, and she removed the bandage, exposing the black threads that stitched her skin. Bluish-purple bruising covered half her midriff, and she examined the dark pink rope burns on her wrists. A sickness swirled in her empty stomach, swaying her footsteps.

Rubbing her eyes, she fanned her lashes, clearing her gummy lids and scoped out the loft space for a clock. Nope. In the darkness, she flicked on the bedside lamp. She collected her phone and shuffled her thick, athletic socks on the hardwood surface, staggering alongside the wall.

Jeanette grasped the handrail overlooking the open concept floor plan below and noticed all the shades drawn closed, and the recessed ceiling lights dimmed. Oh, come on, she just wanted to know the time.

Dragging her fingers along the iron railing for support, she ambled downstairs. Every step irritated her cuts. At the bottom of the staircase, she searched in all directions but still no sight of Tom until she spotted a light coming from the office beside his bedroom.

She set her iPhone on the raised granite counter and clambered down the short hallway. Jeanette tapped her knuckles on the door and pushed it open.

"You're finally awake." Tom peered up from his computer screen. Papers covered the surface of the oak desk, a graduation gift from Mom and Dad, and he had displayed the stones on a cloth in the center. He stood from his chair. "Come in, have a seat."

Jeanette entered the room and averted her gaze from the artifacts. The whirlwind of chaotic events continued to perplex her, and it was best to block the incident from her mind.

"How do you feel?" Tom asked.

"Groggy and thirsty."

Tom selected a bottle of water from the corner of his bookshelf.

"I brewed Bewley's Irish Tea, if you'd like a cup. I bought a box in Ireland."

Conlin... Jeanette checked the current time on Great-Grandad Sjur's wall clock, 3:17 p.m! "I slept for sixteen hours?"

"Well, considering what you went through—"

"The Murphy's appointment at the consulate..." She rummaged through the mess on the desktop for his phone as her pulse quickened. "Did they take care of everything?"

"Whoa, Nettie." He held his arms out and pushed his hands in a downward calming motion. "We can cope without you taking control of every situation."

Did everyone feel that way about her actions? Not Conlin. He valued her strengths and weaknesses, finding a balance in their alliance. Although, she probably ended up with Brian because of her constant organizing—someone else directing her on how to look, act, and think somehow gave her a break from assuming responsibility for all circumstances. Jeanette slumped forward, inhaling a sharp intake of air, and scrunched her face at the throbbing lacerations.

Tom patted her on the back, offering reassurance. "Hey, I only meant we'll be okay if you relaxed once in a while."

She inclined her head in consideration of his statement and slid her backbone against the tweed-fabric upholstered chair. After all the lives affected by both their decisions, she needed a moment of reflection on her reactions to Tom's ventures and attempts at managing every situation.

"And to answer your question"—he stepped behind his desk and eased into the seat—"they made it to their appointment and received replacement passports."

Jeanette smacked a palm against her heart. "Thank God."

"I spoke to Conlin a few hours ago. He tried to contact you more than once."

"Oh yeah, my cell is in the kitchen, and I'll need to borrow your charger." Focused on his monitor, she craned her neck to catch his attention. "Tom?"

"Huh, do you want to hear about our conversation?"

Each tap on the keyboard pinged in her brain and a nerve twitched under her eye, glaring at her aggravating brother. "Yes, please." She bit the inside of her mouth.

"Hmm..." He reclined in his executive chair and scratched his chin. "Let's see, he asked how you're doing, and I explained you had slept for hours. He told me not to wake you and he'd see you later."

The thought of being on Conlin's mind and his concern for her triggered a fluttering in her belly. She pursed her lips, concealing a grin, and angled her head, allowing curls to hide her expression.

Tom bent forward and set an elbow on the desk, pressing a fist against his cheek. "Things are serious between you and Conlin?"

How could she express the extent of her feelings? "Yeah, and we're hoping to continue developing our relationship." Jeanette drew in a thoughtful breath, inhaling the scent of a clove-spice candle. "It already began with plenty of challenges, including the events that brought us together and now we'll have to manage the distance once he leaves..."

Tom's appearance went vacuous, as if his thoughts traveled miles away. A smile swung free, showing a full grid of teeth. "You're in deep."

"What do you mean?"

"You are in *love* with Conlin." He emphasized the vowel in his pronunciation of the word.

A hot flash prickled her nape and soared behind her ears after hearing the truth spoken aloud. Discussing the complexity of relationships with her brother seemed pointless, since the longest he dated someone was eighteen months. The pursuit of ancient relics was his passion, and he committed his life to work years ago. "Are you even capable of having an adult discussion?"

Laughter charged out of his mouth. "For sure, I witnessed your interaction with him, like the longing looks whenever he's around, and now the eagerness for details about everything he said. Reminds me of that guy you had a major crush on in middle school." Tom rocked in his seat and tapped a finger on his lips. "What was his name? Josh—"

"Don't even go there." She waved a dismissive hand. "And I'm done talking to you about this topic." Jeanette vaulted an eyebrow as her lips played at smiling. "So, any updates from Officer Dallas?"

"Nothing new about the case, but ever-loving Adelaide accepted my invitation for dinner on Saturday night." Tom folded his arms over his chest and protruded his chin.

"Good for you. It sounds nice." Would she and Conlin have the chance to go on a date? She stared at the pile of papers until the colors blurred into a sheet of white.

"Nettie—"

"Are you working on your findings report?" She twirled a ringlet around her finger.

"I've been at it all day. I summarized the stones possess the ability for solar energy to pass through and connect when they're activated during the alignment of the sun over the equator." Tom scratched his scalp and combed his fingertips through his hair. "I can't seem to articulate how it's achieved or what happened in the storm."

"Because of the transcendent elements involved?"

"I'm writing and presenting a scientific thesis, not submitting a fantasy novel to a literary agent."

Jeanette's gaze wandered and settled on the three mysterious stones. A chill struck, forming bumps on her skin, and she gulped through a clump of words. "Do you believe the relics contain mystical powers?"

"I witnessed lightning strike Geron, and a tornado carried him off, but..."

Jeanette hoisted herself to her feet and held a soft touch against her rib cage. Moving closer to the relics, she bowed over them as the table lamp shined on the etchings. Glints of light flickered, and her lashes flew high.

"Use your regular method of observation, interpretation and application, working your way up to an adequate concept."

"What do you think took place at Divinity Hill?" Tom said.

"I agree with your assessment about Geron's physical body and part of him remains connected to the artifacts."

A wrinkle cut across the breadth of his forehead. "Like a chemical bond or atoms dispersed?"

"Similar to the petroglyphs we examined at Bellows Falls in Vermont and the Abenaki theory of a dead person's soul traveling through the stones when guided into the afterlife."

"Another folklore." Tom gestured to the stones and the different cultures represented. "All based on storytelling retold throughout their tribes."

Tom always struggled to confront anything he couldn't mathematically solve. "Don't all stories, whether fiction or nonfiction, have an origin of truth?"

"I respect the balance you discovered believing in the supernatural and science. After all, you presented yourself as a blót sacrifice to spare another life and trusted in godly deliverance."

"Faith is stepping into the light, not hiding in the dark. My approach to research in archaeology and biblical studies is similar." Jeanette drank more water and the liquid sloshed in her stomach. "I'm committed to discovering there's more to learn through experiences and use critical thinking to understand both. I allow quantifiable data to reveal patterns for comprehending our natural environments, then apply the same technique of examination based on the historical and divine occurrences recorded in the Bible."

Flat-lipped silence compressed his mouth, and an inquisitive look hooded his eyelids. She didn't want him to miss the fantastic moments of wonder within the universe. "In other words, the physical world is full of surprises, so you can expect God to exceed your expectations in an unexpected way."

For someone living the life of an adventurer, he walked a fine line, always leaning toward the side of skepticism. She embraced all possibilities, and his denial of the supernatural led to the careless handling of the stones.

Tom planted his sight on the document and pinched the bridge of his nose, shutting his eyelids for a lengthy blink. "It's time for a break." He ticked the save icon, closing the Word program and shut off the desk lamp. Standing to his feet, he motioned toward the doorway and Jeanette followed him into the kitchen.

At the countertop, she angled her torso to relieve pressure on her wounds, although more than body aches caused discomfort. Now that she hadn't seen or talked to Conlin, the past week seemed dreamlike.

Tom passed her the phone charger. "Can I make you something to eat?" He hunched his posture and opened the fridge. "There's a tofu wrap, if you are hungry."

"Thanks." Jeanette bit her lower lip, staring at the red battery bar on her screen.

"Mom and Dad called earlier,"—he pulled out two mugs from a cabinet—"and I explained you had an accident but you're fine."

"Then what?"

"Nothing." Tom poured water into a kettle.

"If you suffered injuries, they would've arrived at the crack of dawn."

"Did you want them to come over?"

"No..." The last thing she needed was to face her parents' opinions about her choices. How did Tom have such a dissimilar rapport with Mom and Dad? He really didn't know or understand what she meant. "Seriously though, you've always been the golden child and do no wrong in their eyes. On the other hand, I'm an overachiever, and not once have they recognized my achievements. I can't win."

Tom rested his elbows on the slick surface and slid closer, considering the solemnity of her statement. "Are you joking?"

"Um, we grew up in the same household."

"Exactly." The toaster oven dinged, and he dished her food onto a plate. He served her the meal and gave her a paper napkin. "Nettie, it's not a contest, and they never demanded perfection from you. You placed that expectation on yourself."

Perhaps she did, but it didn't alter her personal experience within their family dynamic. Jeanette lowered her gaze and opened her mouth to make her defense.

Tom held up a single finger. "Hear me out. Mom and Dad are proud of both our accomplishments. But you're not around when I get the constant lecturing about settling down and how I should take responsibility for my actions."

"I'm not the only one receiving parent lectures as an adult? They've suggested I let you figure out your own life so I can work on mine."

"Well..." Tom shrugged his shoulders. "They might be onto something."

Jeanette chewed and swallowed a bite of her wrap. "Okay, I know. I'm an overbearing, controlling perfectionist—"

"Nobody thinks you're all those things... maybe controlling."

"Hey!"

"Honestly, I'm grateful you care enough to watch out for me."

She went misty-eyed, choking back her emotions and gulped a mouthful of water, washing down the thick feeling. In his own way, he granted her freedom from the role of a protective sister, and she released a swoosh of air.

The teapot whistled and he pivoted on his heel. "How's your pain level? I picked up your prescriptions."

"Thanks, I'll hold off on the medications."

Drumming her fingernails on the countertop, Jeanette monitored her vibrating phone, and the missed incoming calls as it recharged. A tingle circulated in her limbs, excited to hear his voice, and she clicked on his goodnight text.

Voicemail notifications popped onto the screen from his Quebec number. The twitch of her fingers pounced on her device, and she unplugged her cell. "I'm going to listen to a couple of messages." Jeanette stepped away from the counter and sauntered into the living room, selecting the top recording.

"Hello Banféinní. Hopefully, ye're feeling better and getting the rest ya need. Looking forward to seeing you later."

A buzzing sensation expanded through her center, and she listened to Conlin's second voicemail, sent at 3:22 p.m. "Hiya Jeanette, I received a call from the airline, and they've changed our flight because of a storm forecasted on Friday. Em, we're leaving tonight. Our departure's at 7:15 p.m., so I'm not sure we'll see each other before we leave." He cleared his throat and there was a pause. "I'll try calling Thomas now..."

The news constricted her heartbeat, and nausea crept up her esophagus. On her home screen, she verified the present time of 4:48 p.m. and clamped a palm on her mouth.

"Nettie, what's wrong?"

"The flight got switched and they're leaving tonight."

"Wait, no." Tom rushed from the kitchen and met her beside the sofa. "Send Conlin a message that we're on our way and tell him not to board the plane." He placed a hand on her shoulder and directed her toward the stairs. "What time is their departure?"

Jeanette scanned her texts and scrolled for the flight information. "At seven o'clock."

"Hurry and get dressed." Tom took a deep breath. "We'll make it to the airport on time."

THIRTY-NINE

Half an hour later, Tom weaved in and out of lanes, pushing almost 40 mph over the speed limit whenever they managed to avoid traffic. Sickness stirred in her stomach with a mixture of the spicy tofu wrap, Tom's driving, and the possibility of missing Conlin. Veering off Route 1A toward I-90, Tom followed the signs for international departures.

"Terminal E," Jenette said.

He pulled alongside the drop-off zone for Aer Lingus. "I'll circle around, park, and meet you inside."

"Okay." Jeanette hopped out of the car, moving faster than she should and ignored the pain. The stab wounds would heal, yet the cut to her heart if she missed Conlin would never close.

The automated doors slid open, and she entered the airport, perusing the sea of faces, hoping to find Conlin. Did she miss them? At a clipped pace through the corridor, she made a straight path for the carrier's check-in counter, and her pulse ramped up into a thundering panic.

A heaviness weighed on her chest as she skimmed the airline company's timetables posted on the display screens above her head and spotted their flight information at gate E7 on L3. Within an hour of departure and thirty minutes before boarding, they must've already passed through security.

Jeanette retrieved her phone from her coat pocket to text Conlin and, for a change, preferred saying goodbye in person rather than writing it in a message. Ignoring the bustling people in the terminals, she shuffled her feet toward a row of empty chairs and moved out of the way to accept the harsh reality that Conlin departed. At least she had beautiful memories to cling to and unforgettable kisses. But when would she see him again?

"Banféinní."

Joy permeated her heart at the sound of his voice and shot a frisson of excitement down her spine. Standing beside her, Conlin angled his body toward her stance and sloped his head to capture her attention.

"You're still here," she said.

"I'd wait till the last bleedin' second for ya."

Her lashes flicked up, and their gazes joined in an impassioned lock. For a minute, she lost herself in the bluest sky revealed in his irises. Jeanette scouted the surrounding area. "Where's Saoirse?"

"In the shops."

"She's doing all right after everything that happened?"

"Ah sure, look, in the strangest circumstances we've ever encountered in our lives, we grew closer and repaired our relationship. Going through these trials helped me gain a healthier perspective on family, work and my personal life"—he interlaced their fingers—"discovering I'm a better man with you."

A warmth infused her core, and his words whisked her away. "There's so much I wanted to say during the afternoon we had planned."

"Though I wish we were together the day, ya needed to rest" Conlin sidled closer and slipped his arm around her, pulling her into a hug.

"The few moments we had alone—"

"When our lives weren't in danger?" he said.

"The time was too short." A yearning look danced between them. "I need more of you."

"Mo stóirín, my sweetheart." The curve of his finger elevated her chin a few inches, bringing their mouths into intimate contact. "I feel the same."

Their lips met, and she inclined against the muscular planes of his body. Conlin's hands landed on her waist, rubbing the arc of her hip bones with his thumbs. Fervency transferred between them, and the thrill of his touch zinged through her center. His kiss wandered and trailed along her lower lip, pecking a path from her jawline, following the curvature of her cheek and ending his kisses on the tip of her nose.

The sweetness of his caress melted her in his arms, and yet her insides tangled into a knot. Her lids flickered open and anchored into the depth of his gaze.

"Ah, that's a right proper send off." He uttered for her ears only, brushing the back of his hand across her cheekbone.

An entire lifetime with him flashed before her eyes, and she had never felt so certain about a future with anyone. "Conlin..." she choked, reining in her emotional responses. *Give it time and wait.* "It's too difficult watching you leave."

Loosening his grip, he edged backward for a full view of her face and his brows compressed in the middle. "A part of me is staying with you."

A wave of hot to cold crashed over her and wobbled her balance. She slumped, bearing the weight of her crushing spirit, and tears pushed against her eyelids, fogging her vision. Jeanette blinked fast to keep from crying. All the events that took place, medications, physical injuries, and the agony of her breaking heart hit with a powerful force at once.

"My OTP, what's the story?" Saoirse said.

"I want to wish you both safe travels home," Jeanette said.

Saoirse stepped forward and gave her a hug. "T'anks for watching out for us."

Conlin reached around and joined their embrace. A contentment flooded her senses as the three of them huddled close together, yet she was falling to pieces. He kissed the top of her scalp and ran his fingers along the length of her hair.

"Take care of yerself, Banféinní. Feicfidh mé go luath thú."

Jeanette believed his Irish words, declaring they'd see each other soon and cleaved to the promise of reuniting. "Will you message me when you've arrived home safely?"

Conlin coiled his fingers around her hand. "I will, so." He took a few steps, overreaching his arm to maintain their handclasp until his fingertips fell from her grasp.

"Slán." Saoirse moved ahead, then made a turnabout on her sole, marching backward and waving.

"Bye." Her voice faded into the announcements over the airport intercom.

Keeping an uninterrupted sightline, she visually followed them to the security checkpoint, progressing at a steady pace in the short queue, and then straight through the metal detectors. Conlin copped a final look before disappearing down the hall. She stared for over a minute at the last spot she saw him before he rounded the corner and an immediate emptiness ensued.

Strangers cruised past her, going about their business, unaware of the devastation she felt, although she knew nothing of the joys and sorrows surrounding her at the moment. Someone nearby understood and suffered a similar pain. The complexity of life represented in an international airport—diverse people from around the world, new destinations, busy routines, overextended schedules, heartrending goodbyes, cheery reunions, all the while undertaking ever-changing circumstances and no matter how distant everyone seemed, a shared connection of human emotions existed.

She rode down the escalator, and noticed Tom near the elevators, leaning against the wall beside the payment machine for parking.

"Well, how did it go?" he asked.

A numbness spread throughout her limbs, and she massaged her hands.

"Good, I guess... I don't know when I'll see him again since we didn't set a date."

"It still sounds hopeful." Tom processed his fee and removed the ticket. He wrapped an arm around her shoulder and guided her out of the exit.

The biting thirty-eight degrees temperature snapped her nose, and she zipped her puffer jacket to the top as they crossed the street into the lot.

Tom clicked the key fob, unlocking the doors to his pristine AC Cobra 140 Charter Edition in light beige exterior and red interior. The fact he drove his car to the airport, helping her make it prior to the Murphy's boarding, proved Tom had his moments of coming to her rescue. Plus, he returned the Honda CR-V rental, and paid the additional fees, otherwise he would've never taken *his baby* into the dangerous environment of a parking garage.

"I have something to tell you." Tom glided into the bucket-seat.

Jeanette eased into the front-passenger side and struggled to latch the safety belt, attempting to avoid pressure on her bruised rib cage. Holding his palms outward, he remained ready to assist her, although his gesture was in all likelihood to prevent any damage to his vehicle.

At the click of the secured seatbelt, Tom relaxed and started the motor, revving the 2.3-liter high-power engine. He scrunched his face and nodded. "Oh, yeah..."

She was used to his level of distractibility, especially when it came to his Cobra and anything concerning artifacts. Jeanette flinched at the buzz of her phone in the back pocket of her jeans and withdrew the device, skimming the notification. A text from Conlin flashed on her screen and brought a smile to flourish as she tapped the message.

Boarded the plane and I already miss you. x

Picturing him in her mind, she shut her eyes and clutched her iPhone, pressing it against her chest, beside her heart.

"Are you awake?" Tom nudged her biceps. "Because the Bostonian Historical Society contacted me earlier and offered me Simon Bonhoeffer's position as Chief Executive of Field Research."

"Wow, congratulations! Did you accept?"

"Absolutely, I was in line for the job as his assistant and prepared to step into the role after his retirement in about eighteen months, but considering his actions..." Gripping the gearbox, he stared out the windshield.

The reactions to Simon's choices revealed how betrayed and troubled he felt about the way things unfolded, even if it benefited him by advancing his career.

"I start immediately and scheduled my fieldwork in Ireland after the holidays," he said.

Jeanette held her breath for half a second at the reminder of Tom's prearranged return, and she didn't know when she would see Conlin. "Busy as usual."

"Yeah, and I'm wondering if you can do me one last favor."

Really, after all they went through, he had the moxie to ask for favors. It had better be a request to water the plants or pick up his mail. "What is it now?"

"I need to get situated in my new job, and there's lots of desk work that's bound to keep me out of the field for a while. So, will you lead the team in Ireland for me?"

Jeanette froze for a moment, paralyzing her tongue and dizziness whirled in her head, processing the request in her thoughts.

"I'm sure you'll want to think about it and consider your options since you'd need to leave your current employment."

Tremors of enthusiasm trundled up her backbone, and she bounced in her seat, forcing contained energy from her body. "Yes, of course I'll go." She grabbed the sleeve of his canvas jacket and rattled him hard. "Thank you!"

Light wafts of laughter escaped as he swayed back and forth. "All right, if you're certain, because you'll probably have to stay for at least six months, perhaps longer."

A hitch caught in her chest, feeling breathless, and she texted Conlin the news. "Tom, you can't imagine what this means to me." She laid a hand on his forearm. "Obviously, I'm beyond excited about spending quality time with Conlin, but also grateful for the opportunity to manage an excavation."

"You deserve it, and after all, I've learned most of what I know from you. But... stay out of trouble. I can't leave on a whim and bail you out."

Jeanette side-eyed him, preventing a grin from showing, and shoved his shoulder. "There's gotta be a diagnosis or at least a term for siblings like us."

Tom shifted the gear into the reverse position and glanced at her before backing out of the space. "I believe it's called family."

Jeanette set free a smile and let out a satisfied sigh. The tautness of her muscles diminished, knowing all the wonderful new beginnings awaiting her in the year ahead. The hopeful future relieved her heartache and would make the wait to see Conlin more tolerable.

FORTY

A late February misty afternoon limited Jeanette's visibility on her drive to Kinsale. After her first experience with the weather in Ireland, she knew to either braid her hair or wear a hat. She parked her black Opel Astra along the fence near Conlin's house at the end of the street on Friary Lane.

Jeanette trekked the stone pathway toward the front door and her heartbeat thrummed wildly. It took every ounce of restraint to keep from running to the entry. Three long months without looking into his eyes or feeling his touch seemed forever.

Technology helped maintain a connection using video calls, emails, shared music playlists, including a recording Saoirse wrote and sang with her dad. Her favorite form of communication was handwritten letters, cards, and items from anywhere—a brochure for a location they discussed visiting, photos, bookmarks, and something as simple yet meaningful as a coaster from the pub they met at on her first night in town. For Christmas, Jeanette mailed her watercolor painting of Conlin's Bavaria 30 Cruiser sailboat docked in Kinsale harbor.

"'Tis yourself!"

At the sound of his voice, she whirled around, and Conlin set his grocery bags on the stones beside the gate. He rushed to meet her at the entrance and her heart dropped with the sensation of lunging off the Cliffs of Moher.

"I hoped I'd find you at home—"

Gathering her into an embrace, he raised her feet off the ground and squeezed her tight. Jeanette fixed her grasp around his torso, and the warmth of his chest against her body weakened her extremities.

Conlin eased his grip, allowing her to slide downward and plant her soles firmly on the cement. He arched backward, resting his palms on her hips, and rocked her gently, as if verifying that she was there in person. "I wasn't aware you were arriving today."

For half a second, she visually examined his appearance. Oh, how she missed gazing at his exquisite facial features and nothing on earth filled her with the tranquility of floating adrift into his eyes.

His expression lifted and he smooched the tip of her nose. Heat dispersed from her neck and across her cheeks. The ache for him to kiss her was almost excruciating. She blinked the thought from her mind and refocused.

"The apartment I'm leasing for six months became available a week early, so I decided to surprise you," she said.

"I am thrilled altogether to see and hold you again. I've missed ya more than words—"

Jeanette pressed her lips against his mouth, unable to resist him anymore. She stood on her tiptoes and fastened her hands on his biceps, luring him into a deeper kiss. As their tongues intermingled, he clutched the fabric of her clothing and tugged her as close as physically possible.

A quake rippled in her chest and throughout her midsection, triggering aftershocks to roll across her belly. The fervency of his caress in perfect harmony with her, creating a rhythmic movement, an orchestrated symphony building and reaching the crescendo. Her palms slid along his arms as the intensity of their embrace weakened her limbs. She lowered her boots flat onto the ground and the height difference broke the seal on their lips.

Air seeped into her mouth, recovering her breath to gain composure, and she straightened her posture. The taste of salt and minty lip balm lingered on her tongue. "Um, I interrupted when you were speaking."

"You can quiet me with a kiss anytime."

"I'll keep that in mind."

Loosening his shirt collar, he cleared his throat and subdued a smile. Conlin dug in a pocket of his navy peacoat and removed the house keys attached to the familiar die-cast sailboat.

"Ya came here straight from Shannon Airport, yeah?"

"Yes, and I couldn't get here fast enough." Jeanette looked through the tips of her lashes and grazed her teeth along her lower lip.

His exploratory gaze settled on her mouth, and he shut his eyelids for a minute, then swung sideways toward the entry. Conlin opened the door and stepped aside. "Come in for a cuppa."

Jeanette entered the cottage, unzipped her jacket, and removed her outerwear. He hung it on the coat rack and yanked off his maroon-knit beanie. She surveyed the pleasing surroundings—the place where it all began, and they first met. Joy overflowed in her heart, reminiscing about the similarities of their initial meeting and the complete circle they made.

"Make yerself at home." He did a double take and raked a palm through his curls. "I left the messages outside."

The clop of his boots splashed through puddles, and he grabbed the two grocery bags, hurrying indoors. Conlin paused, making direct eye contact. "Look what ya do to me. I'm flummoxed."

She enjoyed getting him flustered and tangled inside in the same way he affected her. Heat prickled her nape as she perused the living space and viewed her painting framed above the stone hearth. Jeanette strolled toward the kitchen and propped an elbow on the counter. "How's Saoirse doing?"

"Great." Conlin unloaded the bags and put a kettle on the stove. "She's visiting the coming week for winter-term break, and she'll be excited to see you." He rested his hands on her shoulders, drawing her nearer, and planted a kiss on her forehead. "I sure am."

Weakening in the knees, she shut her eyes and leaned forward, enjoying their closeness. He steadied her and they ambled to the sofa.

"Em, how's Thomas getting on at the new job?"

"The position suits him well, but he'll probably be out in the field within a year. We'll see... Adelaide seems to have helped him mature and find a better balance in life."

"Right, Officer Dallas. Good on him." The teakettle whistled. He patted her knee and moseyed into the kitchen. "And how is Jack?"

Jeanette stood and shadowed his footsteps. "Content and happy, as always. It was wonderful spending the holidays in the mountains at his cabin and enjoying a white Christmas. If only you had been there..."

Conlin rendered an understanding look, followed by an upward tick of his lips. The malty scent of brewed tea and unforgettable smell of burning peat lingered in the air. A homey vibe inundated her senses, chatting about family and friends, and it would be a blessing if they lived the remainder of their days immersed in the environment.

He set a cup in front of her, and deep interest affixed their gazes. "It's almost four o'clock. I'd like to help you get settled at your gaff, then have dinner together."

"Sounds perfect. A proper date."

"Yeah, our courtship has been a bit unconventional."

"Took us a little extra time to arrive here, but we've made it through some serious challenges."

"Sure listen, the difficulties strengthened our relationship and it'll only grow stronger."

A feeling of absolute contentment permeated every part of her being, and she drew a satisfied breath. She agreed with Conlin's assessment of their bond strengthening and believed in the everlasting connection they shared.

Seven months later, after her return to Kinsale, they revisited Kilmalkedar Church on the Dingle Peninsula. Conlin parked his Volkswagen Tiguan, exited the car, and crossed in front of the vehicle to meet her. Jeanette swung her legs outside first and reached for his hand. He gently pulled her upward and she steadied her feet, shifting the fitted side seams on her ivory lace dress.

Conlin's gaze traveled the distance of her entire body and backtracked, following a scenic route along the curves of her form until he arrived at her eyes. "You're a gift."

A warmth kindled across her skin, and she fanned a flat palm over her neck. "I am all yours, Mr. Murphy."

The back of his hand caressed her cheek. "I'm beyond blessed." Conlin wrapped his fingers around her hand and shut the door.

Jeanette raised the sweep train of her sheath gown above her ankles, and they strolled in the sunshine on a fall afternoon. A soft breeze skimmed her bare shoulders with her hair tied into an asymmetrical twisted updo, and a couple of vibrant orange tassel flowers added for color.

Approaching the Ogham Stone at the church ruins, mixed emotions swept over her reminding her of the past. "Strange to think of everything that happened here." Tingles frolicked along her flesh, and she rubbed her forearm. She refused to dwell on those incidents, not today of all days.

Conlin reached around her waist and embraced her from behind. "We're creating new memories now." He slanted his head sideways and nuzzled against her exposed shoulder.

"You're off to a wonderful start." She sank into his touch as he dipped his lips in the shallow pool between her neck and collarbone. The tickle of his facial stubble enlivened every nerve, and she breathed out an agreeable moan.

He glided his palms along the length of her arms and clasped their hands together. "Continuing the tradition of affirming promises at the standing stone."

"Yes, like when we got engaged on our first visit." She enjoyed teasing him about their different perceptions of shared experiences and he always returned the playfulness with a question.

"Em, is that how you interpreted it?" A throaty laugh defined the lines around his eyes. "Then I proposed marriage to ya twice."

The lightheartedness of his tone coaxed her about, and she stared into his striking irises, accentuated by his dark-blue, three-piece-suit. "I would've accepted your offer at that moment since I already surrendered my heart to you."

"The events definitely joined us together on that day." Conlin stroked a thumb against her chin. "And in all certainty, I wanted you, too. 'Tis fitting to make it official at the Ogham Stone."

"The happy bride and groom," Tom called out. He escorted Saoirse up the incline and Pastor Shane trailed behind them.

"The photographer parked and is on her way," Tom said.

Conlin aimed his steps at Saoirse. "You are lovely, dear one."

A rosy hue reddened her complexion, and she fluffed the edges of her navy chiffon A-line dress. "Thanks Da, ye're looking quite handsome."

"You are both stunning," Jeanette said.

"Ah, you're gorgeous." Saoirse passed her the bouquet of three cut sunflowers, two pale-yellow carnations and white baby's breath bundled with an orange ribbon.

Conlin inched closer to Jeanette's ear and uttered for her alone. "Nothing compares to your beauty."

Prepared to argue that his attractiveness surpassed everyone else's, she opened her mouth to make her point.

"Don't bother, you'll never convince me otherwise." He winked and flashed a bold grin.

She shut her eyelids for a second, relishing his voice, words, and the sentiments, valuing all his qualities.

Thirty minutes later, after greetings and pleasantries, the photographer snapped several pictures of the wedding party. Visitors at the attraction stopped and watched in the distance.

Tom clapped his hands together and skidded a glance their way. "Ready to tie the knot?"

Conlin and Jeanette faced each other in the presence of the pastor at the Ogham Stone. Saoirse and Tom stood beside them.

Pastor Shane announced, "Family and friends, we're gathered on this 24th day of September for the joining of these two people." He addressed Conlin. "You may place a finger into the center of the stone and give your word."

Conlin stationed his eyesight on her, setting a palm on top of the ancient structure, and arranged the fourth finger of his left hand in the circular opening. "By the power of Christ, I pray you love me."

An expansive feeling ballooned in her chest, and she passed Saoirse the flower bouquet, positioning her finger to converge with Conlin. "Go deo na ndeor, forever and ever."

"Jeanette LaVonne Hillestad, our union is heaven sent and I praise God for the blessing of bringing us together." His facial features lit up and his eyes gleamed. "I proclaim; heart to heart, hand to hand, flesh and spirit, binding us in unity. Holy Trinity, hear us now, confirming our sacred vow."

Jeanette's heartbeat pulsated through their touch, and she swallowed the emotions welling in her throat. "Conlin Aran Murphy, I thank the Lord for binding our hearts and lives in the spiritual fellowship of marriage. I affirm and accept with our fingers entwined, we are two becoming one, united in body and spirit." She finished by repeating the same vows he professed.

Pastor Shane's rapt attention hopped between them. "Will you promise to love, honor, cherish, provide comfort in trials, and forsake all others for the rest of your lives?"

"I will, so I will," Conlin said.

Each ceremonial procession enriched her soul and sparked a filament of euphoria in her inmost being. "I will."

An unrestrained grin exposed his teeth as he released his grasp, and they removed their fingers from the hole in the Ogham Stone.

Tom passed the rings to Pastor Shane and Conlin retrieved a white-gold-Celtic-warrior band with a round diamond set in the center shield and an engraved inscription on the inside.

Love is stronger than death.

Jeanette selected her chosen Trinity Knot ring for Conlin, encompassing the identical *Song of Songs* inspired biblical verse inscribed on the interior of the band. The displayed quote in Jack's house left an impression on all of them and strengthened their belief at Divinity Hill.

Pastor Shane said, "Let these rings be a symbol before God of Conlin and Jeanette's faith and a reminder of their love for each other. Through Christ our Lord."

Gliding the wedding band on her finger, Conlin declared with ardor in his inflection. "Jeanette, is tú mo ghrá."

Her lids closed for a moment, savoring every phrase, the expressions, the entire ceremony, and treasured it all in her heart. She swept her lashes upward, completely focused on him, and echoed his words.

"Conlin, you are my love... always." Jeanette slipped the symbolic ring on his finger.

"I pronounce ye husband and wife, in the sight of God and witnesses." Pastor Shane confirmed. "May yer joys be as bright as the morning sunrise, and your sorrows fade in the light of God's love."

They clasped hands, puckered their lips, leaning toward one another and kissed. Cheering and clapping erupted. A smile broke through their kiss as they sidled apart and peeked at the intimate group.

"God bless your married life," Pastor Shane said.

Tom strode forward and pecked her cheekbone. "Congratulations, Nettie. Everyone in New Hampshire sends their best wishes." Then turned to Conlin, offering a handshake and patted his shoulder. "Well done, congrats." He breathed a laugh out of his nose. "Funny, I brought you together and made this day possible."

Conlin imparted a knowing look, and they rolled their eyes at the same time. "Of course, thanks Tom," she said.

"Fair enough, lad," Conlin said.

"Finally, me one true pairing." Saoirse approached and gave her a hug. She shuffled a footstep toward her dad and kissed his cheek. "I'm so delira and excira for youse."

"Ah, dearest Cricket…" Conlin, Saoirse and Jeanette gathered, connecting the three of them in a handclasp, signifying their powerful team.

"Ye make a mighty grand pair." Saoirse peered at Tom. "Y'know, they're my OTP. I was the first to point out their obvious interest in each other and encouraged them to get together."

Laughter bubbled in Jeanette's belly, and she tipped her chin in agreement. "Right, and I'm honored to be part of your family now."

Wedged between them, Conlin outstretched his arms across their backs and exhaled a satisfied sigh. "Another member of the Murphy clan."

"The Irish Celts and Vikings… there's a site in Greenland—"

"Thomas!" they said in unison.

"What? I was only going to share an interesting fact." Tom held out his palms skyward. "Okay, newlyweds, enjoy your sailing trip and safe travels."

Conlin's hand rested in the middle of her bare shoulder blades and his fingers danced in a circle on her skin. "We will, so."

The mention of their honeymoon titillated every nerve, sending flutters across her chest and spiraling into her stomach. Seven days alone with her husband on their boat, cruising along the southwest coast of Ireland, was everything she dreamed. Conlin bent nearer and pressed his lips against her temple, beside her eye. She tightened the ends of her mouth and contained a smile as if everyone was privy to her thoughts. Only one tuned into all her mannerisms by listening, observing, caring, and she married the man.

Saoirse waved goodbye. "Slán agat."

"Slán leat," Conlin and Jeanette said.

Saoirse traipsed downhill to join Tom. After the guests departed and a few strangers wished them well, they stood on the grassy hill overlooking the water.

Tethered in a handclasp, he drew her nearer, placing his head against hers, and spoke in a low Irish brogue. "I'll appreciate all the days with you."

"Wherever life leads us, and no matter the circumstances, we'll endure it together."

"Whatever the future holds, we will always support and trust each other." He whirled her around and held her against his chest, caressing her mouth with his lips.

Light-headedness swayed her balance as the kiss grew passionate and heat rose between their bodies. A mutually affectionate sigh escalated, and they gasped in a shared breath.

Conlin maintained an anchored eye connection. "Let's go begin the rest of our lives."

Yes, like Saint Brendan the Navigator setting off on his voyages, their new adventures, trials, joys, and sorrows awaited them. Their promises to one another, including their wedding vows, made her confident that faith and unity would help them persevere.

The End

I hope you enjoyed The Mystery Stone. If you did, please leave a review on Goodreads, BookBub, or wherever you enjoy leaving feedback at your favorite online retailer. You can also like, follow and share my social media pages on Facebook, Twitter and Instagram. Reviews and sharing feedback are the greatest gift you can give to an indie author. I'm grateful for your support and thrilled to share my writing journey with you.

Would you like free and exclusive offers delivered directly to you?

Visit my website at www.victoriamarsell.com and subscribe to my newsletter, which will keep you up to date on my current work, new releases, special promotions and free goodies. While visiting the website, please check out my additional pages; blogs, poetry and getting to know me. I enjoy connecting with my readers, so feel free to connect with me on social media.

Thank you:

Dillon and Rhiannon, for supporting me every step of the way.
My mother, Diane, for inspiring me to write about the strong
women in our family.
To my first reader, Jill, for giving me feedback during a difficult
time.

Thanks, Taija Morgan, for the encouragement to finish my book
and answering so many questions.
Thank you, Marcus Breathnach, for verifying my use of the Irish
language and slang.

A huge thank you to all my readers and newsletter subscribers.
And a special thank you to the writing community.

I'm grateful for all of you.

Victoria Marswell is a romantic suspense author. She started writing poetry and short stories in her early teens. Victoria majored in biblical studies at Hope International University and incorporates inspirational Christian themes into her writings. Victoria is a world traveler and sets her stories in the destinations she visits. She continues traveling the world, creating and writing romantic and thrilling adventures. She lived in Orange County, CA. for 38 years and currently resides in Portsmouth, NH.

Author website: https://www.victoriamarswell.com/

Follow the author on any of the social media platforms:

https://twitter.com/vicmarswell

https://www.facebook.com/VicMarswell/

https://www.instagram.com/victoriamarswell/

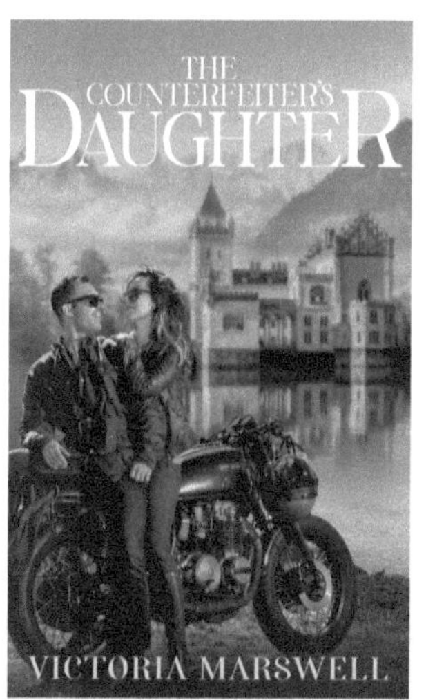

The Counterfeiter's Daughter

A lonely psychologist must travel to Germany and deal with her father's shocking counterfeiting crimes when she secretly inherits a priceless museum piece. Complications arise after she reluctantly partners with a faith-led adventurer. Together, they embark on a thrilling adventure of faith, love, and forgiveness.

https://www.victoriamarswell.com